THE YEAR OF LIVING RAINBOW

SUE PARRITT

Copyright (C) 2024 Sue Parritt

Layout design and Copyright (C) 2024 by Next Chapter

Published 2024 by Next Chapter

Edited by Elizabeth N. Love

Cover art by Lordan June Pinote

This book is a work of fiction. Names, characters, places, and incidents are the product of the author's imagination or are used fictitiously. Any resemblance to actual events, locales, or persons, living or dead, is purely coincidental.

All rights reserved. No part of this book may be reproduced or transmitted in any form or by any means, electronic or mechanical, including photocopying, recording, or by any information storage and retrieval system, without the author's permission.

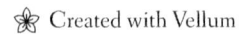

❋ Created with Vellum

ALSO BY SUE PARRITT

Novels

Sannah and the Pilgrim

Pia and the Skyman

The Sky Lines Alliance

Chrysalis

Re-Navigation

Feed Thy Enemy

A Question of Country

28 Days

Next Step

Exposure

Poetry

New Flowering

PROLOGUE
JANUARY 1ST, 1992

A WHITE HOLDEN POLICE CAR TURNS OFF THE MAIN road into one of the leafy streets winding through Brisbane's inner western suburbs. On either side of wet bitumen, the land rises steeply, presenting large brick houses built into the hillside or timber versions perched on stilts like long-legged water birds. Slumped in the passenger seat, a balding man in his sixties blinks to clear a veil of tiredness before asking for the second time, 'Number thirty-six, wasn't it?'

His driver nods but makes no attempt to speak. She's twenty-five and alert as the marmalade cat poised to strike a noisy minor sipping raindrops from a footpath hibiscus.

Turning his head to the right, his gaze alights on black numerals set in a sandstone block. A classy mailbox proclaiming postcode affluence, but not the street side he seeks. He adjusts his position, neck muscles taut, shoulders stiff. 'Fourth on the left, I reckon.'

'Yes, sir.' Her pert ponytail swings.

'White house up ahead.' He suppresses a groan at the sight of steep steps – pine logs restraining square pavers. No handrail. 'We're in luck this time. There's a car on the driveway.'

Drawing to the kerb, she silences the engine before checking her appearance in the rear-vision mirror. Cap straight, expression suitable, hair tidy. Movement alerts her to the passenger seat, where her about-to-retire partner is struggling to open the door. The expected expletive isn't forthcoming, so she opens her door and steps onto drenched grass, which squelches beneath her polished black lace-ups. Rain drips from a tall eucalypt, spotting her blue shirt; she inhales humidity as heat from the rising sun draws moisture from the sodden earth. It has been a long and difficult shift, the usual New Year's Eve problems exacerbated by a severe storm.

He joins her beside the squat mailbox – Besser blocks painted white with black numerals affixed below the usual cast iron insert. Side by side they climb wide steps to the double front doors, terracotta red to match the roof tiles with half-circle chrome handles. No sign of a bell or door knocker. A tall redhead dressed in sleep-rumpled clothes answers his knock but she bears no resemblance to the photograph discovered in the victim's wallet. Have they been driving around half the night calling at the wrong house? 'This is number thirty-six?'

'Yes, yes, it is.' The woman's mouth trembles, her voice ebbing as though she's reluctant to engage in further conversation.

'Mrs Pierce?' he asks, praying they haven't walked into a difficult domestic situation.

A lengthy pause evokes concern, but before he can make further inquiries, she answers in the negative. 'Mrs Pierce is asleep. I'm Elisabeth Coney.'

'May we come in? We must speak to Mrs Pierce.'

Elizabeth Coney ushers them into the house, leaves them standing in a sea of mauve carpet as she crosses the room to access a narrow hallway.

In the middle of what's called a family room in 1990s jargon, the policeman remains stationary, his eyes fixed on the carpet, wishing he were home in bed. Bad luck drawing this shift, especially on his final week. Most likely an attempt by his superior to make him feel guilty about retiring early when they're already short-staffed. Glancing at his partner, he notices her hands are clasped behind her back and her lips move slightly as she bites moist mouth-flesh. First time for her, he trusts she can handle the situation, not that you ever get used to it, but you learn to accept it as part of the job, learn to keep your distance emotionally. He touches her elbow. 'You'll be right, Jane.'

She releases her lower lip to give an unconvincing smile.

Somewhere down the hall, a door opens; he senses familiar phrases rising to the surface, they coat his tongue with a bitter taste. Removing his cap, he holds it in front of his soft stomach with both hands – standard procedure for a call of this nature. The redhead reappears, one thin arm wrapped around an older woman's shoulders. She leads her friend – or employer, you never know in this neighbourhood – over to a grey sofa where they sit close together, cushions squashed to varying degrees beneath their contrasting backsides.

'Mrs Delia Peirce?' he begins, focusing on a face still flushed from sleep.

'Yes.' Her left hand reaches out to grasp the redhead's slender knee.

'I regret to inform you that your husband, Ronald

Pierce, was involved in a road accident just after midnight. He was taken to Royal Brisbane Hospital, but...'

Liz fails to acknowledge the conclusion of the policeman's report; she's conscious only of sudden stiffness followed by ragdoll sagging.

The young policewoman rushes to the sofa, grabbing Delia's limp body to prevent a fall. 'Have you any brandy?'

Words form in Liz's head, but she cannot answer, too afraid to release the question hiding behind her teeth.

The policeman steps forward to assist his partner and together they lay Mrs Pierce against the cushion wedged in a corner. 'Brandy?' he repeats.

Liz hears her own voice as if at a distance, catches the echo of a single word.

'Kay?' the policewoman queries, puzzled.

Delia stirs and raises a hand to her forehead. Beside her, Liz tries to concentrate on blue uniforms rather than turn to face her friend, the unanswered question hovering above her head.

'Why don't you go and make some tea, Constable,' the sergeant suggests, recognising his partner's need to escape.

'Of course, sir.' Backing away from the sofa, she steps towards the adjacent kitchen – gleaming white floor tiles and cupboards, pale grey benchtops.

Exhausted, the sergeant seeks refuge in a matching armchair placed at rightangles to the sofa. 'Mrs Pierce, is there someone you would like me to call?'

'My daughters, Carol and Joanna.' Delia speaks slowly, each word enunciated with care.

'Do they live locally?'

'They're on holiday up the coast. Staying with friends. I've got the number somewhere.'

Liz jumps to her feet. 'It's probably on the notepad next to the phone in your study.' She scurries away down the hall, the policeman's 'Thank you, Ms Coney' trailing behind her.

Relieved that the other woman has recovered from her initial shock, the sergeant leans back in the chair. Now she can make herself useful. It's always helpful if a friend or relative is present to organise matters or at least take some pressure off the newly bereaved. With a bit of luck, they'll soon be on their way back to the station. Hurry up with the tea, Jane, I'm parched.

Mrs Peirce interrupts thoughts of tea. 'Was my husband alone in the car?' Her voice is low, apprehension evident. Raising herself from the cushion, she grips the edge of the sofa with both hands.

Here's trouble, he thinks, recalling the injured man's anguish as he cradled the woman's blood-stained head. 'No, Mrs Peirce, there was a female passenger. A Kay Masters. I'm sorry to report she died instantly.'

'Oh, God, no! I was praying they weren't together.' Delia tips forward but manages to prevent a fall.

'I'm so sorry, Mrs Pierce, I had no idea you knew Miss Masters.' He rises with difficulty and moves across the room to offer comfort. 'We've been trying to trace her next of kin. Would you be able to help us?'

'It's Professor Masters,' Delia retorts. 'And we can both help you. Kay is Liz's partner.'

'I see. They were in business together.'

'No, you don't see at all!' She struggles to her feet, stands facing the puzzled policeman, her brown eyes blazing. 'Liz and Kay lived together; they were lovers.' Turning on her heel, she rushes from the room.

Chastised, the sergeant moves into the kitchen to lean

5

heavily against a cupboard. 'We've got double trouble now,' he reports to his workplace partner.

'I heard. Would you like me to handle this one, sir?'

'Good idea. I'll take the tea.' He gestures towards four matching mugs steaming alongside an electric jug.

———

In the study, the two women cling to one another, hot tears fusing on flushed faces. No words have passed between them, the awful truth apparent from the moment Delia burst into the curtain-dim room where the atmosphere is thick with dust disturbed in a frantic search for numbers scrawled on a notepad.

ONE

Back home hours later – Delia was desperate for her to stay until the girls arrived – Liz replays the events of the previous day, each vivid segment preceded by a phrase often employed by those struggling to come to terms with the sudden death of a loved one. *If only* Delia hadn't nagged Ron all afternoon to deal with her temperamental brakes; *if on*ly they'd waited for Ron and Kay to finish fixing the ancient Datsun, a certainty if Delia hadn't been so determined not to miss out on what she called *Gloria's culinary delights* when *supper* would suffice. Damn Delia and her inability to stick to a diet. What was that limp excuse she made when berated, albeit in a light-hearted manner, for continually thinking about food?

I can't help the way I associate words and images. It's my linguistic training.

Bullshit, Liz remembers replying, the nearest she ever gets to swearing. Unlike Delia, who despite embellishing speech, seems to think that peppering her sentences with expletives demonstrates her ability to embrace contemporary customs. At least that's what she once told Liz when raised eyebrows indicated disapproval.

Ron was no better, Liz reflects, recalling his response to her suggestion that they hurry up, as Delia is about to blow her stack.

Tell Delia she can get stuffed. She told me to fix her fucking car so I'm fixing it. I'll go to the fucking party when I'm ready.

Annoyed by Delia's constant complaining, Liz had descended the steps to the garage to clarify when Ron and Kay would be ready to leave, found them sitting on the garage floor, their grimy hands clasping brown beer bottles. *If only* Kay hadn't suggested Liz and Delia go on ahead, certain she could persuade Ron to postpone further repairs until the morning. The question of transport had been discussed previously – they would take only one car to the party as the police would be hot on New Year's Eve drink driving – yet Kay overturned the decision in a moment, explaining in her rational manner that Ron's car could be left overnight outside Gloria and Roger's house. As the designated driver, Liz readily concurred, yet her subsequent behaviour behind the wheel implied continuing irritation.

On the short journey to the Martins' home – double-storey brick, high on a ridge – Liz dismissed her usual caution on approaching amber traffic lights to sweep across the intersection onto Moggill Road. Her self-excuse that Delia's demeanour showed fury bridled by the taut seatbelt seems ridiculous in the harsh light of day. Did she imagine Delia unbuckling to leap from the car when her demand to *stop at the tavern, I've left the bloody wine behind* was denied?

A change of subject – whether a mutual friend would

be attending the party – failed to lighten the mood, Delia accusing Liz of prudishness when she remarked, *I thought Bobbie would have had enough of brief intense affairs by now,* after learning of yet another new lover.

'Why would anyone tire of affairs,' Delia added as they turned into a side street, 'when they're so invigorating?' A series of sensual sighs hung in the air like the tiny raindrop-bombs threatening to explode on the windscreen.

Liz can never decide whether Delia really indulges in extra-marital affairs or simply enjoys regaling stories of steamy relationships to her monogamous friend. In recent years, Delia has favoured visiting academics. 'No worries about future repercussions,' she said in relation to the *delicious* – her description – Frenchman seconded to the French Department last winter. How Liz cringed when witness to outrageous flirting in the university Staff Club! And she wasn't the only one embarrassed by Delia's behaviour, Ron, returning from the bar with drinks for the four of them, almost dropping the tray!

'She's playing with him,' Kay said at home that evening when Liz broached the subject of Delia's infidelity. 'Stirring the shit, getting Ron uptight. They probably have a flaming row, then spend a passionate hour making up.'

Maybe it *is* just a game, Liz thinks, before acknowledging with a start that whatever the extent of Delia's past betrayals, it doesn't matter now. A widow can do as she pleases once a reasonable period of mourning has elapsed. She considers her own status, similar yet completely different in the eyes of the public. Despite her loss of a long-term partner, the term 'widow' won't be applied to unmarried Elisabeth Coney, who dared to flout convention by embracing a lesbian lifestyle. Liz recalls that lesbianism has never been unlawful in colonised Australia, although her home state, Queensland, remains socially conservative. Her mournful expression alters slightly as she thinks of the myth surrounding this anomaly, Queen Victoria supposedly stating that it would be impossible for women to engage in such acts. Lack of a penis doesn't preclude a satisfactory sex life, Your Majesty, Liz muses, prompting a vision of Kay's magnificent full breasts, soft skin beneath her fingers, nipples responding to her touch.

Late afternoon sun disappears behind a dark cloud, erasing the light patterns shimmering on polished floorboards, and the shrubs planted to hide an ugly side fence shudder in a sudden breeze, shadowing storm-soiled windows and fly-screens. Since returning home, Liz has retreated to the study located at the rear of the house to avoid social interaction. Neighbours may have heard reports of the accident on television or radio news, but she can't face well-meant hugs or offers to keep her company until her parents arrive from mid-coast New South Wales. So far, she's been spared telephone calls, the service still unavailable. Just before the storm struck, she used the Martins' phone to call home in case Kay had decided not to bother attending the party. When the call went unanswered, Liz assumed Ron had suggested a few more beers to celebrate new year, with Kay snoozing on the spare bed until Liz brought Delia home. A second call to Ron failed to connect, suggesting the storm had disrupted telecommunications.

'Dead phone, dead bodies,' Liz says aloud, the memory of Delia's scream thick in her dry throat. As expected, the house was in darkness when they pulled onto the driveway, the garage door closed against the late-night storm. Sodden leaves and small branches littered the lawn and the terraced garden beds either side of unlit steps, making the ascent

THE YEAR OF LIVING RAINBOW

problematic with an inebriated Delia in tow. Inside, the family room remained as they'd left it, empty glasses on the pine table, a glossy magazine open on the sofa.

'Do you want a coffee or a nightcap?' Delia asked, heading for the kitchen.

'Neither, thanks, I'm too tired. I assume Kay is fast asleep in your spare room, so I might as well join her. Night.' After removing her shoes, Liz tip-toed down the hall to the second bedroom. The room was hot and airless as though the louvres hadn't been opened for days. Kay must have gone to bed during the storm and decided to leave the windows shut. Loath to disturb her, Liz felt along the adjacent wall for the fan switch and turned it on high before peeling off her clothes. As she straightened up, fan blades whirring overhead stirred the flimsy curtains, sending a faint strip of moonlight across the bed. Snapping on the light, Liz stared at the unruffled bedspread and shivered. Don't be ridiculous, she told herself, Kay would have gone home. She was always complaining that Delia's spare bed gave her backache. Calmed by logical explanation, Liz skirted the bed to open the window, stood listening to the drip of raindrops from tall trees. A cool breeze dried the beads of perspiration flecking her forehead.

Woken from deep sleep by a scream that seemed to be coming from the adjoining bedroom, she tensed at the thought of Delia and Ron having yet another of their loud arguments. Sometimes she wondered why they stayed together. Heavy footsteps smothered her thoughts, Delia flinging open the bedroom door to yell, 'He's not in bed!'

'Neither is Kay. Perhaps they went to our place on the way to the party and decided to stay put once the storm struck.'

'I'll phone to check.' Delia raced from the room into the hall.

'The phone's out of order,' Liz called after her. 'I tried earlier.'

TWO

Waves run ragged along the shoreline, dragging sand into a heaving indigo ocean. Further along the beach, Pacific gulls cluster near the coal-black rocks that litter the base of a small promontory, their feathers ruffled by blustery wind, red beaks pointing to their preferred environment. This morning, the birds are silent sentinels, reluctant perhaps to waste energy on their usual raucous cawing.

In similar fashion, the single human present on this wild-weather January day stands staring out to sea, her bare feet planted on moist sand dotted with the flimsy foam left behind by retreating waves. Oblivious to her surroundings, she fails to notice that two bottle-nosed dolphins have rounded the point, their grey fins rising in unison above the swell. Undeterred by weather patterns, the playful animals swim together like best friends sharing summer school holidays.

Every January since 1981, Liz Coney and Kay Masters have spent two weeks here, staying with Liz's parents in their modest retirement home located amongst a smattering of similar dwellings lining the streets of the small beachside settlement on the other side of the headland. Beyond the houses, the land slopes down to a strip of beach where a creek enters an estuary protected by tide-sculpted sandbanks, providing a safe place for small children to play in the shallows, or create sandcastles while mothers sit on towels beneath the shade of eucalypts, sipping cold drinks and exchanging news.

Each morning, Liz and Kay would cross the shallow creek to climb the narrow path that generations of swimmers have pushed through tangled bush to the grass-topped headland, which, on a clear day, offers stunning views of ocean and a wide beach that stretches as far as the eye can see. After a few minutes spent inhaling sea-wind, the pair would descend a sandy track winding down to the beach, where they dumped day-packs on a smooth rock before stripping off their clothes to run into surf, squealing as cold water slapped hot bodies. In noonday heat, they would sit in the shade cast by huge boulders, sharing cold drinks and sandwiches.

'I come alive here,' Kay always said on the first day of their holiday. 'It must be the sense of absolute freedom. Throw off your clothes, and problems melt in the hot sun. No clothes, no hang-ups, it's as simple as that.'

Liz recalls her initial reluctance to lie naked in sun or shade, despite Kay assuring her that nobody minded on this unofficial nudist beach where the long climb over the headland deterred all but the most determined peeping Toms. Eventually, Liz overcame her prudery, learning to love the feel of sun and sea on her naked body. Occasionally, other couples arrived, nodding hello before strolling along the beach to set up beach umbrellas at a discrete distance.

Today the beach is deserted, strong winds and grey skies keeping sunworshippers indoors, but Liz had to escape the close atmosphere of her parents' home, her mother's cloying compassion. Grief hangs like a black shawl over the small house, preventing summer sun from erasing interior gloom. On slippered feet, her mother glides through rooms making unnecessary adjustments to vases of flowers, dusting ornaments, smoothing cushions. In the living room, television and radio stay silent, the intrusion of music or smiling faces off-limit. Unable to cope, Liz's father, Bill, retreats daily to the bowls club, returning at dusk to eat the evening meal. Left alone with her mother, Liz has made several attempts to induce normal conversation, but to no avail, responses restricted to monosyllables or a strained smile. Each morning, her mother brings Liz breakfast in bed as though she's recovering from a long illness.

This morning, the sight of yet another soft-boiled egg surrounded by toast fingers and a cup of insipid tea incensed, Liz pushing the tray aside to shout, 'I'll scream if you give me one more boiled egg! I'm not an invalid, I just need some time to think before I go back home. And it's not a sin to smile, Mum. Kay's dead but my life must go on. *I'm* alive. Do you hear me? *I'm* alive.'

'That's the way, darling, let those tears fall. Don't worry, Mummy will fetch you some toast and marmalade.'

'Mum, you're not listening. I'm not a ten-year-old who's lost her best playmate. I'm a thirty-eight-year-old woman trying to come to terms with the death of her lover.'

Her mother flinched at the word 'lover,' picked up the breakfast tray and rushed from the room.

Exasperated, Liz flung on yesterday's clothes and stormed out of the house.

―――

Facing the ocean, Liz tries to comprehend her mother's odd reaction. Why this sudden refusal to accept the truth? From the start she'd known theirs was a lesbian relationship – both Liz and Kay believed in complete honesty. Kay's death didn't alter past events, reduce their relationship to mere friendship. 'Why did you have to die?' Liz shouts, running into the waves. 'Why have you left me alone?' Surf pounds her thin body, foaming around her face as she pushes forward. Knocked off her feet by a huge breaker, she tumbles over and over in swirling white water like clothes in their frontload washing machine. Dumped in the shallows, she winces as coarse sand grazes her thighs. Staggering to her feet, she propels herself away from the angry sea to collapse on soft sand.

'It's a bit bloody rough for swimming,' a man's voice calls from somewhere nearby. 'Get yourself drowned in them rollers.'

Liz looks up to see an elderly man approaching, fishing rod in one hand, a canvas bag slung over one shoulder.

He looks down at her dripping shorts and T-shirt. 'You alright, miss?'

Liz nods, unwilling to explain herself to a stranger.

'Got a towel?' he persists.

Feeling foolish, she shakes her head.

'Borrow mine then, you don't want to get cold.' He unclasps his bag and rummages around to extract a thin towel. 'Here, dry yourself with this.' He hands over an old, grubby towel, then sits down beside her. A packet of cigarettes emerges from his shorts' pocket, he sticks one in his mouth, then pulls out a lighter – old-fashioned, the metal tarnished from frequent use. Cupping his free hand around the lighter's flame, he inhales deeply, followed by a spate of coughing. A plug of thick phlegm slaps the sand.

Wrapped in his towel, Liz observes a wrinkled face and wisps of white hair protruding from a battered towelling hat. His shorts are stained, his check shirt is riddled with holes. Fishing clothes, she assumes, imagining the look on her mother's face should her father dress this way. Thank goodness Dad prefers bowls; Mum likes to see him decked out in his whites.

'You weren't trying to do nothing stupid, I hope,' the old man asks when coughing subsides.

'I don't think so.'

'Terrible way to die,' he declares, staring at breaking waves.

'Death is always terrible. At least for those left behind.'

'Too right. I thought I'd go first. Doc said I only had a couple of years. Bloody smokes are killing me. Not much point in giving 'em up now my Katy's gone.'

Liz hesitates, uncertain whether to continue this line of conversation.

'One year ago, heart attack. Right as rain one day, dead the next.' He grinds the cigarette butt into the sand.

'I'm sorry,' she says, sensing the inadequacy of her words.

'First few months are the worst. You feel numb, sorta frozen.' He turns to look into her eyes. 'You'll get over it, mark my words. It won't be easy but someday you'll feel like smiling again.'

'How did you know about Kay?'

'Written in your eyes. Besides, I watched you fling yourself into that surf. Grief or anger, I thought to myself.'

'It was both.'

'Natural enough, we blame 'em for leaving us alone.'

'It wasn't just that, it's my mother's behaviour. Bad

enough her treating me like a sick kid, but now I think she's trying to pretend Kay and I were friends, not lovers.'

The fisherman lights another cigarette, draws smoke into his diseased lungs. 'Parents and kids never understand if you don't follow standard practice. Take my Dawn, for instance, she won't forgive me for not marrying her mother. Says she'll never get over the shock of finding out at forty that she's illegitimate.'

'I didn't think anyone bothered about that these days.'

'Oh, they worry, I can tell you, but mainly 'bout what other people will think. Same as your mother.'

'But we come down here every January. Some of Mum's friends must have realised we were a couple.'

'Sure, they did, same as me and Katy's friends knew we weren't married. It's the new situation your mother can't handle. You've lost your partner, but you can't draw a widow's pension, can you?'

Liz shook her head.

'So, your mother's at a loss how to discuss the matter. Probably worried too 'bout how she'll deal with any future partners.'

'You're right. I guess the only way she can deal with the circumstances is to pretend I'm a child. A pre-pubescent innocent, asexual.'

He takes another drag before saying wistfully, 'I can't help thinking of all the trouble sex got me into when I was young. Not even out of me teens and forced down the aisle by an irate father. Six months later a stillborn baby and a wife that hated me. Stuck it out for years 'cos they said you made your bed you must lie on it. Then I met Katy. Another baby, only this time I wanted to live with her, support our child. No one understood when I walked out of my loveless marriage. Family and friends shunned us, we had to leave town. Best move we ever made; we loved this place.' A smile flits across his weathered face. 'Our Dawn loved the beach when she was a kid. Not now though, she's always on about the dangers of being out in the sun. Says she'll blame me if she gets skin cancer.'

Liz has no response to his lengthy monologue; she's thinking of Kay's olive skin, her beautiful all-over tan.

'Don't be too hard on your mum,' he says, turning to face her. 'Family's important, often all you've got when you're old like me. Dawn and me, we have our moments, but I'd rather listen to her raving on than live out my old age alone.'

Liz leans towards the old man to plant a kiss on his stubbled cheek. 'Thanks for telling me your story. I hope the fish bite.'

'So do I. Dawn loves a bit of fresh fish for tea. See you again sometime. I come here most days.'

'Maybe next year.' Liz gets to her feet. 'I've decided to go home tomorrow. I've got to face that empty house sometime.'

The fisherman smiles. 'You'll be right.' He stands and walks slowly towards the ocean, scanning the water for the deep gutter where fish are often plentiful.

THREE

High above the winding street in her architect-designed home – first prize in the 'building on a difficult site' category, 1979 – Delia Pierce spends hours in front of the TV watching previously scorned soaps, alternately laughing and crying over melodramatic scenes. During sleepless nights, she pads around the house, wishing she could turn on the television to watch the old movies often shown at this hour, but reluctant to disturb her daughters. They have yet to come to terms with their father's death, seventeen-year-old Joanna even offering to defer her nursing course to support her mother through this first year of widowhood. A ridiculous suggestion, Delia thought, and said so in no uncertain terms. The University of Southern Queensland is in Toowoomba, a country town no more than two hours' drive west of Brisbane, so visiting at weekends won't be an issue.

Elder daughter, Carol, about to begin her final year in marine biology at James Cook University in Townsville, has made no such offer, although once or twice she's mentioned trying to get a job locally instead of pursuing post-graduate studies, as previously discussed with her parents. Another idea Delia dismissed immediately – both she and Ron having doctorates in their respective fields.

'Do come and look at this, Carol,' Delia calls from the family room. 'It's so amusing.'

'In a minute, Mum, I'm loading the dishwasher.'

'You've missed it now, darling. Come and sit with me. You'll love the next programme.'

In the kitchen, cutlery clatters into place and a metal door slams. 'Mum, we need to talk,' Carol shouts over the hum and vibration of economy cycle. She strides into the family room to turn off the TV.

'Hey, I was watching that.'

'We can't talk properly with that thing on.' Carol takes the seat opposite her mother. 'I'm worried about you, Mum. How can I go back to uni with you in this state?'

'I'm coping very well. I've done my grieving and now I'm getting on with life just like I did before. As a person, I remain unchanged. I'm still Dr Delia Pierce, university lecturer, wife, mother.'

'That's the problem, you're acting as if Dad's going to walk through the door any moment. You won't even let me take his clothes to the op shop. Yesterday, you bought his favourite biscuits, and you know Jo and I hate custard creams.'

'They were on special.'

'Face facts, Mum. Dad's not coming back and that means you're a widow, not a wife.'

Delia's face freezes at this unwelcome change of status.

'And another thing.' Carol takes a deep breath before continuing in a gentler tone. 'The message I gave you yesterday. Have you rung the bank manager? He did say the matter was urgent.'

'No, I haven't. Dad always handled financial matters.'

'But *you're* in charge of the money now. In a few weeks, Jo and I are going to uni. We'll need money for textbooks, fees, accommodation. Don't you think it would be a good idea to see if there's a problem? I'll come with you.'

Tears trickle down Delia's pale cheeks and her mouth quivers. 'I can't face the future without him. Most nights I can't sleep, and if I do snatch a couple of hours, my dreams are filled with tangled wreckage and blood-soaked bodies. Waking up's another nightmare. I reach out to hold him and there's no one beside me. I'm so tired, so tired I can't think.'

'You need professional help, Mum,' Carol says, moving to the sofa, where she lifts her mother's drooping head to kiss moist cheeks. 'Jo and I hoped we could supply the emotional support you need, but I guess we've been too preoccupied with our own grief. You ring the doctor, then I'll call the bank manager and try to stall him a bit.'

Delia sniffs. 'You're right, darling, I do need some help. How foolish to believe I could manage on my own.'

'No man is an island.'

'Person,' Delia corrects automatically.

'That isn't what Donne wrote.'

Delia's face relaxes a little, a slight smile lifting the corners of her mouth. 'I can't help the way I think,' she counters. 'Now be a dear and make me a cup of tea.'

———

Doctor Barclay prescribes Valium and sleeping tablets, stressing that Delia should take the latter medication only for a limited period. If the chronic insomnia continues for more than a few weeks, he advises her to visit the surgery again, so he can refer her to a psychiatrist.

THE YEAR OF LIVING RAINBOW

Relieved to have found a medical solution, Delia hurries across the shopping centre carpark to the pharmacy.

'Next stop, the bank,' she mutters, zipping up her handbag to conceal tell-tale pharmaceuticals. She has dressed for the interview – light grey summer-weight culottes teamed with a pale pink blouse and black low-heeled sandals. The insipid blouse accentuates her pallid complexion, the result of weeks spent watching television with the family room curtains closed to keep out heat and light. Despite an initial refusal to acknowledge her new status, this afternoon, Delia wishes to present as *washed-out widow* at her meeting with the florid-faced bank manager, who a decade earlier refused them a second mortgage on the grounds that the second Dr Pierce – her doctorate newly-conferred – had yet to gain tenure at the university. Whatever the problem with Pierce family finances, her demeanour must engender compassion, her state of mind is too brittle to deal with a staunch chauvinist.

Outside the bank, she pauses to catch her breath, a sprint to the other end of the shopping centre having confirmed her lack of fitness. She must join the university gym, or at the very least walk sometimes instead of always taking the car. A brisk walk before breakfast should be possible once the girls have departed, her suburb's hilly terrain certain to strengthen long-neglected muscles. Her goal could be climbing the steep street around the corner that leads to the nearest bus stop. The bus to the university takes that route, she's often seen students disembarking when forced to wait behind the bus on her drive back from the shops, the road too narrow for overtaking. Once a week to start with – there's no point in over-exerting herself – increasing to twice or three times as fitness improves. Satisfied with her plan, Delia steps towards tinted glass doors that open into a dim space, where bank tellers stand guard behind a highly polished timber counter.

Unable to face the open bonnet of her disabled Datsun, Delia parks the red Mazda on the sloping driveway instead of securing it in the two-car garage, where Carol left it the previous day. Following Kay's funeral, Liz travelled south with her parents – you're not in a fit state to drive, her mother said – prompting Liz to insist Delia borrow her car. Lack of transport will be a problem when Liz returns home, the insurance claim for Ron's written-off Holden station wagon is still in progress.

Moisture lingers in the cracks between pavers, but Delia is too intent on reaching the front door to notice such trifles, her sandals slapping each step as though she has already started her new exercise regime. 'I'm home, girls,' she calls on entering the house, redundant advice given Carol is sitting in the family room no more than a metre from the small entry space.

'Hi, Mum, how did it go?'

'Bloody awful! Get me a stiff drink.' Delia kicks off her sandals and crosses the room to the sofa, where she collapses against soft cushions.

Carol complies at once, hurrying into the adjoining lounge/dining room to fetch whiskey from the sideboard.

Down the hall, a door opens, and Joanna pokes her head out. 'Mum?'

'Why are hiding in your bedroom?'

'I'm not hiding.' The door closes behind her.

'Scotch on the rocks,' Carol announces, returning from the kitchen to hand her mother a tumbler.

'Thanks, darling.' Delia takes a swig, then thumps her tumbler down on the pine coffee table. 'Something very strange is going on, girls. There's hardly any money in the cheque account, only a couple of thousand in the savings account, and the mortgage is two months in arrears!'

Joanna slides into the chair opposite her sister. 'I thought you said the other day that mortgage payments were deducted automatically?'

Delia sighs. 'They are but there must be sufficient funds in the account. Mr bloody po-faced Gordon said non-payment in December had been overlooked over the Christmas New Year period, and given the circumstances, he hadn't wanted to disturb me when the next payment was due. Hence the command to visit the bank.'

'So, what happens now?' Carol asks.

'I told him to take the mortgage payments from the savings account. That leaves us with nine hundred dollars plus a bit in the cheque account to last until I return to work in February.'

Carol struggles to contain her anger. 'Where's it all gone?'

'That's what I'd like to know.' Delia takes another swig of whiskey. 'I rather overspent before Christmas but that doesn't explain all of it. Bank records show a dozen cheques for five hundred dollars each drawn between the end of August and Christmas. Fortunately, I took the chequebook with me, so I was able to check the butts, not that I found what your father had written enlightening. Just the date and the initials SZ. Any idea who or what SZ is?'

Joanna leaned forward. 'You don't think Dad had a girlfriend?'

'How could you say such a thing, Jo? Apologise to Mum at once!'

But Delia ignores her younger daughter's hasty apology; she's remembering her all too obvious attraction for Pierre Lavigne. Maybe Ron felt neglected, so he sought comfort in another's arms? Now she would never know. 'What does it matter, girls,' she says quietly. 'The fact is we're broke and you two need books and accommodation in a few weeks. Any suggestions?'

Carol slaps the arm of her chair. 'The insurance money for the Holden should come through soon.'

'I only sent it in last week, I'm afraid. Perhaps they could speed things up if I phone to explain the situation.' She glances at her watch. 'It's a bit late now. Never mind, I'll try tomorrow. Come on, let's forget about money and organise some tea.'

At the dinner table, Delia mulls over their financial difficulties, conscious that the insurance payout won't entirely resolve the matter. She had intended using the money to purchase a decent car, not pay for the girls' uni expenses, the Datsun's innards still littering the workbench at the rear of the garage. Sharing a crowded bus with university students five days a week seems inevitable. She looks across at Jo, toying with her food, green beans pushed into a neat pile at one side of her plate. 'I thought you liked beans, Jo?'

'Not hungry. I can't stop thinking about our money worries.'

'I'll soon have them sorted out. Eat up.'

Joanna prods a bean with her fork. 'What about a car, Mum? Liz will be back in a couple of days.'

'Shit, I'd forgotten she's coming home early. I'll have to get Daisy fixed after all. I'll ring Roger this evening to see if he can recommend a good mechanic.'

When Delia phones, Roger insists on finishing the brake repairs himself, saying it's the least he can do under the circumstances.

'Why don't you speak plainly?' she almost retorts, sick of the way all and sundry refuse to utter any vocabulary associated with death. Are they afraid the truth will summon the Grim Reaper, star of the 1987 commercial aimed to increase the Australian public's awareness of the AIDS epidemic and send him scurrying in their direction? Instead, she thanks Roger profusely.

Early the following evening, Roger arrives, attired in an odd selection of clothes – an old business shirt, faded boardshorts and highly polished hiking boots. After refusing the offer of a cold drink, he descends to the garage to begin work on the old Datsun affectionately known as Daisy. Delia leaves him alone – she doesn't know one end of a screwdriver from the other – plus she needs to study the pile of bank statements discovered in the bottom drawer of Ron's desk. When Carol left home to attend university in Townsville, Ron had decamped from the study he shared with Delia to the small space adjoining Carol's bedroom, which featured a built-in desk with cupboards either side. The long narrow room utilising the upper half of the sloping garage roof was labelled 'storage area' on the architect's drawings, but Carol claimed it once she entered her teens, persuading her father it was a suitable space for sleep and study. Armed with paint, brushes and a roller, father and daughter had redecorated the walls, then laid carpet and hung gingham curtains at the single window. Later, Delia suspected Carol had an ulterior motive – an exterior entrance door enabled access late at night without disturbing the rest of the household. As expected, Ron disagreed, maintaining his favourite daughter was an open book incapable of keeping secrets. 'It's Jo you should be worrying about,' he said when Joanna turned fifteen. 'The quiet ones have hidden depths.'

Surrounded by a sea of bank statements, Delia grimaces at the memory of numerous disagreements over raising teenage daughters. So far, timorous Joanna hasn't given them any cause for concern; no interest in smoking, alcohol or obsessing over her appearance, and although not as smart as her sister, she's a diligent student. As for dating boys, or girls for that matter, Jo shies away from social events that might lead to anything more than brief conversation. Delia trusts her younger daughter will find her feet once away from home at university.

Prior to leaving home, extrovert Carol might have indulged in the occasional drunken night out, but she believed taking drugs was for idiots and wouldn't entertain smoking cigarettes. Scuba divers keep their lungs pristine, Mum. As for sexual relationships, Carol assured her mother she would never risk pregnancy. Delia made certain her girls were well-informed about contraception, so assumed Carol was on the Pill.

Delia glances at her watch; it's nearly eleven and Roger's still working. Rising slowly, she stretches before opening the small door set into the opposite wall to descend a steep flight of steps into the garage. 'Time you called it quits, Roger, or you'll never get up for work tomorrow.' At the bottom of the steps, she walks over to the old wardrobe that serves as a wine cellar to rummage around for a good red.

Head under the bonnet, Roger grunts an unintelligible response.

'A small thank you,' Delia calls, placing a bottle of Hunter Valley cabernet sauvignon on the workbench. 'One of your favourites, I believe.'

Roger backs away from the car before straightening up. 'Yes, it is, but I haven't finished yet. I'll come back tomorrow, then Daisy Datsun will be as good as new. They made cars to last back then.'

Delia nods, her mind moving beyond the quality of cars or Hunter Valley reds. 'Roger, have you ever heard Ron mention anyone with the initials SZ?'

Roger stiffens. 'Er, can't say I have.' Taking a rag from his shorts' pocket, he wipes perspiration from his forehead and glowing cheeks.

'A company perhaps?' Delia persists.

Roger focuses on the tools scattered across the garage floor. 'No idea.'

'Oh well, the mystery remains unsolved,' Delia says half to herself. 'Don't worry about clearing up, just shut the garage door behind you. And thanks again, I really appreciate it. Money's a bit tight at present what with uni expenses for the girls and....' She hesitates, reluctant to mention funerals costs. 'Night, Roger.'

'Night, Delia,' he calls, waiting until she has mounted the stairs before raising his head.

FOUR

Exhaust fumes hang in humid January air, trapped between tightly packed buses and the thick concrete walls of Brisbane Transit Centre. Passengers preparing to embark mill around aimlessly, creating havoc for the newly arrived. Exasperated by the long delay, an elderly woman waves her walking stick to attract a bus driver, in the process she strikes a wailing toddler on the head.

Wails rise to a crescendo as Delia tries to locate the inter-state bus. She should have left home earlier, the traffic is horrendous, even though a week remains until the new school year begins. University students have another month's break, semester one starting at the end of February with Orientation week. Returning to work will be a blessing in many ways. Apart from a dire need to replenish bank accounts, Delia craves distraction.

At last, she spots a helpful sign, so pushes through the crowd, noting with relief that the Coffs Harbour bus has just arrived, and passengers are yet to disembark. Positioning herself as close to the door as possible, Delia cranes her neck to look for a familiar face. Passengers stream from the bus, forcing quick sidesteps to avoid being crushed. Hearing her name, she inches forward to fling her arms around Liz's slender frame. 'Thank God you're back home. I really missed you.' She kisses suntanned cheeks. 'You look fit. I hope the break helped.'

'A little.' Liz disentangles herself. 'Let's get out of here.'

'What about your luggage?'

Liz points over her shoulder at her backpack. 'I only took a few things as I didn't intend to stay more than a couple of days. I had a dreadful row with Mum yesterday when I announced I was coming home.'

'I shouldn't say it, but I'm so relieved *my* mother couldn't come over from Perth. I wouldn't have coped with her fussing.'

'I know what you mean. Mum treated me like a ten-year-old!' Liz grabs Delia's arm to steer her through a gap in the crowd.

'Do you want to drive?' Delia asks when they reach the carpark.

'No thanks, I'm too tired. Just drop me home and bring the car round in the morning.'

'I thought you might like a meal at my place first. You must be hungry after that long bus trip.'

'Thanks, Delia, but I need to be alone. I hope you understand.'

Delia nods and looks around for the red Mazda.

———

Perched on another of the suburb's steep slopes, the timber pole house smells musty as if it's been uninhabited for months not weeks. Leaving her backpack in the living room,

Liz strides through the house, opening doors and windows. The breeze has dropped with the onset of evening, the heavy curtains hardly stir. She leaves the main bedroom until last, hesitating before opening the door. Signs of her hasty departure are everywhere – the unmade bed, discarded clothes on the cane chair in the corner, shoes spilling from the open wardrobe.

Whisked away by her parents only hours after Kay's funeral, Liz had no chance to tidy up, her pleas to remain home for a couple of days falling on deaf ears. 'You need a complete break,' her mother insisted. 'Staying in the house will only intensify your grief.' Liz felt too fragile to argue.

Now, she sits on their comfortable double bed, running her fingers over the crumpled cotton bedspread. Plump pillows draw her attention – one smooth, one creased. On arrival, her mother insisted on changing the sheets and pillowcases, as though Kay had died in bed, leaving behind unpleasant body fluids. Reaching under the pristine pillow, Liz's fingers touch the sheet beneath – cool cotton smooth as silk. What did she expect to find in the third week of January, Kay's winter PJs? They always sleep naked in summer, even adjusting their 'banana' sleeping positions to allow air from the ceiling fan to circulate around bodies still cool from late evening showers.

She tries to withdraw her hand, but it appears to have a mind of its own, travelling towards the headboard until her fingers encounter wrinkled cotton. Retrieving a large handkerchief, Liz studies her handiwork, a carefully embroidered K in one corner, but when she holds it against her cheek, tears refuse to flow. Has she already spilt the obligatory quota? Automatically, she folds the handkerchief into a neat square and tucks it under the creased pillow.

Comprehension dawns: she is emotionally drained, her reservoir bone dry.

Irritation surfaces, directed at the sheet-stripper who should have found the handkerchief and removed it to the laundry basket. Glancing at the wardrobe, Liz recalls Fran Masters' suggestion she ask a friend to clear out Kay's half while she was staying with her parents. 'It will be too upsetting for you, dear. I know how grateful I was when Kay cleared out her father's things.' Although Liz never met Harold Masters, he remains a presence in the modest home once shared with Fran, photographs from a formal wedding portrait to holiday snaps adorning every room. A tall, slim man with a shock of unruly brown hair, Harold was popular with workmates, neighbours and anyone who knew him, Fran said. Just like Kay, Liz reflects, rueing her own timidity, her tendency to linger on the periphery of parties, nursing a drink for hours, while her gregarious partner engaged in conversation with one and all. Liz is terrified at the thought of meeting new people and answering polite but prosaic questions about her occupation, her marital status, etcetera. Meeting the 'public', as she labels those outside her small circle of friends, must be avoided if at all possible. Reticence also colours her career path, compelling her to remain within the semi-basement haven of Main Library Cataloguing Department, where the public never venture, although she acknowledges promotion is unlikely unless she broadens her experience. Facing a heaving sea of students and impatient academics daily, like her friend upstairs in Reference, doesn't bear thinking about.

Her thoughts return to the hidden handkerchief, but she quickly concedes that one small personal item is of no consequence when the entire house is filled with Kay's presence. Every room she enters whispers Kay's name, each painting she passes taunts her with Kay's face' and she's beginning to doubt her ability to continue living in the house they shared for a decade. On the beach with the fisherman, she'd spoken of her determination to face the empty house, yet now she fears courage will falter, her nerves snap under the strain.

Catching sight of her reflection in the dressing table mirror, her glowing, suntanned face surprises, despite Delia's earlier comment. Surprise isn't the sole reaction, she feels cheated; bereavement should have caused a radical change in her appearance. On the journey from the transit centre, she noticed a profound change in Delia: dark circles under her eyes, cheeks devoid of colour, hands shaking when she lessened her grip on the steering wheel. Conversation seemed strained, Liz's questions regarding Carol and Joanna answered in monosyllables. Perhaps the girls are having difficulty coming to terms with their father's death. Carol was very close to Ron, sharing his love of the natural world and his passion for science. As a schoolgirl, Carol often accompanied Ron on bush weekends, Lamington National Park their favourite camping spot. Delia refused to join these expeditions, complaining the bush was a dangerous place full of venomous snakes and biting insects. 'I'm a city person,' she would say whenever the question of camping arose, as though this prevented her from leaving the built environment. Joanna preferred the beach, staying with her paternal grandparents on the Sunshine Coast within walking distance of sand and surf her idea of a good weekend.

Camping in Giraween National Park over Easter the previous year was a marvellous experience, Ron and Carol eager to teach the novices basic skills, which included climbing some of the massive granite tors and outcrops protruding from dense bush. Liz remembers the joy of inhaling fresh air – Brisbane still suffering summer's high humidity – cooling off in rock pools after a long bushwalk, singing songs around a campfire each night, toasting marshmallows stuck on twigs. Before they retired for the night to their respective tents, Ron would carefully extinguish the fire, a sensible precaution given the dry environment. Liz wasn't afraid of the dark, but when the embers died, she felt threatened by an inky sky devoid of the ambient light witnessed in the suburbs. In the darkness of their tent, she fell asleep each night clutching her torch, single sleeping bags and camp stretchers preventing their usual nocturnal embrace.

Sitting cross-legged on their double ensemble, Liz can almost smell the aroma of burning pine and gum, see familiar faces flickering in firelight. A memory to savour; she closes her eyes against fading January light. Night has fallen when she returns to bleak present, the mirror no longer taunting her with a suntanned, healthy reflection. Alarmed by imagined shadows, she snaps on the nearest bedside lamp to focus her attention on its warm glow. Fear subsides slowly, to be replaced by text from a small green sticker Kay once stuck on the wall above their computer: *It's better to light one small candle than to curse the dark.*

Uncurling her long legs, Liz slips from the bed and walks purposely into the hall to retrieve her backpack. It's time to unpack, confront the empty space in the wardrobe.

———

In the insipid light of early morning, Delia wakes from a long, dreamless sleep, her mouth bone dry, her mind cottonwool. Rubbing her eyes, she struggles to clear both vision and brain, then notices two pill boxes propped against a glass of water on the bedside table. Vaguely, she recalls talk of side effects that could persist for a few hours. She'll be back to normal after breakfast. Floral curtains flutter in morning breeze, attracting still-clouded attention. Carefully, she counts petals and stems, dimly aware of pink, white and grey shapes drifting through haze. Soft pillows absorb her heavy head.

Morning dreams come swiftly, primary colours erasing tranquil pastel shades. Solid slabs of red, black and blue saturate her mind, bearing pain with each brush stroke. She wants to shatter the canvas with sound. Her lips part, her tongue shifts for speech, but nothing emerges, the scream is barricaded within.

She wakes clutching her head, her body quivering with fear. Speech explodes as she reaches out to grab the strips of tablets protruding from torn cardboard boxes. 'Never, never again!' she cries, throwing prescribed medication across the room.

'What's up, Mum?' Carol calls, racing into the bedroom wearing only the bottom half of summer pyjamas.

Delia buries her head under the crumpled sheet.

'It's alright, Mum, I'm here.' Carol loosens the sheet to stroke her mother's forehead. 'Did you have a bad dream?'

'I can cope with *my* nightmares, they're of my own making.' Delia pronounces each word with care. 'I tried to banish them with drugs, but the horror grew like a tumour. I can't endure that sort of pain.'

'How many tablets did you take last night?' Carol asks quietly.

Delia holds up four fingers.

'Four? Christ, you weren't trying to...' Her voice trails off.

'No, no, I just wanted to obliterate the present for a few hours. Sweet dreamless sleep. Dr Barclay said the tablets would destroy the dream element of sleep.'

'They obviously didn't.'

Delia pouts. 'Yes, they did, but I fell asleep for a second time early this morning. That's when the nightmares began.'

'Why take more when you said yesterday that one of each has been helping you sleep these past few nights?'

Delia turns her head to avoid Carol's penetrating gaze.

'Come on, Mum, you can talk to me. Let me help you.'

'I don't know how to tell you, darling. I don't understand what's going on and no one seems have any explanation.'

'About the bank accounts?'

'No, now it's the car insurance. The policy wasn't renewed last October. I was relying on the insurance money to tide us over until my next pay.'

Carol stares straight ahead at mirrored wardrobe doors, sees her mother's slumped shoulders, her expression of defeat. Post-graduate dreams shatter, distorting her own reflection.

'Don't worry about your course, darling. I'm sure I can get a loan; it's imperative you finish your degree.'

'What about Jo?'

'I'm afraid I can't fund both courses this year. Jo will have to defer and get a job. She has good keyboard skills, perhaps she could find a secretarial position.'

Carol remains silent.

'Roger might have a position coming up in his office,' Delia continues, her tone brightening. 'I'm sure he said his secretary was leaving. I'll speak to him this evening when he comes to finish the repairs.'

'It might be better to break the news to Jo first.'

Delia waits until Carol has left the house to visit friends to raise the difficult subject of deferral. Despite efforts to encourage Jo to get some fresh air, or go out with her own friends, she persists in spending hours in her bedroom, leaving Delia no option but to knock on the closed door before entering a stuffy space darkened by drawn curtains.

Jo is sitting at her desk holding a terracotta picture frame containing her father's photograph and doesn't acknowledge her mother's arrival, so Delia perches on the end of the double bed, set at right-angles to the desk. She dislikes speaking to Jo's back but a suggestion that they adjourn to the family room is also ignored.

When there's no reaction to news of the latest financial dilemma, Delia gets straight to the point, asking rather than telling Jo to defer university for one year and apologising for having to choose between daughters. The response is unexpected, Jo lifting one hand to reach forward and draw back the left-hand curtain, then, as afternoon heat surges into the room, she begins to address the smiling face bordered by a patterned frame. 'You deliberately ran the car into that light pole, didn't you, Dad? You were in big trouble, so you took the easy way out. Now you've ruined all our lives. Why the hell didn't you shoot yourself or take some pills, then at least we could have sold the car?' Raising her right arm, she throws the photo frame against the wall and bursts into tears.

Rushing to her side, Delia hugs taut shoulders, but Jo will not be comforted, hastily detaching her mother's arms to retrieve terracotta and glass fragments from the carpeted floor. Her father's face is pitted with small scars; red dust coats her fingers. 'I'm sorry, Daddy,' she whispers in a little-girl voice. 'I didn't mean it. I know it was an accident, you never would have put Kay's life in danger.'

Unseen, Delia retreats to fetch dustpan and brush from the laundry cupboard but once outside Jo's bedroom, she hesitates, loathe to re-enter even though the door remains open. Sneaking a peek inside, she sees Jo lying on the carpet, one hand stroking the place where adolescent dreams shattered along with a belief in parental wisdom. On the adjacent wall, a red scar defines downfall. Slipped inside the room, cleaning tools rest on unstained carpet.

When the phone rings later in the afternoon, Delia is retrieving washing from the line in front of a retaining wall, a shady spot that prevents clothes from becoming stiff with summer heat. Aware that Jo can't bear to leave a phone unanswered, she continues to unpeg flimsy underwear. The kitchen door is open, so she'll hear if the call is for her.

Jo answers quickly, repeating the number instead of her usual bright greeting. 'No, I'm bloody pissed off,' she snaps, indicating the caller is a friend. The response must be a suggestion to lighten up, Delia thinks, still straining to learn the caller's identity. But it seems Jo has no intention of obeying, sounding off instead about hating her father and why, then saying she feels guilty for speaking ill of the dead. A lengthy silence ensues, broken eventually by Jo's apology for upsetting her paternal grandmother. 'I should know better,' she adds, 'it's just as hard for you and Grandpa, losing your only son.'

Delia considers whether to attempt a quiet withdrawal by creeping along the path into the fernery, where she can enter the house via her bedroom, but she can't remember if she unlocked the screen door this morning. The alternative, bumping into the kitchen door with the laundry trolley, seems too obvious, Jo certain to realise her mother has been eavesdropping. She settles on a third method – running the trolley back and forth over exposed aggregate concrete – before heading into the kitchen.

'See you soon,' Jo says as the trolley slides over smooth tiles. 'Love you, Gran.' She replaces the receiver and, completely ignoring her mother, moves to open the fridge.

'Are Nancy and George coming down tomorrow?' Delia asks Jo's back.

'No, this evening.'

'Then I'll have to go to the shops. There isn't enough meat for an additional two.'

'No worries. Gran said they'd buy pizza for our tea.'

Delia glances at the kitchen clock. 'Why tonight, George doesn't like night driving?'

'They can stay over.'

'Then you'd better tidy your room. You can sleep on the study bed.'

Jo shakes her head. 'You're the one with the ensuite. Essential for the elderly.'

Delia concurs, recalling the squeak of doors and a flushing toilet that disturbed her so much on Christmas Eve, she insisted they give up their bedroom the following night. Not that it would have mattered in the end, excess drinking during the evening ensuring instant sleep.

―――――

Night descends swiftly, twilight brief in sub-tropical Brisbane. Inside number 36, the Pierce family give a collective sigh of relief. 'Bloody daylight saving,' George Pierce mutters. 'I know which way I'll be voting when this trial ends.'

'I think it's great,' Jo contradicts.

'You don't have to live in the tropics,' her sister retorts.

'Don't start arguing again, girls,' their grandmother pleads, her voice weary from the strain of earlier emotive discussion.

Delia is quick to diffuse the situation, suggesting a cold drink before bed, but her mother-in-law would prefer a cold shower. 'I'll say goodnight, then.' Delia leans across the sofa to kiss a papery cheek.

Nancy Pierce smiles at her daughter-in-law. 'Try not to worry too much. As we said before, George and I can help with Jo's expenses, if you'll let us.'

'I appreciate your offer, but....' Delia hesitates, aware that pride alone prevents her from accepting their hard-earned savings. 'Let me start again.' She reaches out to squeeze Nancy's hand. 'I accept your offer with grateful thanks. But only for this year. After that, I want to support Jo, and I'll pay you back with interest.'

Rendered speechless with relief, Jo beams at her mother and grandmother, while Grandpa George directs his attention to the elder granddaughter. 'Carol, see if you can locate a bottle of bubbly in the garage wardrobe. We need more than cordial to toast the launch of Joanna's university studies.'

'I'll see what I can find, Grandpa.'

FIVE

Downstairs in the garage, Delia and Liz are attempting to sort out the jumble of tools on the workbench, Roger having departed the previous evening – almost a week later than promised, his excuse the need to catch up on paperwork – as soon as he finished the repairs. Earlier, Liz had called to offer her car for shopping, then accepted an invitation to lunch. Three-day weekends alone remain tough.

'Roger seemed on edge from the moment he arrived,' Delia remarks. 'Going on and on about Gloria's incompetence. Apparently, she's a lousy typist and her manner on the phone is off-putting to customers. He said she sounds stuck up.'

'Gloria maintains it's a clash of cultures. She cringes when listening to some of the customers, bad language and sexist comments being common. She didn't want to take his secretary's place but Roger insisted, as she hasn't been able to find another library position.'

'Do you think his business is in trouble?'

'It's more than likely. According to the news, the recession's biting hard and economists are predicting it will get worse this year.'

'Thank God I've got tenure.'

'And I'm permanent staff.'

'Will you be able to manage on a three-quarter time salary?'

'I believe so.' Given Delia's circumstances, Liz doesn't wish to mention that they paid off their mortgage last year, Kay being concerned about the recession. 'But I am considering advertising for a student boarder. It feels wrong rattling around in a three-bedroom house when students find it so difficult to find affordable accommodation.'

'I could do the same, I suppose. I'll soon have two spare rooms.'

'Carol's study and bedroom would be the perfect arrangement for a student. Jo's room is also a reasonable size and you won't have to share a bathroom. Boarders would enable you to repay the loan from George and Nancy quickly and provide company.'

'True, but I want the girls, particularly Jo, to be able to come home at any time.'

'One boarder then.'

Delia nods. 'I'll think about it.'

The telephone's intrusive ring reverberates throughout the house and garage, but Delia makes no move to answer it. 'Jo's closer,' she says in response to Liz's questioning look. 'Besides, I can't bear yet another condolence call from someone I haven't seen in years.' Soon, they hear Jo thumping down the hall to the kitchen. 'I do wish that girl would learn to move quietly. God knows why she continues to wear her Doc Martens' in the middle of summer!'

'There's no accounting for a teenager's taste,' Liz

replies, grateful that she doesn't have daughters, or sons for that matter. It's hard enough dealing with her own grief.

A door creaks and Jo appears at the top of the short flight of steps leading to Carol's rooms. 'It's for you, Mum.'

'Who is it?'

'I didn't catch the name.'

Delia sighs and turns to Liz. 'We can finish down here later. It's almost time for lunch.'

'Sure. I'll give you five minutes to take the call.'

'Hurry up, Mum. He sounded impatient.'

'I'm coming.'

———

Upstairs, Delia stands barefoot on cool kitchen tiles, the receiver clamped to her ear, wishing the caller would give her the opportunity to explain. So far, he's been rabbiting on about debts needing to be paid on time and how he only extended credit as Ron was one of his best customers and he didn't want him to take his business elsewhere. At last, he pauses for breath. 'I can't give Ron a message,' Delia says in an authoritative tone. 'My husband was killed in a road accident on New Year's Eve. As it's a financial matter perhaps I can help?' Delia notices that Jo is loitering nearby and signals her to be quiet. 'Are you still there, Mr Zampa?' She replaces the receiver. 'Strange guy, he hung up.'

'Who was that?' Jo asks.

'A Santo Zampa. He asked where the money was, something about a monthly cheque. I guess he felt embarrassed learning Ron was dead.'

'SZ, Mum. Those were the initials on the cheque butts. Dad must have owed him a lot of money.'

Delia flops in a nearby chair in the family room. 'First

the mortgage in arrears, then cancelled car insurance, now this! I wish I knew what on earth Ron was mixed up in.'

'Blackmail,' Jo says breathlessly. 'Remember when Dad went rushing off to Sydney just before Christmas? Something to do with experiments at Lucas Heights nuclear power station, he said. Perhaps Dad was selling secrets to the Russians?'

'What a ridiculous suggestion, Jo! Don't you read the paper? The Cold War's over.'

Jo scuttles to the sofa, where she sits cross-legged hugging a cushion. 'How do you know Santo Zampa isn't a corrupt ASIO agent.'

The screen door squeaks as Liz steps into the room from the front patio. 'Don't tell me that was ASIO on the phone?'

Delia shakes her head. 'No, a Mr Santo Zampa. He didn't mention the name of his business, only that Ron owes him thousands.'

'Thousands?' Liz tries to recall where she's heard the name before. Not heard, she remembers, read about.

'You know the name, Liz?' Delia asks.

Liz ponders whether to reveal distasteful information that may or may not be relevant.

'Go on then, tell me what you know.'

'I'll have to check at work to confirm the details,' she begins, thinking of the microfiche collection housing past newspaper issues, 'but I remember reading about a Santo Zampa in the Courier Mail. He was charged with operating an illegal casino in the Valley and is facing trial in a few months. Remember all those police raids last year?

Delia nods and turns her head to the wall. 'An extra-marital affair would have been easier to deal with. I've never thought of Ron as a gambler.'

Liz hurries to Delia's side. 'I could be wrong, there's no proof. Look, I'm sorry I mentioned it.'

'It's fine, I'm pleased you remembered the article, it explains a great deal. All those evenings when Ron said he was keeping Roger company at the tavern. I worried about him getting done for drink-driving.'

'Mystery solved,' Jo says, sounding disappointed. 'A sleazy gambling joint in the Valley. I thought Dad had better taste.'

'Enough of that, Joanna. Go and make us some coffee.'

'Yes, Mum.' Jo scurries into the kitchen.

Liz kneels besides Delia's chair to whisper in her ear. 'This could explain Roger's behaviour towards Gloria. Nothing to do with business problems. He probably owes money to Santo Zampa, too.'

'It also explains why he insisted on fixing Daisy. He must have felt guilty about my being left with debts.'

'Perhaps Roger instigated the gambling sessions?'

'I'm not about to ask him.' Delia sighs. 'Liz, do you know if a widow is responsible for her husband's debts?'

'Sorry, I've no idea.'

'I could ask our solicitor but he charges an arm and a leg for every phone call.'

'Don't worry, I'll ask my friend at the Law Library. No need to mention any names.' Liz gets to her feet before Jo can return from the kitchen and settles in the matching armchair the other side of a square pine coffee table. 'I'll go Monday lunchtime. You need to know where you stand.'

Delia smiles her thanks to Liz, as Jo brings coffee and biscuits.

———

THE YEAR OF LIVING RAINBOW

As the day draws to a close, Delia lies awake listening to night noises filtering through the wide screen door leading into the lush fernery. High in the branches of a nearby eucalypt, a mother possum hisses at her offspring, a peculiar rasping sound, designed to discourage further dependence, while in the neighbouring garden, fruit bats squabble over ripening native berries. Morning light will reveal purple flightpath decorations from one end of the rear patio to the other, food passing through the bats' digestive systems in less than half an hour. A nuisance for many Brisbane householders, but tonight Delia is focused on the natural world rather than future chores. Likewise, she's reluctant to close the sliding door and turn on the air-conditioner, even though the atmosphere remains humid and the temperature is still twenty-three Celsius according to her bedside clock.

Strangely calm, she senses her myriad problems have dissipated with the descent of darkness, probably the result of the smooth Burgundy Carol retrieved from the garage wardrobe after listening to the latest segment of the family saga. Delia had expected outrage that other family members accepted Ron's gambling as a given irrespective of proof, but Carol simply commented that he must have been a poor player to lose thousands and expressed a fervent wish that her mother wouldn't have to repay the debts.

For a moment, Delia remembers the sleeping tablets and Valium secreted amongst underwear in a chest of drawers. In the morning she must retrieve them, flush every pill down the toilet. Out of harm's way, carried along pipes to dissolve in vast ocean. Waves lap the rim of thought, roll her forward into dream.

SIX

Morning brings heavy showers followed by brilliant sunshine. Leaves stir in a light breeze, shedding raindrops over sodden earth and flora. From the kitchen window, Liz surveys her neglected garden with a heavy heart. Weeds sprout between trees and shrubs; grass has invaded the vegetable plot and dead leaves litter the deck. Leaving her few breakfast dishes to drain, she locates her old straw hat and heads into the back garden.

    She works steadily for hours, filling the wheelbarrow with weeds more times than she can count, then pushing it down the steep path by the side of the house to the compost bin tucked beside the fence. Moist earth has clogged her fingernails and stained her hands; her knees bear more resemblance to elephant hide than human skin. She straightens up to stretch her aching back and inspect the morning's toil, the sense of satisfaction evoking momentary cheerfulness. What was it her father said about weeding during her recent visit? She can't recall, but she does remember reading somewhere that gardening can be therapeutic, outdoor physical activity helping to dissipate negative emotions. *Cheaper than grief counselling,* she thinks, looking forward to the many days it will take to return the garden to its former glory.

Gardening has never been a chore, even though the steep slope is a challenge, requiring careful terracing to prevent soil and mulch from washing down to the road during summer storms. After more than twenty years of cultivation – Kay had the house built years before they met – the front garden is a mass of native trees and flowering shrubs with lawn relegated to the footpath. Apart from retaining walls constructed from old railway sleepers, the back garden – accessed via stairs from the timber deck – is given over to native bush, the only concession to domestic life being a portable washing line Kay lashed to the deck railing with a length of rope.

Perspiration drips from Liz's face and neck as she repositions the empty wheelbarrow at the highest point of the front garden, further dampening a thin cotton shirt spattered by raindrops from overhanging branches. Gardening tools remain on the gravel path at the base of the deck steps, but she needs to rehydrate, so runs over to the tap attached to a supporting pole. Traffic noise filters up the slope as she quenches her thirst; she takes no notice until she realises that a car has turned into the driveway. Raising her head, she sees Gloria Martin step from her white Mazda. A welcome interruption, given Liz's rumbling stomach is telling her it's time for lunch. 'Hi, Gloria,' she calls, stepping out of the shade.

Gloria waves. 'What are you doing under the house, Liz?'

'Having a drink from the tap. I've been gardening since eight. It was like a jungle out the back.'

'Don't overdo it in this heat,' Gloria calls back.

'I won't. Go inside. I'll clean up and join you in a minute.'

Gloria nods and turns towards the steps leading to the front door.

―――

On the shady back deck, the two friends sit side by side on weathered teak chairs, their feet resting on damp deck railings. Between them is a small square table, constructed by Kay years earlier from old fence palings. Crumb-riddled plates cover half its surface, Gloria having insisted on preparing sandwiches while Liz showered and changed. Conversation about the relentless heat and other undemanding topics keep Liz relaxed, which is more than can be said for Gloria, who fidgets with her empty glass like a smoker needing to occupy her hands.

'Just as well it's Sunday tomorrow.' Liz stretches her weary limbs. 'I'll need a sleep-in after today's effort.'

'Yet another Sunday listening to Roger whine about my failure to come up to his former secretary's standard and the lack of customers.'

'I'm sorry. I didn't realise business was bad.'

'To put it bluntly, the business is in a heap of shit. Creditors are hounding him night and day and now his best customer has threatened to take his business elsewhere. Probably to an Italian-owned business, Roger says, blood being thicker than water. Vince Zampa has cousins all over Brisbane.'

Liz stiffens at the mention of Italian families. Santo Zampa could be threatening Roger on two fronts if Delia isn't legally responsible for Ron's debts. 'Italian immigrants do stick together,' Liz answers, echoing Gloria's comments. 'I guess that's why they do so well in business.'

Gloria grimaces and almost drops her glass. 'This isn't just a social call, Liz. May I ask you a personal question?'

Liz nods, hoping it doesn't involve bereavement.

'Are you contemplating full-time work now you're on your own?'

A relatively easy question, Liz thinks, turning to face her friend. 'I have considered it, but right now I need the extra day at home. There's so much to do at this time of year.'

Gloria sighs with relief. 'So, I might stand a chance of some casual work at the library this year?'

'Your chances are pretty good, I'd say. We've recently accepted a large bequest, fifty cartons, I think James said, so there'll be plenty of work. Why don't you give him a call? He said he'd be working today to sort the wheat from the chaff.'

'Are you sure he wouldn't mind my calling on a Saturday?'

'Why not? With the office closed he won't have any other interruptions. Besides, it would be to his advantage to employ someone who knows the system. Use the phone in the study while I clear up the lunch dishes.'

Still clutching the glass, Gloria shifts her sandaled feet. 'I'll drop this in the kitchen.' She rushes indoors, leaving Liz to trust she doesn't mean literally drop into the sink.

Washing dishes and cutlery, Liz muses on Gloria's possible reappointment, the Cataloguing department hasn't been the same this past six months without her friend's vivacious presence. Since returning to work, Liz has sensed an aloofness in some of her colleagues. They remain polite, but if she's sitting alone in the tearoom, approach her in pairs or threesomes. Perhaps they're unwilling to risk the intimate dialogue a one-on-one meeting can evoke. Reticence to raise the subject of death is understandable, it remains taboo, a late twentieth-century hang-up as acute as the Victorian attitude toward sex. Liz imagines starting a conversation by declaring that the death of a loved one is a fact everyone present must face at some stage of their lives. Like sex, death exists, it can't be swept under the carpet.

Company at lunchtime would be most welcome too, she could explore the market with Gloria on Wednesdays. Orange-robed monks from the Hare Krishna movement are often present, selling freshly cooked vegetarian dishes served on paper plates. A cheap alternative to homemade sandwiches and one Gloria would approve of given her propensity for healthy eating.

So far, Liz has yet to brave the crowded Staff Club with its vivid memories of countless lunches eaten at a table for four, Ron and Kay discussing scientific matters, Delia waxing lyrical over the works of George Eliot or the Bronte sisters. Against her wishes, Liz's thoughts return to the New Year's Eve party and an overheard exchange between Delia and mutual friend, Sheila Grey, who's just completed her master's thesis on Charles Dickens. He wasn't Delia's favourite Victorian author, but she seemed content to indulge the recently appointed English tutor. 'I concur that his pathos had a social purpose,' Delia said, pronouncing each word carefully as befitted an inebriated party guest. 'But I do feel the death-bed scenes are somewhat overdone.'

'Excruciating sentimentality,' Sheila agreed, 'but nevertheless expected by the reading public of the period. One must consider the Victorian frame of mind.'

Their discussion deteriorated following Delia's attempt to pronounce 'excruciating,' and ended entirely when she admitted she was pissed.

Footsteps reverberate on polished floorboards. 'I start on Monday,' Gloria declares, rushing into the kitchen. 'James said he was going to call me next week to see if I was free. Three-quarter time for twelve months. Oh, thank God!' She grabs suds-soaked hands to dance Liz across the room.

'That's wonderful, I'll be so pleased to have you back. Lunchtimes are a bit lonely.'

'You haven't joined anyone else at the Staff Club?'

Liz shakes her head.

'Sandwiches by the fountain, then. We can watch the world go by.' Gloria gives Liz another twirl. 'Do you mind if I get going now? I want to tell Roger about the job.'

Liz smiles. 'Off you go. See you Monday.'

———

Delia sits on Carol's bed watching her fling clothes into a suitcase. 'Monday? Short notice, isn't it? I thought you'd be home for at least another week.'

'I can't turn up a job offer, Mum. Kate said her uncle needs someone immediately. Thank God I've had some experience in a coffee shop.'

'Don't work too hard and neglect your studies. This final year is very important.'

'It's only three evenings a week, Mum. Anyway, it will take the pressure off you. I won't need spending money now.'

Delia picks up a pair of shorts to fold them neatly. 'Are you sure you don't mind living with Kate's family? I thought you said their house was rather small.'

'It is, but her brother's moved out. I'm having his room.'

'What if he wants to move back in?'

Carol raises her head. 'Mum, will you stop worrying? I'm almost twenty-one. I can look after myself.'

'Sorry, darling. I'll be better when I'm back at work, saturating my mind with the vagaries of Victorian literature. A good way to blot out the present, eh?'

Carol drops a shoe into the case, then turns to face her mother. 'Mum, you must try to accept the present. I know it's difficult, but you won't always feel this way. Why don't you plan a holiday for mid-year break? Come up north to visit me. It would give you something to look forward to.'

'Maybe. I'll have to see what I'm up to in July. You never know, I might have a new lover by then.' Delia straightens her shoulders to display ample breasts straining against shirt buttons.

Carol raises her eyebrows and slips off the bed to rummage in the wardrobe.

'I suppose you think I'm too old for a sexual relationship. Forty-eight years young in fact, darling, so I refuse to remain celibate for the rest of my life.'

'How can you even contemplate another relationship, Mum?' Carol backs out of the wardrobe. 'Dad's only been dead for six weeks!'

'Just because I'm a widow doesn't mean I've suddenly become asexual, you know. None of Shakespeare's "get thee to a nunnery," for me, darling!'

'I can't find my other sandshoe. I'll see if it's in Jo's room.' Pushing the door leading into Jo's wardrobe, she disappears in a tangle of clothing. Years before, Ron cut an opening in the back of the wardrobe and installed a sliding door, insisting that in an emergency, Carol must be able to access the house internally, as well as through the front door.

Idly folding a crumpled t-shirt, Delia contemplates

daughter Joanna, still spending most days lying on her bed in between meals – eating together at the dining room table is mandatory these days – headphones clamped over her ears, engrossed in her CD collection.

'Hey, what the hell are you doing?' Delia hears Jo shout.

'I was listening to the Pet Shop Boys.'

'Well, listen to me for a change. I'm really concerned about Mum. One minute she's so grief-stricken I think she'll never get over it, next minute she's talking about a new lover! These mood swings can't be normal.'

'Perhaps it's her way of coping. Why are you so upset anyway? What does it matter if she finds a lover, it's none of our business?'

'I don't think it's appropriate to be talking like that when Dad died only weeks ago.'

'Since when has Mum been concerned with appropriate behaviour? Have you forgotten Monsieur Pierre? She went on and on about him for months!'

'She was just having a bit of fun. Teasing Dad. Our parents had a great relationship.'

'You really believe that?'

'Don't you?'

'Not since I read those articles Liz found. If they were so happy, why did Dad wreck all our lives by gambling away everything they'd worked for?'

'Perhaps it started as something small and got out of hand?'

'You can't bear to think of your precious Daddy being less than perfect,' Jo retorts, her voice rising. 'Daddy's girl, Daddy's girl, you even chose your career to please him!'

'Keep your smart-arsed comments to yourself, you little bitch!'

Sitting opposite the hole in the wall, Delia resists the

urge to run into Jo's bedroom to rebuke or pacify. Her girls are young women now, they must fight their own battles. Moreover, Jo is right, Carol worshipped her physicist father, her study of marine science a deliberate decision to gain his approval. Scientists on the same side, stuff the English department. Delia sighs as a door slams. It all seems so pointless now. The ocean and its myriad creatures hold little interest for her, and she fails to understand Carol's passion for scuba diving, especially in treacherous waters teeming with person-eating sharks. Ron always encouraged Carol in her endeavours, even providing funds for a two-week instructor's course on the reef during last year's July break. Hellishly expensive. He must have had a win on the pokies or the roulette wheel. Perhaps Carol could make a career as a diving instructor, given she won't be embarking on post-graduate study. For a start, she could assist the guy that taught her to dive. An Italian-sounding name, Marti something or other, owner of a smart dive boat. A while back, he offered Carol free diving in exchange for deckhand duties.

Satisfied with a plausible solution, Delia flops back on the pillows, oblivious to the multicoloured underwear tangled between her legs. Carol will return before long; the bus to Townsville departs tomorrow morning.

SEVEN

Bus travel to Toowoomba isn't expensive, but Delia is driving Joanna to her new abode, more to check the performance of her repaired Datsun on a long trip than a maternal gesture to assist a seventeen-year-old who's leaving home for the first time. In the two weeks since Carol departed, Jo has continued to spend most days in her bedroom, allegedly reading the anatomy textbook Delia acquired from a colleague whose daughter graduated from nursing several years earlier. Attempts to lure Jo to the movies or the local Pizza Hut have come to nothing, as though first semester has started already, and she lives far from her childhood home. Leaving without a backward glance like her mother, whose own mother had sobbed when Delia accepted a tutoring position at an east coast university.

So far, the car has carried them west at an acceptable speed with minimal groans from the engine, although Delia will be relieved to reach her top-of-the-range destination, the road ahead a tortuous combination of steep climb and hairpin bends. After glancing at the temperature gauge for reassurance, her gaze is drawn to a red-roofed homestead lying comatose adjacent to a sun-dried paddock, where cattle languish in the shade of the few remaining trees. City-woman Delia soon returns her scrutiny to the road; she does not love the sunburnt country of Dorothea Mackellar's poem. 'It's not far now,' she remarks, hoping to rouse her moody daughter. 'There's a good view from the top. Remember?'

'Why would I? It's years since I've been to Toowoomba.'

'Five years. We came up for Diana and Graham's wedding. A lovely service, I even enjoyed the hymns.'

'I wasn't invited.' Jo turns her head away from the window. 'No children, the invitation said. Bloody cheek, I was thirteen.'

'Well, there's no need to mention that. It was kind of them to offer you accommodation. Diana's giving up her sewing room for you.'

'I'd rather have stayed on campus in student accommodation.'

'That isn't possible now, student residences are too costly, as I explained. Diana and Graham are charging me for food only and you can easily walk to uni.'

'But what about the baby? How on earth am I going to study with him around?'

'Joseph's not a baby, darling. He's nearly three.'

'Oh God, the terrible twos! If he's anything like that kid across the road, I'll never get any peace.'

'Try not to be so negative, Jo. You can always study in the library.'

'I guess so.'

The engine labours as they begin the steep ascent, Delia pushing her foot to the floor to change down a gear. 'Come on, Daisy, you can do it. There's a girl, good old dependable Daisy.'

Jo peers at the temperature gauge. 'Shouldn't we stop for a few minutes to let her cool down?'

'She'll be right. No confidence, that's your trouble.'

Around the next bend, they encounter an enormous truck creeping painfully up the range. 'Bugger it!' Delia exclaims, braking hard. 'I've got no power to overtake. Now we'll be stuck behind this bloody thing all the way to the top!'

Jo watches the temperature stabilise. 'Patience, Mum. A few more minutes won't make any difference.'

'Better late than never, eh?' Delia shudders, dismayed by her thoughtless remark. Images of twisted metal and bloodied bodies could be running through her daughter's mind. A sideways glance reassures; Jo seems fixated on the Woolworth's logo dominating the truck's rear end. Perhaps she's hungry. 'Don't worry, Diana will fix you something to eat.'

'What now?' Jo demands.

'Nothing, I was just thinking aloud.'

———

Behind the truck, the Datsun crawls like a tortoise, her faded paintwork eclipsed by gleaming rear doors. 'Well done, Daisy girl,' Delia declares by way of compensation. 'I knew you could do it!'

A wide flat surface lies ahead; thankfully the truck gathers speed.

'We'll soon be there,' Delia says brightly. 'Look for a sign to the uni. Diana said if we head towards the campus, we'll have no problem finding their place.'

Following several wrong turns – Joanna's observation skills are worse than useless – they pull up outside a modest brick home surrounded by neat lawns and colourful flowerbeds. The front door opens and a small boy runs down the path to greet them. 'Hi, my name's Joe.'

Joanna smiles despite her aversion to small children. 'Hi there, Joe. My name's Jo too.'

Puzzled, the child frowns and turns to his mother standing in the doorway. 'Come on in,' Diana calls. 'The kettle's on.'

Joe trails behind the visitors sucking his thumb. Reaching the entrance hall, he stops abruptly to hold up one pudgy finger and then another. 'Jo two,' he shouts. 'Me Joe one, you Jo two!'

'That's right,' his mother responds.

'Smart thinking for a two-year-old,' Joanna remarks, prompting the child to run towards her, arms outstretched. Lifting him up, Jo plants a kiss on his pink cheek.

Watching this unforeseen scenario, Delia sinks into a nearby armchair, relieved that her daughter's negativity appears to have abated.

———

Night has fallen when Delia leaves Toowoomba, Diana having suggested she stay for the evening meal. The tempting aromas wafting from the kitchen were impossible to resist, and besides, it would have been impolite to decline the invitation. Descending the range, Delia feels momentary contentment; another problem solved, another daughter settled for the year. She must consider her own future, her imminent return to work. Preoccupied with her daughters, she has neglected to prepare lecture notes for her students but familiarity with the set texts is no excuse for churning out last year's efforts. When did she last think about Victorian literature?

A conversation with Sheila Gray comes to mind, nonchalant remarks about deathbed scenes expressed from the safety of comfortable bean-bags in Gloria and Roger's rumpus room. Ideas tossed idly into smoke-filled air as she drained yet another glass of wine, while Ron lay dying in Emergency. How can she view death from an exclusively literary point of view?

Her fingers grip the steering wheel as she envisages the lecture hall, more than one hundred students, pens poised, waiting for illuminating information. They will expect her to present lectures in her usual self-possessed manner, her voice authoritative, controlled. But how can she convey the tragedy of Cathy and Heathcliff and remain dry-eyed, when passionate prose evokes such intense emotion? In private, Delia has wept often over Emily Brontë's narrative.

It's far too late to alter the course, or even delete her lecture on the Victorian attitude to death. She must learn to leave personal tragedy at home behind locked doors; breaking down in public would cause embarrassment for herself and her students. Second-year students can't be expected to comprehend the complexities of grief, they consider themselves invincible. 'May they remain untouched by tragedy, at least for a few years,' she says aloud, remembering her daughters' desolation.

Ahead, lies the long straight road dissecting the Lockyer Valley. Flexing her stiff fingers, Delia gives maximum attention to driving, conscious that warm night air and a full stomach could induce much-needed sleep. Adjusting the car radio to her favourite station, 4BH, she sings along to sixties songs, as Daisy moves easily through the miles.

Melancholia – a constant for forty-nine days – drifts through the open window to descend like welcome rain on the parched fields.

———

Screwed-up notepaper litters the study floor, while on the desk, empty coffee mugs, an apple core and chocolate wrappers surround the computer. 'No food or drink near the computer,' Ron announced three years earlier when they purchased the IBM XT286. The girls protested, saying they couldn't possibly produce assignments without regular snacks, but he refused to yield. Rules are meant to be broken, Delia reflects, pushing debris aside.

The screen flickers and changes colour, a frequent occurrence, so Delia thumps the VDU and makes a mental note to arrange a service. After six hours in front of the screen, her eyes are sore and changes of colour only serve to further irritate. Removing her glasses, she rests her head on the desk and closes her eyes for a brief rest. Her lecture notes are almost complete; another half hour and she'll be able to print out a good copy.

When she wakes, the screen has turned a lurid green, but despite several whacks of the VDU, it refuses to return to the pale grey she favours. 'Shit,' she says aloud, 'I'd better call it a day.' She presses function keys to jerk the printer into action, sighing with relief as it spews out a lengthy ribbon. Text blurs into a grey mass as she stares at the printout, prompting the unwelcome thought that she needs new glasses. Silencing the infernal machine, Delia gathers the coffee cups and staggers into the kitchen.

The digital clock shows nineteen-ten; it's much too early to consider going to bed. Leaving the cups in the sink,

Delia wanders into the family room to consult the TV guide. As usual during the summer months, there's nothing worth watching and her eyes are too tired to read, so she stares blankly at the wall opposite. In a neighbouring pool, children splash and squeal with delight, summer sounds that fuse with the buzz of insects and the rustle of nocturnal creatures feeding in nearby trees. Enveloped by night noise, she feels conscious of the silence within her home; not even a ticking clock to break the monotony.

Empty nest, indifferent, deserted, deathly quiet. Last year they discussed the subject frequently, looking forward to the day when parental responsibilities diminished. Back to the beginning, Ron said, running his hand along her thigh. No more closed doors or suppressed cries or wondering whether Jo can hear the bed creaking. Love in the lounge, the family room, even the kitchen; endless possibilities once both girls have left home. Deprived of a vital stage of life, Delia feels cheated of the opportunity to rebuild their tired relationship, to walk along a deserted beach at sunset, four footprints in the sand. Perhaps Ron stood too close to the water, trying to imitate Canute. Two footprints erased; sand smoothed by the rush of an incoming tide. Two remain, uncertain how to take the next step.

———

Rain falls steadily, creating countless brown rivulets as clear water merges with muddy footprints. Sheltered by the overhanging roof, Liz perches on an old teak chair, hoping the downpour is temporary, a summer shower enforcing a brief rest. Despite hours of work, her garden still resembles a jungle. Glancing at her dirty feet, she ponders whether to risk soiling indoor floorboards; a cup of coffee would be most welcome. Sheets of rain sweep across the garden and distant thunder rumbles around the hills. She gets to her feet, carefully wiping her feet on the mat before entering the house.

Last year, days at home alone were cherished; she loved the tranquillity of Fridays, with Kay lecturing until mid-afternoon and the neighbourhood children yet to return from school. Now, as each Friday draws near, she becomes tense at the thought of three days alone in the house. Friends drop in sometimes, and she tries to socialise, but shyness prevents her from seeking out new activities to fill the empty hours. Only in the garden can she accept enforced solitude, where natural cycles temper inexorable grief for a brief period.

The garden has always been her territory, Kay preferring to tinker in the space under the house, her reputation for fixing anything from small appliances to car engines well known. She'd constructed a wall between two poles, attached shelving to hold all manner of manual and power tools. Once, Liz remarked that Kay possessed every tool known to woman! Subsequently, they passed most Saturdays pursuing separate interests, only meeting for meals and cups of coffee. Sundays they always spent together; on fine days packing a picnic lunch and driving to bush or beach, swimming and bushwalking their favourite leisure activities.

Grains of sand blow through Liz's head and her bare toes tingle; it's a long walk through the national park to Alexandra Bay. On arrival, they'll discard sweat-soaked shorts and singlets, run swiftly across searing sand to immerse hot bodies in the cool ocean. Kay loves to skinny-dip, hence the need for a trek to this unofficial clothes-optional beach. Unlike Liz, she tans easily, her olive skin darkening throughout summer. Her breasts are nut-brown, round and ripe, underneath, a crescent moon where the sun never penetrates.

In the bedroom, Liz peels off her damp shirt. Untouched by this year's sun, her small breasts have reverted to insipid skin patterned with blue veins. Pensive, she rubs a pink nipple between finger and thumb, a gesture designed to comfort rather than arouse. Past and present merge, becoming hazy as mid-summer sun. Shorts and undies join a shirt on the floor as Liz shifts her position to lie beside her shadowy lover. A brown hand slips between her pale thighs, neglected flesh responding instantly as she swells with desire. Pressure increases, she shudders as heat suffuses naked limbs.

Motionless, she lies listening to her pounding heart, inhaling short sharp breaths through an open mouth. When her breathing returns to normal, she becomes aware of empty space, the lightness of air around a solitary body. Draped across her thigh, her white hand displays the deception of dream. Guilt traverses mind and veins; she stares at her glistening fingers as tears stream down flushed cheeks.

The telephone's shrill call reverberates through the house, an intrusion prompting a subdued response. Slowly lifting the receiver, Liz asks nervously, 'Who is it?'

'What's the matter, you sound upset?'

'It's nothing, Delia, nothing at all.'

'Oh, come on, Liz, I can tell something wrong.'

'Something strange has happened. I saw her, I felt her touch, I....'

Delia hesitates, unsure how to handle the situation. 'I'll come round; you shouldn't be alone. Dreams like that can be distressing.'

'I wasn't asleep.'

'I'll be five minutes.'

———

The front door is unlocked. 'I'm here,' Delia calls, walking towards the bedroom, where she finds Liz trembling on the bed still clutching the handset. Gently removing taut fingers, she replaces the handset in its cradle before sitting beside her friend to stroke a perspiring forehead. 'Too much gardening in the heat, I'd say. Never know when to stop, do you?'

Locked in misery and guilt, Liz cannot answer.

'Stay there, I'll put the fan on and fetch a cold drink.' Stretching out her arm, she turns the controller on the wall to high.

On the bed, Liz's tear-filled eyes follow the white blades, her thoughts spiralling towards the ceiling.

Delia returns from the kitchen carrying a glass of iced water. 'Ironic, isn't it? I phoned because *I* was upset and I find you in distress. Do you want to tell me about the dream?'

Liz shook her before reaching for the glass. 'I can't, it's too painful.'

'I understand. Do you want me to stay or would you prefer to be alone?'

'Please don't leave.' Liz gripped Delia's wrist. 'I can't bear this empty house. I'm crushed by the silence.'

Felled by the echo of her own thoughts, Delia casts aside her role as carer to rest her head on Liz's shoulder. 'I too am defeated by quiet, vacant rooms whose walls resonate with the hollow sound of monologue. Every day I listen for laughter, for the shrill of argument, for footsteps on the stairs.'

'For the din of an electric drill or the pounding of a hammer,' Liz continues softly. 'The chink of wine glasses across the table, the clatter of plates in the sink, the scrape of chairs on polished floorboards.'

Delia brushes Liz's neck with her lips. 'Dear friend, will this agony ever diminish?'

'I guess, in time, we'll learn to cope with the silence and begin to live again.'

Delia raises her head and together they study their reflections in the dressing table mirror. Two melancholy faces held in proximity as befits their longstanding friendship, yet for both women, the intimate setting only serves to emphasise absence.

EIGHT

Secure behind her closed office door, Delia kicks off her sandals to wiggle tired toes. Hours spent on her feet, two lectures given within the sandstone walls of the Forgan Smith building, have tested her resilience but at least she's cleared the first hurdle without faltering. It feels good to be back at work surrounded by familiar faces. She had dreaded sugary sympathy, lowered eyes and glum expressions but her fears were unfounded, colleagues asking direct questions, offering help and expressing genuine concern for her welfare. Crucially, they continue to behave as usual, unlike some of her neighbours who seem to think that widowhood is a contagious disease.

Right-hand neighbour, Caroline, avoids contact whenever possible, speaking only when forced to acknowledge Delia's over-the-fence greeting, then fleeing immediately to the safety of her house. The same can't be said for husband, Keith – muscular but beer-bellied – who appears keen to develop what has been a superficial relationship until recently. On three occasions he has called to see if Delia needs company, yet never offered to mow the lawn or do any odd jobs. Delia shudders at the thought of his beefy arms around her waist, the smell of stale beer on his breath.

A knock on the door suspends this train of thought. 'Come in,' she calls, hoping it isn't yet another student who has lost the reading list for Victorian literature.

The door opens to reveal newly-arrived Professor Powell, on exchange from a British university. 'Good afternoon, Dr Pierce. I was just passing, so I thought I would drop in to see how your first day has unfolded.'

'All good, thanks, and please call me Delia.'

'So sorry, I'm finding Australian informality a little difficult.' His pale cheeks redden. 'Er, my name's Charles.'

'More importantly, how are *you* settling in?'

'Not as well as I'd hoped, I'm afraid.'

'Is the hot weather getting you down?'

'Yes, but that's not the real problem.' He hesitates, his hands tapping the back of a visitor's chair positioned near the desk.

'Why don't you sit down and talk about it? Maybe I can help. I've been in this department for more than twenty years, so I understand its idiosyncrasies.'

Charles sits down heavily, knocking her naked foot with his shoe. 'Oh, do forgive me, Delia. I'm so clumsy.'

She smiles. 'Forgiven. Besides, it's my fault for removing my shoes. Now, Charles, what's the problem?'

'It's not really *my* problem, it's my wife. She refuses to assimilate in any way, insisting on serving roast beef and Yorkshire pudding in thirty-degree heat! She's terrified of flying insects, so she refuses to go into the garden for fear of being bitten.' He sighs loudly. 'The trouble is she didn't want me to take this position.'

'Only for a year, isn't it? She could have stayed in England.'

'I suggested that but she said it was her duty to accompany me.'

Delia envisages a carbon copy of the Queen, twin-set and pearls teamed with a tailored skirt. Unsuitable attire for sub-tropical Brisbane. 'Perhaps she's lonely. Have you any children?'

'Two adult children. Toby is at Oxford; Jane is teaching in Zambia.'

'Then your wife would be feeling redundant, I imagine. Empty nest syndrome. I miss my daughters, the younger one left home for uni only a few weeks ago.'

'That's understandable in your case, but Joan is accustomed to their absence. Colin's in his third year and Jane has been in Africa for two years.'

'I can't imagine not seeing my daughters for two years!'

'It isn't possible for Jane to take extended leave.'

'You haven't considered visiting her?'

'Life has been rather hectic recently,' Charles says defensively.

'No time like the present.'

'I can't get away until the mid-year break.'

'I realise that, Charles. I was referring to your wife.'

'I doubt Joan would agree, but I suppose there's no harm in suggesting a visit.' Charles leans forward. 'Thank you so much for listening, Delia. I didn't intend to burden you with my personal problems.'

'No worries, Charles.' Delia glances at her watch. 'Why don't you join me for a drink at the Staff Club? I'm meeting Sheila Grey, the department's new tutor. She's an old friend of mine. Have you met her yet?'

Charles shakes his head. 'It would be a pleasure to join you both. I'll just pop into my office to ring Joan. She serves dinner at seven on the dot.'

Dinner on the dot amuses, so Delia ducks her head under the desk as Charles takes his leave. Slipping on her sandals, she ponders the folly of a rigid existence.

―――

Narrow rectangular windows line the library wall facing the lawn in front of the Forgan Smith building, limiting the view of impending dusk. Inside the semi-basement Cataloguing department two women remain at their workstations, one tapping at a keyboard, the other tidying pens and pencils. 'We should leave, Liz,' the latter calls. 'The doors will be locked in a few minutes, and I have no desire to spend the night in here.'

'Sorry, Pam,' Liz replies. 'I forgot the time. I'll logoff now.' Her fingers move deftly over the keys to silence the computer's relentless whirr. Picking up her bag, she follows the senior librarian to the door.

'It's not like you to work until six,' Pam remarks as they walk briskly towards the line of cars parked either side of the road.

'I'm making up time so I can take a few hours off on Monday.'

'Are you doing anything interesting?'

'Not really. I'm interviewing prospective boarders. I've decided to let the spare bedroom to a student.'

'A good idea but be sure to choose carefully. You don't want one that can't live without constant loud music, it gets on your nerves.'

Liz smiles. 'So, Scott's still distracting you with Madonna?'

Pam nods. 'Bloody teenagers! Oh well, I guess I'll miss him when he leaves home.'

'I'm sure you will.' Liz fumbles in her bag for her car keys. 'Night, Pam.'

'Night, Liz. Don't overdo it with the gardening this weekend.' She crosses the road before Liz can respond.

Several metres away, Liz notices a familiar figure walking in the direction of the Staff Club. Delia is deep in conversation with a tall, silver-haired man wearing a tweed jacket – odd get-up for late February heat. A new colleague perhaps or could he be a new friend? Surely not, it's far too soon, even for Delia. Curiosity compels, so Liz calls out a greeting.

Delia turns abruptly to peer short-sightedly at the row of cars. 'Oh, it's you, Liz. I don't often see you around campus this late.'

'I'm making up time,' Liz calls.

Delia catches sight of her new colleague standing politely to one side. 'Charles, come and meet my friend Liz.'

Charles steps forward, his right hand extended. 'Charles Powell, English Department,' he declares in a voice reminiscent of a mid-century BBC newsreader.

'Elizabeth Coney, Library,' Liz responds, echoing his formality.

'Charles is visiting professor for this year. He's researching contemporary Australian poetry for his sins.' Delia dislikes modern verse, the Australian variety in particular.

Charles beams. 'Actually, I'm rather enjoying the different slant on life, the fresh new voices.'

'I'm interested in contemporary poetry,' Liz remarks quietly.

'Do you have any favourites?'

'Yes. Gwen Harwood, Judith Wright and Bruce Dawe.'

'Dawe is a local poet, I believe?'

'Yes, he lives in Toowoomba, west of Brisbane.'

Bored, Delia wishes she hadn't mentioned poetry. 'Liz, why don't you join us for a drink, then you can continue this conversation in the comfort of the Staff Club? I'm meeting Sheila.'

Colour rises in Liz's cheeks at the thought of prolonged conversation with a total stranger. 'Thanks, but I'm busy this evening.'

'Another time then.' Delia turns to leave.

'It was a pleasure meeting you, Ms Coney.'

'And you, Professor Powell.'

Safe inside her car, Liz presses cool palms to her burning cheeks, wishing she could overcome lifelong timidity. During the short journey home, she considers attending a course on communication and assertiveness. Toastmasters, perhaps, there must be a branch in Brisbane. But when she pulls into the drive and glances up at her welcoming home tenderly embraced by tall eucalypts, she acknowledges her ongoing need for sanctuary.

After parking the car in its space between poles under the house, she retrieves the mail and runs up the steps to the front door. Once inside, she drops her bag on the floor before sinking into a comfortable chair. The mail comprises several bills, various advertising blurbs and an envelope postmarked Canberra. Although her address is typed, she senses this isn't a government communication. Kay's older brother, Colin, a high-ranking public servant reputed to advise the prime minister on economic matters, lives in Canberra, and apart from a sympathy card in his wife's handwriting, he hasn't made contact since Christmas. Colin hadn't even bothered to attend his sister's funeral, citing pressure of work, according to his mother.

The small knife shakes as Liz slits the envelope to reveal

a single sheet of paper, also typed. As usual, Colin wastes no space on pleasantries, stating that in his opinion Liz cajoled his sister into leaving her the house and threatening to contest the will if she remains in residence for longer than six months. His concluding sentence, "I shall do everything in my power, which I remind you is considerable, to ensure that my mother receives her rightful inheritance," has been underlined in red ink.

Timidity evaporates as Liz flings the letter across the room. For ten years she and Kay have suffered the increasingly malicious tone of Colin's correspondence and the cuttings from fundamentalist journals included to substantiate his view that same-sex relations are sinful. Ten years tolerating his occasional presence in their home – his mother's house is too small to accommodate his family – playing the perfect hosts, repressing the desire to answer back for the sake of family harmony. 'No need to endure your homophobia any longer,' she yells at the walls. 'You can't hurt Kay now, Colin Masters!'

Rigid with anger, she runs down the hall to fling herself onto the bed, where she pummels the pillows with clenched fists. Fury subsides, replaced by a sobbing fit so intense it soaks the sheet clutched in her hands. Spent, her body collapses on creased bedding, perspiration pooling beneath flattened breasts. Calm descends but instead of serenity, words begin to form in her mind, long-suppressed feelings demanding release. Why hadn't they confronted Colin years before, told him frankly they found his behaviour insensitive, his concern for Kay's moral welfare a sham? Colin refused to believe that his sister had formed a lesbian relationship of her own free will, once accusing Liz of coercing Kay to jettison her heterosexuality. Unwilling to discuss intimacy, Liz had mumbled something about love taking many different forms and retreated to the garden, where she knew Colin wouldn't follow. A gardener tended his immaculate lawns, clipped shrubs and ordered flowerbeds, Colin and his designer-dressed wife preferring to host dinner parties for Canberra's elite. As for his letters, they often went unanswered to the point that he believed his sister was a poor correspondent and rebuked her whenever they met. 'I leave that sort of thing to Liz,' Kay would reply nonchalantly before changing the subject.

At last, Liz acknowledges not only the extent of past suffering but her failure to demonstrate her deep love for Kay. She considers replying to his letter, writing the truth about their relationship, the promise made in the privacy of their home to live together in loving partnership "till death do us part."

Seated as the desk once shared with Kay, Liz attempts to write legibly but her hand is shaking so much, she's forced to steady it by clasping her wrist with her free hand. Even so, the writing becomes a spidery scrawl, leading her to conclude that a computer-generated document would be preferable to allay misinterpretation. She's about to turn on the computer when the phone rings, sending her scurrying to the kitchen instead of reaching for the extra extension installed months earlier to give Kay privacy when communicating with students. 'Liz Coney,' she answers, breathlessly.

'I can't cope with any more lecturing,' Fran Masters begins, her voice fraught with emotion. 'This morning he said I should consider going into a nursing home, just because I won't do as he demands and contest Kay's will.'

'I received a letter today telling me to vacate the house within six months.'

'How on earth did I produce such a bigot?' Fran's voice

is shrill, sorrow banished by maternal ire. 'Political power has gone to his head!'

Liz ponders whether she should offer to drive over, but a glance at the kitchen clock changes her mind. By the time she's eaten, it will be gone eight and she doesn't trust herself to drive right now in an agitated state. 'Why don't I come over tomorrow, Fran? It's my day off, I could take you out for lunch if you like.'

Silence suggests deliberation, but Liz feels a sudden need to sit down and wishes the telephone cord reached as far as a dining chair.

'I'll make lunch, my dear,' Fran answers in her usual mild-mannered tone. 'It will occupy my morning.'

'Lovely. What time?'

'Come around twelve. Goodnight, dear Liz. So sorry to have interrupted your evening.'

'No problem, Fran. I understand.' She almost adds 'the situation,' as though reluctant to label Colin's unacceptable behaviour. Coercion, intimidation, bullying, cruelty, her mind responds thesaurus-fashion, too late for the mother grieving alone in an airless brick-veneer house squatting on baked earth. Thirty minutes' drive west from Liz's leafy suburb, Fran's home is one of hundreds lining almost tree-less streets, fifties' dwellings set in the centre of so-called lawns surrounded by low wire fences. Behind each house, a second patch of grass, intersected by a concrete path, leads to the obligatory Hill's hoist. Houses erected during the post-war population boom with little thought for climatic conditions: small rooms and windows, a narrow veranda if you were lucky. Old-style Queenslanders – high-set weatherboard with roofed verandas on at least three sides – rejected by the designers of public housing. One model for all suburbs regardless of location, built for the migrants arriving by the shipload, enticed by posters of detached houses peopled by smiling families thriving under the Australian sun. Pale-skinned Liz shivers at the thought of living in such a hot-box and silently gives thanks for Kay's foresight in choosing an architect in tune with the natural environment. No clear-felling of native trees on her hillside block, the pole house designed to fit around existing flora, not vice versa. Replacing the handset, Liz heads for the fridge where yesterday's leftovers – she still cooks enough for two – await reheating in the microwave purchased as a Christmas gift. A gift to themselves, to enable quick meal warming when Kay had evening lectures. Liz did most of the cooking, only fair as she worked eight to four three days a week with nine to five on Thursdays. Before Liz moved in, Kay would spend Saturday mornings making huge pots of spaghetti bolognaise or in winter, casseroles to be divided into six single portions and frozen for future use. Liz had been appalled by Kay's monotonous diet and soon suggested a change of menu.

Housework, never Kay's strong point, was divided into segments, with Liz cleaning bathrooms and kitchen, while Kay zoomed around the house with an old Hoover she'd found discarded on the street and brought home to repair. Apart from being university educated professional women they were chalk and cheese: Liz tidy, Kay untidy; Liz neatly dressed even in casual clothes, Kay, when not at work, happiest in a pair of old denim shorts, a t-shirt and elastic-sided work boots. *Chalk and Cheese*, the title of a poem written years earlier, a refutation – although never shared with those that doubted the relationship would last – of their apparent incompatibility. As she waits for leftovers to heat, Liz recalls the final stanza:

Poles apart to outward view
Magnets we are drawn inexorably together
By the electric current of love

On the bench, a ping announces end-time, but Liz remains oblivious, a lone woman standing in her kitchen making no attempt to stem the tide of tears.

NINE

Friday lunch passes pleasantly with no mention of the obnoxious son, so Liz is taken aback when Fran Masters announces over cups of tea in the lounge, that yesterday's conversation was in part dishonest. 'My foolishness prompted Colin to suggest a nursing home,' Fran explains, placing her cup and saucer on the small table beside her chair.

'Were you rude to him?' Liz asks to fill the lengthy pause.

'Nothing as simple as that, my dear.' Fran sighs before continuing in a low voice, 'I'm still finding it difficult to believe that my brilliant girl has gone. Sometimes when the phone rings, I half-assume it's Kay calling from some faraway place to apologise for having left so suddenly. When I lifted the receiver and heard the STD beeps, I said, "Kay, thank God, you've called at last."'

'And he questioned your sanity?'

Fran nods. 'I managed to mumble something about being very tired, which he seemed to accept, as he immediately launched into a tirade about Kay leaving you the house. I've told him repeatedly that I have no intention of contesting the will, I respect Kay's wishes. Besides, she left me her savings *and* her superannuation, which is far more than I'll ever need at my age.' Fran brightens. 'I'm going to have the house painted inside and out. No point in waiting for the Housing Commission to get around to it. I could be dead by then.'

Memories of Fran's eightieth birthday the previous year flit through Liz' mind. Kay arranged the party, Fran's friends gathering in a local hall hired for the occasion, decked out by Liz with balloons and streamers. Café-style round tables adorned with gingham tablecloths, caterers ladling out soup from huge pots, chunks of French bread in baskets, followed by cake and heartfelt toasts to the birthday girl. Thank God Colin hadn't been able to make it, he wouldn't have approved of the simple meal or the band from Fran's sister's church playing tunes from the forties and fifties, the pastor on drums in blue jeans and check shirt. 'Have you seen much of May?' she asks, eager to progress the conversation from inheritance spending.

Fran nods. 'I know she means well, calling round every few days with a cake or a casserole as though I haven't been looking after myself for nigh on twenty years, but I find her visits an intrusion. She wants me to join her bible study group, says it would do me good to meet new people and engage in lively discussions. But I'm certainly not in the mood for discussing God's word. He let Kay die, didn't he? It should have been me. I've had more than my threescore years and ten.'

Liz reaches out to take Fran's hand. 'Try not to get upset, Fran. Would you like me to clear up now, so you can have a rest?'

'No, I don't need a lie down,' Fran retorts. 'What I need

is to find out if Colin, as my next of kin, can contest the will on my behalf. I'm worried he'll explain to his solicitor that I can't make a rational decision as grief has sent me senile!'

Liz remembers her intention to visit the Law Library on Delia's behalf to determine whether a widow is responsible for her husband's debts. A visit that hadn't eventuated, Delia seeking advice from her solicitor. 'I could ask the Law librarian for you. No need to mention any names.'

Fran squeezes her hand. 'Thank you, my dear. That would be most helpful.'

'Right, it's time we made a move,' Liz says, deciding to take control. 'Washing up, followed by a cup of tea and another slice of May's cake. We could both do with a bit of meat on our bones.'

Fran smiles her agreement and they both adjourn to the small kitchen.

―――

Monday morning and Liz is drawing back freshly-washed curtains to survey her weekend's work. The spare bedroom looks clean and neat, even Fran's desk, used by Kay during her schooldays, shines in the brilliant light of a cloudless summer day. Three students have answered the advertisement Liz pinned to the Student Union noticeboard, with each one arranging to inspect the room on Monday. First-year students, they are currently living in temporary accommodation, the number of places available in residential colleges exceeding the demand. Cheap accommodation close to the university can be difficult to find, so Liz hopes the modest rent she's charging will help defray the cost of transport. Depending on the student's timetable, she could always offer a lift.

Colleagues warn her against having a boarder, saying a teenage student could prove problematic, what with late-night partying, general untidiness and loud music. Her response that the arrangement will work well with a little give and take, draws further adverse comments, but Liz remains undeterred. After all, her primary reason for placing the advertisement is a need to eliminate the deathly quiet pervading the house. If that entails putting up with a messy bathroom or the occasional burst of contemporary music, so be it. A second examination confirms the room is satisfactory, so Liz returns to the lounge to await the first applicant.

At eleven, Janet Burgess telephones to say she won't be coming, as her cousin has offered free accommodation in return for house and dog-sitting while he undertakes a lengthy overseas trip. Liz is disappointed – Janet, an arts student majoring in English literature and French, sounded most suitable.

When the second applicant fails to keep her noon appointment or even telephone, Liz begins to worry that the third student won't bother to turn up. Then she remembers that Paula Valli isn't due until one-thirty, so she wanders into the kitchen to make a sandwich for lunch.

A light breeze tempers early afternoon heat as Liz slouches in an old deckchair on the front patio. Mesmerised by swaying palm fronds and fluttering hibiscus flowers, her head falls forward, a curtain of auburn hair shielding her face from harsh summer light. Drowsy, she drifts into daydream, revisiting pleasant scenarios of previous March afternoons, cold drinks with Kay as they wait for friends to arrive, ice-cubes melting on the tongue.

Down in the street, a blue Volvo pulls up to the kerb. Doors open and two dark-haired women step onto thick grass, one middle-aged, short and stout, the other petite and decades younger. 'No stamina these city types,' the older woman remarks loudly, pointing at Liz. 'She wouldn't last a week on the farm.'

'Mum, please, she'll hear you.' Paula looks up at the terraced garden. 'She's probably been gardening all morning. It looks very neat.'

They move over to the steep steps leading to the patio and the front door, Mrs Valli clasping the timber hand-rail to ease her ascent. Behind her, Paula is forced to climb slowly, her dark eyes darting from side to side as she surveys the foliage-filled environment.

Disturbed by the creak of wooden steps, Liz reluctantly returns to the present, and pushing hair from her face, risks a glance at the strangers. Rising from the deckchair, she calls out a greeting and hurries to greet the girl, who is bounding past her mother to the top of the stairs. 'I do apologise. I must have fallen asleep. You must be Paula.'

'Yes, I am. Pleased to meet you, Elizabeth.'

Liz smiles, and looking over the top of Paula's head asks, 'Is this your mother?'

But Paula has no chance of reply, her mother pushing in front to shake Liz's hand. 'Mrs Valli. I've come to inspect the room.'

'Do come in.' Liz gestures towards the door with her free hand, prompting a stare at her ringless fingers.

'Thank you, Miss Coney.'

Liz ushers them into the house, slowing her steps when Mrs Valli pauses to run a plump finger over the pine plant stand in the entry.

'What a lovely Kentia palm,' Paula says, turning slightly. Her cheeks are flushed with embarrassment.

'Enjoy gardening, do you?' her mother asks, tossing the question over her shoulder.

'Yes, I spend hours working in the garden.' Liz slips in front of mother and daughter to stand in the open plan lounge.

'How fortunate you are to have the time.' Mrs Valli casts a discerning look over the uncluttered room.

'This way, please.' Liz moves towards the hall leading off the lounge. 'It's the first door on the right.' Behind her, sensible sandals slap the polished floorboards. Looking down, Liz is alarmed to see that she remains barefoot, her thongs discarded on the patio. Not a good impression; she can sense the elder Valli's disapproval. 'Here we are.' Liz opens the door, standing aside as Mrs Valli sweeps into the room, her bulk almost filling the space between the bed and the wardrobe.

'Rather small, isn't it?'

'What a beautiful little desk!' Paula exclaims. 'It looks really old.'

'It's about seventy years old. Made for an old friend when she was a child, I believe.'

'They don't make furniture to last these days,' Mrs Valli remarks. 'It's all chipboard and Laminex now. Absolute rubbish.' She bustles over to Fran's desk, opening each drawer until she encounters the Gideon New Testament Liz had meant to remove when dusting. 'What a lovely gesture,' she says, holding up the faded red book unopened since Kay's schooldays. 'We'll take the room. I just know Paula will be happy in a Christian home.'

Liz blushes. 'I'm so pleased you like the room. How about a cup of tea or a cold drink while we discuss the arrangements?'

'Tea will be lovely, dear.'

THE YEAR OF LIVING RAINBOW

―――

A shy studious girl of eighteen, Paula Valli settles in quickly, barely ruffling the surface of Liz's quiet life. But before long, she overcomes her shyness to speak about her former life on the family wheat property, west of Toowoomba, a conversation that, by its conclusion, discloses why she vacated the accommodation secured by her mother after only a week in residence. The third of six children, Paula, as the only girl, was expected to help her mother in the house and supervise her youngest brother after school. Frankie is a mischievous eight-year-old who loves playing practical jokes on his sister. A few hours after Paula's arrival at the home of the second or third cousin – she could never remember which – who'd agreed to accommodate her, Paula discovered a cane toad in her toilet bag. Her screams reverberated throughout the small house, causing the elderly woman great distress. Following this episode, the relationship between the cousins deteriorated rapidly – having never married or had children, Maria found sharing difficult – culminating in a request that Paula find alternative accommodation. 'Luckily there's no problems with toads here,' Paula remarks as she washes dishes while Liz dries and puts everything away.

"Don't bank on it,' Liz replies, flicking the tea-towel at Paula's shoulders. 'On occasion, I've found a few half-eaten bodies in the garden, probably the work of a snake or crow.'

'None in the bathroom though.'

Liz laughs. 'I did find a green frog in the toilet once.'

'I love green frogs.'

'So do I. Sometimes at night they can be found clinging to the screen door.' Liz points to the door leading to the rear deck. 'I imagine they're attracted by the kitchen lights.'

Paula peers out the window, her hands resting in warm water as leaves rustle in the evening breeze and the lower branches of a tall eucalypt brush against the deck railing. A sudden lull brings the sound of scratching, followed by loud hissing. 'Cats, I suppose?'

'No, it's a possum. Come over to the door but move slowly and quietly.'

Dripping suds, Paula shadows Liz and together they watch a ringtail possum scramble down the branch to jump onto the patio table, where a small dish containing slices of apple awaits. Lifting a slice with delicate paws, the possum munches noisily. 'I didn't expect to see possums in the city,' Paula whispers.

'I call him Marmalade on account of his red-tinged fur. He's been around for several years. I leave fruit out for him most nights.'

'He's beautiful.'

'Quite tame, too. Sometimes I can get quite close if I move very slowly.'

Suddenly Marmalade stops eating, drops the apple and beats a hasty retreat into thick foliage.

'Did we scare him?'

'No. He probably heard next door's cat. He'll be back when we've finished here and turned out the light.'

Paula returns to the sink to pull out the plug and wipe underneath the dish drainer with the cloth hung on a nearby rack.

'Tea or coffee before you tackle New Testament study?' Liz asks, crossing the kitchen to access the electric jug.

'Tea please, thank you so much, Liz.'

'It's no trouble, I'm having one myself.'

'I meant thanks for your company, it's such a refreshing

change. At home, it was all men's talk. Cars, rugby league and the price of wheat.'

'Didn't you ever share a quiet conversation with your mother?'

Paula shakes her head. 'She never has time. Anyhow, she prefers boys.'

'Oh well, you have plenty of opportunity now to make new friends. Feel free to bring anyone home.'

'Thanks, but right now I want to concentrate on study. Uni assignments are tougher than I imagined.' She opens the cupboard above the bench to extract two mugs.

'They're meant to be. Uni isn't a continuation of school. First year sorts out the wheat from the chaff if you'll pardon the pun.'

'I will.' Paula deposits the mugs beside the jug. 'You're right, Liz. Some students seem to think uni is for partying all night!'

'Surely not those studying theology?'

Paula grins. 'You'd be surprised who's hungover on Monday morning.'

'Nothing's changed since my day, then. I knew girls who appeared studious on the surface but ran wild once they tasted the freedom of living away from home. Not me, in case you're wondering. I was too scared of failing to risk getting drunk or experimenting with drugs. Uni was a hard grind, I'm not super-intelligent like some.' She thinks of Kay who admitted to breezing through her first degree, cutting classes to go to the beach and handing in assignments at the last possible moment.

'You must be smart to work in the Uni library.'

Liz would prefer "methodical" or "efficient" but she doesn't wish to contradict, so says nothing. Paula will encounter the real world soon enough.

TEN

In a shadowed children's playground, two women run towards empty swings hanging limply in the humid air. Slipping into seats designed for small bottoms – their own fit this category – soon they're swinging skyward, their hair flowing like the ribbons once tied to the ends of childhood plaits. The younger woman possesses long straight hair, black as the night sky, the other shoulder-length auburn with a slight wave. Pale and olive skin glow in the moonlight; legs, long and short, stretch as the pull of muscles send swings higher and higher.

A cone of light from an adjacent street denotes scuffed ground beneath the swings but with their faces tilted to the sky, the women fail to register the presence of a grey-haired man sprawled on a bench at the far end of the playground. Before long, he leaves the bench to make a dash for a large shrub on the perimeter, the sound of dry leaves crunching beneath his heavy shoes. 'Let's go home,' Liz calls to Paula. 'I think there's something over there.' She points to the dense bottle-brush.

'It might be another possum. Shall we go and look?'

'I'd rather not. Too much noise for a possum and I don't feel like confronting a large dog.' Or a man, she wants to add, but reluctant to alarm, she leaves the thought unsaid.

Paula slows her swing by scuffing the ground with the toes of her trainers, an action that Liz feels certain the formidable Mrs Valli would not condone. Then, Paula risks a jump, landing on all fours like next door's cat leaping from roof to patio, trying to snare one of the rainbow lorikeets perched on the railing. Liz hopes the damn cat never succeeds.

Safe on the ground, Paula gets to her feet and saunters over to the swings' metal supports, where she grasps the horizontal rail with both hands, as though about to attempt a somersault.

Amused by Paula's antics, Liz turns her head to smile, feels instead a faint flutter of fear in the pit of her stomach. Dark eyes are following her slow-motion legs from thigh to ankle.

'What a pity we had to leave,' Paula remarks as they head across a patch of grass to the well-lit road. 'I was really enjoying myself.'

'Me too. I'd forgotten how much fun a playground can be. Occasionally, it's good to revisit childhood.'

'Sometimes I think I haven't left it.'

'Nonsense, Paula, you're eighteen. Old enough to vote.'

'But I don't want to think about that sort of responsibility. Uni life is too hectic to worry about politics.'

'Perhaps, but with a state election later this year, you should at least acquaint yourself with the policies of the different parties.'

'I don't need to. I'll be voting green. That Bob Brown is right; we've got to look after the planet. Besides, I intend to have my threescore years and ten.'

'So did Kay,' Liz murmurs to herself.

They walk on in silence, Liz hoping her previous remark hasn't registered. Last Sunday morning, Paula brought her a cup of tea in bed and after placing the mug on the bedside table, she admired the carved picture frame containing a photograph of Kay. 'Present from a friend,' Liz said and thanked Paula for the tea. No doubt, the girl was too polite to ask whose smiling face filled the frame. Liz regretted her brusque tone – most likely it was the reason Paula left her alone afterwards.

The house is in sight when Paula asks tentatively if Kay is the woman in the photo by Liz's bed.

Liz can only nod.

'I bet she's great fun.'

'She was.'

'I'm so sorry, Liz, I didn't mean to pry.'

'It's okay, you weren't to know.' Liz considers how much to reveal. 'I lived with Kay for ten years. She was killed in a road accident on New Year's Eve.'

'Oh, how tragic! Was she your best friend?'

'Kay was more than that, Paula.'

'How do you mean?'

'We were lovers.'

'Oh.'

'Are you shocked?'

'No, no, of course not. But please don't tell my mother. She says that sort of relationship is sinful and she'd never let me stay here with you.'

Liz turns to face her. 'Don't worry, I won't say a word. But what do you think?'

'I think it's rather wonderful that these days people don't have to disguise their feelings.'

Liz smiles, although unwelcome thoughts are crowding

her mind: Colin Masters in self-righteous mode, scathing comments juxtaposed with quotes from the Old Testament delivered in a clerical manner. She shudders. 'But we're still not accepted by those of a fundamentalist bent.'

'It's time the church embraced late twentieth-century life.' Paula thumps a nearby mailbox with her fist. 'Who wants to listen to an elderly priest spouting the same platitudes every week?'

'I thought you valued your faith?'

'I value theology, not what I've been forced to believe all my life. Mass every Sunday, recite the prayers like automatons, sip the bitter wine, confess your sins to a man hiding behind a screen. My mother says God knows everything about me, so it's no use trying to hide my sins behind an innocent smile.' Paula stops walking to wipe her cheeks with her fingers. 'She used to hit me with a cane if I questioned anything about Catholicism. That is until my oldest brother broke it in front of her when I was twelve.'

Moonlight illuminates dark eyes shining with tears. Liz rejects words of comfort that could be misconstrued, reaching out instead to stroke the girl's bowed shoulders. 'Enough serious talk for one night. How about a race home? The winner gets the last ice block.'

'You're on!' Paula exclaims, taking off before Liz can make a move.

Long legs soon prevail and they're neck and neck when they reach the bottom of the steps. Side by side, they climb quickly, taking two steps at a time, but when they reach the front door, Liz hangs back clutching her aching side. 'You won,' she says breathlessly as Paula fumbles in her shorts' pocket for the key.

———

The sound of breaking glass startles Delia, other staff sharing the corridor having vacated their office hours earlier. She's sitting at her office desk marking assignments and should have left too, taken the pile of papers to deal with at home after dinner, but she couldn't face yet another dish of leftover pasta. All her favourite recipes were devised for families, and initial attempts to divide the ingredients by four failed to produce anything appetising. Reverting to student days, she now cooks mainly one-pot dinners once a week, splitting them into three or four, depending on her hunger level. Evidence of her new regime is stacked in the freezer – brightly coloured plastic boxes purchased at the supermarket underneath equally gaudy bags of frozen vegetables. On evening lecture days, she treats herself to a takeaway from KFC or the Chinese restaurant halfway home. Weekends provide an opportunity to cook, but Delia prefers to socialise with friends, the house too quiet, the garden of little interest.

In the absence of further noise, Delia concludes that something could have fallen from the cleaner's trolley as she passed by on the way to the kitchenette at the end of the corridor. Re-positioning the red pen abandoned mid-comment, she decides to leave the moment she's finished examining the current offering.

A light knock on the door is ignored, Delia engrossed in a final page that redeems the otherwise mediocre assignment, but a second attempt demands her attention. 'Come in,' she calls without turning around.

'I trust my accident with a water glass did not disturb?' Charles begins, his clipped English consonants punching holes in Delia's concentration. 'I was attempting to locate my water glass to tend a pot plant I purchased recently. Its leaves are already drooping. I dare say the air-conditioning disagrees with it.'

'No worries, Charles, I was going soon. I've had enough of marking assignments. I haven't even eaten yet and it's too late to go to the Staff Club.'

Charles glances at his watch. 'How about sharing a pizza? I haven't eaten either.'

'Now you're talking!' Delia swivels around until she's facing him. 'Give me five minutes.'

Charles lingers in the doorway, his lips parted slightly as if he wants to continue the conversation.

'Dustpan and brush in the kitchenette cupboard under the sink,' Delia advises. 'And you might as well water your plant while you're about it.'

Charles smiles and scurries away, leaving Delia to apply a fresh coat of lipstick and comb her hair. Takeaway pizza could be interesting; she imagines his wife is out this evening. My place or yours, she muses, unsure whether he travels to campus via car or public transport. If he lives on the other side of the river, he might use the ferry. Does he expect a lift home? By now, the ferry will be tied up for the night on the Dutton Park side. Slipping on her sandals, she contemplates how to evade a lengthy round trip without appearing impolite.

A warm wind blows across the deserted campus as they walk towards her car. There's a pizza place at nearby Toowong with a few tables and chairs for outdoor dining, plus plenty of buses to transport her colleague over the bridge to the southside. Charles agrees to her suggestion at once, being unacquainted with the ferry's after-five timetable. Unlike Delia, he has no evening lectures or tutorials.

'What a beautiful sight,' Charles remarks, his gaze

embracing the star-studded canopy above. 'I love the tropic night sky. So clear, so many stars.'

'Beacons of light in a pitch-black universe,' Delia murmurs, sensing the imminent descent of late-day melancholy. She lowers her eyes from the Southern Cross to shadowed grass.

'Southern hemisphere only, your crux constellation.' Charles moves a step closer, prompting Delia to raise her head. 'In the north we have the Plough amongst others, although too often light pollution prevents a clear view. Have you visited England?'

'No, though I would like to. I have British heritage on my father's side.'

'Have you ever considered working overseas? An exchange, perhaps, like me?'

Delia shakes her head. 'Daughters restrict one's career moves somewhat.'

'Both away at university, aren't they?'

'Yes. Carol's in her final year of marine science at James Cook. That's in Townsville, North Queensland. Joanna has just started first-year nursing in Toowoomba.'

'So, you're free now. Why not consider an exchange with a British academic?'

Delia scans the night sky. 'Freedom is an ambivalent concept. For years I craved it, yearned to claw my way out of the domestic box. But now that the carton has collapsed, I feel overwhelmed by infinite liberty.'

'We become accustomed to imprisonment,' Charles replies sadly. 'Like caged birds, we cannot fly far when the door is opened.'

Over pizza and ice-cold Coca-Cola, Delia learns that Charles took her advice to suggest his wife visit their daughter in Zambia. Joan Powell departed three days ago, which explains why Charles was working late. In the days prior to leaving, Joan drove him mad with her endless preoccupation with how he would manage alone for an entire month.

'A ridiculous performance,' Charles concludes, pushing his plate to the centre of the table, 'that resulted in pages of instructions. Detailed descriptions of every aspect of housework, what appeared to be a map of the pantry and a list of useful telephone numbers, including that of the local vet!' Charles pauses to sip his drink. 'As we don't possess a pet, I failed to see the value of that information, but I made no comment.'

'Very wise. So, what are you up to on the weekend? Beach, bush or do your tastes run to museums and art galleries?'

'I haven't decided yet, it depends on the weather.'

'Twenty-nine and sunny, according to the forecast.' Delia resists the urge to recommend the clothes-optional beach Liz and Kay favoured. 'Whatever you choose, I hope it's enjoyable.'

Charles smiles before glancing at the nearby bus, its engine idling. 'I should leave now. Excellent pizza, and your company was most welcome.'

'Likewise. Goodnight, Charles.' She tilts her head skyward in case he wishes to kiss her cheek, but the professor is a dyed-in-the-wool English gentleman, so after raising his hand in farewell, he strides towards the waiting bus.

The Pacific Ocean shimmers in morning sunshine and a light breeze ruffles the waves' white frills. Sand has compacted close to the water, making walking easier there than on powdery dunes. Four footprints pit the sand, the walkers ambling along the beach pausing frequently to pick up shells or admire the view.

'Carol's out on the ocean today,' Delia remarks, pausing to watch a ship cruise far out to sea. 'She phoned me last night. Said she was working on the dive boat again this weekend.'

'Carol?' Charles queries.

'My elder daughter. She's mad on scuba diving. She works as a deckhand to make a bit of money and get a free dive.' Delia shudders. 'It scares me half to death thinking of all those sharks waiting to gnaw unsuspecting divers.'

'Surely, they don't attack unless provoked?'

Delia shrugs. 'I wouldn't take the risk.'

'Are there sharks in these waters?' Charles peers anxiously at azure water.

'Probably, but don't let that deter you from swimming. It's safe enough if you swim between the flags.'

'What flags?'

'Really, Charles, you amaze me! Three months' residence in Australia and you haven't visited a beach before.'

'Joan doesn't like the beach.'

Delia wriggles her toes in the wet sand, then bends over to test the water temperature with her fingers. 'It feels great. Fancy a swim?'

'I am rather hot, but I thought you said we should swim between the flags?'

'No worries provided we don't swim out too far.' Delia peels off her shirt and shorts, then walks up the beach to deposit them on dry sand along with her beach bag.

'I'll join you shortly,' Charles calls after her.

She waves and strolls back down the beach, pausing at the high-water mark to slip off her thongs. From the shallows, she watches the pantomime that is Charles attempting to change into swimming trunks under a towel that shields very little of his large body. 'Hurry up, Charles,' she calls, as he begins to anoint his pale skin with suntan cream.

Leaving his sandals beside his bag, he dashes across burning sand, only to pitch forward at the water's edge, landing at Delia's feet like a beached whale.

'Enjoy your trip?' She barely suppresses a giggle.

'At least I'm thoroughly soaked,' he splutters. 'You haven't even got your hair wet!'

In response, she pushes through small waves to plunge into deep water. Surfacing, she slices the swell with powerful strokes. Contrary to appearances – flabby skin around her middle and thighs displaying patches of cellulite – Delia, like most Australians brought up on the coast, remains a good swimmer. Beyond the breakers, she continues her swim, unaware that a large wave has dumped Charles in the shallows, where he lies half-submerged, delighting in clear cool water.

The ball of wet sand hits his stomach with a resounding smack.

'Two can play that game,' he retorts, scooping up a handful of sand and throwing it before Delia can reach for a second missile.

Laughing, she steps backwards to rinse sand-spattered thighs. Charles stays on his back, as though reluctant to continue the game, but Delia refuses to accept a draw, so bends to fill both her hands. Advancing purposefully, she grinds sand into his chest, her large breasts threatening to spill from the size-too-small one-piece retrieved that morning from the back of a drawer. 'Oh dear, you've gone quite pink,' she says, splashing water on his face. 'We should find some shade; otherwise, you'll be feeling queer in the head.' Extending an arm, she helps him to his feet.

'I do feel a trifle light-headed,' he admits, clinging to her hand as they walk up the beach.

On the far side of the dunes, several pandanus trees offer respite from the midday sun, plus the opportunity to retrieve cold drinks from the small esky Delia packed earlier. She spreads her large beach towel over a patch of thin grass beneath a tree to prevent sand from infiltrating the rest of their lunch – ham and cheese sandwiches with an apple each. Charles can buy ice-cream cones for dessert from the shop across the road.

In front of them, clusters of sun-worshippers dot the sand, oblivious to the danger of ultraviolet rays, while further along, a few fishermen try their luck on the edge of deep gutters. 'No sandcastles on this beach,' Charles remarks, his eyes fixed on shimmering sand. 'I used to hate it when the incoming tide wrecked hours of work in minutes.'

'Sometimes I think it's a shame we have to grow up,' Delia responds, staring at breaking waves. 'It was fun playing in the water. I was able to forget the world with its myriad problems and just enjoy the present.'

'We could forget for a while longer,' he says quietly, running pale fingers over a tanned thigh.

Melancholy surfaces swiftly, dark stain on an otherwise cloudless sky. Delia recalls past infidelities, surges of passion followed by guilt or the emptiness of sudden loss. 'I don't think so,' she says, her gaze fixed on the incoming tide. 'Reality always returns with haste to topple my fragile dreams.'

ELEVEN

Following the obligatory small-talk, Delia leans across the narrow table, even though there are few other diners in their section of the restaurant. 'Last Saturday I went to Peregian Beach with Charles Powell.' She sits back in her seat.

'And?' Liz queries.

'And nothing.'

'Then why are you whispering?'

'Because this a private conversation.'

Liz sips her wine as she waits for the inevitable elaboration.

'Charles made advances and I rebuffed him.'

'I thought you liked him.'

'I do. As a colleague.'

'Is it because he's married?'

Delia shakes her head and turns her attention to the menu. 'What about fish tonight?'

'I'm going to try vegetarian for a change.'

'It doesn't feel right.'

'Then have something else. We don't have to eat the same things.'

'Liz, I'm talking about Charles, not the bloody main course.'

'Sorry, I thought you'd finished *that* conversation.'

Delia tosses the menu aside. 'We were sitting in the shade of pandanus trees to eat lunch. Side by side, as I'd spread out my towel to flatten the coarse grass and keep sand from infiltrating the sandwiches I'd made. *His* towel was soaked, being rather small. When we finished eating, he stroked my thigh. It was half-expected. Musing about my sliding through the waves like a mermaid, instead of mentioning my swimming prowess, his eyes glued to my breasts as I left the water. But when I felt his fingers on my skin, I wanted to run into the water to wash the stains from my body.'

'I would have felt the same.'

Delia laughs. 'Of course you would, silly. You're not attracted to men.'

'You misunderstand. I meant I would have felt uncomfortable, disturbed by the implied intimacy.'

'Disturbed, yes, that's the right adjective. It was as though an interior voice were saying no.' She pauses to take a sip of wine. 'But I don't understand my reaction.'

'Don't worry, just give it time. It was too soon that's all. Grieving is a lengthy process.'

'I thought I was doing well, coping with work and the girls' absence. These days, I can even look at Ron's photo without bursting into tears. But this business with Charles has made me extremely apprehensive about the future. I feel as if everything's falling apart again.'

'Don't be so hard on yourself. You're adjusting, that's all.' Liz studies the menu. 'Come on, let's order.'

Delia returns to her discarded menu. 'Barramundi, salad and chips. And pavlova for dessert. That will cheer me up.'

'Make that two pavlovas.'

Delia looks up. 'Is this my sensible friend Elizabeth talking?'

'I'll walk it off tomorrow. I'm taking Paula to Brisbane Forest Park for a bush walk.'

'She seems to have settled in well.'

'Yes, she's no trouble at all. She keeps her room tidy and helps with housework without being asked. When she's not studying, we have some interesting discussions, given she's majoring in theology and I haven't opened a Bible since schooldays.'

Unbidden, funeral images stir, Joanna reading, at her insistence, from St Paul's letter to the Corinthians. Delia forces a return to present-day text, bold black script on white cardboard. 'We're ready to order,' she informs the hovering waiter.

Rain spatters window glass and insect screen, a light breeze sending droplets splashing to the sill beneath. Listening to monotonous patter, Liz acknowledges that the bush walk will have to be abandoned. She buries her head in the pillow to gain further sleep but the rain intrudes, wearing away the protective coating of dreams. Images form in her restless mind, long black ribbons shiny with moisture that blot out the night's restful hues. She tries to banish them by turning on her back to focus on the bright floral curtains drawn back halfway to admit cooler night air. Patterns blur, scarlet petals fall from green stems, staining the plain white hem. Pain hammers her head; she hears the crack of breaking glass. Falling back on the pillow, she winces as stars dance behind closed eyes.

Paula bursts into the room and runs to the bed. 'Whatever's the matter, Liz? Your scream woke me.'

Liz struggles to focus. 'Paula?'

'I'm here. Did you have a bad dream?'

'I wasn't asleep.'

'You must have been.'

Liz glances at the curtains; their patterns remain intact. 'Yes, a nightmare. Sorry to have disturbed you.'

'It doesn't matter. Would you like a cup of tea?'

'Yes, please.'

'I won't be a minute.'

The rain has intensified, water is streaming down glass and screen. Small puddles form on the windowsill, drip down to polished floorboards. Unable to bear the sound, Liz leaps out of bed and pulls the curtains aside to shut the window.

'Here you are.' Paula places a mug on the bedside table, lingers next to the bed until Liz is slipping between crumpled sheets. 'Do you want to talk about your nightmare? I'm a good listener.'

'A saturated suburb,' Liz murmurs, lifting the mug of tea. 'Blood washing over a wet road. Smashed metal and a broken windscreen. How can I see what I didn't experience?' The mug shakes and splashes of tea stain the sheet.

Paula bends over to ease the mug from Liz's trembling hands and holds it to her lips. 'Drink, you'll feel better.'

Swallowing hard, Liz feels warm tea soothe her raw throat. 'I thought I was doing fine, Paula, but now I'm not so sure.'

'It was just a dream. You're safe. Dreams can't hurt you.'

'But sleep should be a refuge.'

'Perhaps it was something you ate last night?'

'Perhaps. I did try a vegetarian curry.'

Paula smiles as she smooths the top sheet, her small hands taking care not to touch the long legs stretched out beneath. Crossing to the window, she stares out at dripping foliage. 'Rain washes the wounds, but love heals them.' Turning around, she adds brusquely, 'Bloody rain. I'll have to study now.'

'Yes, there's no point in walking in this weather. I'm going to read for a bit. You have the first shower.'

'I'd better tidy up first. I'm afraid I left the lounge in a mess. I fell asleep watching a movie and couldn't face tidying when I woke up.'

'No hurry.' Liz reaches for her book.

———

When the book falls from her hands, Liz admits she hasn't absorbed a single word, even though the narrative seemed promising last night. Soon after returning from the restaurant – she dropped Delia home but refused the offer of coffee – she retired to bed as Paula was watching a movie that didn't appeal. Her hands touch unruffled bedclothes. She lifts her head to glance around the room, notices the skirt and top worn to the restaurant hanging over the bedroom chair to air, her black sandals arranged neatly below. A place for everything and everything in its place. An ordered life, the pigeon-hole world she inhabits by choice. A carbon-copy of her work environment where rules dominate every task. AACRII, LC, ALA filing rules – *Anglo-American Cataloguing Rules 2nd edition*, Library of Congress Classification, and American Library Association to the uninitiated. She remembers her first week in the library, the filing test mandatory for all new staff irrespective of position, the "alphabetiser," a narrow plastic gadget with A to Z slots used to facilitate the process.

Black letters printed on white 5 x 3 cards.

Kay was so untidy: books scattered over the dining room table, dirty coffee mugs and apple cores in the study, screwed-up paper on the floor. It was one of the few things they argued about.

Black letters scrawled on scraps of paper. Notes fastened to the fridge door with a magnet. *Gone to Mum's. See you about 5. Love you. Datsun issues again. Gone to help Ron. Love you.* Brief messages read hurriedly, then tossed in the pedal bin without a second glance. Hot tears flood her face and she shakes as Kay's words repeat in her head. *Love you, love you, love you.*

Springing out of bed, she dashes over to the cane chair, throws clothes on the floor before turning to the dressing table, where she scatters brush, comb and hair clips with a sweep of her hand. Knocked by her elbow, a bottle of perfume falls to the floor and smashes against the cane chair. Liz sinks to her knees, inhaling flagrance through a wide-open mouth. Last year's birthday present, gaudy wrapping paper, an amusing card, laughing over ridiculous words – had Kay even read the greeting with its sugary sentiment and forced rhymes? Raising champagne flutes to another good year.

Piece by piece, Liz collects the larger glass fragments, and reaching to the other side of the chair, places them carefully in the cane wastepaper basket. Another broken dream, another shattered illusion. Rising stiffly, she sits on the end of the bed, observing with indifference the blood trickling down her left leg. Further down the hall, a door opens and small feet pad past the bedroom – Paula on her way to the shower. Did she hear the perfume bottle break? No, if she had, curiosity or concern would have propelled her into the room for a second time.

Feet back-pedal, a sheet of black hair skims the door-frame. 'Liz, there's blood on the floor. What on earth happened?'

'Smashed,' Liz answers, without turning her head.

'I'll fetch a cloth and some band-aids. Keep still.' Paula rushes down the hall, returning moments later carrying a bottle of Dettol and several clean hand-towels. 'I couldn't find any antiseptic cream or band-aids.'

Liz doesn't reveal their whereabouts.

'Can you wriggle up the bed a bit? It might help if your leg is horizontal.' Paula hands her a towel. 'I'll fix you up, then mop the floor.'

Liz shifts her position but makes no attempt to staunch the flow of blood. Scarlet spots dot the sheet. 'I had to make a mess,' she tells Paula as the girl cleans the wound, her small hands competent but gentle. 'I had to break the containers to let the contents flow free.'

'What containers?'

'The little boxes.'

'I don't follow you?'

'I tried to categorise my grief,' Liz continues, her gaze fixed on the curtains, 'bundle it up into little boxes. Out of sight, out of mind. Surprise, surprise, it didn't work!' A tear slides down one cheek.

'It's best to release your emotions,' Paula replies, leaning forward to stroke Liz's forehead with her free hand. 'Bottling them up never does any good.'

'But I broke the perfume bottle!' Liz cries. 'Kay bought it for my birthday and now it's gone, every drop wasted!'

'I'll buy you some more,' Paula says quietly.

'No need but thank you. You're a sweet girl.'

Paula moves away from the bed to take several deep breaths. 'Now then, take off your nightdress so I can wash out the blood. And where *do* you keep the band-aids?'

'In the bathroom cabinet. Sorry to be such a nuisance.'

'No trouble, I'll be back in a minute.'

The wound stops bleeding, so Liz eases the soiled nightdress over her head, bundling it into a ball before tossing it on the floor. Only the hem is stained but she can't bear to see such blatant evidence of uncontrolled resentment.

When Paula returns bearing a box of band-aids, Liz has regained her equilibrium and is quick to point out that the wound isn't as bad as she first thought. 'It just bled rather a lot,' she adds, as Paula applies antiseptic cream followed by several band-aids.

'Can I fetch you a clean nightie?' Paula asks, straightening up to admire her handiwork.

'No thanks, I'll get up soon and go straight to the bathroom.'

Paula gives a small smile before bending to pick up the nightdress and hand-towels. 'Mum says salt is best on blood stains.' She bustles out the door as though desperate to leave the room.

TWELVE

DELIA CAN'T WAIT TO SHARE HER NEWS, ROMANCE A welcome change from grumbles that the small bedroom with its single window makes her elder daughter feel like a chicken on a spit when the dying sun edges down the steep rocky hill behind the house to engulf the space with light and heat. Closing the curtains is a waste of time; it increases the sense of suffocation. Tacked on to the back of the house as an afterthought, the room once occupied by a teenage boy lacks adequate insulation as well as ventilation. During recent phone calls, the litany of complaints has grown to encompass mould in hard-to-reach corners, high humidity following torrential rain and swarms of mosquitoes should Carol venture onto the front patio to escape the worst of late afternoon heat.

Final-year studies are also proving onerous, dissatisfaction with marine science and a yearning to escape the university system frequent topics of conversation. Delia worries that this late-stage change of heart could lead to a hasty departure, although Carol assures her this won't happen. A face-to-face meeting could help to dispel discontent – but there's very little in the savings account since she settled the backlog of mortgage payments and other overdue bills. Although her salary would seem more than adequate to an outsider, it's proving difficult to pay all the household bills as well as support two daughters living away from home. Working at a local coffee shop enables Carol to buy a few clothes and go out with friends, but other than the occasional baby-sitting, Joanna has yet to find a part-time job to supplement her small allowance.

Delia decides to visit instead of telephoning, Liz bound to be at home tending her garden on a Saturday afternoon. Leaving the comfortable sofa in the family room, she rummages in the pantry for an unopened packet of biscuits to take for afternoon tea, small recompense for Liz treating her to dinner the weekend before last, but a gesture, nevertheless.

Liz has other ideas, producing three varieties of cheese along with crackers and chilled white wine. 'No problem today about drink-driving as you walked over,' she remarks, her tone revealing surprise.

'I couldn't be bothered to get the car out,' Delia lies, a desire to conserve fuel too embarrassing to mention. Fortunately, Liz has her back turned, being occupied with pouring a glass of cold water from the jug in the fridge.

'There's some shade on the back patio,' Liz says, handing over the glass. 'Goodness, you're very red in the face. I trust you didn't run in this heat?'

'Of course not.' Delia quaffs her water, suddenly grateful for over-exertion.

They sit on faded director's chairs either side of the old table. Liz has spread a gingham cloth over its mottled surface – victim of rain and sun over many years – while bright orange plastic plates with matching wine glasses complete the picture of an early seventies picnic. Apart from sipping wine, Delia munches several biscuits topped with generous slices of cheese before beginning her disclosure. 'I heard from Carol again this morning. Of course, I guessed she had a boyfriend the moment she waxed lyrical about sunsets slipping into navy-blue water.'

'One of the divers?'

'No, the dive boat's owner. Marti something or other.'

'Do you think it's serious?'

'Possibly. They've slept together.'

'Carol told you that?'

'Not in so many words, but when she was talking about a night dive with him, her voice softened.'

'Perhaps Carol's in love with the seascape?'

Delia helped herself to more cheese. 'Next, you'll be saying she wants to write romantic poetry!'

'Nothing wrong with that.'

'No, you know I adore your poems. But Carol hasn't a poetic bone in her body, so it must be love.' She takes another sip of wine. 'Oh, to be young again and in love!'

Liz shivers. 'I'd hate to turn back the clock. I went through hell as an adolescent.'

'Because of your sexual preferences?'

Liz nods, reluctant to revisit trauma.

'It must be easier these days. At least one can be open about same-sex relationships.'

'You misunderstand me, Delia. I wasn't referring to problems I had with my parents or my peers.' She sighs and touches her head. 'The battle was in here. I had to convince myself I wasn't mad or wicked or warped. It was only when I met Kay in my mid-twenties that I fully acknowledged it was appropriate for me to love a woman.'

'You two had a wonderful relationship,' Delia says wistfully. 'I envied your absolute devotion to one another, the strength of your love. Ron and I were never like that.'

'Maybe not, but you loved one another, didn't you?'

Delia shrugs. 'I suppose one could call it love, though sometimes I felt more like his friend than his lover. We were comfortable together, good mates.'

Liz smiles her approval. 'Don't forget, we all need a good mate.'

Fighting back tears, Delia buries her face in her hands, triggering an immediate 'good mate' response. Abandoning her wine, Liz hurries to Delia's side, where she lifts the curtain of hair from damp cheeks, then bends to drop a kiss on her friend's flushed forehead.

Not far from the deck, a narrow path comprising compacted sand and gravel, meanders through trees and shrubs to the highest point of the rear garden, providing a clear view of the rear deck. Hidden from view between two overgrown hibiscus shrubs, Paula Valli stands on damp soil, secateurs in one hand, scarlet blooms in the other. The resumption of deck conversation prompts swift downward action, undergrowth tumbling as she slashes thick foliage with the secateurs.

'Is that you, Paula?' Liz calls.

'I'm just clearing up some dead flowers,' she calls back.

'Don't bother about that, let them fall into the garden. They make good mulch.'

Secateurs land on the path; petals glide like scarlet butterflies. Four more steps and Paula is approaching the deck.

'Hi, Paula,' Delia calls, peering over the railing. 'How's the study going?'

'Very well, thank you,' Paula answers politely.

'Excellent! Keep up the good work. Build a solid foundation in first year and you'll find second and third year much easier to deal with.'

'Thanks for the advice.' Paula turns to access the deck steps.

'I hope you leave some time for socialising,' Delia says when Paula reaches the deck. 'All work and no play make Jill a dull girl.'

'I enjoy helping Liz.' Paula runs across the deck and into the house.

But Delia has already noted flushed cheeks and the puppy eyes directed at Liz. 'Do I detect a bad case of hero-worship?'

'She'll get over it once she's made friends at uni.' Liz leans forward. 'I don't want to admonish her, she's such a sensitive girl. The wrong words now could scar her for life. I know what she's going through.'

'Be careful, Liz. She may mistake your silence for consent.'

'I don't think so. I've done nothing to encourage her.'

'I didn't encourage Charles Powell.'

'I thought you'd put a lid on that one?'

Delia sighs. 'I tried to but he's still dropping hints. Bloody sex, it causes nothing but trouble!'

Liz wants to laugh but a sudden surge of anger provokes a curt response. 'We wouldn't have to worry about new relationships if Kay and Ron hadn't died. Why us, what did we do to warrant such sorrow?'

'I know what I did. I behaved selfishly as usual. Insisted Ron fix my brakes, insisted on going to the bloody party.'

'Stop berating yourself, Delia. It won't bring them back.'

'I know but I can't stop thinking about that evening, my inability to see beyond entertainment and enjoyment. Stuff Ron and his pig-headedness, stuff my diet, stuff my bloody car! All I wanted was to get pissed, drown the old year in a river of chateau cardboard, washed down with Gloria's vol-au-vents and party pies!

'I broke one of Gloria's good glasses on the patio,' Liz says quietly, recalling shards of glass glistening on terracotta tiles. Hurrying into the laundry to find a dustpan and brush, a streak of lightning illuminating the garden, palm trees around the pool bent almost double, their fronds shredded, pink and white frangipani petals flying. 'Portent of disaster, yet all I could think about was sweeping up the evidence of my carelessness.'

'It's a wonder we didn't all drop our glasses when Bobbie and that hunky American were cavorting in the pool like lovesick dolphins!'

'After that,' Liz corrects. 'I was watching the storm unleash its fury.'

'But we'd all gone back inside by then.'

'Not all of us.'

Despite a statement inviting further conversation, Delia is reluctant to hang around, so she stands and begins to clear the table. She must return home to finish cleaning in preparation for her mother's arrival from Perth late the following day. It's her mother's first visit since Ron died, illness preventing attendance at his funeral for which Delia was grateful, the relationship between mother and elder daughter strained at the best of times. Jean Andrews has always favoured younger daughter, Anna, a wisp of a woman prone to bouts of severe depression since adolescence. Marriage and children have done little to improve Anna's mental health; she remains fragile and needy, relying on her mother for everything from babysitting to choosing her clothes. Trained in high school teaching, Anna has

THE YEAR OF LIVING RAINBOW

worked for years as a supply teacher, the casual nature of the position enabling her to manage her mental health and her domestic duties, or so she maintains. Her only daughter is sixteen, preoccupied with friends and sport, yet Anna refuses to acknowledge the imminent empty nest, should Angela wish to live in student accommodation next year.

The sisters, being poles apart in every way, weren't close even during childhood, preferring to spend time with their separate friends unless no one was available. In recent years, they have communicated for birthdays and Christmas only, Delia for one, thankful for the three-thousand-plus kilometres between their homes.

After less than three days, Delia feels exhausted, her mother determined to organise every aspect of her post-Ron life, excluding her university career. Since returning home from work on this third evening, Jean has been extolling the benefits of joining a self-help group for widows as she had done following her husband's death fourteen years before. Like Liz, Delia has no desire to discuss her grief with strangers, even though her mother assures her that outsiders are preferable to friends, given they have no knowledge of one's past.

'As I said before, Liz understands,' Delia says, hoping her mother will take the hint and change the subject.

Her mother bristles. 'You spend far too much time with her. It can't do either of you any good sitting around brooding about the past. It's time you faced up to the present, dear.'

'We don't brood. Sure, we sometimes mention what

happened, but it's not the primary focus of our conversation. We enjoy each other's company as we always have.'

'And you don't enjoy mine, I suppose.' Jean turns her attention to the casserole simmering on the stove.

'I didn't say that, Mother.'

'Lovely bit of lamb I got at the local butcher's. Cheap too.'

'Liz doesn't like lamb.'

'I didn't realise she was coming for tea.'

'I told you yesterday. I thought Liz would like to join us as she doesn't cook on Tuesdays. Paula eats at the refec, as she has an evening lecture.'

'Who's Paula?'

'Liz's boarder. She's a student at UQ.'

'Liz didn't waste any time. I've always thought gay relationships lack commitment.'

'How dare you! They're friends not lovers!'

Jean stops stirring and turns to face her daughter. 'Aren't you being a trifle naïve, dear?'

'No, I'm not. Liz and I have been close friends for years. I couldn't have survived the last few months without her.'

'We could have been closer, Delia. If only you had been willing to forgive.'

'You betrayed a confidence, Mother,' Delia retorts, unable to resist raising a subject that has coloured their relationship for nearly fifteen years. 'You judged me and found me guilty *before* you'd heard all the evidence.'

'You know perfectly well I acted to protect our family. Divorce would have been most unpleasant for everyone concerned. I had no choice but to tell Ron. Anna had to be spared any trauma, whereas you were strong enough to deal with the consequences.'

Furious, Delia seizes her mother's shoulders. 'Get off that high moral pedestal for a minute and listen.'

'You're hurting me, Delia.'

'Sorry.' Backing away, Delia spins around, clutching the rim of the sink as if she's about to vomit. 'Give me credit for a little commonsense. An affair with my brother-in-law, I'd never consider it.'

'But you told me he....'

'Fucked me, Mother. He fucked me!'

Jean winces. 'Don't be so coarse. I'm sure you said made love.'

Delia slams her fist against the cupboard below the sink. 'I know what I said. Love didn't come into it. I was pissed and he took advantage.'

'You're not trying to say he raped you?'

Cradling her throbbing fist, Delia turns back to her mother. 'No, it wasn't rape. I'd been flirting with him all evening. Just a game to be played until the end of the party. Only he didn't keep to the rules and I was too drunk to stop him.'

'Why didn't you tell me this at the time?'

'Because you went off at a tangent as soon as I mentioned sex. Raved on about scandal and the children and how could you face your friends at church. I was scared, Mother, and all you could think of was yourself.'

'Scared of Michael?'

Delia shakes her head and focuses her attention on the white-tiled floor.

'Come on, dear. It would help to talk.' Jean steps forward to stroke tightly clasped hands. 'I promise to listen to every word.'

'I was scared for Anna. I knew she wouldn't act rationally if she found out.'

'She would never harm you, darling. Anna wouldn't hurt a fly.'

Delia sighed. 'I was referring to her fragile mental health. Michael's infidelity could have pushed her over the edge.'

'My poor, poor Anna. She might have succeeded a second time.'

'So, you knew about her suicide attempt?'

'Yes, but I wasn't aware that you did.'

'If only we'd been honest with each other.'

'If only I'd heard what you were saying and not the words I wanted to hear.'

Abandoning years of perfunctory gestures, Mother and daughter embrace lovingly, neither wishing to be the first to separate.

THIRTEEN

Preoccupied with the pile of bills on her desk, Delia absorbs little of her younger daughter's excited chatter. 'It sounds lovely, darling,' she murmurs into the phone whenever Joanna pauses for breath.

'I've made some great friends at the youth group and next week we're going to organise a camp up the coast. I'm sure you know the place, as it's not far from Gran and Grandpa's, tucked behind that big fence just before the shops and Big Rooster or is it KFC? Anyway, we're going for a full weekend and it won't cost much 'cos the church has special funds for us. We're the future you see, we're the ones who can spread the word. After all, Pastor Eames has so much work to do, he could do with a bit of a hand. Such a special man, he never thinks of himself. He's always ready to listen, offer a bit of advice, not preaching at you, mind. He's not stuffy at all like that boring vicar we had at Dad's funeral. 'Course I shouldn't say that about a man of God but I do think the mainstream churches have got way out of touch with youth. No wonder the churches are full of old people like Grandma Andrews done up in their best clothes as if God cares what you wear; it's what's inside that's important. The spirit, I mean, the condition of the spirit. Pastor Eames says God knows if you've been untruthful or dishonest or thinking evil thoughts about someone. Not that he comes down on you like a ton of bricks, I mean God, not Pastor Eames, but he makes you feel bad. Praying helps though and especially if you ask for forgiveness, God knows no one can be perfect all the time. Except Jesus of course, but then he's different, he's special.' She pauses, asks sharply, 'Mum, you are listening, aren't you? Only you haven't said anything for ages.'

'Yes, darling, I'm listening. You were telling me about a special friend.'

'Well, I hope he's my special friend, even though I've only known him for a few weeks. Some of the others have known him all their lives. It makes me feel as if I've been missing out, but still better late than never, don't you agree?'

'Yes, darling, but please don't go rushing into anything. Relationships take time to evolve.'

'I've got the rest of my life to work on this one!'

Delia sighs.

'Anything wrong, Mum?'

'No, darling. I just hoped you would concentrate on your studies for a while before becoming involved with someone.'

Loud laughter assaults Delia's ear.

'Oh good, you're not serious then. I was only saying to Carol the other day that I wish she hadn't got herself...'

'Mum, I'm talking about my special friend Jesus, not some zit-faced student.'

'Oh, Lord,' Delia mutters, following a lengthy pause. At

this time of night, she lacks the energy to engage in theological argument.

'You still there, Mum?'

'Yes, but I must go now, marking to do.'

'Bye then. Love you.'

'I love you too.'

'Oh, and, Mum, don't forget that Jesus loves you too.'

'I won't, darling.'

Thankful for silence, Delia considers her daughters and their separate obsessions. She can't decide which is worse, sex or religion. In the end, it seems irrelevant when both can ensnare. Yawning, she opens her chequebook, praying that the account holds sufficient funds.

———

Several cheques bounce, triggering another phone call from the bank manager to arrange a meeting. Their encounter is brief, his manner terse. There will be no extension of credit; Delia must learn to live within her means.

Driving home from the bank, Delia considers his parting advice to sell the house and move to something smaller in a less up-market suburb. She wanted to tell him it wasn't just bricks and mortar, it was the home they'd built to raise their family, packed to the rafters with priceless memories, but then, he went on to say how foolish it was for one person to rattle around in a large family home, so she kept quiet.

Over twenty years have passed since she and Ron stood in the street watching an excavator bite into the steep hillside to expose black earth heavy with moisture. 'Full of nutrients,' Ron remarked, bending to scoop up a handful of soil. 'I'll soon have a garden established. Flowering shrubs, a veggie patch, Hill's hoist in the back and a strip of lawn for the kids to play.'

'Aren't you jumping the gun?' She patted her swollen stomach. 'It'll be months and months before it's running around.'

'Contentment makes time fly,' he assured her, leaning forward to kiss her moist mouth.

Her lips are dry this afternoon, the hastily applied lipstick caked in the corners. Inside her mouth, soft flesh is pitted with small lumps where she'd bitten repeatedly during the bank interview. As her tongue explores rough terrain, she tastes blood, wincing at the thought of future pain. Within days, the lumps would be covered with stinging ulcers. Biting the inside of her cheeks and lips is a foolish habit but one she seems unable to break.

At the next red traffic light, she peers into the rear-view mirror to remove the lipstick with a tissue. Minus a scarlet line, her face appears anaemic, a white mask cracked with age. Dismayed, she glances at the traffic lights, readying the car for a swift take-off, but when the lights change, Daisy leaps across the white line, shudders and stops. Turning the key produces an unhealthy whine. Behind her, an impatient driver leans on his horn, so she tries a second time, willing the car to start. Not even a whine, so she bends to release the bonnet catch before stepping from the car and signalling the driver to pull out into the other lane.

Head bent under the rusting bonnet, Delia surveys oil-stained metal and promptly curses her ignorance.

'Need a hand, darl?' a male voice asks.

Careful not to bump her head, Delia backs out to see that a truckie has climbed from his cab and is strolling towards her. 'Thanks. I don't know where to begin. She just died.'

The truckie peers at the engine. 'Bloody mess in here. Lost a fair bit of oil, I'd say.'

'She always uses a lot of oil. Roger says I need a new engine.'

'Reckon he's right.' The truckie straightens up. 'How about I push you into that side street? Then you can use the phone in my truck to call your husband.'

'My husband,' Delia begins, then decides this isn't the time or place for a lengthy explanation. 'Thanks, I really appreciate your help.'

'No worries. I'll just park my truck.'

Before long, Delia is sitting in his cab calling Roger's office. 'Engaged,' she says, handing back the phone. 'I'll call again from a friend's place. She lives around the corner.'

'Righto, darl. See ya.'

'Bye, thanks again.' Delia climbs down from the truck, conscious that her tight skirt has risen halfway up her thighs.

Roger's verdict is grim. Daisy's days are numbered. 'Had it,' he repeats, 'clapped out like me.'

'Daisy's demise may be imminent, Roger, but there's plenty of life left in you.'

'It's got to be worth living though.'

'Business troubles?'

'Amongst other things.'

'Want to talk about it?'

He shrugs. 'Another time. I've got to get back to work.'

'Thanks again for towing Daisy home.'

'No worries.'

Watching Roger approach his ute, she notes stooped shoulders and a bowed head as though he's navigating her steep driveway for the first time. Does he, too, owe Santo Zampa a large amount of money?

The girls seem indifferent when Delia tells them that the only home they have ever known will have to be sold, their only concern being strict instructions not to discard any of their belongings. Although Delia reassures them that she intends to purchase a three-bedroom unit, only Joanna expresses an interest in returning home during university holidays. All Carol can talk about is Marti and his boat. If only Delia could afford a visit to Townsville, see for herself the man her daughter professes to love madly. Other than Italian parents and hordes of siblings, Carol has disclosed few facts about Marti apart from his physical appearance. Ensnared by Latin charm, Delia suspects, recalling smouldering dark eyes and a honey-smooth voice. She'd made a fool of herself over that Frenchman, even breaking her own rules by allowing the affair to interfere with her work. Called in to the Dean's office one afternoon, she was reprimanded for behaving like a love-sick student and told to remember her position and her age.

Her thoughts turn to another visiting lecturer, dear Charles, the soul of discretion with his guarded comments and an invitation to the theatre sealed in a brown envelope and pushed under her office door. How easy it would be to respond, assuage her grief in his arms. She has nothing to lose anymore, no one waiting at home to demand an explanation or feign indifference. Nothing to gain either, a brief affair pointless – she can't imagine Charles having the stomach to continue once his wife has returned from Zambia.

The evening light catches the edge of a gilt frame propped against some textbooks. 'Are you laughing at me?' she asks Ron's photograph. 'I don't blame you. It is rather amusing considering my reputation, your wanton wife, celibate by choice. I must have buried my libido along with your battered body. Perhaps I'll always prefer the men in my life to be just friends.'

Locked in the frame, his face retains its amiable expression, a verbal response impossible.

FOURTEEN

CREDITS CONTINUE TO ROLL UP THE SCREEN AS LIZ manipulates the remote control. She's hunched forward, her right hand outstretched, her expression one of intense concentration. An exercise that once evoked amusement, Kay using exaggerated gestures to mimic Liz's attempts to manage their latest device.

'I think it's important they were friends first,' Paula remarks, stretching legs stiff from being curled up on the sofa next to Liz.

'I don't think it made any difference in their case.' The VCR drawer opens to eject the video, but Liz remains seated, her thoughts fixed on the miniseries they've just finished watching. 'Vita and Violet were drawn together by a force more powerful than friendship or love. Wonderful actresses, you could almost hear the electricity between them crackling.'

'Why do you think Vita got married?' Paula heads for the TV to extract the video and close the drawer. 'She must have realised she was gay.'

'In those days it was easier to hide behind the mask of

marriage than acknowledge your sexual preferences. Women weren't free to run their own lives like we are today.'

Paula sighs. 'I knew nothing of freedom until I came to live with you. Mum would never have allowed me to watch programmes like that.'

Liz nods. 'I thought you'd appreciate *Portrait of a Marriage*. I taped it months ago because Kay had a late lecture, then forgot all about it.'

Paula hands over the videotape. 'How did you know I was grappling with my sexuality?'

'I remembered my own struggles.' Liz motions Paula to sit down again. 'Crying myself to sleep because I couldn't comprehend my feelings, too scared to share my secret in case I was called wicked or worse. Girls at schools used to say that only ugly old spinsters who couldn't get a man loved other women.'

'When I asked Mum about same-sex relationships she said they were sinful and I must take care never to mix with gay people. I prayed for absolution, begged God to alter my emotions. But next morning, I still felt the same way.'

'It's impossible to change who you are.'

'I know that now. Living with you has altered everything!'

Liz frowns. 'Everything?'

'You've taught me honesty and acceptance and most important of all, helped me to like myself.'

Liz recalls lines from a poem she wrote in the early seventies, typed on a portable Olivetti, then hidden in a manila folder until the advent of her one and only love.

> *Above all lead me to abandon self-pity*
> *Teach me the lesson of self-love*
> *That I may learn to like myself*

'To love others, you must first love yourself,' Liz says quietly. 'Self-love is a difficult task; it took me years. Slow learner, I guess.'

'It would have taken me the rest of my life if I hadn't met you!'

Liz reaches out to pat her knee. 'Don't be silly, Paula. Soon you'll make friends at uni who are happy to discuss anything. Or maybe a special friend who understands exactly how you feel.'

'No one else could have made me face the whole truth.' Paula fidgets with her hair until the clip holding it away from her neck falls to the floor. 'Liz, it's wrong to suppress your feelings, isn't it?'

Liz sighs. 'I thought that's what we were discussing.'

Pushing a curtain of hair from her face, Paula says breathlessly, 'I love you, Liz. I really love you.'

The admission comes as no surprise given Paula's recent behaviour, but Liz acknowledges the need for a considered response. The wrong words could destroy the girl's fragile self-esteem. But before she can speak, Paula has embraced her passionately and is bombarding her face with hot kisses. Careful not to use force, Liz manages to disentangle herself and hold the panting girl at arm's length. 'Listen to me, Paula, and please try to understand. I love you as a friend but I can't be your lover. Not now, not....'

'Why not?' Paula interrupts. 'I can wait. For years and years if that's what you want.'

Liz shakes her head. How to convince the girl without hurting her that there can be no possibility of a future sexual relationship? 'Please don't put your life on hold for me, Paula. Just accept my friendship; I'm not interested in anything else.'

'Friendship is sufficient for now. I realise your emotional life is all over the place at present, but please let me love you, Liz. I can ease the pain and make you forget your sorrow. Then you'll be able to think of Kay in the past tense.'

At the mention of her dead lover, Liz abandons her resolve to be gentle. 'How dare you be so arrogant as to suggest your love could supplant hers. You're just playing at love, toying with romantic words, enjoying newly-sanctioned sensations. No one can replace Kay. Do you hear me? No one.'

'I'll leave in the morning,' Paula declares, and without a glance at Liz, slips off the sofa to creep away to her room.

―――

In the privacy of her bedroom, Liz presses Kay's photograph to her breast and weeps. Salt tears sting her flushed face, but she cannot stop until the residue of unwelcome kisses has been washed away.

Outside in the garden, tall trees moan in sympathy, a strong southerly pummelling their limbs. Closer to the house, leaves brush against a fly-screen, even the Japanese maple is making its presence known. Wind whistles through the open window, emphasising aloneness and vulnerability. Unbidden, a recent news bulletin replays in her head:

Last night, knife-wielding intruders gained access to a residential property in the inner suburb of Toowong. A considerable amount of jewellery as well as cash was stolen.

The thieves were disturbed by the owners' teenage son whose face was slashed during a struggle. The boy, aged seventeen, is recovering in the Royal Brisbane Hospital. A neighbour heard the commotion and called police but the thieves managed to escape.

Suddenly, Liz sits bolt upright, the photo-frame still clutched to her chest. Was that footsteps on the back deck? Did she leave the kitchen door open, too distracted by the confrontation with Paula to exercise her usual caution? Breath escapes her tight mouth; she shivers uncontrollably as something raps repeatedly on the closed half of her bedroom window. Placing Kay's photo on the pillow, she slips out of bed and pads to the window, where she almost laughs out loud at the cause of her foolish fears. A branch is tapping the glass, its russet leaves dancing in a futile attempt to remain in place. Lodged on the fly-screen, a single leaf flutters like an insect trapped in a spider's web. Paper-thin, it would crumble into dust if held in her hand. Soon it will fall to the earth, another victim of the changing seasons.

Drawing the curtains to conceal the scene, Liz turns to retrace her steps. She cannot cope with bare branches and dry leaves when her world is locked behind timber-framed glass, its colour undimmed by the passage of time.

———

In the spare bedroom, Liz strips off sheets and pillowcases, dumping them on the floor while she folds the quilt neatly and places it across the end of the bed. On the old desk, flowers from the garden wilt in a vase, green-tinged water and bare stems where a handful of brown-tipped petals have fallen in front of a white envelope inscribed with her name. A week has passed since Paula's hasty departure, but

Liz refuses to read the contents and subject herself to further pangs of remorse. Disturbed sleep is sufficient punishment for the callous way she has treated Paula. After extending the hand of friendship, she snatched it away just when the girl needed help to overcome her infatuation. So much for the desire to smooth Paula's path to emotional maturity; it would take months for her to recover from brusque rejection. Why hadn't she asked her to stay?

Abandoning dying flowers, Liz lifts the bundle of dirty linen and carries it to the laundry – more of a large cupboard than a room – built into the kitchen. After loading the washing machine, she crosses the kitchen to the sink, where she stands scrutinising a sapphire sky typical of Brisbane's cooler months. Strong wind has chased away the clouds of yesterday and bright sunshine promises a good drying day. Good weather too, for clearing away late summer debris in the garden.

———

Tired of hammering on Liz's front door, Delia clatters down the stairs to make her way around the side of the house to the back garden. 'Oh, there you are,' she says, spotting Liz hunched over a pile of dead leaves. 'I almost broke your door down. Why don't you get a bell, or are you trying to discourage visitors?'

'There's nothing wrong with wanting a bit of solitude,' Liz retorts as Delia strides up the path towards her.

'Then pardon me for intruding! I'll come back when you're feeling more sociable.'

Liz straightens up and smiles sheepishly. 'I didn't mean to growl at you. Please don't go. It's been one hell of a week.' A grimy hand reaches out to stay Delia's departure.

'I'll put the kettle on while you clean yourself up.' Delia makes a show of brushing dirt from her shirt sleeve.

After downing a mug of strong tea and one of the brownies Delia produced from her cavernous handbag, Liz is content to listen to practical talk of real estate, the depressed domestic market and the need to entice buyers with a realistic price.

'A couple came round twice yesterday, the agent said. They seem very interested, asking about schools and public transport.'

'That sounds promising,' Liz murmurs, stretching out her legs to catch the last rays of autumn sunshine.

'It does indeed. The agent reckons the first month is the most important, so I've agreed to an open house next Saturday and advertising in the *Courier-Mail*.'

'Have you had any more thoughts about what you'll purchase?'

'I'm still considering a unit, although I'm beginning to think a townhouse would suit me better. Less cramped and it would give me a bit of garden to potter around.'

Liz stifles a laugh. 'I wasn't aware you'd developed an interest in gardening.'

'I haven't, but I don't want to feel hemmed in. I need some space to spread my wings.'

'I'm not ready for flight,' Liz says with a tinge of regret. 'I'm stuck in a cocoon, bound tightly to the past.'

'Oh, my poor butterfly!' Delia reaches across the table to brush Liz's cheek with her fingertips. 'Please try to emerge into the light. We can't cling to our memories forever.'

'Paula said something like that. But how do I begin to look forward?'

'Take a lesson from the young,' Delia says, moving her hand away from the crumbs dotting her plate. 'That's what

I'm trying to do. From what I observed in my girls, their grieving was intense but they refused to let it dominate the rest of their lives. It's as though they allocated a certain time-span for mourning their father, then pushed tragedy aside to concentrate on the present.'

'But I wasn't prepared to learn from an adolescent or even admit that her words carried a degree of truth. I screamed at her and told her she was emotionally immature.'

'You screamed at Paula?' Delia repeats, astounded by the admission.

Liz hangs her head in shame. 'We hardly spoke after that. She left the next morning. Seven days ago. I don't know where she is. If anything happens to her it will be all my fault. She's so vulnerable, so much in need of a helping hand.'

Delia moves fast to comfort, wrapping her arms around Liz's hunched shoulders to pull her close. 'We all need a helping hand. I didn't say I could fly alone.'

After making a third mug of tea, Delia carries it into the living room where Liz has adjourned to lie on the sofa drowning in guilt, despite practical suggestions that might reveal Paula's whereabouts. 'Here you are, darling,' she coos, reverting to maternal mode. 'Sit up and drink this. Then we'll concoct an action plan.'

Obedient, Liz sips her tea while Delia parks herself on the chair furthest from the sofa. A little distance is welcome, she has already spent half an hour stroking a forehead hot and damp from repeated bouts of sobbing. Grief-tears she can comprehend, but she's baffled by atypical behaviour over a girl who shared the house for less than three months. Although Liz has a limited circle of friends, most are close relationships valued for their longevity.

Roused by movement on the sofa, Delia notes that Liz has shifted to a sitting position and is stretching out to place her pottery mug on the adjacent coffee table. 'Ready for the action plan?'

'Yes, although I would prefer not to speak to Mrs Valli.'

'Didn't you tell me that Paula initially stayed with a cousin?'

Liz nods. 'I think her name was Maria.'

'Same surname.'

Liz shrugs.

'Right, I suggest we adjourn to the study to peruse the phonebook. I assume you keep it in there?' Delia rises with uncharacteristic speed.

'In a magazine holder on the desk. But what if her surname isn't Valli?'

'Then we think again, or I speak to the formidable Mrs Valli on your behalf.'

'Won't that seem odd?'

'Laryngitis,' Delia declares as she passes the sofa. 'Come along, there's been enough lying about for one day.'

Liz follows meekly. In the study she stands to one side of the desk as if afraid to search the already open phonebook for clues.

'Only six.' Delia traces names with a plump finger. 'Here we are, Valli, M. Taringa.'

'Could be, I suppose.'

Delia lifts the handset to punch in the number. The response is immediate, a male voice repeating the number but not a name. 'Good afternoon, have I reached Maria Valli?'

'No, I'm Marco Valli.'

'So sorry to disturb you, Mr Valli, but you may be able to help me. My name is Dr Delia Pierce, a lecturer from the University of Queensland. I'm trying to trace the whereabouts of one of my students, a Paula Valli.'

'Never heard of her.'

The dial tone replaces his gruff voice. 'He hung up.' Delia looks down the list. 'There's a C M Valli.' She repeats the process to no avail. 'I'll try the other four.'

'No.' Liz steps forward to grab the handset. 'I must take responsibility. I'll call Mrs Valli.'

'Are you sure you're up to it?'

Liz concentrates on pressing buttons.

'Hi, Vince Valli here.' The voice seems young but not childish, which suggests it's one of Paula's teenage brothers.

'Elizabeth Coney here. Your sister boarded with me recently. I was wondering if you have a forwarding address for her?'

'No, but Mum said she had a phone number. Paula's staying with a uni friend. Give me a minute.'

'Sure.' Liz reaches for one of the biros stacked in an old pottery mug, then looks around for a piece of paper.

Beside her, Delia tugs at the parchment writing paper protruding from under the desk lamp.

'Leave that,' Liz says curtly, brandishing a notebook. 'Right, Vince, fire away.'

As Liz transcribes numbers, Delia can't resist a peek. It appears to be a typed letter from a government department, not that she can read upside down or risk Liz's ire by lifting the lamp. Feeling guilty for prying, she flattens the paper.

'Thanks so much, Vince. I'm relieved to know that Paula has found somewhere to stay. Bye for now.'

'Problem solved,' Delia remarks brightly. 'It's getting late. I'd better get on home.'

'Please stay for dinner.' Liz reaches out to clutch Delia's arm. 'I'm sure I can rustle up something.'

'Okay by me.'

'Good. I'm sure there a packet of pasta in the pantry and a tin of tomatoes. Maybe some veggies in the fridge.'

'Comfort food.' Delia smiles, despite her unease at sudden incompetence. Liz has always been super-organised, her pantry and refrigerator well-stocked and orderly. Ron once remarked that he wouldn't be surprised to find labels stuck to the edge of each shelf, all bearing the correct cataloguing classification!

FIFTEEN

Since returning home, Delia has begun to suspect that guilt over Paula's hasty departure is only part of Liz's current dilemma. Prior to the girl's arrival, Liz seemed to be coping well with living alone, keeping herself occupied at the weekend with her usual household chores and gardening, while making sure to leave sufficient time for meeting friends. Writing poetry – initially the reason for reducing her working week to four days – hasn't been mentioned lately, but that's understandable. As Delia well knows, there's so much business to attend to when a partner dies – name changes on bills and bank accounts, advising all manner of government departments plus dealing with university administration. Delia has yet to reach the bottom of the list supplied by her helpful solicitor.

At least Liz can remain in her home, although she expressed a wish to find another boarder as they ate a concoction of pasta, tomato sauce and the few bedraggled vegetables discovered languishing in the crisper. More for company than financial reasons, she assured Delia, telling her that Kay paid off the mortgage the previous year. A sensible decision, Delia concurred, wishing her own circumstances were similar. Five months after Ron's death, she still can't forgive him for leaving her with an almost empty savings account, a pile of bills and the mortgage in arrears. As for the money owing the mysterious SZ, thank God the law is on her side, a widow not responsible for her husband's debts. She has no idea of the amount involved, a thorough search of Ron's study, his bedside cupboard and the garage having failed to uncover an invoice or a handwritten note. Roger might be able to enlighten her, but Delia lacks the courage to raise such a contentious issue.

The telephone's shrill tones suspend all thought of gambling debts and Liz's odd behaviour.

'Hi, Mum, I've just got back from a day on *Reef Star*,' her elder daughter announces, her voice lacking the breathlessness of recent calls.

'Hi, darling.' Delia retires to the sofa, figuring she might as well be comfortable while listening to yet another lengthy description of reef-diving and the delights of Marti's company. 'Busy day? I imagine there are plenty of tourists around at this time of year.'

'Yes, and some of them are downright rude. As if it's our fault the wind picked up and we had to curtail the last dive. Safety first, Marti says.'

'Quite right, you wouldn't want to be caught out on the reef in a storm.'

'Someone was in trouble. The coastguard sped past us as we were coming into port.'

Delia hears a sharp intake of breath but makes no comment, sensing Carol has more to say.

'That's what set him off,' Carol continues, her tone implying irritation. 'He was raving on about bloody fools going out in bad weather, risking their lives and those of the coastguard crew. Then, as we were approaching the wharf, he snapped at me because some yacht had pinched his mooring. A beautiful yacht, such sleek lines, all white except for the name *Lady Julia* sign-written in flowing black letters like a wave. Not that Marti would have noticed, he was too busy shouting at the owner. Poor guy, I'm sure it was a mistake and he did apologise. And move his boat quickly.'

So, no amorous doings on a narrow bunk tonight, Delia muses, as Carol reports on a subsequent argument about diving equipment not being stowed properly and Marti's refusal to apologise for being unreasonable. 'Don't worry, darling, just turn up for work tomorrow. If your relationship doesn't work out, you can always find another weekend job.'

'How can I?'

'What's happened?' Delia dreads asking a more direct question, pregnancy would wreck Carol's career prospects. Abortion would solve the problem, but she fears an Italian and most likely Catholic boyfriend might want to marry her daughter instead.

'Don't worry, Mum,' Carol answers quickly. 'I'm on the Pill. And I'm not sick or behind in my studies. It's just that I love Marti so much and it really hurt to be pushed away.'

Delia puts her hand over the receiver to disguise a sigh of relief.

'Are you still there, Mum?'

'Yes, darling. My advice is to forget about the silly argument. He'll be all smiles tomorrow, I'm sure and apologising for his bad mood.'

'Thanks for listening, Mum. I miss you and....' She hesitates, then adds, 'and Jo, of course.'

'I miss you too, darling, but don't forget you graduate in less than six months, so we'll all be together for Christmas.'

The moment she finishes the sentence, Delia rebukes herself for indiscriminate inclusion. All implies four not three and even if Marti were to join them, their family won't be complete over Christmas or at any other future gathering. 'Bye for now,' she says hurriedly, 'and take care.'

On the other side of the ridge that dissects the suburb, Liz watches a boring movie rather than pick up the library book lying on the coffee table. *Wild Swans* is a fascinating tale of three women, spanning a century of life in China, but she cannot cope with text tonight, black letters on white paper reminding her of the letter half-hidden beneath her desk lamp. Four weeks until a dreaded arrival, Colin Masters visiting his mother in person to expedite the legal proceedings for contesting Kay's will. Does Fran know her son is planning to visit or comprehend the nature of his visit? When the letter arrived on Monday, Liz considered phoning Fran but on reflection felt it would be unwise given the circumstances. Since then, the matter has festered and become an insurmountable sore, concerns regarding Paula Valli paling into insignificance when compared to losing her home. Yet, Liz has chosen not to confide in Delia, the only one of her friends who would completely understand, neither has she consulted the kindly solicitor who handled Kay's will and the legal matters pertaining to the change of name on the house deeds. However, a recent visit to the Law Library has answered one query. Under the Queensland Succession Act, Colin Masters can only contest Kay's will on his mother's behalf with Fran's written consent, and only if Fran were financially dependent on Kay.

Advertisements distract for a few minutes, Liz focusing on items she has no intention of purchasing but when the movie resumes, she abandons self-pity to walk into the study, where she compiles a list of tasks to be completed within the next forty-eight hours in order of priority. Top of the list is buying food from the corner store to last until she can visit the supermarket after work on Monday – Brisbane is yet to embrace Sunday trading. The next item is two-fold, the first being to call Delia to ask if it's possible to meet the next day, the second to apologise for self-indulgent behaviour and a sub-standard meal. Item 2b is swiftly erased, Liz acknowledging its irrelevance. Third on the list is a call to her solicitor seeking advice regarding Colin's letter – should it be answered or ignored, does it have legal standing, etc. Liz appreciates that it may be necessary to take time off work for a face-to-face meeting given the seriousness of the matter. Items seven to ten are less important, being household chores neglected during the past week and added to the list to ensure a swift return to an orderly existence.

Satisfied, Liz retrieves the letter from beneath the lamp and carries it along with her list into the kitchen, where she places both on the bench nearest the wall-mounted telephone, ready to be acted upon come morning. Then, she turns off the TV to begin her usual pre-bedtime routine of checking door locks, putting her mug in the sink and looking at the weekly menu to see if she needs to defrost any meat for tomorrow's dinner. Except, of course, there isn't a handwritten menu attached to the fridge with the magnet purchased during a Tasmanian holiday. Resolve wavers; she bites her lower lip to prevent a return of soggy tears. Perhaps it's not too late to phone Delia about lunch tomorrow.

Although wide awake, Delia is unable to take the call, being already engaged with listening to an excited daughter recount a second Marti instalment. The man in question visited Carol at home soon after the first call to her mother, his mission to ask for forgiveness, rationalise his unwarranted anger and most important of all, to express undying love – Carol's words, not his, Delia imagines. The explanation, while understandable, was a revelation, Marti describing how the name of a yacht evoked long-suppressed memories of his fiancé Julia's tragic death in a boating accident ten years earlier. Not for the first time, Delia suspects that Marti is considerably older than Carol, but decides to leave that question for another day rather than upset her with comments about the folly of a twenty-year-old dating a thirty-something man.

'I was shocked, too,' Carol continues before Delia can think of a suitable response, 'but now I know the truth, so much about Marti makes sense. Lovers shouldn't have secrets.'

'No, darling, but that's easier said than done.' Delia suppresses a yawn, wishing the call would end. Her right ear feels sore, having been pressed against inflexible plastic for what seems like hours, and she's longing for a glass of wine before bed. Maybe a few crackers and cheese as well, the meal with Liz barely enough to sustain her until morning. Other people's problems are so draining!

'Got to go, Mum,' Carol says, 'or I'll get into trouble for tying up the phone all evening.'

'I hope you're paying Mrs Harris enough for your calls?'

'Yes, Mum. We go through the bill together, so I know what I owe. Bye.'

Beeps indicate a message, but Delia is too weary to risk another lengthy call. After replacing the handset, she staggers into the kitchen to prepare a well-earned supper. Early mornings don't agree with her and today she rose at seven to tidy the house prior to the Open House scheduled for ten. Five couples attended, the real estate agent reported afterwards, with two expressing an interest in a second inspection. Delia detests having her home on show and the thought of strangers tramping through her private spaces making comments about size and décor, is extremely unsettling. She prays for a quick sale with a short contract. The sooner she can buy a new property, the sooner she can begin to move on. Eminent psychologists – she's read several books about the grieving process – might advise not to move house for at least a year following the death of a spouse, but what choice does she have? The house is too big, too expensive to maintain and, if she's honest, too full of memories that constantly remind her of all she has lost.

SIXTEEN

Gloria's news comes as a complete shock to Liz. Preoccupied with the CM issue – at present, she can't bear to even think his name – she has failed to notice her friend's mounting distress. At work, Gloria appears professional as usual, with no mention made of marital trouble during their on-campus lunches or when they meet for weekend coffee and cake at a local café. This morning, Liz should have realised something was amiss when Gloria insisted on sitting at a pavement table, even though a chill wind was blowing up the street and they know from experience that the wrought-iron chairs are hard and cold.

'Have you thought about the reality of living alone?' Liz asks, following a second revelation that the children will remain with Roger in the family home, only joining Gloria for weekends.

'It won't be easy, but I'll cope. It can't be worse than the current situation. Roger and I hardly speak and when we do, we argue.'

Unsure how to respond, Liz toys with her cake.

'I've spoken to James,' Gloria continues, 'and he's

offered me full-time work from July. A twelve-month contract, so I can manage the rent on a small flat, and at least the kids won't have to give up their home for now.'

'Is divorce a certainty?' Liz ignores the inner voice that's prodding her to offer Gloria the spare room. No way could she cope with two boisterous children every weekend.

'Let's say it's a likely outcome. I would have been more understanding if the business problems were the only issue, but I can't forgive Roger for gambling debts. Tens of thousands owed to one of his best customers, or should I say former customer, who in turn persuaded *his* mates to take their business elsewhere. Christ, I wouldn't even know about the gambling now if I hadn't answered the phone when the bank manager called back in February to advise that our personal account was overdrawn! What went wrong, Liz? Roger and I used to discuss everything!'

'I don't know, Gloria. Everything seems to be falling apart this year.' Liz considers whether to mention that Delia was also in the dark regarding Ron's gambling, but Gloria powers on before she can gather her thoughts.

'So, I had to talk to someone, the whole thing was eating me up. I've tried talking to Mum – not about the gambling – but she said I was overreacting, that naturally Roger was preoccupied, as the business is in trouble. She accused me of being utterly selfish, said that was the problem with women today, we want the lot, kids, career and a perfect marriage. But you know I'm not like that. I put my career on hold when the kids were young and I've never expected marriage to be perfect, although honesty and some sort of affinity would have been good this past year. We're not even friends, just two people who happen to live in the same house!'

'Two people who promised to live together through thick and thin until death parted them,' Liz says quietly.

Gloria reacts with wide eyes and a downturned mouth. 'You disappoint me, Liz. I thought you'd be more sympathetic but you sound just like my mother.'

'Sorry, I didn't mean to preach. I guess what I meant to say is why not give your marriage another chance? Surely a relationship that's lasted fifteen years is worth saving?'

'Right now, we're travelling different roads and there seems no possibility of a convergence.'

Liz nods and picks up her coffee mug. She needs a few moments to make sense of sudden trepidation and to fashion her question in a way that won't alarm. Perhaps Roger is repaying his debts, having come to an arrangement with the gambling establishment. Perhaps the threatening figure she read about in the *Courier-Mail* last year has been jailed for his crimes or has nothing to do with Roger's debts. Ron and Roger might have used the excuse of meeting each other at the local pub to hide their gambling addiction, but it's anyone's guess whether they actually spent several evenings a week together. 'Are you sure the kids will be alright with their father during the week?' she asks, a weak question unworthy of expression.

'No problems on that score. Roger will be working from home soon. The lease on the office and warehouse expires at the end of June, thank God. He's already cleared out the garage to accommodate his stock and he'll be using the rumpus room as an office instead of a bedroom.'

'A bedroom?'

'He's been sleeping down there for the last couple of months.' Gloria gets to her feet. 'Thanks so much for listening, Liz, and sorry I growled at you. I'll be better when all this is sorted.'

So will I, Liz almost says, as the image of an angry man barrels into her brain. 'Take care, Gloria, and please call me if you need to talk.'

'Will do. See you Monday.'

Alone at the table, Liz lingers over the last mouthful of coffee as she contemplates a beautiful partnership. Thank God, there was no time for disenchantment.

Relocation dominates a second weekend conversation, Liz and Delia sitting on the deck sharing a quiche, courtesy of the latter's well-stocked freezer. The accompanying salad – prepacked and somewhat limp – came from the corner store. Prior to lunch, Liz shared the CM issue – no surprise to Delia, given she had observed the man's hostility over many years. Real estate news can wait until they've finished eating and are sipping the last of the Sauvignon Blanc. As usual, Delia is the first to place her glass on the table. 'I've had a busy morning,' she remarks, settling back in her chair. 'The agent came round at ten with a contract.'

Liz beams. 'Congratulations!'

'A pleasant couple, he said. Both academics. I think they come from Sydney uni. One child, a boy of twelve. I didn't get quite what I wanted, but one can't be fussy in this economic climate. The only problem is the short contract. Thirty days, which doesn't give me much time to find a unit, so I'm thinking of renting for a while.'

'Why not come here? I've plenty of room. You can put your furniture in storage for a few months.'

'Are you sure? I don't want to become another problem boarder.'

'That's unlikely. We've been friends for twelve years.'

'I'm cranky in the mornings and not very tidy.'

'Well, I don't exactly leap out of bed with a smile and I could do with a few things out of place.'

'Then I accept with deep gratitude. Do you know if there are any storage facilities locally?'

'There's one not far from the shops. On the left.'

'Great, I'll look them up in the *Yellow Pages* when I get home.'

'Have a look in the study while I clear up.' Liz pushes her glass into the middle of the table. 'And don't feel you have to find a new place quickly. No finite lease here.'

'Thanks, I would prefer to be selective. My knowledge of living in a unit is limited. I shared a house when I first came to Brisbane.' She thinks of the rundown unit Ron and a mate were living in when they met. Mould on the bathroom walls, cracked concrete tubs in the shared laundry, thick grease on the kitchen hotplate. 'Not exactly pleasant memories.'

'Student accommodation is rarely good unless one has wealthy parents. I was stuck in a tumbledown place in Taringa for years. Rotten windowsills and always a plague of ants in the kitchen. Still, there were good times, and as the three of us were in the same boat it didn't seem so bad.'

'Good times,' Delia muses, thinking not of shared accommodation but of passionate couplings on a sagging mattress, drunk on sex and whatever cheap wine Ron had bought at the Regatta Hotel. 'In those days, we considered ourselves invincible. Access to the Pill courtesy of a friendly campus doctor, a plethora of part-time jobs while we pursued post-graduate study, with the promise of an academic position once we had a masters under our belts.' Delia sighs. 'What bloody fools we were to think the good times would last forever.'

'Not fools, Delia, we were young and idealistic.'

———

There are innumerable jobs to be done before Delia moves in, so following a dinner reminiscent of student days – cheese on toast – Liz sits at her desk writing another list. The storage space under the house needs a good clear-out, bookshelves must be weeded to provide room for Delia's essential titles and the linen cupboard sorted to make room for more bedding. Liz wants Delia to surround herself with familiar objects as she adjusts to yet another unplanned development. Shutting the door on her home of twenty years could feel like another death.

After numbering the tasks in order of importance, Liz turns her attention to the desk calendar. They have already agreed on a date, but when she lifts her pen, the square labelled Saturday 27 already contains a set of initials. Her pen scrawls across a multitude of squares, her body shaking uncontrollably as truth descends. What is the matter with her, has she suffered amnesia for the past few hours? Legal matters take months to reach a conclusion, but if a judge finds in CM's favour, she will be homeless, and unlike Delia, lack the means to purchase another property!

SEVENTEEN

Cardboard boxes litter the carpet, and a pile of old newspapers leans precariously against a dining chair, Delia using the living room for packing purposes. The family room is ample for day to day living, meals already eaten while watching TV or perched on a high stool at the breakfast bar. Since the contract became unconditional, she has filled one or two boxes after work each day, with weekends reserved for mass sorting and packing. A meal of any kind has been overlooked tonight; she's too engrossed in sorting the family's extensive book collection into Keep, Discard (Op shop), and Donate to UQ library.

At the weekend, Joanna is visiting to clear out her room with a promise to help with other packing should time permit. On Sunday afternoon, Pastor Peter Eames will be arriving to transport Jo and her belongings back to Toowoomba. Delia trusts he has a large car. As for Carol's few remaining possessions, they will be boxed up and stored until she deigns to return home, Marti taking precedence during the coming semester break. Although relieved that neither daughter seems upset about the forced sale of their childhood home, Delia would have appreciated a little empathy.

Reading a textbook slows decision-making, but Delia feels reluctant to part with Ron's words. The scientific jargon she's struggling to comprehend epitomises an important period when they worked together for a common goal. Weeks spent typing a decent draft of his manuscript from handwritten pages, her annoyance when he decided to alter the first three chapters and she had to begin again. On-line editing didn't exist in the late seventies, and her head throbbed as she struggled to decipher his scribble. But she refused to give in or employ a professional typist as he suggested. How could she? It was a labour of love.

When she turns the page, her attention is drawn to a white-coated physicist photographed conducting experiments in a laboratory, her earnest young husband, his face unlined, bushy brown hair reaching to his shoulders. Touching the shiny paper, she traces his youthful shape with dusty fingertips. *Promise of a golden future,* she hears his senior colleague remark at the book launch, *a brilliant mind well ahead of his contemporaries.*

Research dollars delighted the department, and before long, America beckoned, a wealthy East Coast university offering a mind-boggling salary. But Delia refused to go, her career too precious to risk a third disruption. Three years after resuming full-time work, she had obtained tenure at last and her doctoral thesis was almost completed. Besides, the girls were ten and eight, both doing well at primary school; it would be unwise to uproot them.

Night after night they argued, his voice harsh and unyielding, her own shrill and demanding. Illogical woman-talk, he maintained, accusing her of disloyalty and selfishness. A week of discord culminated in his reaching for the telephone to dial a string of numbers and accept the two-year position. Six weeks later, he kissed three sulky mouths goodbye to soar high into a clear September sky.

Pale blue envelopes streamed across oceans; small girls hurried to the mailbox each afternoon in anticipation of colourful postcards. Months passed, Delia suggested a Christmas visit, spent hours with a travel agent. At home, the girls gazed wistfully at library books depicting snowmen and Santa arriving in a sleigh pulled by reindeer instead of kangaroos. Later, they tried on borrowed parkas, their mother laughing as they paraded in front of the bedroom mirror, their hot faces framed with fur.

Three days before their departure, Delia rose from sweat-soaked sheets to answer the telephone's persistent ring. Surely Ron realised it was the middle of the night! But as she flew across the family room, a second thought entered her head. He might be lonely, need to hear her voice, her love ringing down the wires. She lifted the handset, heard the beep, beep of a long-distance call. 'Hello, hello, my love.'

Mute, she absorbed the message, her white Christmas melting in hot December sun. A distant hospital, a dying man. 'He's slipping away with barely a whimper,' her mother said, her voice choked with emotion. 'You must come over, he's waiting for his other girl, he can't leave until you're here.'

Words tumbled out before Delia considered their impact.

'You can't ignore death,' her mother shouted across the continent. 'You can't draw the curtains around your father's hospital bed and pretend he isn't there!'

A subsequent barrage of anger and disappointment

THE YEAR OF LIVING RAINBOW

prevented an apology or further dialogue, Delia recalling similar treatment when announcing her intention to accept a position at the University of Queensland. Leaving family and friends to forge a new life in Brisbane was beyond her mother's comprehension. Why couldn't Delia be like her sister, marry a local man and settle down in suburban Perth?

When her mother reverted to a little girl whimper interspersed with sobs, Delia's tough mid-thirties skin split, exposing a malleable core that instantly yielded to maternal authority. And then the child in *her* cried out for the broad-shouldered father who'd carried her up winding stairs, whispering stories of fairies and wishing her teddy-bear dreams.

Early morning phone calls organised child-minding with paternal grandparents and air-hostess assistance for unaccompanied minors. A flight was cancelled, another booked, Delia flew west to death and childhood.

———

The textbook falls to the floor, his face vanishing, trapped between early eighties pages. Relief floods, she has no desire to relive further memories. Stretching limbs stiff from sitting cross-legged on the carpet, she's about to leave the packing room when a high-pitched voice calls from a corner of her mind. 'Mary, I said Mary, Mum. Aren't you listening?'

Delia shakes her head to dislodge the painful memory, but the voice persists, eight-year-old Joanna determined to recount her version of their American adventure. 'Pretty lady, lots of blond hair like bubbles. Mary plays games with us in the snow and gives us hot chocolate in bed.'

'A girl from the lab,' she hears him murmur. 'Mary's helping me out with the kids.'

She remembers the questions that buzzed in her head,

the sleepless nights, her refusal to interrogate innocent children on their return home. His distraction during phone calls, pathetic excuses for not returning home during the long northern summer break, a second Christmas in Perth, the children fractious, missing their father and their friends.

A benevolent sun shone in a cloudless winter sky when Dr Ronald Pierce finally landed at Brisbane airport, surprising his family with his bushy beard and Yankee Doodle speech. The girls listened wide-eyed, swallowing candy-wrapped lies of solo travel to distant states, while their mother smiled sweetly and tossed his words into the wind. By then, she had moved beyond pain, assuaged her grief in another's arms.

Closing the penultimate box of books, Delia seals it, using the packing tape purchased from the removalist. 'End of an era,' she says aloud, noting there are eight boxes to be transported to the library. Two car trips will be required.

'End of what, Mum?' Jo calls from the kitchen, where she's washing up the lunch dishes.

Delia joins her in the kitchen, the last of Ron's textbooks tucked under one arm. 'I said end of an era.'

Jo nods. 'I knew you would be terribly upset to leave the house, so I asked Pastor Eames to say a special prayer for you.'

'Thank you, darling.'

'Pastor Eames really cares, you know.'

'I'm sure he does, darling.' She throws the book through the doorway into the living room.

'You're not throwing textbooks away, surely?'

'No, I'm donating them to the library.'

'I can't imagine old ladies reading books on physics.'
'The uni library, of course.'
Jo grimaces. 'That won't please Liz.'
'What's it got to do with Liz?'
'She'll have to catalogue them.'
'Liz doesn't catalogue science books. Her subject areas are literature and religion.'
'I must ask Pastor Eames if he wants all the books in *his* house,' Jo muses. 'It seems such a waste to leave them lying about when there are so many people needing help.'
'Why were you…' Delia begins, then decides she prefers not to know what Jo was doing in the pastor's house. 'What do you mean by needing help?'
'Salvation. They need to open their hearts to Jesus and renounce their sins before it's too late.'
Delia dismisses medieval images of Hell to grab a tea-towel.
'He suffered for us, Mum, that we might be saved.'
Delia continues to wipe a plate. 'Who, Pastor Eames?'
'Jesus, Mum, not Pastor Eames. Aren't you listening?'
'Sorry, I'm a bit preoccupied.' She sets the dry plate on the counter.
Jo lifts her hands from the sink to fold them across her chest. 'His death on the cross was a supreme act of selflessness, you know. He died that we might have eternal life.'
'Threescore years and ten will do me.'
'Don't you believe in life after death?'
Delia shakes her head, then reaches for another plate.
'Because of what happened to Dad, I suppose?'
'Nothing to do with that.'
'It's quite natural to blame God for taking your husband. And your friend, Kay.'

Delia sniffs. 'It's hardly God's fault that your father drove too fast on a wet road.'

'God sent the storm,' Jo declares, her voice chock-full of conviction. 'It was a necessary death. Pastor Eames said so.'

'How dare that pastor fill your head with such rubbish!' The plate falls to the tiled floor, shattering on impact.

Ignoring broken pottery, Jo ploughs on. 'God had to rescue Dad from sin. The gambling tainted him. Pastor Eames said death was the only way to save Dad's soul.'

Delia struggles to contain her fury. 'I don't believe I'm hearing this from my own daughter. Next, you'll be saying that Kay's death was also part of God's plan!'

'It was.'

Delia reaches out to grab her daughter's shoulders. 'So, what sin had Kay committed?'

Jo blushes and lowers her eyes. 'The Bible forbids sex between two women or two men.'

'And eating pork and coveting your neighbour's donkey. Get real, Joanna. It's nineteen ninety-two.' Rushing from the room, Delia heads for the box labelled *Children's Books, Op Shop,* slashes tape with her Stanley knife and proceeds to empty the contents. 'It's here somewhere,' she mutters to herself, 'and I'm going to make damn sure no other child is brainwashed.'

Bent over the box, she fails to notice that Jo is standing behind her, hands on hips, following the flight of each book with disbelief. 'Don't you dare toss out my children's Bible,' Jo cries, snatching the book from her mother's hands. 'Pastor Eames is right, not you. He knows his Bible off by heart.'

Delia twists around, her expression one of absolute exasperation. 'Then I suggest he reads with a little more discernment instead of picking out bits that suit his cause and quoting them out of context.'

'He wouldn't do that, Mum. You don't understand, you don't know him.'

Frustration deflates like a pricked balloon. 'No, but I do know my daughter. Forget all this talk of saving sinners, Joanna. You were the lost sheep wandering in the wilderness, seeking another reason for your father's death.'

'Okay, I can relate to that one. But can't you see that Pastor Eames has given me the answers and taught me to accept the will of God?'

'He also took advantage of your vulnerability to fill your head with images of a vengeful Old Testament God. An unyielding patriarch who demands an eye for an eye and a tooth for a tooth.'

'No, Mum, you've got it all wrong. God loves us and cares for us. Only the wicked suffer. If I'm free from sin, I know I'll be saved.'

Delia sighs, and getting to her feet, wraps her arm around her daughter's thin body.' 'Tell me something,' she says gently. 'Are the children dying in Bosnia wicked, have they committed some unforgivable sin?'

Jo lays her head on her mother's breast. 'No, of course not.'

'Then I suggest you think very carefully before you sound off again about sin and divine retribution.'

'I guess I've got a lot to learn.'

Delia strokes her hair. 'You can't expect to know everything at eighteen.'

Harmony restored, mother and daughter continue to sort and pack, sometimes together, sometimes in separate rooms. Dinner – pizza purchased from a local shop – is eaten straight from the box to save on washing up, Jo giggling like the schoolgirl she was only months earlier when a piece of greasy cheese falls onto the mauve carpet.

After demolishing a huge amount of ice-cream, also eaten straight from the carton, Delia announces that it's time for a bit of fun. 'The smashing of hideous ornaments,' she explains, leading Jo over to the dining room sideboard where two decades of unwanted gifts languish behind the best crockery.

'Four China ducks!' Jo lifts the in-flight birds from their hiding place. 'Where on Earth did these come from?'

'My great-aunt, Ethel. One a year. Just as well she died four years after we got married.'

Jo places the ducks on the carpet. 'Where are we going to smash them?'

'In the garage. We don't want to alarm the neighbours. Put them in a cardboard box for now, then we can carry them downstairs to do the dastardly deed all at once.'

Jo retrieves the nearest box. 'Here you go, guys.'

Next to emerge is a mock-ivory elephant glued to a wooden base, its pale glass eyes staring disapproval. Holding the beast at arm's length, Delia drops it into the box.

Jo shivers. 'I hope it doesn't return to haunt your dreams, Mum.'

'I don't believe in that sort of nonsense.'

Jo smiles and reaches for a pottery ashtray. It should have been tossed out years ago, being stained and chipped. 'Ugh! Who used that?'

'Dad. He smoked a pipe when we first met. I imagine he thought it enhanced his earnest scientist image.'

'Disgusting!' Jo throws the ashtray into the box with such force, they hear the crack of elephant hide.

Saturday evening television and doors closed against the evening chill prevent the sound of demolition from reaching the neighbouring houses. Jo appears to enjoy the process, laughing as each item shatters on the concrete floor. When the task is completed, she fetches a dustpan and brush to sweep up the debris and throw it into the nearby dustbin, Delia surprised by her diligence.

Upstairs, weary from unaccustomed physical labour, they prepare for bed, Jo borrowing a pair of pyjamas, having forgotten to bring hers. Laughter fills Delia's bedroom when Jo prances in clutching size sixteen pyjama bottoms to prevent them falling to the floor.

'I'll lend you a belt,' Delia says, making a move to leave her warm bed.

'No need, Mum. I'll just wear the top.'

'Night, darling. Thanks for all your help today.'

'Pleasure, Mum.' Jo bounces out of the room.

Relieved to see that her daughter has cast off the cloak of piety, at least for tonight, Delia switches off the bedside light and snuggles under the duvet, but as she drifts off to sleep, loud sobs, reminiscent of childhood nightmares, sweep down the hall to invade her maternal mind. Sighing, she prepares to comfort her frightened child by pushing the duvet aside to swing her legs around.

Sobs diminish as she nears Jo's bedroom, halting her progress. Reluctant to disturb her melancholy teenager, she's about to retreat when grief reignites.

'Smashed, smashed to bits, just like my Daddy,' Jo cries in the darkness. 'Oh God, why did you have to take him away?'

———

By Sunday morning, Roger has joined them, bringing his ute to transport a load of boxes to Liz's house, Delia wanting to avoid a last-minute rush. Then, out of the blue, Charles Powell arrives, eager to help. Dressed in long baggy shorts and a t-shirt depicting Zambian wildlife, with his wavy silver hair uncombed and face flushed from a sprint up the front steps, he resembles a mad professor rather than the serious-minded academic he presents in the English department.

Following introductions, Jo rushes off to her room on the pretext of last-minute packing, but Delia has already noticed her daughter's attempt to prevent a burst of laughter. At least Charles has provided a distraction and restored Jo's equilibrium. Pastor Eames is due to arrive within the hour; it would be preferable if his convert appeared reasonably composed. Any residual sorrow that surfaces as they drive up the range can be attributed to Jo's leaving her childhood home.

Pastor Eames isn't what Delia expected. For a start he's much younger – early thirties, she guesses – and despite it being Sunday, he isn't wearing a dog-collar. His handshake is firm, his manner friendly and there's no God-talk during the half-hour he spends in and around the house. When his car is full to the brim, Delia offers a cold drink and he stands in the kitchen leaning against the counter, chatting about the trials of moving house in between gulps of lemon cordial. She gathers he has moved often during the past decade and ponders whether being transitory is the reason for his single status, acknowledged when Delia remarked that frequent moves would be difficult for a family.

During their conversation, Jo is nowhere to be seen – a final look around her bedroom, Delia assumes, perhaps to shed a tear or two. Other than a hope that Joanna will enjoy the upcoming break with Delia and her friend, Pastor Eames makes no mention of her daughter. Reassured, Delia concludes that Jo's heavenward gaze whenever she invokes the pastor's name, has nothing to do with physical attraction to the man standing in her kitchen. Her daughter is in love with a Jewish prophet, two millennia dead, not a balding, moon-faced man with insipid grey eyes and thick legs stuffed into a pair of worn denim shorts.

Waving to the departing car, Delia retains her smile until the old brown Holden has disappeared, then turns to climb the steep steps to her soon-to-be ex-front doors.

EIGHTEEN

Peace descends along with early winter darkness as helpers depart for their own homes. Charles lingers longest, offering dinner at a local restaurant, and more besides, Delia imagines, assigning him top marks for perseverance. Pleading exhaustion, she abandons him at the top of the steps and adjourns to the kitchen, where cardboard boxes are out of sight and she can pretend that the fabric of her life remains undisturbed. Wine beckons along with cheese and crackers, a simple meal for one. Cradling a large glass, she slumps in an armchair, barely focusing on the images of wildlife streaming across the TV screen, her mind blank despite the presenter's enthusiastic commentary.

She lacks the energy to close the curtains, so almost spills her wine when a thump on the sliding door alerts her to a nocturnal visitor. Tiny feet cling to the insect screen, bright eyes staring into human habitat. 'Have you come to bid me farewell?' she asks the brushtail possum, but apart from a twitching nose, there's no audible response, the door shut against night's chill. Years before, the girls would leave pieces of fruit on the patio table, then turn out the lights to await the descent of any possum resident in the eucalypt Ron planted for summer shade.

Memory brings regret for complaints about gum nuts lying in wait for tender feet – the girls didn't mind, Brisbane children accustomed to walking barefoot – but Delia queries her ability to create a new life in another suburb where unaccustomed night noises could accentuate her empty nest. Thank God for Liz, a few months' residence within familiar boundaries should ease the transition.

The possum retreats empty-handed, Delia too weary to fetch an apple from the fruit bowl, or has she reached the melancholy stage often experienced during the evening before a fourth glass tips her into blessed torpor? Some nights, she awakes around midnight to find herself sprawled on the sofa, an empty wine glass spilling its dregs on the carpet. Is she becoming an alcoholic? Wine was always a feature of their shared life, a glass or two over dinner but only Ron drank a third or fourth during winter evenings. In summer he preferred beer straight from the bottle, condensation moistening brown glass and the yellow label displaying its trademark red XXXX.

Delia ponders the reasons for Australia's big drinking culture – a hot climate, mateship, the acceptability of alcohol in every social setting. Beer bellies are a constant in most men over forty, initially taut as a mid-term pregnancy, then hanging over shorts as age softens muscles. How often has she wanted to ask a man when baby is due? Her hands roam over the flabby stomach blamed on two pregnancies, a poor excuse for the climb from size twelve to sixteen. She has never been thin, her curvaceous figure delighting the hands that explore, be they husband's or lover's, but gravity is beginning to take its toll. Rising from the oversoft armchair, Delia vows to visit the gym and reform her diet.

Satisfied by alcohol-fuelled promises, she staggers to the bedroom, forgetting to brush her teeth or visit the toilet. Sleep descends with the swiftness of tropic night, dreamless until a shrill sound near her right ear, induces swift awakening. She considers letting the telephone ring out – it could be a crank call at this hour – then realises she has no idea of the time. A glance at the alarm clock on the bedside cupboard puts her mind at rest. The midnight hour has yet to arrive, the digital alarm clock showing 10:03. Lifting the handset, she gives her number rather than her name.

'Hope I didn't wake you, Mum, but I couldn't wait for morning.'

Carol's voice seems distant, as though she's relocated beyond state borders to the shallow waters of the Torres Strait, Delia certain she can hear waves slapping a fibreglass hull. Her murmured response sinks in the rush to impart important news.

'But you're only twenty,' Delia answers, unable to share her daughter's delight.

'Old enough to vote, old enough to get married. Anyway, you were only twenty-one.'

'It was different back then. Couples didn't cohabit before marriage.'

'Are you suggesting Marti and I live together first?'

'Yes, it would be a good test of compatibility.'

'Marti would never agree.'

'Why ever not? Most guys would jump at the chance and you two already have sex.'

'We make love, Mum.'

Delia has no desire to engage in semantic games. 'Whatever,' she says, stifling a sigh.

'Anyway, Marti's a bit old-fashioned.'

'Not another Fundamentalist!' Delia groans.

'No, a lapsed Catholic. Anyway, we were thinking of September.'

Delia does a quick calculation. Fourteen months would give her ample time to find a suitable property and ensure she's settled before wedding arrangements must be considered. 'That sounds good, darling. Another year will enable you to get to know one another better.'

'Mum, this year, not next.'

'But that's only weeks away. I can't possibly organise a wedding and move house!'

'No need for you to worry about the wedding. We've decided to get married up here. A small gathering, we know your finances are stretched, and Mrs Tonelli would really like us to be married in her local church, not that I'm turning Catholic, but she's waited so long and I feel it would be a lovely gesture on my part.'

Puzzled, Delia attempts a second calculation but fails, her mind awash with unforeseen detail and the lingering effects of alcohol. 'You're not making sense, Carol. I thought you and Marti got together only months ago?'

'I wasn't referring to me. Marti was engaged before, but there was a boating accident and she drowned. It's taken him ten years to get over it. He was with her, so he blamed himself, not that he was responsible or anything. The storm came out of nowhere; he was lucky to survive.'

'How old is Marti?' Delia asks, suspecting the reason for haste.

'Thirty-nine last month. I bought him a bright red t-shirt for his birthday. Kate knows someone who does screen printing, so I had *Reef Star* printed on the front and a dolphin on the back. Marti loved it! I've got one now, 'cos it's great advertising.'

'Are you pregnant, Carol?'

'No, Mum, I'm on the Pill. We're getting married because we love each other.' Carol takes a deep breath. 'I know you're about to say Marti is old enough to be my father, well not quite, but I can assure you age doesn't make any difference to either of us.'

Delia sighs. There's little point in arguing when Carol has made up her mind. 'Please settle down and listen for a minute.'

'Sorry, Mum. I didn't mean to go on, but I'm so happy! Cloud nine has nothing on me!'

'Cloud what?'

'Nine. You know, high as a kite.'

'I get it, but could you manage a brief return to Earth? We need to discuss your course. I trust you'll finish it?'

'Sure. I'd have Marti on my back if I dropped out. He nags me about study more than Dad did.'

'Thank God for that, I'd....' Delia falters, suddenly aware of past tense. In less than six months, Carol has eliminated her need for a father figure, exorcised the ghost who haunts her mother's dreams. 'Who will give you away, darling?'

'I hadn't thought about that,' Carol says quietly.

'Grandpa,' Delia declares, grateful for a suitable replacement. George Pierce will be delighted.

'Brilliant, Mum! Should I ask him, or will you?'

'I'll call him tomorrow.'

'Great! I'll write you a long letter with all the details and a photo of my ring. I'm so relieved that you understand. I thought we might have a bit of a blue about it. Bye now.'

———

Delia stares at the handset, as a single word repeats in her head. Understand, of course she understands, that's what worries her. The rationale is obvious, Daddy's girl has found a new daddy to rock her to sleep and kiss the tears from her eyes. Anger surges through her, washing away the thin layer of composure she's fought so hard to attain. 'It's alright for you,' she says to Ron's photograph. 'You won't have to pick up the pieces when she hits the ground.'

The bedroom reverberates with ghost-addressed speech, and conscious of her foolishness, Delia blushes like a bride. Her constant conversation with a photograph is futile. Yes, Ron would have disapproved of Carol marrying a man almost twenty years her senior; yes, he would have tried to talk her out of it; and failing that, he would have insisted, no, indicated his preference for a lengthy engagement. But his opinion is irrelevant; the dead are not concerned with the here and now. Stopped by the clock, they are trapped in a time-warp and nothing she says or does can wind back the hands. The present and future are her responsibility and hers alone.

NINETEEN

JUNE 27TH, 1992

After giving the removalists directions to the storage facility, Delia closes the front doors and walks through the family room to collect her bucket and mop from the kitchen. An empty shell, the house appears forlorn, stripped of character and vitality. Cobwebs cling to grimy paintwork and layers of dust top the carpet where heavy furniture stood for decades. Never much of a housekeeper, for years Delia has employed a cleaner to do the basics and ignored the rest, but months ago she dismissed Joyce due to lack of funds. Pushing the mop over grubby tiles, Delia vows to take more care of her next home.

Wind whistles through the open kitchen window, lifting suds from the bucket. A bubble settles on her arm, rainbow-bright it shimmers for a moment before collapsing on winter-pale skin. She touches the damp patch, shivers as another gust sends currents of cold air sweeping past her to the rooms beyond. Naked walls swallow the breeze, the resultant sighs drawing Delia into vacant space where she half-expects to see a familiar face. Silence mocks her hopeful anticipation, nothing remaining but cobweb strands too high to reach. The solid substance of her life has disintegrated into brittle particles.

Her feet push forward until she's standing in the corner where Ron sat each evening waiting for night to obscure his beloved trees. Unable to sense his presence, she turns to face the wall, crying, 'Have you left me forever?' Her question smacks the dusty surface, rebounding to sting her mouth. Then, limbs loosen to welcome liberty, as the ties that bound them together snap and fall in a heap at her feet.

A straining engine alerts her to outdoor activity; she moves to the sliding doors, peers sideways as Roger's ute struggles to climb her steep driveway. Startled – she's forgotten that Daisy Datsun has already relocated to 6 Tamarin Street – Delia rushes to open the front door. 'Won't be long,' she calls as Roger climbs from the cab.

'Anything else to come?' he asks from the bottom of the steps.

'Only a few cleaning things. There's no need to come up.'

'Righto.' Roger retreats to the cab.

Pleased she has managed to deter him so easily, Delia walks slowly through the rooms to bid a silent farewell, drawing each set of curtains against the midday sun. In her bedroom, filtered sun casts a rosy glow over cream walls, softening the sorrow that threatens to overwhelm. Memories linger, sweet and sour strands drifting with dust motes, but now the moment of leaving has arrived, Delia knows she must not delay. Beyond the open door lies the way to her future.

Beside the single red rose, elegant in a tall-stemmed vase, Liz leaves a card on Fran's old desk, bearing the simple message *Welcome friend*. Tidying the already neat house has occupied both body and mind for most of the morning, enabling her to push the date's other significance into the background. Despite vowing not to contact Fran prior to her son's visit, Liz has telephoned twice to ask after her health and make general conversation, such as preparations for Delia's arrival. She made no mention of a threatening letter, feigning surprise when Fran told her that Colin would be visiting soon for a few days.

During their second telephone conversation, Fran expressed relief that Colin would be arriving without the usual baggage of wife and children. At eighty-one, she finds the children tiresome and has nothing in common with her social-climbing daughter-in-law. The real reason for Colin's visit remains unspoken, leaving Liz pondering whether he has raised the subject at all during the past few months. His strategy could be to catch Fran unawares by spending the first couple of days playing the devoted son, then thrusting the papers under her nose when she's weary following an extended lunch at an upmarket restaurant.

Reluctantly, Liz acknowledges that her thoughts are uncharitable. For all she knows, Fran could enjoy being spoilt on occasion. Moreover, Colin is now her only child, the remaining link with her earlier life as a young mother of two. Liz finds it difficult to envisage motherhood at the best of times, but impossible to imagine having a fifty-year-old son and wonders if all mothers continue to regard their adult offspring as children. 'You will always be my baby,' her own mother said when Liz left home for university, 'so I'm entitled to worry about you.'

Maternal solicitude has continued throughout the intervening years with Liz, for the most part, an agreeable recipient, although she shudders at the memory of January's visit when soft-boiled eggs and toast fingers tried her patience, forcing an early return home.

A final pat of the bedspread, and Liz leaves the room, determined that her adult relationship with Delia won't descend to childish depths no matter how many tears her friend sheds over leaving the home she shared with Ron and their girls for twenty years.

———

Delia inhales rose perfume, then reaches for the white envelope bearing her name. She appreciates the handmade card with its simple message; profuse greetings could have engendered tears. Wisely, Liz has left her alone to settle in, murmuring something about preparing lunch, although a glance at the kitchen as they passed by carrying the suitcases, revealed a bowl of colourful salad laid out on a benchtop along with plates and cutlery.

Jaded by the morning's activity, Delia sits on the end of the bed next to a fluffy white towel, reminiscent of those found in hotels. As she reaches out to stroke soft towelling, memories surface of a long-ago seminar held at an Auckland hotel and conference complex. White bathrobes, a deep white bath, crisp white sheets on a king-size bed. Cheeks still flushed from unaccustomed housework, she recalls champagne bubbles on her tongue, dark hands on her breasts. 'I wonder what happened to…?'

'Did you say something, Delia?' Liz stands in the doorway, her arms full of clothes retrieved from washing lines.

'Nothing important, I was just thinking I'd love a long soak in the bath.'

'Go on then, there's plenty of hot water. You must be worn out after all that cleaning.'

'I'm shattered.'

'I'll sort out my washing while you're in the bath. Then we can have lunch.' Liz moves into the hallway.

'Oh, Liz,' Delia calls after her. 'Thanks so much for the rose and the card. Beautiful gestures.'

'I wanted you to feel welcome.'

'I do.'

―――

Immersed in warm water, Delia closes her eyes and drifts into dream. Hot sun beats down on the back of her neck as she runs naked across white sand to a cool blue ocean, where she ploughs through breakers to reach calm depths. On surfacing, she becomes aware of other swimmers, their strong arms rising and dipping in unison. Tanned faces tip momentarily to the sun as she struggles to distinguish watery features, their rhythm unbroken as they swim past her. Giving chase, she pushes her body through the deep water, but as the distance between them increases, she acknowledges that she will never catch up. Breathless, she rolls onto her back to float on the gentle swell, but when she turns over to begin the swim to shore, the swimmers have surrounded her, their black fins slicing through the water like knives.

Opening her mouth to scream, Delia splutters as tepid water floods her throat. How foolish she is to have fallen asleep in the bath! She grabs the sides of the bath to pull herself upright.

Liz taps lightly. 'Are you ready for lunch?'

'Give me a couple of minutes.' Delia reaches for the soap.

The two women sit in a sheltered corner of the rear deck, munching crispy cheese-topped bread and salad. At their feet, empty soup bowls are stacked on a tray.

'I sure needed that,' Delia remarks through a mouthful of lettuce. 'I hadn't eaten since breakfast.'

Liz smiles. 'There's nothing like home-made soup to fill you up after a hard morning's work.'

'And soup is so warming. I was getting a bit chilly in the bath.

'I'm not surprised, you were in there for ages! I thought you'd fallen asleep.'

'I had.'

'You should be more careful, it's possible to drown in a bath.'

'I know, I did.'

Liz directs her gaze to her careless friend, confusion and concern juxtaposed in sea-green eyes.

'I had a strange dream about swimming in the ocean,' Delia explains, her brown eyes glazing over. 'I was trying to join some other swimmers, but as fast as I swam, I couldn't reach them. So, I floated for a while to catch my breath before returning to shore. When I turned over, they were circling me and their arms had changed into fins. Then, I woke up to find I had slipped beneath the surface. What do you think it means?'

'Perhaps it's a warning about the dangers of swimming into unknown waters.'

Delia toys with a lettuce leaf. 'A reflection on changed

circumstances, more likely. Creditors circling like sharks.' She picks up the lettuce and chews thoughtfully. 'There was something else. I was naked. Do you think that's relevant?'

'It probably means you have a secret desire to go skinny-dipping.'

'Trust you to think of that!'

'Seriously, would you like to go? Come summer, we could go to Alexandra Bay.'

'Why not? It's time for a new experience. What's it like swimming nude?'

'There's an immense feeling of liberty. Saltwater flowing over, under and between, smooth as silk. You become a natural being completely at ease in a watery environment.' Liz hesitates before adding, 'Afterwards, running back up the beach, the salt air makes your breasts tingle and water streams from folds and furrows.'

'Very poetic.' Delia studies her pale-skinned friend. 'But *you* must have to take care not to get sunburnt.'

Liz grimaces. 'I spend most of the time sitting under the beach brolly.'

'What else do you expect with Scottish ancestry?'

'I didn't choose my genes!' Liz retorts, tossing her red hair.

Delia reaches out to touch her arm. 'Hey, don't get mad. I was only teasing.'

'I know, I didn't mean to growl at you. It's just that talking about the ocean made me think of Kay. She loved nude swimming and sunbathing. Oh, Delia, why can't I reflect on the past without anger or grief?'

'Chains of love, I suppose.'

'Something like that.' Liz picks up her fork to stab a

piece of tomato but makes no attempt to eat it. 'Are you still tied to Ron?' she asks tentatively, reluctant to upset.

Delia raises her head to stare over Liz's head at the native trees and shrubs climbing the steep slope beyond the deck. 'I thought I was, but I think I left him behind today.'

'In the house?'

Delia shakes her head but continues to stare at the bush garden. 'He had already gone when I awoke this morning.'

TWENTY

Above-average height and a stern expression augment the intimidating presence Liz recalls from previous visits. Standing on the narrow patio at the top of her steps, Colin Masters resembles a praying mantis with his bulging eyes and long thin limbs encased in a tight-fitting pale green suit. Determined not to be spooked – there was no advance warning this morning of his arrival – she ushers him inside, depositing him on the living room sofa while she makes coffee.

Five days have passed since he flew up from the nation's capital, suggesting it has taken longer than anticipated to persuade his mother to sign legal papers, his letter having implied only a brief stay. Liz hasn't heard from Fran, but that isn't surprising, given CM is resident in her home. As she spoons instant coffee into mugs – why waste the percolated variety on him – Liz decides to contact her solicitor if she sights any signed documents, verbal confirmation being unacceptable. On opening the door, she saw no sign of a briefcase or even a manila folder, but either could have been left in the BMW she spotted parked on her driveway. If Delia were home, there wouldn't be any room on the concrete drive for a large vehicle, an observation that amuses as she envisages CM forced to step onto damp grass to avoid the ancient Datsun. Grass stains on pristine suede shoes would never do!

She carries the mugs on a tray, willing her hands to remain steady as she places it on the coffee table. 'I don't have any biscuits. Delia's on a diet,' she announces in a crisp tone, deliberately omitting an apology.

Colin dismisses the information with a wave of the hand, waiting until Liz is seated in the armchair opposite before lifting the remaining mug.

'So, have you come to evict me?' Liz asks, settling on plain speech.

Thin lips curl slightly, giving an impression of amusement. 'No, Elizabeth, these matters take time.'

Liz refrains from comment. No signed document could mean failure.

Silence hangs in the cool winter air, heavy as a window blind that refuses to fall despite numerous tugs on the cord. Amplified, sips of coffee become gulps followed by the smacking of lips, sounds that remind Liz of Kay's deliberately exaggerated response to tasting a welcome beer on a hot afternoon.

Before she can finish her coffee, Colin places his cup on the tray and fixes her with a look that could be interpreted as friendly if one remained ignorant of their history. 'Elizabeth,' he begins, settling back against the cushion to appear relaxed. 'I understand that you communicate with my mother on a regular basis and, on occasion, visit her home.'

'That's correct. Fran and I have been friends for more than twelve years.' Liz would like to add that Kay's death hasn't altered their "pseudo-in-law" relationship, but she is determined to limit herself to hard facts.

'I doubt it is that long, but no matter, suffice to say you are fond of my mother.'

'Yes.'

Colin offers a small smile that wilts instantly. 'Therefore, I'm certain you would wish her to spend her remaining years in comfort.'

'I would.'

'More comfort than she has been accustomed to in recent years.'

Liz can sense where this is going; he wants her to give up the house voluntarily to save Fran the strain of a legal challenge or, more likely, because she won't sign the papers. Instead of repeating her previous response, she inclines her head.

'I am not a heartless man, Elizabeth, so after much thought and prayer, I propose a perfect solution to this impasse.'

An impasse of your making, Liz thinks, recalling unequivocal *Last Will and Testament* instructions.

'Simplicity will be beneficial to both parties, so I suggest a straightforward reversal. My mother will inherit this house, which, as it is most unsuitable for an elderly woman, can be sold to enable the purchase of appropriate accommodation. As the other beneficiary, you will have the benefit of my sister's savings and superannuation.'

It would be so easy to accept his offer and get him off her back forever, but Liz knows for certain that this "solution" to a fabricated problem wasn't Kay's wish. Against her better judgment, she acknowledges that hitherto private aspects of her life with Kay must be shared at this point, even though her statements will be regarded as mercenary. 'From the moment Kay and I began living together, ten years ago, we split all our expenses including the mortgage payments, which means that I possess equity in this property. Proof of mortgage payments made by me are available from my bank, Kay and I having held separate accounts throughout our partnership. We felt this was necessary as federal law defines couples who are married or living in de-facto relationships as members of the opposite sex.' She pauses to glance at her unwelcome visitor. As expected, Colin appears ill at ease, although it's impossible to tell whether this is due to her change of tone or because he believes such information could be detrimental to his case. 'Furthermore, I would not dream of contravening Kay's wishes, which we discussed long before her untimely death. You may recall that her will was made two years ago, by which time we had lived together as equal partners for eight years.' Getting to her feet, she crosses to the sofa, where she stands peering down at him, thankful for her own above-average height. 'So, I'm afraid you have wasted both your time and your energy.' She raises her hand to indicate the front door, clearly visible from this angle.

But CM will not be hurried. Brushing non-existent crumbs from his suit pants with long pale fingers, he then smooths the fabric with the palms of his hands. Although his head remains bowed, slow deep breathing suggests he remains calm. In some respects, anger would be preferable, his temper tantrums familiar territory. Self-control seems more menacing, so Liz takes a step backwards, carefully avoiding the sharp edges of the coffee table. Several more steps and she's leaning over to lift the tray, his empty mug steady as she adds her own. Confident she can maintain her composure until he departs, she walks into the kitchen to place the tray on a bench. Then, she's turning on the tap to disguise the sound of her ragged breaths.

As her breathing returns to normal, she shuts off the flow of water to listen for the door opening and closing, hears nothing but the wind whipping through backyard trees and the steady beat of a branch against the deck railing. When answering the door to CM, she'd deliberately left it unlocked to prevent her hands fumbling with the key as he left, yet now she fears he could take advantage by locking them both inside. The neighbours on either side are at work and the house opposite remains shuttered, the owners on holiday. Moving away from the sink, she creeps to the narrow space beside the fridge, which will give her a glimpse of the living room.

CM is standing in front of the sliding doors leading to the front patio These doors are locked but have no key, the flick of a catch all that's needed to open or close.

Resolved to eject him one way or another, Liz steps away from the dividing wall into the living room. 'Admiring my garden, I see,' she remarks, stressing the possessive adjective.

'A credit to you,' he answers without altering his position.

'Thank you.' Skirting the sofa, she approaches the front door. 'Now then, Colin, I'm sure you wish to return to your mother, and I have chores to attend to.' A gust of wind tries to snatch the door from her hand, but she holds on, shifting a sneakered foot to impede its progress.

At long last, he takes the hint, crossing to the doorway and descending the steps without a farewell glance or further comment. She watches until the hire car has disappeared around the corner before closing the door, even though instinct tells her to barricade herself inside.

THE YEAR OF LIVING RAINBOW

Safe behind a double-locked door – she slid the bolt across as an extra precaution – Liz makes a second cup of coffee to counter nerves, it being far too early for a shot of the whisky kept in the pantry for those friends that preferred spirits. Early on in their relationship, Kay admitted she didn't touch spirits anymore, having got into a fight following a night of over-indulgence at a party. Liz was appalled to learn that 'fight' meant two women wrestling in a swimming pool following offensive remarks about Kay's inability to sustain a sexual relationship. 'Fortunately, I came to my senses after a few minutes,' Kay had remarked in conclusion. 'I could have easily drowned the skinny little rat!'

Liz shudders as she envisages pale hands around her throat, then rebukes herself for unworthy thoughts. Sticks and stones aren't CM's style – he prefers the written or spoken word – but whatever the proverb says, his insults hurt!

For the rest of the morning, Liz keeps herself fully occupied with physical activity, there being no possibility of clearing her mind sufficiently to sit at her computer composing poetry, her usual Friday pursuit. Raking leaves and twigs from the front lawn is a thankless task while the wind continues to gust, but she needs to burn the rage building inside. CM's solution is more than an affront to his dead sister, it's preposterous and downright illegal!

Apart from eliminating anger, she wants to be calm and pleasantly tired when Delia returns from work to ensure a relaxing evening, so plans to prune wayward branches after a short break for lunch. The mid-year break has already started, but this morning, Delia mentioned having a day in her office to create order in a much-neglected space before preparing material for the second half of the teaching year. 'Four days of indulging myself by sleeping late and lying on the sofa reading for pleasure is enough,' she told Liz as they sat side-by-side at the breakfast bar eating muesli. 'By the end of today, I intend to see the surface of my desk!'

'A worthwhile goal,' Liz managed to respond once she swallowed a mouthful of muesli and astonishment. Like Kay, tidiness has never been one of Delia's strong points.

TWENTY-ONE

Sunlight filters through the curtains as Delia pushes the heavy quilt away from her face. Raising herself on one elbow, she glances at the digital clock on the bedside cabinet, noting with dismay that the flashing green numerals read 8:15. Shit, she's slept in again, despite her determination to share breakfast with Liz and ask what needs to be done during the day. It's the least she can do when Liz is so generously sharing her home and has already offered to accommodate Joanna when she returns from spending the first two weeks of vacation up the coast with her grandparents. There's a folding single bed stored behind the bookshelves in the study, so Delia won't have to share her bed. Disappointed at the prospect of breakfast alone, she lies back on the pillows to make plans for her day.

Half the teaching year lies behind her, buried under a pile of lecture notes and tutorial topics. Moving forward on automatic pilot from one day to the next, she has barely noticed the passage of time. Relying on the previous year's research, she has injected nothing new into her lectures, the few notes made at the beginning of first semester not expanded into worthwhile material. Colleagues have been most supportive, assisting her with assignment marking and administrative tasks whenever she felt unable to summon the requisite intellectual energy. The Dean – renowned as a sticker for protocol – has even overlooked her absences at staff meetings, and recently, Charles insisted on marking her examination papers when he heard she was moving house. She remains grateful for assistance, but with the house sold and debts settled, it's imperative she revitalise her teaching curriculum and consider research.

Towards the end of semester, Charles floated the idea of a joint project comparing nineteenth- and twentieth-century migrants' attitudes to Australia, as expressed in the literature of each period. Preoccupied with her move, Delia suggested he approach someone else in the department. Since then, Charles hasn't raised the subject, so she has no idea if he's co-opted another colleague. If only she'd expressed some interest, the topic could be absorbing. Perhaps she should call him, or will the Powells have gone away for the break?

Halfway through her breakfast, she recalls his complaints about lack of funds for a holiday, his wife's trip to Zambia having cost more than anticipated. The nine o'clock news has just started, so Charles should be up and about, but where did she put the home phone number he'd given her months ago? Leaving toast and tea, she returns to the bedroom to retrieve her handbag from the old desk positioned in front of the window. Grumbling to herself, she rummages through crumpled tissues, lipsticks, pens and receipts looking for her diary. There's no sign of it, so she tips the entire contents onto the bed. 'Got you!' she exclaims as the diary surfaces from a tangled scarf.

Joan Powell answers the phone, advising that Charles is

out jogging in the park. Her perfectly pronounced syllables remind Delia of the Queen's Christmas broadcast to *my peoples of the Commonwealth.* Joan promises to pass on the message when Charles returns home.

———

A rap on the door annoys, Delia fully immersed in lecture notes on *Bleak House,* Dickens' satirical novel about a long-standing law case that takes decades to resolve. Insistent, the caller knocks again, prompting a dash for the front door. 'Charles, this is a surprise.'

'Joan gave me your message, so I thought, I'll call around to give you more details of my proposed project.'

Remembering her manners, Delia ushers him inside. 'I hope you didn't make a special trip. I just wanted to let you I'm interested after all.'

'I was at a loose end anyway. Have you time to discuss the project now?'

'Yes, it will be a pleasant change from the interminable legal proceedings of Jarndyce and Jarndyce.'

'*Bleak House* can be grim, if you'll pardon the pun.'

Reading glasses slip down her nose as she raises her eyebrows. 'Take a seat, while I go and save my document. Then I suggest coffee on the back deck. It's much warmer there than in the house.'

'Could I possibly have tea?'

'Sure, I won't be long.'

———

Settled in old canvas chairs either side of Kay's handmade table, the two colleagues demolish slices of Liz's rich chocolate cake while, beyond the deck, noisy minors quarrel in a flowering grevillea, sending blossom tumbling to the ground. 'Raucous little chaps,' Charles remarks, placing his cake fork neatly on the empty plate.

Delia smiles. 'No lilting birdsong here, I'm afraid.'

'I shall miss them, and the colourful parrots. Sometimes I wish I could stay on this side of the world.'

'Perhaps you could extend your contract?'

'That is possible, but Joan would never forgive me.'

'She's still having problems adjusting to the Australian way of life?'

'Yes, but enough of me. How are you settling in here?'

'Very well. It's not as if I must adjust to a new environment. I've been visiting this house for years; Ron and Kay were colleagues and friends long before Liz came on the scene.'

'Pardon me for asking, but who is Kay?'

Unwilling to provide a lengthy explanation, Delia says, 'Oh sorry, didn't I tell you that Kay was Liz's partner?'

Charles shakes his head.

'Liz is such a thoughtful person,' Delia continues, grateful that Charles is too polite to ask further questions. 'On the day I moved in, I found a single red rose in my room and a handmade card with the simple greeting, welcome friend.'

'Kind gestures,' Charles murmurs.

'Indeed, but I discerned more than kindness.' Leaning back in her chair, Delia tilts her face to the morning sun. 'On moving day, I spent hours scrubbing and sweeping to leave the house in good condition for the new owners, but as I looked around for the last time, I felt not only exhausted but also drained of all emotion as though my actions had erased twenty years of my life. I didn't even look back as

THE YEAR OF LIVING RAINBOW

Roger drove away from the kerb. When I arrived here, Liz appeared fully aware of my feelings, even though I said nothing. There was no effusive welcome, no clinging arms around my neck or sobbing on my shoulder in sympathy. Instead, she helped me to carry my suitcases to my room, then left me alone. But the rose and the card were waiting for me, symbols of authentic compassion.' Lowering her head, Delia picks up her coffee mug, conscious that she has said more than enough.

Charles appears deep in thought, although it's impossible to tell whether he's reflecting on her words or contemplating something else entirely. 'Years ago,' he begins, following a brief silence, 'I misunderstood the friendship between women. I considered it shallow, an excuse for trivial chatter about fashion and babies.'

Delia frowns over her coffee mug. 'Really, Charles, that's such...'

'Let me finish,' he interrupts, reaching across the table to touch her arm. 'I admit I'm a chauvinist, although I would refute the further appellation of 'pig.' So, it took me considerable time to come to a different conclusion or, as I prefer to think of it, learn to look below the surface.'

'And what did you see beneath the mask of meaningless prattle?' Delia asks, unable to resist a contemptuous tone.

'Empathy, loyalty, love,' he answers evenly, either oblivious to her scorn or choosing to ignore it. 'Most women seem to possess an ability to give of themselves without holding back. To be an open book.' He sighs and removes his hand from Delia's arm. 'I wish I could be the same.'

'What prevents you?'

'Men fear exposure, we dread the discovery of weakness.'

'It's okay for men to cry nowadays, you know.'

185

'I'm aware of that, but I would find it almost impossible to alter the habits of a lifetime.'

'Stiff upper lip and all that,' Delia says, imitating his English accent without thinking. 'I guess you'll never be a SNAG, Charles.'

'A what?'

'Sensitive New Age Guy. Have you not heard the acronym before?'

Mellow laughter wafts across the table. 'Oh, my dear Dr Pierce, our research project promises to be exhilarating. You are more than a match for me!'

'I do hope so, dear Professor Powell,' she replies, her eyes brimming with mischief.

TWENTY-TWO

Darkness descends early in July. By five the winter sun has almost slipped over the horizon. Driving straight into the setting sun, Liz shields her eyes with one hand as she strains to see the road ahead. She intended to leave work half an hour earlier, but department manager James detained her, asking whether Gloria and her husband's separation were permanent. Liz felt uncomfortable and, for a fleeting moment, wondered if he was attracted to her friend and colleague, then banished the thought when she recalled his recent marriage. As it turned out, James wanted to offer Gloria a longer contract but didn't want to pressure her if she and Roger were trying to patch up their marriage. Unsure of Gloria's long-term plans, Liz could only suggest James ask her himself.

Waiting for the lights to change, she considers the high number of failed marriages –one in three, according to the Australian Bureau of Statistics. Nothing seems immutable these days, the world whirling in a constant state of flux as nations and peoples struggle to assert their identity. No wonder we fail on a one-to-one basis, she reflects, ignoring the green light. Behind her, a driver sounds his horn, prompting a swift move across the intersection.

Sinking into her favourite chair, Liz reaches for the glass of wine Delia has thoughtfully placed on the coffee table.

'Difficult day?' Delia asks when Liz has taken several mouthfuls.

'It was fine until James started asking me questions about Gloria's marital problems. On the way home I started thinking about failed relationships and all the hate in the world, which has left me a bit depressed.'

'Oh darling, like all poets, you take life too seriously.' Delia scuttles across the room to wrap her arms around Liz's shoulders.

In response, Liz clutches her glass, telling Delia to be careful not to spill red wine on her white blouse.

'Sorry, I just thought you needed a hug.'

'I did. Apologies for snapping at you.'

'Forgiven.' Delia returns to the sofa. 'Let me cheer you up by recounting further tales of Charles Powell and his quaint, old-fashioned ways.'

Liz settles back in her chair as Delia begins her tale of an unexpected visit. 'Poor Charles,' she interjects when Delia pauses to sip her wine.

'Why poor?'

'Isn't it obvious? He's still yearning for you.'

'I'm not interested in the slightest.'

'Then you need to let him know, not make remarks that could be misconstrued.'

Delia pouts. 'I'm sure he knows I'm just being mischievous.'

'So, you wouldn't consider an affair even if he were free?'

Delia shakes her head.

'Because you're grieving,' Liz persists.

Delia turns sideways to fiddle with a magazine lying on the sofa.

'Sorry, it was wrong of me to pry.'

Delia raises her head. 'I don't understand my attitude, either. Perhaps I'm scared of intimacy.'

'You mean sex?'

'Not entirely, I'm not trying to deny past infidelities. But previously, when I gave my body, I often gave my heart as well, even if it was for a limited period. These days, I feel reluctant to share my innermost thoughts with a stranger.'

'Is that how you think of Charles Powell?'

'Yes, he's not and never could be part of my world.'

Liz looks puzzled. 'But you see him at work five days a week and now you're going to be his research partner. Surely that makes him less of an outsider?'

Delia pushes the magazine aside, then fixes her gaze to a spot above Liz's head. 'When Ron died, I felt as though a protective barrier had been torn down, leaving me defenceless. For the first time in my life, I craved a sanctuary where no one would ask awkward questions or expect rational answers.' Looking down, she studies the familiar contours of Liz's face as though expecting to find an answer in sea-green eyes or the pale skin stripped of summer's faint blush. 'Six months on, I'm afraid to step outside the box I've created and reveal my true self. So, instead of outrageous flirtation that once promised and often delivered results, I resort to playful remarks that mean nothing at all.'

Unnerved by Delia's strange admission, Liz picks up the wine bottle to pour another drink. 'Don't worry, it's early days. Grieving can take years. Most likely your fears will subside when you're settled in a new home.'

The real estate agent flicks through a thick wad of cards. 'I'm afraid there's not much around here under one hundred and fifty, Mrs Pierce.'

'Dr Pierce,' Delia corrects, having decided to drop Mrs as it belies her status.

The agent – wide-shouldered suit jacket and pleated pants – tosses a remorseful smile. 'I do apologise, Dr Pierce.'

'What about Toowong or Taringa?' Liz suggests, turning to Delia. 'You could catch a bus to work.'

The agent lifts another pile of cards. 'I've a unit near the shops at Taringa and another opposite the cemet... I mean the park at Toowong.'

'Can we inspect them today?'

'Certainly. If you'll excuse me, I'll call to see if anyone's at home. We prefer to give our vendors a little warning.'

Liz notes his even teeth as he supplies a second insincere smile.

Before long they're drawing to the kerb outside a block of units – cream brick and narrow balconies edged with wrought-iron railings. At the agent's insistence – do call me Damien – they have travelled in his car, a late model Holden with leather seats. He must be successful.

'A bloody six-pack,' Delia murmurs to Liz.

'Did you say something, Dr Pierce?'

'Er, how old is the block?'

'Built in the early seventies. Sound construction. Cavity brick with plaster walls and aluminium windows.'

'Which one is for sale?'

'Second floor, facing the street.'

'Okay, we'll take a look.'

The concrete steps are smeared with dried mud, and cigarette butts have gathered in dusty corners. Delia and Liz exchange glances as they follow Damien to the second floor.

'Here we are, Dr Pierce,' he says, opening a faded orange door, then standing aside to let them pass into a narrow hall. 'The living area is spacious. It needs a little TLC, that's all.'

Ignoring the average-sized living area, Delia turns into the kitchen where floral wallpaper crowds the tiny space. Beneath the giant yellow flowers, orange benchtops, stained and chipped. She feels like a character trapped in *The Day of the Triffids*. 'Liz, you must see this.'

'Good Lord!' Liz exclaims. 'Are the owners colour blind?'

'The unit has been let to students in recent years,' Damien says from the carpet side of the living room. 'You could easily alter the colour scheme.'

'But not the size of this kitchen.' Delia sighs. 'Could you please show me the other unit?'

'Of course, Dr Pierce.'

Delia collapses on the sofa, kicking off her shoes and running her fingers through her hair. 'Christ, however many stairs have we climbed today?'

'Thousands, or at least it seems that many.' Liz slumps in her chair.

'Why were both units on the second floor?'

'Luck of the draw. At least the exercise would keep you fit.'

'I'd rather go to the gym.'

'What about that Damien? He couldn't keep his eyes off you.'

'Or his hands. Palms pressing against my back as he guided me through that second place.' Delia grimaces. 'Do call again, dear Dr Pierce. I'm sure I can help you find the perfect abode. Pompous ass!'

'And what about his blond-tipped hair? I suppose he goes to Stefan's.'

Delia laughs. 'Remember the eighties perm? I looked like a giant poodle!'

'It wasn't that bad. At least you only tried it once.'

'Seriously though, it's going to take ages to find something decent at my price.'

'Don't be so negative. You can't expect to find the perfect abode on the first day.'

'True, but I don't want to intrude for too long.'

'You're not intruding. I love having you here.'

'Even though my books are cluttering your bookshelves and Daisy is leaking oil on your driveway.'

'I welcomed you with all your encumbrances.' Liz gets to her feet. 'Come on, Dr Pierce, let's go buy a pizza to team with another bottle of red.'

'You're on, my dear Ms Coney.'

TWENTY-THREE

Days melt into one another at 6 Tamarin Street and Delia no longer fears night's sombre shadows or the dark depths of nightmare. Dreams are sweet interludes briefly recalled as she wakes to birds proclaiming new dawn and ridge-top wind whistling through nearby branches. Each morning, Ron's smiling face greets her and she returns the smile, holding his image in her mind for a few minutes before rising for breakfast. The need to address him has passed away with the advent of daily companionship.

In the kitchen, Liz's serene presence warms the chill morning air, her footsteps barely registering on the polished floorboards. Few words are exchanged over breakfast, yet the scrape of cutlery on cereal bowls and the crunch of toast provide immense comfort. When the girls departed for their respective universities, everyday sounds would echo through Delia's house, amplifying her solitude. Meals, especially dinner, became hurried affairs, eaten for sustenance but rarely enjoyed, dirty dishes tossed in the sink to be left overnight, as though the cockroaches that often invade Brisbane homes have also abandoned the nest.

These days, Delia looks forward to evening meals, Liz preparing a variety of food that looks appealing and tastes scrumptious. At weekends, her host concocts delicious desserts as a special treat, which they eat greedily like children at a party.

'I should be doing the cooking when I'm not teaching,' Delia protested at the start of semester break, but Liz declined the offer, saying she enjoyed making meals for her guest. For her part, Delia is effusive in her praise of each culinary effort, devouring every meal as though her life depends on it! Afterwards, she insists on washing and drying the dishes.

———

Undressing for a shower one Sunday evening, Delia catches sight of her body in the bathroom mirror: white, flabby flesh escaping blue denim as she tugs jeans over her ample behind, solid thighs fusing when the garment finally falls to the floor. Dismayed, she turns away from the mirror to release her bra, wincing as heavy breasts hang towards her stomach.

Voluptuous, Ron called her, a real woman, not like the skinny, flat-chested models parading like storks on narrow catwalks. He would cradle her breasts with care, lifting each one in turn to nuzzle nipples with his warm, wet mouth. Sometimes she'd say he should be weaned by now and he'd plead for more, his voice husky. Stroking his bushy brown hair, she would whisper endearments, then guide his lips back to her breasts.

Trapped in the past, she steps into the shower. Needles of heat prick her cool skin, water streams over her breasts, stomach and legs. Droplets cling to black pubic curls, she notes the contrast with pale thigh-folds. Clutching the soap, she lathers her body, taking care to cleanse every part. Nipples stiffen, her fingers linger in pink warmth, but as her body heaves, hot tears flood her face, washing salt into her open mouth.

Wrapped in a thick towelling dressing gown, Delia sits on the sofa pretending to read a magazine while Liz curls in her armchair studying a literary journal borrowed from UQ library. 'I'm fat,' Delia declares, 'gross, obese, corpulent.'

Liz looks up. 'Have you swallowed a thesaurus?'

'No, but I'm like an old sofa, lumpy and sagging towards the floor.'

'I prefer to think of old sofas as well-loved, comfortable and moulded to my shape.'

'You're only saying that to console me.'

Liz sighs and returns to her journal.

'I want to be loved,' Delia continues, staring at the wall opposite. 'But not like an old sofa.'

Liz closes the journal. 'You are loved. You mean the world to Carol and Joanna.'

'Carol has Marti and Joanna's in love with Jesus.'

'What's bothering you, Delia?'

'I feel so guilty about the state of my body, all those rolls of fat and breasts hanging down like ripe melons.'

Liz tosses a smile across the room. 'We can soon fix that problem. We'll start walking after dinner and I'll stop making desserts.'

'Dieting and exercise won't help.' Delia pulls the dressing gown over her knees.

'Don't be so pessimistic. At least give them a go.'

'You don't understand. My guilt is double-edged.'

Liz frowns. 'What's caused this sudden self-reproach? You were fine an hour ago.'

'Promise you won't laugh or chastise me?'

'I promise.'

Unwilling to face her friend, Delia lowers her eyes to focus on her slippers. In a small voice, she relates her shower experience, disgust followed by delightful memory, followed by an urgent need for release.

'And now you feel guilty?'

'More than guilty. It seemed so wrong to experience such pleasure by my own hand.'

Liz rises from her chair to join Delia on the sofa. 'At first, I felt so ashamed, it was as if I'd committed a crime and tarnished Kay's memory.'

'So, it wasn't an isolated incident?'

Liz shakes her head. 'I have feelings and needs like anyone else. My sexuality didn't die with Kay.'

'I hadn't thought of it like that.'

'Initially, neither did I, but I hadn't counted on dreams.' Sea-green eyes gleam in the lamplight. 'Kay was calling my name, holding out her hand, begging me to join her. I ran towards her, but the distance between us lengthened with each stride. I woke up as she faded into mist, panting as though I'd run for miles. For a few minutes, I tried to recapture the dream, but when I opened my eyes, daylight was filtering through the curtains. The dream taught me to accept that I belong in a different world, a world where both spirit and body reside, so it would be wrong to deny my desires.'

'Is, er, I mean, do you imagine Kay is with you?'

'Not now, it's no longer necessary.'

'Because she's in another world?'

Liz nods. 'I must face all of this life alone.'

Tears spill from Delia's eyes, splashing onto her dressing gown like drops from wet hair. She makes no attempt to stem the flow.

Fearing she's caused this outburst, Liz retreats to her armchair. 'I'm so sorry, Delia. I didn't mean to upset you. I was only trying to help.' She blinks to check her own tears.

Delia gives a final shudder, then wipes her face with her hand. 'It's my fault for blubbering. Something snapped when you spoke of facing life alone. I can't accept the single life forever; the loneliness would be unbearable!'

'I agree, but I'd rather tolerate loneliness than deliberately seek out another partner. The result could be disastrous! I'm not ready for all that's involved in a new relationship, the nitty gritty of getting to know someone, discovering their likes and dislikes, their idiosyncrasies.'

'And vicissitudes,' Delia adds, recalling a Victorian novel.

Laughter bubbles in Liz's throat, threatening to spoil contemplative dialogue. She clamps a hand over her mouth.

'What's so funny?'

Liz removes her hand. 'Remember the Christmas before last when we all had too much wine?'

'Vaguely.'

'You were sounding off about Victorian literature, quoting Thackeray. You just about managed "idiosyncrasies" but fell apart when it came to "vicissitudes."'

'Then, we all tried to say it, gave up and opened another bottle of red.'

'That's a good idea.'

Delia grins. 'I'll fetch the glasses while you go down to the cellar.'

Cut deep into the cool earth, the space under the house

behind Liz's car provides the ideal location for a cellar. Built by Kay, the three-sided block wall is lined with wide, grooved shelves, accessed via an old piece of fencing secured with a padlock. Liz recalls friends asking why Kay built a cellar when it would be easier to drive to the bottle shop down the road? 'It's not the same,' she would reply. 'You can't beat rummaging around in a cellar brushing aside cobwebs to find a favourite wine.'

Switching on the light, Liz opens the gate to scan the shelves for a bottle of Lindeman's Shiraz Cabernet. Last year, Roger and Gloria gave her a mixed dozen for her birthday. A cobweb brushes her cheek as she bends down, prompting a decision to sweep and dust the following weekend. Liz never shared Kay's romanticised view of dark, grimy spaces; to her the cellar embodies neglect. Lifting a bottle from the rear shelf, she shudders as thick dust coats her hand. Old wine, blood-red, layers of dust obscuring bright glass. 'Can I pour new wine into an old bottle?' she asks, stepping away from shadows.

———

Daylight is fading as Delia stirs the remaining wine into the beef casserole she's prepared for their evening meal. Lifting the spoon to her lips, she blows gently before sipping the rich sauce. Satisfied with her efforts, she covers the dish and returns it to the oven before setting the automatic timer. Liz will be surprised to discover dinner waiting for her when she returns home from work. What a pity they can't share the meal together, but Delia has an evening lecture on *Bleak House*.

Dickensian images crowd her head as she clears up the kitchen. Broom in hand, she recalls the crossing-sweeper, pitiful child eking out a living on bleak London streets. Unloved and homeless, he seeks shelter each night in draughty doorways, his thin body curled foetal-fashion against hard timber.

Suddenly, she remembers her juvenile outburst the previous evening, her irrational demand for love. How could she be so egocentric, so insensitive? Has she forgotten the love written at the end of each letter, their caring questions over the phone? Unlike Liz, she is not alone, she has two loving daughters. Mother-daughters, lifelong bonds, strong, unbreakable, an abundance of love.

More than enough love for one person, she reflects, returning the broom to its cupboard. Closing the door, she knocks the edge of the wipeable noticeboard that hangs on a nail, sending the felt-tip pen swinging on its string.

DEAR LIZ
DINNER IN OVEN BON APPETIT
HOME ABOUT NINE
LOVE D

Her message lacks the punctuation she demands of her students. Is she learning to embrace less structured syntax?

———

Liz pushes her plate to the centre of the table, then leans against the chair, her fingers curled around a crystal wine-glass. Lifting the glass to her lips, she savours a last mouthful. Blood-red wine washes through her mouth, colouring the pink flesh of gums, tongue and palate. I should rinse the bottle, she thinks, toss it in a box for recycling.

Full-bodied, cabernet was the perfect accompaniment to a hearty casserole or the ripe camembert and crackers once enjoyed in bed on chill winter evenings when wild westerlies tossed the branches of tall trees and timber walls creaked. Escaping to bed at eight – a single-bar electric heater was useless in an open-plan living room – they would laugh when crumbs in the bedclothes tickled naked legs or wine-stained matching oversize t-shirts, their favoured nightwear. Eyelids grew heavy as dreams beckoned, moist mouths met to relish the taste of wine and desire.

Last of the Hunter reds, Liz reflects, placing her glass on the table. Last night, she'd noticed several empty shelves in the cellar, so must replenish the stocks, particularly the old favourites like claret, burgundy and tawny port. She reaches into her handbag, dropped carelessly by the dining chair, to retrieve the small notebook and pencil kept for jotting down poetic ideas or shopping lists.

Friday's lunch comes to mind, a pasta dish served with salad and crisp white wine. Light, clear wine frothing in tall-stemmed glasses, raising glasses to friendship, giggling like adolescents as bubbles tickled their noses. Delia said lunch was a reward for a week of cataloguing tedious Danish philosophy, Liz having bemoaned a recent donation of Soren Kierkegaard's entire oeuvre. Dismissing existentialism, Liz rips a half-completed list from her notebook.

An hour later, she remains hunched over the notebook, scrunched-up pages littering the table, her eyes aching from the poor light. Her wine-poem is almost complete, almost ready to be entered into the computer sitting in state on her desk in the study. How strange this sudden compulsion to write on paper, the need to feel a wooden pencil dig into her soft palm, when it would be so much easier to use a keyboard. Most Fridays, she has no trouble creating poetry on-line, watching contentedly as the pale grey screen fills with her thoughts and feelings. After signing her name and the date, she eases the pencil from stiff fingers.

Curled on the sofa, Liz warms her hands around her favourite coffee mug, wishing she could share the poem, even in its handwritten state. A glance at the clock reveals it's half past nine; Delia should have been home by now. Perhaps a student has delayed her or Charles Powell wanted to discuss their research project.

Suddenly, she recalls the note inserted with a recent payslip, advising female staff not to walk alone on campus after dark as several assaults have been reported. UQ campus covers a vast area, with the paths to carparks badly lit and often bordered by dense shrubs. To reduce the risk, security staff are now available at night to accompany female staff and students to their cars. Liz trusts that Delia has the sense to call Security if she's parked Daisy any distance from the well-lit lecture theatre. A second glance at the clock amplifies anxiety; Liz decides to call Delia's office followed by Security if she's not home by ten.

Rain spatters the living room windows, a welcome sound for a thirsty garden. As wind gusts around the house, she hears a loud crack that seems to be coming from the front garden. Too late she remembers dead limbs in the tall eucalypt that shades the patio. Weeks ago, she should have arranged for an arborist to visit. Crossing to the sliding doors, she peers into darkness, but there's no visible damage at this level. Down in the street, car headlights reveal a mess of damp leaves and small branches stretching from one kerb to the other, the usual wet weather damage. Headlights draw her attention to the driveway where a taxi lingers, its engine running. Delia emerges, laden with books and papers.

'Bloody car,' Delia calls up the stairs as Liz opens the front door. 'Trust Daisy to give up the ghost after a small shower!'

'You should have called me. I'd have picked you up.'

'I didn't want to trouble you.'

'It's no trouble.' Liz backs into the living room to avoid a collision.

The front door slams, caught by a gust of wind. 'I should have listened to Roger and bought another car,' Delia mutters, dropping books on the table.

'We could look at some on Saturday if you like?'

Delia sighs. 'There's no point. I need all my funds for a new home. That's if I can ever find one at my price.'

'Cheer up, you'll find one soon. Didn't that agent from Ashgrove mention a unit coming on the market shortly?'

'Yes, he did. A refurbished unit. The price is right, but I'm concerned about the distance from work.'

'Delia, it can't be more than ten ks!'

'I realise that, but there's no direct bus to uni and I can't rely on Daisy when it's raining.'

'I could…' Liz begins, then remembers Delia's aversion to borrowing more money. The loan from her in-laws is already causing her angst, even though they haven't pressured her to repay quickly. 'I could make coffee, or would you prefer to eat first? It won't take a moment to heat up the casserole, which was delicious, thank you.'

'Not hungry,' Delia answers, then leads for the sofa. 'I'll take a glass of wine instead, if we've got any left.' She kicks off her shoes and leans back against the cushion.

'I can fetch another bottle from the cellar. Any preferences?'

Delia shakes her head. 'Don't go down there in this weather. Coffee will be fine.'

They share biscuits and cheese with the coffee but conversation is limited, Delia preoccupied with a letter from Joanna. Reluctant to ask if all is well in Toowoomba, Liz carries used crockery into the kitchen for washing and drying.

Afterwards, she returns to the notebook lying open on the table. Her poem lacks a title, or rather an appropriate title, several having been discarded earlier. She crosses out, rewrites, struggles to find space, turns the page.

'Having trouble with the menu?' Delia asks, recalling feverish scribblings the previous week. Liz abhors unnecessary trips to the supermarket, so always writes a menu followed by a shopping list, unlike Delia who rarely plans meals, adopting a 'whatever I feel like at the time' attitude towards food.

'No, I'm trying to finish a poem I wrote this evening. The title's evading me.'

'Why don't you read it to me? I might have some ideas.'

'It's a bit depressing.'

Delia shrugs. 'I promise not to burst into tears.'

'Okay.' Liz picks up the notebook. 'There is an...' She coughs as though the words are sticking in her throat.

'Go on, I want to hear it.'

There is an emptiness within
that echoes with the hollow sound
of absent conversation

I am drained, depleted, a vacant vessel
tossed in a cardboard box
for later recycling

All that remains are the dregs
blood red droplets
staining the base

Shall I rinse the bottle
observe the old wine
float down the sink?
My new wine is clear and crisp
light white frothing
in a tall-stemmed glass

Can I pour new wine into an old bottle?
I lift the decanter
with trembling hands

'Empty vessel,' Delia declares, as Liz continues to stare at her creation. 'Your poem speaks to me. It poses questions I haven't dared ask myself, let alone answer. And I didn't find it depressing, the final stanza eradicates any trace of melancholy.'

Liz looks up. 'I love the title and your positive interpretation. When I started writing, my mood was unduly melancholic.'

'What made you change the tone?'

'I thought of Friday's lunch.'

'That doesn't make sense.'

Liz smiles. 'You served a white wine, crisp and light.'

'Fresh taste for a fresh start, if we can only push the past aside.'

'The past is inordinately heavy.'

Delia rises to take a seat at the table opposite Liz. 'I know, my friend, but four hands are better than two.'

Their hands meet across the table.

———

The following week, Liz insists on picking up Delia from the lecture theatre on Thursday evenings, dismissing the complaint that *I'm perfectly capable of walking alone to my car after dark* by threatening to hide Daisy's keys or let down a tyre.

Surprised by Liz's atypical resolve, Delia quickly capitulates, offering in return to cook dinner during the week and do the ironing.

For her part, Liz discovers she enjoys being pampered, and it's fun returning from work not knowing what's for dinner.

TWENTY-FOUR

The Ashgrove unit might be refurbished and the price reasonable, but Delia is appalled by its size and outlook. Small bedrooms face the adjacent block of flats, and the long narrow living area, leading to a tiny balcony tacked on like an afterthought, is shadowed by the trees in the neighbouring property.

Against their better judgment, Delia and Liz return to the Toowong agency, where blond-tipped hair bobs as Agent Damien grasps their hands in effusive greeting. Following a gap of several weeks, he has two properties to show them, both within Delia's price range.

The first – an old house divided into two – is rejected outright on the footpath, both women deterred by weatherboards patched with rough-cut fibro and a patio roof leaning drunkenly towards the minuscule garden. 'A distinct health hazard,' Delia remarks to a disappointed Damien before he can recite his mantra of *just needs a little TLC.*

The second property is on the other side of a hill that dips to a roundabout before rising steeply away from the entrance to Toowong cemetery, opened in 1875 and once

Brisbane's largest. No graves are visible from the street, which pleases Delia as she stands waiting for Liz on a wide concrete driveway leading to a sixties block of units. Despite its *six-pack status*, the building appears well-maintained and there are lawns and garden beds on three sides. Individual verandas extend over garage doors, promising light and breeze, each one high enough to see over the roof of the adjacent single-storey house lower down the slope.

They follow Agent Damien up concrete steps to a narrow elevated walkway with wrought iron railings that run the length of the building. After unlocking the first door, he ushers them into a short, carpeted hall with doors on either side. The left-hand door opens into an out-dated bathroom: handbasin, toilet and bath in pale green, the floor composed of tiny white and green tiles. A tarnished showerhead juts out from the wall above the two sets of taps. 'Good dimensions in here, Dr Pierce,' Damien says, as though Delia is incapable of judging size. 'A little refurbishment and you'd have a sparkling modern bathroom.'

Delia trips on loose tiles and grabs the towel rail to prevent a fall. The rail wobbles but remains tethered to the wall.

'Easily fixed,' Liz remarks, referring to floor tiles rather than the entire space.

Agent Damien tosses her a grateful smile before crossing the hall to open the door opposite. 'Second bedroom, or it could be used as a study.'

The first thing Delia notices as she steps inside is the windows facing the walkway – four timber-framed panes made of frosted glass like those in the bathroom. A claustrophobic space completely unsuitable as a research environment. Still, the glass could be changed and there's always her light-filled departmental office. But where would visitors sleep, the room isn't large enough for more than one single bed? 'Adequate,' she murmurs, trying to remain positive.

Liz focuses on the carpet – worn sage green that reminds her of wilting plants.

'Shall we view the living area?' Agent Damien backs out of the room.

Apart from depressing carpet, the lounge and dining area is light and spacious. Floor-length cream curtains frame the large sliding doors leading to a concrete patio with wrought-iron railings painted green. Delia brightens and instead of heading for the kitchen, crosses to the patio doors.

'Allow me, Dr Pierce.' Agent Damien overtakes her to unlock and tug on a cumbersome handle that initially refuses to budge. 'A good-sized patio with views,' he says breathlessly.

Delia agrees, although the overall outlook of a rusty corrugated-iron roof leaves much to be desired. At least tall trees disguise part of the adjoining house. She ventures to the railing, turning to the right where the driveway ends in lawn edged with well-trimmed shrubs. 'Are there any washing lines?'

'Three Hills' hoists, tucked neatly behind the block. Each unit has its own laundry at the rear of the garage.'

Delia nods in his direction before returning to the living area. 'The main bedroom, please, Damien.'

'Come this way, Dr Pierce.'

She follows him around a corner to a good-sized room containing a built-in wardroom. The window is large with openings at either end; a strip of winter sun distracts from sage green carpet. There's also a ceiling fan. 'I could sleep in here,' Delia remarks, half to herself, sliding open a wardrobe door to reveal ample hanging space with deep shelves at one end.

Unable to believe his luck, Agent Damien beams. 'Would you like to view the kitchen now and then we can go downstairs to the garage and laundry?'

'Yes, please.'

As expected, the kitchen – original sixties style – is shabby, its black and white vinyl floor tiles cracked in places, Laminex bench tops faded, and pale green cupboard doors needing a fresh coat of paint. The upright stove shows signs of wear but appears clean as does the single stainless steel sink and draining board. Undeterred – Delia is already envisioning a new kitchen if the vendors will accept less than the asking price – she's stepping back to survey the room when Liz touches her shoulder.

'A new kitchen wouldn't cost much, it's a small space.'

'It is, but as you know, I'm not exactly a gourmet chef.'

'Maybe not, but I'm enjoying coming home from work to dinner on the table.'

Agent Damien hovers nearby, the toe of one highly-polished shoe tapping the carpet edge as though he's contemplating whether to join them.

Delia turns to face him. 'We're ready for the garage now, Damien.' She tosses a smile in his direction before slipping her hand into Liz's. 'Off we go, my friend.'

Downstairs – the rear door to the garage is tucked under the walkway – both women comment on the extensive space, there being room for two medium-sized cars parked side by side, with laundry tubs positioned against the back wall under a window.

'Yes, it's most unusual to find garages of this size in Toowong.'

'This is definitely the most suitable property I've seen so

far,' Delia remarks as Agent Damien escorts them back to his car. 'Are the vendors open to offers?'

'The vendors are keen to sell, so I imagine they would be open to a reasonable offer. They inherited the property from their late mother.'

'I wish to sleep on the matter and discuss it with Liz.'

'And your daughters,' Liz adds.

'Of course, Dr Pierce. Please feel free to contact me tomorrow if you decide to make an offer. The office isn't open on Sundays but I'm happy to give you my private number.'

'If you're certain it wouldn't be too much of an imposition?'

Agent Damien offers his most charming expression. 'It's no imposition, I can assure you, dear Dr Pierce. I'm here to serve my clients.'

Delia responds with a grateful smile and a light touch to his wrist.

Following a brief discussion over a takeaway fish and chip dinner, the two women settle down to tackle the pros and cons of the Toowong unit, Liz insisting she make a list to ensure nothing is overlooked. She draws columns with a ruler fetched from the study, then labels each one with neat capital letters. They sit side by side at the dining table, empty plates pushed out of the way along with an unfinished bottle of wine.

As usual, Delia is impressed with the order Liz brings to decision-making and declares her *scribe extraordinaire* when a second sheet of paper is required.

Liz brushes off the compliment, maintaining it's simply

the result of librarianship training coupled with an extant pigeon-hole brain.

'Everything in its place and a place for everything,' Delia remarks, wishing she possessed such admirable traits.

'Some would find my methods tedious,' Liz replies, thinking of the disorder Kay once brought to her life. Welcome disorder, she now believes, although at times it seemed as if Kay's knee-jerk remarks and perpetual untidiness were deliberate, a way to evoke a moment of discord, dispel the serenity her partner displayed. Having grown up in a house where, despite its small size, the inhabitants shouted at one another, mother calling to shed-bound husband from the back step, siblings arguing over anything and everything, Kay failed to comprehend Liz's even-tempered existence.

'Sensible is the word I would use.' Delia studies the list. 'Right, let's determine the winner.'

Unwilling to take chances, Liz begins to count out loud, running a finger down each column.

'Pros!' Delia exclaims, reaching for the wine bottle.

―――

By Tuesday afternoon, the vendors have accepted Delia's offer and she's driving to the real estate office to sign a contract. Despite intermittent showers, Daisy started first time and covers the short distance from the university without missing a beat. Finding a parking space proves easy for a change, boosting the feeling that she's making the right decision.

Agent Damien is standing in the doorway, his angular frame held military-fashion as though he's awaiting her inspection. Bemused, Delia approaches slowly, averting her eyes from rigidity to transfer her briefcase from right to left hand. A handshake would suffice, dear Damien, she muses, adopting a suitable expression. 'Good afternoon, Damien,' she calls, 'the sun's out at last.'

He jerks into life, almost tripping over his shoes in his haste to exit the doorway.

Puppet on a string, Delia thinks, recalling the Sandy Shaw song that won the Eurovision Song contest back in the sixties. She envisages Damien barefoot, skinny ankles and long, thin feet protruding from suit pants.

'And good afternoon to you, Dr Pierce. Ready to do business, I see.' He indicates her briefcase with his free hand.

She almost enlightens him by unfastening the worn leather strap to reveal student assignments and research papers from Charles. In recent weeks she's taken to using Ron's larger briefcase, there being extra material to accommodate now that joint research has begun in earnest. Instead, she extricates her hand from Damien's to march into his office.

'Conference room today, Dr Pierce,' he calls after her, gesturing towards an open door to the right, even though she has her back to him.

Stopped in her tracks, Delia swivels around. 'My apologies.'

'No need to apologise. I should have mentioned that we always sign contracts in the conference room.' He steps forward to take her arm. 'This way.'

The room is a miniature version of his office, a corner space with floor-to-ceiling glass on three sides and no blinds to soften the spears of sunlight striking a round glass-topped table and metal-framed chairs. Lacking sunglasses, Delia sits with her back to the sun, leaving Damien to squint as he pushes a pile of paper towards her, before taking the adjoining seat. 'Please take your time to read thoroughly,' he instructs, 'then sign where indicated.'

After retrieving her reading glasses from the depths of the briefcase, Delia settles to her task, adopting the method she employs when reading student assignments. But no matter how hard she tries, memory insists on breaking her concentration and instead of a modern office, she sees a small, rectangular building – more a site-shed than an office – furnished with a filing cabinet, a Laminex-topped table and three vinyl chairs in a depressing shade of brown. Unlike dapper Damien, the land agent supervising this early seventy's contract signing is casually dressed in flared jeans and a check shirt. Mud clings to his work boots, although that's understandable, given they have just returned from tramping over recently developed blocks of land. Practical Ron insisted on taking gumboots to change into; they're lined up outside the temporary office set on a patch of grass a few streets from the one where they hope to build their new home. Shaking her head to dislodge unwelcome images, Delia resumes her reading.

'A problem, Dr Pierce?'

Delia raises her head. 'No, everything is clear. Tired eyes, that's all. The consequence of hours spent researching old documents. I need new glasses, but life has been rather hectic lately.'

'There will be plenty of time now you've chosen a property. As your belongings are already packed and in storage, you can arrange furniture removalists, then sit back and wait for settlement.'

'When is that?' Delia asks, suddenly remembering Carol's September wedding.

'It's a standard thirty-day contract, so that makes it

around the end of August.' He leans over her to check the date on the last page. 'August 24th. A Monday.'

'That's cutting it a bit fine, my daughter's getting married on the fifth of September in Townsville.'

'You could delay moving in until your return to Brisbane. Didn't you say you're staying with your friend?'

'Yes. I'm sure Liz won't mind my staying on for a few days.' Conscious of his continuing proximity, she covers her left cheek with her hand to prevent further minty breaths from alighting on her skin.

Post-signing, Damien offers a celebratory drink, but Delia prefers to wait until her new mortgage has been approved by the bank. She envisages dour Mr Gordon scrutinising her bank statements, a magnifying glass held in pale fingers to ensure he doesn't miss a withdrawal. There shouldn't be a problem, she earns a decent salary and he remains unaware that the February cheque from her in-laws is a loan she intends to repay within a year. After cashing the cheque, Delia paid Jo's entire year's board in advance, Diana pleased to have cash. Textbooks took another chunk, then she stashed the remainder in an unwashed sock discovered in an old hiking boot. At present, boot and loot lie in the bottom of the wardrobe along with jumbled pairs of shoes.

―――

Leaving Daisy parked on the street – Liz's car is already parked under the house and she'll be first to leave in the morning – Delia checks for mail. A letter postmarked Perth, and a bill for Liz; she transfers them to her left hand before picking up the briefcase to make the steep climb to the front door.

Inside, Liz is seated in an armchair reading. 'Hi there, is it all done and dusted?'

'It sure is.' Delia dumps her briefcase on the floor. 'The thirty-day contract's a bit of a problem, as settlement is so close to Carol's wedding. I wanted to have the unit re-carpeted before I move in.' She kicks off her shoes to collapse on the sofa.

Liz closes her book. 'You don't have to move in on settlement day. Why not stay here until after the wedding?'

'Are you sure you don't mind?'

'Of course not. Besides, we were talking about taking a short holiday while we're up north. A few days on Magnetic Island would be lovely.'

'I'm not sure I can afford it now.'

'I'm happy to pay for the accommodation; it won't be much more than paying the single supplement and I could really do with a break.'

'So could I.'

'That's settled then,' Liz declares, having decided it's high time she became more assertive. 'Now, a pre-dinner glass of wine to celebrate your purchase.'

Delia shakes her head. 'I'd prefer to wait until the bank have approved my mortgage.'

'Okay, we'll celebrate contract signing instead.'

Delia grins. 'You organise drinks while I prepare dinner.'

'No need for preparation, last night's pasta bake was enormous, so there's plenty left over for tonight.'

'I might make a small salad.'

'I can do it later. You sit and read your mail.'

Delia glances at the letters clasped in her hand. 'One's for you. It looks like a bill.'

'Then it can wait.' Liz gets to her feet and crosses to the

kitchen. Leftovers from last night include a half-bottle of white wine.

When Liz returns with the wine, Delia is frowning over her mother's letter. 'Not bad news, I hope?'

'My mother has changed her flight arrangements for the wedding. Now, she's flying to Brisbane first, as she wants to catch up with some old friends.' Delia lays the letter on the coffee table. 'Can you think of a decent motel near here?'

'That's not necessary, she can have the fold-up bed Jo used, or you could give up your bed and sleep in the study.'

'Thanks, but I don't want to inflict any more of my relatives on you. It's bad enough that you've had to put up with me for so long.'

'So, you think I'm just putting up with you, that I can't wait until you leave?'

'No, but I don't want to…' Delia hesitates, loath to further upset.

'Don't say impose, please, or I'll blow my stack!'

Delia decides it would be best to remain silent, so she picks up her mother's letter and pretends to read.

'Sorry, I just wanted you to feel at home, invite friends over or have family to stay,' Liz says softly, acknowledging that her assertion-attempt has backfired.

'I'm happy staying here with you, but this is your home, not mine.' Delia folds the letter, then picks up her wine glass and crosses to Liz's armchair. 'A toast to our futures. May we both learn to love our altered environments.'

Reluctantly, Liz lifts her glass and turns to face Delia, but eye contact brings sorrow rather than equilibrium. If only she could answer her poem-question in the affirmative by pouring new wine into an old bottle.

TWENTY-FIVE

Suspended over a steep gully, the house belonging to Liz's friend, Bev, juts into a dense canopy of eucalypts. Tossed by strong westerly wind, grey-green leaves graze the edge of hardwood boards while tree-top branches tap morse messages on sturdy timber railings. Dotted around the wide rear deck, kentia palms, secure in heavy terracotta pots, push fresh green fronds into a sable sky. Inside the open plan living room, uncurtained glass doors and floor-to-ceiling windows ensure uninterrupted views of swaying foliage from the cane chairs arranged in a semi-circle facing the deck.

Sipping red wine, Delia searches for silver stars in the slits of sky between branches, but none are visible, and she ponders whether clouds have gathered. Earlier, there was no hint of cloud as they drove through shadowed suburbs, the taxi driver remarking in lyrical fashion on the yellow moon warming the winter sky. High above the solid entrance at street level, listening to trees and old timbers creaking, Delia suddenly feels vulnerable, as if this slight exposure to nature has cracked her city-bound skin. To counteract fragility, she closes her eyes, envisaging the view from her office, Helidon stone walls, sturdy columns and archways. Walking through stone cloisters to a lecture theatre, she often glances up at the shields carved into each column. They remind her of another era, another country steeped in tradition. A world where knights rescued maidens from tower imprisonment and scribes sat hunched over parchment transcribing ancient tales.

Musing on antiquity, she experiences a fierce desire to flee her birthplace, her old/new land struggling to find its place in the world. Two hundred years of so-called civilisation, a thin veneer covering primeval earth, a new Britain under pellucid southern skies. The wholesale transplantation of British culture seems redundant now, nineties media reverberating with the buzzword *multiculturalism*. Each week she teaches nineteenth-century English literature to Asian students along with second-generation Australians named Dimitri, Francesco and Gerda. Watching eager faces absorb language and landscapes far removed from their present reality, she concludes that the young can transcend national boundaries with ease and voyage through the centuries like Doctor Who.

Despite her love for the Australian way of life – at least that lived in a city built on the green rim – she resolves to break out of her British colonial past, open her eyes to other cultures, listen to the rhythm of diverse languages. Work-wise, she's spent too many years in the nineteenth century with only the occasional foray into the modern world. She must adopt global citizenship, acknowledge her place on a planet spinning towards a new millennium, according to the calendar proclaimed over five centuries earlier by a Pope:

Gregorian replacing Julian, man-made titles of no consequence to an ancient planet. She blinks and the room surfaces, drawing her attention to untouched wine. Lifting her glass, she recalls Liz's poem, trusting she possesses sufficient strength to uncork a new vintage.

Footsteps alert her to Liz returning from the kitchen with a cheese platter. She turns away from the trees to present a warm smile.

'Enjoying the trees?' Liz asks, placing the platter on a low table nearby.

'I'm not sure. They make me feel insecure. It's the constant movement, I suppose.'

'I rather like the idea of swaying in the treetops. The house is perfectly safe.'

'I realise that, although I'm not certain I would want to be here during a storm.'

'Storms frightened Leah at first,' Bev declares from the kitchen doorway. She tosses a smile over her shoulder to the tall blond woman standing behind her. 'Didn't they, love?'

'Scared me half to death! But Bev taught me to overcome my fears and learn to love the trees.' Inclining her head, Leah kisses the back of her lover's neck.

'I'll fetch the coffee.' Bev turns back to the kitchen.

Acknowledging the offer with a distracted wave, Leah wanders over to the doors to stand staring out at palms illuminated by spotlights hanging from the soffit. 'Bev helped me face all my fears,' she says, her usually forthright tone soft as the cashmere sweater that hugs her slim torso. 'Surrounded by her love, I felt empowered to raise a subject I'd kept hidden for years, camouflaged beneath a tough-as-nails demeanour.'

Against her will, Delia remembers past vocabulary:

suspicion, lies, infidelity. Language she believed erased, language that should no longer cause her pain.

Leah turns towards Bev's long-time friend and the woman currently sharing her house. 'Incest, rape,' she remarks, indifferently.

Disturbed, Delia waits for further statements, but there are none, Leah walks to a nearby chair to stretch out long slender legs.

Returning from the kitchen with four mugs balanced on a tray, Bev serves her guests, then makes a beeline for Leah. 'Are you okay, love?'

'I had to repeat them,' Leah answers defiantly. 'I had to tell other women, to prove I've genuinely conquered my demons.'

Bev sets the tray on the small table. 'I'm sure Liz and Delia understand.'

Liz takes a sip of coffee as she searches for a careful response. 'Leah, I don't pretend to understand, I have no such experience. But I understand your need to express your pain, and I'm pleased that you felt able to do so.'

Unable to augment Liz's remarks, Delia nods in agreement. Leah has humbled her, made her feel ashamed of her petulance, her inability to forget events in the distant past, her refusal to forgive, even though she had wasted little time in treading the same path. She knows nothing of Leah's life, can only guess at the depth of suffering.

'It's okay to smile,' Leah says brightly. 'I didn't mean to put a damper on the evening. How about a bottle of port with our coffee? That should raise the spirits.'

'Lovely.' Liz turns to Delia. 'Thank God we didn't drive. Port would really put us over the limit.'

Leah holds out her hand. 'Come and help me choose, Bev.'

When they have left the room, Liz asks if Leah sparked uncomfortable memories, her voice low, caring.

Delia shakes her head. 'Like you, I have no experience of those matters.' Unlike Leah, she can't repeat the words. 'She made me realise how fortunate I've been.'

'Me too. The only real hurt I've experienced is the pain of losing Kay, and I do believe that wound is beginning to heal.'

'I'm not so sure mine is.' Delia sighs. 'Sometimes I think the knife cut too deep.'

'Be patient, time will lessen the pain.'

'I know you're right.'

Bev calls from the kitchen that she's found a bottle of port. 'Fancy getting merry, you two?' she asks, appearing in the doorway clutching a large bottle. Behind her, Leah carries four port glasses.

'I'd prefer to get pissed,' Delia answers.

Liz opens her mouth to reproach but thinks better of it. Delia isn't a child.

'So would I.' Leah advances into the room, flashing a smile in Delia's direction as she places glasses on a dining table still littered with the remnants of dinner. 'Come on, Liz, it's time to let your hair down. Even librarians are allowed to get pissed!'

Blushing, Liz tries to think of a witty reply.

'I can see the headline now,' Delia remarks with mock-solemnity. 'Librarian drunk in charge of on-line catalogue. Red-head's revels produce information glitches!'

Laughing, Liz extends one hand. 'A large port, please.'

Somehow, Delia and Liz manage to sit demurely in the back seat of the taxi, their lips clamped shut to prevent giggles betraying an inebriated state. The taxi driver prattles on, seemingly unconcerned by their failure to response to his innocuous questions. 'Here we are, ladies,' he remarks as the taxi turns into Tamarin Street.

Liz fumbles in her purse to find a note. 'Thank you. Keep the change.'

On the footpath, Delia collapses in a heap, sniggering as the taxi drives away. Behind her, Liz echoes her laughter, although she has no idea what's so amusing. At last, Delia regains sufficient self-control to ask if Liz noticed the driver's hair.

'Yes, a pony.' Liz struggles to suppress a giggle. 'A thin grey ponytail with nothing on top.'

'No,' Delia retorts, wagging a finger at Liz. 'There was something on top.' She searches her befuddled brain for the correct vocabulary. 'Red like Gorbachev.'

'Communism is dead!' Liz shouts to the street.

Delia points to her head. 'Red, a red mark.'

'Port wine,' Liz answers, recalling cartoons of the former Soviet leader.

'No more port, I'm full to the brim! I need my bed.'

Having consumed slightly less alcohol, Liz helps Delia to her feet and together they negotiate the steep steps, sighing with relief when they reach the front door. Fortunately, Liz has minimal trouble with the key, so they are soon safely inside with the added protection of a bolt pulled into place.

Swaying a little, Delia crosses to the hall, where she hesitates in front of a closed door to hang her handbag on its round wooden handle. 'Around the corner,' she murmurs, retrieving a mind-map of her recent purchase. A second, open door aids her passage, she staggers inside to strip off her clothes and tumble into bed.

Liz heads straight for the bathroom to lean over the handbasin, one hand turning a tap, the other splashing cold water over her face. Then, she lowers her head to gulp a mouthful of water, before turning off the tap. Backing out of the bathroom, she collides with the cane linen basket, so begins to remove her clothes, forgetting to open the lid in her haste to fold neatly. Naked, she scurries across the hall to her bedroom, groaning when she spots Delia curled up in her bed. 'Don't go to sleep, Delia. This is *my* bed and you're lying on my pyjamas.'

'Warm in here,' Delia says sleepily. 'Warm as toast.'

Liz remembers switching on her electric blanket before leaving the house. Resigned to sharing her bed, she says, 'I still want my pjs. Move over.'

'No pjs here. Gone to the Op shop.' Delia throws back the duvet. 'See.' Her full breasts glow in a shaft of moonlight, dusky nipples firming as night air chills.

Shivering, Liz runs over to the window to close the curtains before lemon light can sting. Two steps and she's reached her side of the bed. 'Night,' she mutters, and curling into a ball, turns away from Delia's warmth.

'You're freezing!' Delia exclaims. 'You need warming up. You'll never sleep if you're cold.' Rolling over, she throws plump arms around thin shoulders.

Nipples prick Liz's bare back; thick thighs envelop her lean backside. In a vain attempt to stop shaking, she bites her lower lip. Blood mingles with saliva, subsequent tears adding salt to the wound. Somewhere a soft voice urges her not to cry, but Liz cannot comply, more tears falling as a lock of brown hair brushes her shoulder and moist lips slide across her neck. Her breath is short and sharp, expelled deep into dark night; she waits with mounting expectation, her neglected flesh brimming. Strong arms turn her, cradle her against full breasts like a suckling infant. Slowly, her body withdraws from its foetal form, long legs unfolding, clenched fists relaxing to release stiff fingers. Tentatively, she raises her head, presses trembling lips to smooth skin.

TWENTY-SIX

Saturday morning and Delia wakes early, her bare shoulders tense with cold. A headache pricks her scalp and her tongue feels thick, her lips dry. Another hangover, proof that she's drinking too much; after seven months she has failed to come to terms with changed circumstances. As soon as she's moved into her new home, she must curtail her alcohol intake or stop altogether. Drinking alone would be asking for trouble. She's been down that road before, back when Ron left her alone with the girls to pursue his career in the U.S. An affair resolved the problem, a history lecturer eager to assuage his lust while his wife struggled with a newborn baby. Delia knew the relationship wouldn't last, guilt – on his part not hers – certain to surface once he acknowledged their affair was based entirely on sexual attraction. She didn't mourn his departure; there were plenty of other sex-starved academics around the campus.

Leaving Liz asleep, she slips out of bed, gathering her clothes from the floor before creeping out of the room. Safe in her own bedroom, she remembers that Joanna is visiting for the day, something about getting a lift from a friend.

Dog-tired, Delia tries to resist the lure of sleep by propping herself against the pillows; it's much too early to risk waking Liz by having a shower.

When she wakes at ten, Liz is clattering about in the kitchen, obviously none the worse for last night's binge. Heaving herself out of bed, she reaches for her dressing-gown slung over the old wooden chair in one corner.

By the time she's finished showering, Liz is out in the back garden, raking up leaves with a vigour Delia would love to emulate, but all she's capable of is making black coffee and toast. Bread soaks up the alcohol, she remembers Ron advising early on in their relationship, when he handed her burnt toast made in his grubby share-house kitchen. Delighted by his thoughtfulness – he'd also prepared strong black coffee – she perched on a stool at the breakfast bar, her eyes half-closed to block late morning light.

Seated at Liz's dining table, Delia dismisses late-night happenings to focus on meal matters. She's tempted to take Jo and her friend – if he or she wishes to stay for lunch – to a local café but on reflection feels reluctant to make unnecessary purchases during the mortgage approval process.

———

Down in the street she hears voices and presuming Jo has arrived, strains to determine the gender of her daughter's friend. But in the absence of car door slamming or engine idling, she realises it's Liz chatting to a neighbour. She must have completed back garden raking and moved to the front. Where does she find the energy?

When Liz returns to the house for a coffee, she solves the lunch problem, opening the fridge to reveal a quiche made the previous day in anticipation of guests.

A quick trip to the shops to buy salad ingredients and fresh bread is all that's needed to complete the meal. Grateful, Delia thanks Liz and hurries to fetch her purse and car keys.

'I'll go to the shops,' Liz calls after her. 'I need some cream from the chemist. You stay for Jo.'

Waiting for her daughter, Delia ponders last night's intimacy. Has Liz dismissed drunken sex as a one-off, almost non-event, or is she too embarrassed to raise the subject? For her part, Delia needs to explain her reckless behaviour. Unaccustomed to guilt – at least as far as casual sex is concerned – today she senses an overwhelming desire to apologise.

The groan of mismanaged gears push culpability to a corner of her mind. It sounds as if a truck is struggling to negotiate the sharp turn into the driveway. Don't say Jo's friend is a truckie? Leaving her breakfast dishes on the table, Delia rushes to open the front door. An old Nissan Patrol is backing out of the driveway, the driver's head turned, making it impossible to establish gender. Her daughter is standing on the lawn talking to Liz, who's returned from the shops. 'Hi, Jo,' Delia calls from the top of the steps, as the Nissan straightens up, then accelerates towards Moggill Road.

Jo waves but continues her conversation with Liz.

'Come on up,' Delia persists, 'I'll put the jug on.' Retreating inside, she snatches mug and plate from the table before heading to the kitchen where she dumps them in the sink.

The jug is boiling when Jo waltzes into the room. 'I drove all the way from Toowoomba,' she announces proudly. 'Peter says I managed well considering it's my first time driving his new four-wheel drive.'

Delia frowns. 'It didn't look new to me. Is Peter a new friend?'

'New to him, I mean.'

'You haven't answered my question.'

Jo removes her back-pack and sets it on the floor. 'He's a good friend. My best friend, in fact. After Jesus of course.'

Delia decides to ignore Jo's last remark. 'A boy from uni?'

'No, from church. And Peter's a man.'

Delia sighs. Another older man, another surrogate father. Why this rush to restore the status quo, this desperate need for fatherly affection? Her daughters are behaving like small children that have broken their favourite dolls and won't be placated until replacements are placed in their empty arms.

'It's not what you're thinking, Mum. I'm not like Carol. Peter and I aren't sleeping together.'

'But he is your boyfriend?'

'We prefer to think of ourselves as soulmates.'

'So, this relationship is serious?'

Jo's eyes glaze over. 'We are united in faith and love. We walk the same road towards salvation. There can be no division, no splitting of the sacred path.'

'Darling, I appreciate the depth of your feelings but please don't overlook your studies.'

'I won't, Mum. Besides, Peter believes it's important for me to qualify as a nurse so that I can help him in the future. He feels led to work in a remote Aboriginal community.'

'Very commendable.' Delia envisages an outback clinic staffed by Nurse Joanna and Doctor Peter. Red dirt and flies. Sweat-soaked uniforms and dust-streaked children. 'But surely he won't want to wait until you've finished your studies?'

'Maybe not, but Peter always consults the Lord before making major life decisions.'

Resisting the urge to ask if Peter has a private line to the Almighty, Delia says evenly, 'I'd like to meet Peter. We need to talk about *your* future.'

'You've already met him, Mum, when we were packing up the house.'

'Oh Christ, not Pastor Eames!'

Jo looks horrified, although whether on account of blasphemy or disapproval, it's difficult for her mother to tell. 'I thought you had more sense, Joanna,' Delia continues, determined to discover if pastor and convert have discussed marriage. 'You're eighteen, far too young to be tying yourself to anyone, let alone a much older man. You've hardly lived!'

'I'm not tying myself to Peter, Mum, and age is irrelevant. We believe we're destined to carry out God's work together but that doesn't mean a fancy wedding followed by a bloody great mortgage and two kids!' Snatching up her backpack, Jo flounces out of the kitchen. The front door slams behind her.

'Oh shit, I've done it now,' Delia says as Liz enters the kitchen from the rear deck.

'I heard raised voices, so I waited round the back. What's happened?'

Delia relays the information, her expression one of exasperation.

'Stop fretting, it's probably just a passing phase.' Liz offers a comforting smile. 'Did Jo mention marriage?'

'No, but she said it was serious.'

'It always is when you're eighteen.' Liz scoots over to the jug, which is boiling furiously, steam rising from beneath its lid. 'I'll make the tea. Or were you making coffee?'

'Tea is good.' Delia heads for the living room, changes her mind and wheels around. 'I thought Gen X women would think and act independently, not fall for the first man to offer love and security. We raised them to focus on higher education and careers.'

'I think you're misjudging them, Delia. Sure, many young women still want to get married and have children but most want a career as well. And let's face it, these days with maternity leave and childcare centres, they can easily combine parenting and a career, just like you did.'

'In theory, yes, but they don't realise how onerous it is trying to balance career, housework and kids. Plus bolstering a husband's fragile ego.'

Liz hoots with laughter as she picks up two mugs, sending tea slopping over the rims.

'Careful, you'll burn yourself.'

'I'm not as delicate as the male psyche.' Side-stepping spilt tea, she heads for the doorway. 'Go and sit down before I'm forced to push you out of the way.'

Delia pouts. 'It's alright for you to laugh. You haven't had to pander to the male of the species.'

'No, there are advantages to being lesbian.'

———

Joanna returns for lunch, looking sheepish, and ends up staying overnight, Peter Eames tied up with matters ecumenical until late in the evening. Fortunately, she doesn't have a morning lecture, so she's spared a maternal sermon on the importance of not missing out on vital knowledge. Meals pass without further drama, a relief to Liz, who values peaceful Sundays.

Over Monday's dinner Delia and Liz comment on their

respective workdays, each waiting for the other to broach the subject of impromptu sex. 'Washing up or watching the news,' Liz asks when every morsel has been consumed and cutlery placed neatly in the centre of each plate.

'Neither.' Delia's tone is harsher than she intended. 'We need to talk about Friday night.'

Liz tilts her head to fix her gaze on the wall above Delia's head. 'What can I say except sorry, but that's such an inadequate word.'

'Why do you feel obliged to apologise? I made the first move.'

'You were drunk. You didn't realise what you were doing.'

'I knew exactly what I was doing.'

'Then why? Were you feeling sorry for me?'

Delia fiddles with the buttons on her shirt.

'Sorry. I have no right to demand an explanation.'

'There you go again. Stop berating yourself. Just listen. Help me make sense of this. And please look at me. I can't talk to your neck!'

Sniffing, Liz pulls out a handkerchief to blow her nose. Washed with tears, her green eyes glisten like forest leaves after rain.

'When we were with Bev and Leah,' Delia begins, looking directly into Liz's eyes, 'I experienced a string of conflicting emotions, initially apprehension. As I told you, the location intimidated, making me aware of my vulnerability. But it wasn't only the swaying trees and the house perched precariously on a steep hillside that threatened, it was the interior atmosphere, their rock-solid relationship working in antithesis to the external environment. As the evening wore on, jealousy pierced my mask of geniality. Bev and Leah had each other, they could laugh and cry together, love together while we had only memories. I wanted to shout out that it wasn't fair, ask Joanna's precious God why we had to suffer. Then Leah stood by the window to utter her once-secret words, and suddenly I found myself praying to that same God. Seeking forgiveness for copious sins, giving thanks that Leah had found Bev and could confront her past.'

'And having dealt with the past,' Liz interjects softly, 'she could face both present and future, which we haven't yet learned to do.'

Tears sting Delia's cheeks as she pushes back her chair and hurries to the other side of the table, where she kneels to lay her head on Liz's lap. 'Can we learn together? I'm not strong enough to work through this alone.'

Lifting Delia's head, Liz whispers assent.

———

Unaccustomed to sharing her bed, Liz wakes long before crisp September dawn. She's lying on her side facing the wardrobe, home to a single set of clothes. After spending the evening watching a movie, she and Delia had adjourned to the same bedroom as though from habit, with no mention made of total relocation. Turning onto her back, she contemplates the previous eight months, the extraordinary chain of events that led to the moment when friendship and passion fused. Is their new relationship merely the result of shared suffering? When first engulfed by dark days, they clung to one another instinctively, sheltering from unremitting grief within the solid walls of their longstanding friendship.

Destiny could explain the sudden shift from friend to lover, Ron's unexplained debts and Delia's subsequent financial troubles the catalyst for change. Yet in Liz's mind, external circumstances fail to explain the intensity of shared emotion, the depth of love. God is love, she muses, recalling a long-neglected phrase. Biblical images thread through thought, impeding further relationship contemplation. God the Father, God the Son, God the Holy ghost, the patriarchal trinity that dogged her Sunday school years. Suddenly, she's a small girl asking what happened to God the Mother and God the Daughter? A sharp response insinuates ignorance and stupidity, destroying a child's simple faith.

Months earlier, when she emerged from the initial numbness of grief, Liz resurrected her childhood deity to spend hours venting her anger at cold-hearted God the Father. Not that her rants brought comfort or relief. On the contrary, sorrow intensified, and after several weeks, she abandoned yelling at a white-bearded old man in the sky. Kay's death was the result of human error, nothing whatsoever to do with the hypothetical image Sunday school teachers taught her to worship.

Spring sunshine filters through the curtains, diminishing morning melancholy. In the few minutes remaining before the alarm clock emits buzzes, her thoughts turn to an article discovered the previous week when cataloguing a book on contemporary religious studies. The author, a feminist theologian, had revived the concept of a feminine divine, stressing the need for contemporary women to worship a goddess rather than an obsolete father figure. Liz likes the idea of an Earth-Mother nurturing her children and protecting the planet.

Flickers of lemon light stroke her face as she senses the genesis of new spirituality, the opportunity to release her soul from childhood rhetoric. Closing her eyes, she moves warm hands from beneath the bedclothes to hold them steady, fingertips almost touching her chin. Her prayers are unpretentious, brief expressions of gratitude and joy. She gives thanks for sunshine, sanctuary, sustenance, and for a rich seam of love, damaged but not destroyed by death, lodged forever in her memory. New love is growing in cool earth, waiting for spring warmth to unfurl its tender shoots. 'Happy is she who has acceptance, for she will have all she needs.' She sighs contentedly before adding, 'And happy is she who listens and hears and extends her hands, for she has understanding.'

'Beatitudes of a woman,' Delia murmurs.

Liz opens her eyes. 'You remember.'

'Women's group, a few years back. An interesting bunch.'

'Why did we stop attending?'

'Too much theology if I remember correctly.'

'Yes, that was it.'

'Were you praying just now?' Delia asks, snuggling into her lover.

'Yes, to God the Mother.'

Delia strokes the thin wrist protruding from Liz's pyjama sleeve. 'A feminine deity appeals to me, too. Mother Nature if you will, Ceres with her corn-ripe yellow hair scattering seed over fertile fields.'

'The bread of life. That's what I was thanking her for, amongst other things.'

'May I ask what else?'

'Love.' Liz tucks her hands under the bedclothes. 'That's the greatest gift of all.'

'I know. Love heals deep wounds and knits damaged flesh.' Searching beneath the covers, Delia lifts a warming hand to place it over her left breast. 'Hand on heart, a holy sacrament.'

Repeated buzzing foils extended loving gestures. Surrendering to workday requirements, new lovers depart for separate rooms – Liz to the bathroom, Delia to her bedroom, where she retrieves suitable clothing from a jam-packed wardrobe. Circumstances may have changed but she must present the same public image to her students. Confident experienced lecturer, tailored jeans and a sky-blue linen jacket unbuttoned to reveal a crisp white cotton shirt. Delia refuses to use the word 'blouse' with its connotations of feminine fussiness. Shoes are an easy decision – she possesses only two winter pairs, sneakers and black slip-ons with low heels. She gave up lecturing in high-heels long ago, the resultant pinched toes and aching legs too painful. Sometimes, she considers borrowing a Victorian outfit from the Drama department. A high-necked, floor-length dress teamed with button-up boots would lift her first-year students from their usual morning stupor without a doubt!

'Bathroom's free,' Liz calls from the hall.

'Thanks,' Delia calls back, grateful that she lives in the late twentieth century, so won't be sharing a jug of hot water placed on a marble-topped washstand!

TWENTY-SEVEN

Their clothes remain in separate wardrobes, both women weary following the day's work, so preferring to relax by watching television or reading until it's time for bed.

By contrast, love-making lingers long into cool night, Friday's demanding passion vanquished as they take time to discover all the secret places, their hands wandering over soft skin. Lips meet repeatedly to kiss or whisper endearments; limbs entwine languidly in a delicate dance. Drawn together by a need deeper than love or the hunger for sexual gratification, they embrace the intimate world with absolute surety, surrendering to exquisite ecstasy only when their bodies can no longer resist.

Throughout the week, Delia makes no reference to her forthcoming move, so Liz assumes they'll discuss the matter over the weekend. Renting out the unit is an option; students are always looking for accommodation close to campus. Furnished flats attract higher rents, so the bulk of Delia's stored belongings could be transported to Toowong with the remainder moved to Tamarin Street. If Delia swaps the double bed brought from her former home for one of the girls' singles, there will be plenty of room in the second bedroom for Delia's large desk. A senior lecturer can't be expected to share a small study or use an old-fashioned desk more suited to a schoolgirl.

Satisfied with her deliberations and forgetting that Professor Kay was happy to mark students' papers at the dining table, Liz sets aside potential problems to focus on daytime cataloguing and evening togetherness. That is, until Friday afternoon when she surfaces from poem creation to retrieve the day's mail. Perched on the timber mailbox built by Kay from old railway sleepers, she tears open an envelope postmarked Canberra, fearing further vitriol from Kay's brother. The solicitor's letter is succinct, advising the date and time of a court case to contest Kay's will. Colin Masters on behalf of Frances Masters vs Elizabeth Coney, the case to be heard in Brisbane District court. The letter falls to the grass as Liz grips the sides of the mailbox. How could she have forgotten his threat to instigate legal proceedings if she didn't vacate the house within six months? Fran must have signed the documents, succumbed to his constant moralising about her right to inherit the bulk of Kay's estate.

She bends to pick up the letter before beginning a slow climb to the front door, her legs heavy, her head pounding with the onset of headache. Not now, she pleads with her body, I need my wits about me. Her solicitor will be closing his office for the weekend within the hour; she can't wait until Monday to discuss her options.

Inside the house, she rushes to the bathroom to swallow a couple of Panadol with a glass of water, then heads to her bedroom to fetch shoes and car keys. A glance in the mirror, a quick comb of her hair and she's flying out of the door and down the steps as though her life depends on Olympic speed. In a way it does, the future would be an unmitigated disaster if she lost the house. Sharing a small unit is out of the question, they would get under one another's feet, argue about study space. And retreating to the garden would be impossible, she can't imagine the other unit owners allowing her to dig up the lawns to plant vegetables!

Behind the car, Liz skids to a halt on under-house gravel as she remembers visiting the Law library months earlier to discover whether CM could legally contest Kay's will on his mother's behalf. Information for herself and Fran, who told Liz that a legal challenge was entirely unwarranted, the inheritance of Kay's savings and superannuation being more than adequate for an elderly woman's needs. Liz tries to recall if she phoned Fran to tell her what the Law Librarian unearthed, or whether she called around, not that it matters, but the former would mean she still possesses the photo-copied extract from the Queensland Succession Act (1981). She's particular about storing important papers, so it's probably in the grey metal filing cabinet under M for Masters. Abandoning her visit to the solicitor, she heads back upstairs.

In the study, she searches thoroughly – including the desk drawers – but there's no sign of the paper, and she's forced to acknowledge that whatever the exact wording, CM has triumphed. No reputable solicitor would take on the case otherwise. Seated on her office chair, she stares out of the window trying to envisage a different outlook, one lacking the comforting presence of trees. When the November court case comes around, jacarandas will be blooming on campus in time for end-of-year exams. It's said that failure is a certainty if a purple blossom falls on your head prior to an exam. Despite her sombre mood, Liz smiles at the memory of giving jacarandas a wide berth, especially during windy weather.

Meal preparation calms, Liz determined not to bombard Delia with court case news the moment she walks in the door. Over dinner, they discuss their planned drive to Toowoomba the following day, Delia wanting to see for herself the extent of her daughter's relationship with Peter Eames. Joanna has offered lunch at the pastor's house, saying it's too noisy for conversation at her own accommodation with toddler Joseph asking endless questions.

Following the usual post-dinner chores, they settle in the living room with mugs of tea and custard creams – Liz's favourite biscuit although, unlike Delia, she limits herself to one per evening. Delia has shed a few kilos since implementing a physical exercise routine in the form of weekend walks and climbing the hill to the bus stop on the day she has evening lectures but dismissed the idea of serious dieting when Liz retrieved *New Theories on Diet and Nutrition* from the study. Her excuse remains pertinent: she can't afford to replace all her clothes.

Before they discuss evening viewing, Liz produces the solicitor's letter, handing it to Delia without a word. The response is unexpected – no rushing over from the sofa to deliver hugs and sympathy – instead, what Liz assumes is Delia's lecturer voice, advising the appointment of a solicitor experienced in family law.

'I'll contact Mr Melling's office on Monday,' Liz answers, preferring to deal with a local solicitor.

'Prior to seeing him, you need to document any conversation you've had with Frances Masters regarding Kay's will.'

'Fran was perfectly content with her inheritance and said she'd told Colin repeatedly contesting the will was out of the question. She also said she was pleased that Kay left me the house.'

'Then I foresee success on your part.' Delia places the letter on the coffee table before moving to the sofa. 'Now my love, I suggest we go through your stack of videos and choose a comedy to take our minds off Colin Masters and Peter Eames.'

Liz accepts this advice with a kiss.

———

Leaving the sanctuary of 6 Tamarin Street, they drive west towards the Dividing Range and Pastor Eames. Out here the country aches for rain, grasses burnt brown by winter sun swishing in a strong westerly wind. Cloudless sky seems to smother the land, a tight cerulean cap encircling bone-dry earth. High on the range, Toowoomba, known as *the garden city*, also waits patiently for rain. Soon, the city will hold its annual Festival of Flowers, drawing visitors from hundreds of kilometres around.

From the passenger seat, Delia surveys the drought-stricken fields, relieved that she lives in a suburb where sprinklers can still be used three times a week. 'They sure need some rain out here.'

'The trouble is the region needs more than the odd shower, and I believe that's all they've forecast for the rest of this month.'

'Yes, it's tough on the farmers. I knew there was drought out west but I had no idea it had spread this far east.'

THE YEAR OF LIVING RAINBOW

'Brisbane needs rain too. Our garden is very dry.'

'I must confess I hadn't noticed.'

Liz sighs. 'You mean to say I spend hours gardening and you don't even notice the results?'

'The garden is beautiful, a credit to you. But I tend to look above the earth, to focus on green leaves and brilliant blooms.'

'Then it's time you felt the earth between your fingers.'

Delia reaches out to touch the hands gripping the steering wheel. 'I would like that, but are you sure I wouldn't be intruding? The garden has always been your domain.'

'I would love to share it with you.'

'Even though Ron said I had brown fingers and wouldn't let me touch the garden. I only stepped outside to hang up washing.'

Liz gives a wistful smile. 'That sounds like Kay, although I don't recall her ever doing the washing.'

Delia is surprised to learn that a lesbian partnership comprised clearly defined roles. She'd expected flexibility, not a repeat of heterosexual marriage.

'We were an old-fashioned pair,' Liz continues. 'I was the femme; Kay wore the pants. These days, I believe the roles are interchangeable or even non-existent.'

'Did you ever wish for a role change?'

'Now and then, but the feeling didn't persist. Besides, I was reluctant to alter the status quo.'

'Fair enough.'

Turning her head, Delia's eyes reconnect with the passing landscape but her mind focuses on their nascent relationship. She wants an equal partnership not a repeat of her marriage, where outsiders believed she was the dominant partner but behind closed doors, Ron made all the major decisions. Sometimes, this split personality seemed pointless, yet she persevered for twenty-odd years, anxious to project an acceptable image to colleagues and friends. A committed feminist, how could she have confessed to condoning a traditional marriage?

As for Ron, Delia knew he enjoyed playing the henpecked husband in public; it ensured an abundance of sympathy, especially from his female staff. She remembers the day a lab technician answered his campus phone, the comments to a colleague overheard as the young woman went to fetch Ron. *It's Delia Dragon again. Poor man, no wonder he's always the last to leave at the end of the day.* Silly girl forgot to press the mute button!

Beside her, Liz is pondering infidelity, Delia having made no secret over the years of on or off-campus lovers. Did Ron play the same game, and if so, why did their marriage endure? From what Liz understands, divorce has been a simple exercise since a no-fault clause was added to the Marriage Act in the mid-seventies.

Present tense returns to remind her that the past is over and done with, no longer can she rest secure behind the thick walls of a long-term relationship. Walls built to last, impervious to cyclone, hail or heat. They, she, overlooked earthquakes – no fault-line at 6 Tamarin Street. Even so, tremors came without warning, cracking the concrete foundations, crumbling the plasterboard walls. Eight months on she's still knee-deep in rubble, yet she has already engaged in rebuilding, albeit without definitive drawings. She must clear the ground if a new dwelling is to rise from the earth.

A host of tomorrows beckon, tasks to be shared, financial arrangements made, compromises to be negotiated. Annoying traits, such as Delia's propensity for dramatising every issue from whether she can pay a bill to burnt toast, can be tolerated, but on one subject Liz refuses to compromise. Fidelity is paramount; there can be no half-measures, no tearful apology and promises not to stray in future.

When they reach the top of the range, low cloud is blanketing the city and rain is falling, obscuring views of the plain below. Prayers have been answered, dust washed from spring flowers before the festival. 'I hope it's raining down there as well,' Delia remarks.

Reverting to poetic mode, Liz replies, 'High above an ocean of undulating grass, the goddess tossed her flaxen hair, sending a million raindrops cascading to parched earth.'

'Write that down soon. You'll lose the words before next Friday,' Delia urges.

Seated in an armchair close to an open fire, Peter Eames adjusts his dog-collar with pale hands that exhibit no signs of manual labour. Beneath the collar, a triangle of white shirt protrudes from a V-neck sweater in sombre grey. Black trousers and highly polished black shoes complete the image of reputable cleric. The pastor's house is red-brick with small sash windows and polished floors – one of those old houses that's freezing in winter, baking hot in summer.

Opposite him, Delia and Liz sit side by side on a sagging sofa, waiting for Joanna to bring coffee from the adjoining kitchen. Less than five minutes after she welcomed them at the door, they feel tongue-tied, the pastor's greeting troubling in its candour. After rising from his chair and extending his hands to enfold each of theirs in turn, he announced that he felt familiar with them both, Joanna having spoken at length about their long-standing friendship and the way they were helping one another to overcome the loss of their respective partners. After inviting them to take a seat, he went on to say that they often entered his thoughts late at night as he prepared for sleep; an innocuous statement, if he hadn't then apologised for thinking of them as "the bereaved" instead of separate entities. This, he explained, enables him to transcend the physical and concern himself fully with the condition of their souls as he prays for their redemption.

After an uncomfortable silence, the pastor stretches his legs, nudging a corner of the grate with his shoes. Grey ash peppers black leather. 'Joanna,' he calls to the open doorway. 'Bring a duster, please. I've got ash on my shoes.'

The visitors exchange glances while his head is turned.

Almost immediately, Joanna materialises at his side, kneeling to carefully remove the offending ash. 'All bright and shiny again,' she assures him in a little girl voice.

'Just like your soul, my dearest,' he answers before nuzzling her left ear.

Joanna blushes. 'I try to be good for the Lord.'

'You are, my little angel.' The tip of his tongue emerges to moisten dry lips. Then, he bends to kiss her upturned face, beginning with her smooth forehead and ending with an extended caress of her silky mouth.

Appalled by possessive language and inappropriate gestures, Delia struggles to remain seated. Angel, my arse, she thinks, the man's using his position to seduce, convince his latest 'faithful servant' that her newly-discovered Lord sanctifies the union of their bodies. How many other young female converts have ended up in the pastor's bed?

―――

The road's steep descent with its numerous hairpin bends requires careful negotiation, so despite a churning stomach and a host of furious thoughts, Delia remains silent until they have reached the plain below. Liz's response to maternal anxiety is out of character, minimal empathy followed by a reminder that at eighteen, Joanna is an adult capable of making her own decisions about sexual partners.

'But what if she gets pregnant?' Delia asks, determined to pursue the matter of her daughter's stupidity. 'It would wreck her career plans. I can't imagine a bloody fundamentalist pastor agreeing to an abortion.'

'Knowing you, I imagine Joanna has been informed about contraception. Besides, hasn't it occurred to you that love may form the basis of their relationship?'

'Love? How could she love such an unattractive specimen?'

Liz drums her fingers on the steering wheel.

'And don't insult my intelligence by saying that love is in the eye of the beholder.'

'I have no intention of spouting platitudes.' Liz shifts her right hand to the indicator stem, checking the rearvision mirror before slowing to pull onto the hard shoulder. 'If we're going to argue, there's no point in risking an accident.' After silencing the engine, she sits back in the seat, arms folded across her chest.

'I don't want to argue with you, Liz,' Delia begins, unbuckling her seatbelt to facilitate proximity. 'And I apologise for raving on about Joanna. You're right, she must make her own decisions. My approval is irrelevant.'

Liz turns to offer a smile. 'But your concern is understandable and you're not the only one with misgivings about Peter Eames. I felt extremely uncomfortable. There was something about him that set off warning bells. Those cold blue eyes, that holier-than-thou manner.' She shudders. 'I pray I won't have to meet him again.'

Shocked by blatant fear, Delia reaches out to squeeze trembling hands. 'He can't harm you, Liz. He may be a pastor but that doesn't give him the right to influence either your spiritual or your secular life. Were you worried he guessed about us?'

Liz shakes her head. 'No, he hardly noticed me. I'm probably overreacting but I couldn't help thinking of Colin Masters.'

Delia reaches out to stroke her cheek. 'I realise this court case is hanging over you, but please try to push it aside until November, otherwise whatever the outcome, Colin Masters will have succeeded in destroying months of your life.'

Pushing her hand away, Liz splutters, 'How can I push it aside? The implications are horrendous. If the court overturns Kay's will, I stand to lose the house! Everything Kay and I worked for!'

TWENTY-EIGHT

The old weatherboard church gleams as afternoon sunlight illuminates the stained-glass windows installed decades before, courtesy of pious parishioners. On the neatly mown front lawn, relatives and friends of the bride and groom greet one another before making their way into the cool interior, their sun-dazzled eyes blinking as they adjust to diminished light. Rows of dark wooden pews fill the small space, each one decorated at the aisle end with a bouquet of tropical flowers.

In her new ensemble of A-line dress and short-sleeved jacket – Delia refuses to think of it as a mother-of-the-bride outfit – high-heeled shoes prove problematic as she negotiates uneven floorboards on her way to the front pew. Safely installed beside Liz, sensibly shod in low-heeled shoes, she runs a hand over worn timber, speculating on how many generations have worshipped in this weathered timber structure once surrounded by farmland carved from virgin soil. How alien tropical savannah must have seemed to those accustomed to the green fields of England or Ireland. Later immigrants who came to work the work were mostly from southern Italy, so at least would have found the climate familiar. The same can't be said for those South Sea islanders known as Kanakas, forcibly removed from their homes to toil in the cane fields and cotton plantations of north Queensland. Virtual slaves, she's read that they suffered appalling working conditions, with most deported in the early 1900s in line with the newly adopted White Australia policy.

Abandoning dark history, Delia turns her head and is surprised to see almost every pew fully occupied. 'I thought this was supposed to be a small wedding,' she whispers to Liz.

Liz smiles. 'I guess Marti has a big family.'

On Delia's other side, her mother-in-law fidgets with her handbag. 'I wish Carol would hurry up; I'm getting nervous. Poor George must be so hot in that suit. I do hope he doesn't feel queer in the head.' She leans towards Delia. 'His blood pressure's unpredictable, you know.'

Delia pats a gloved hand. 'He'll be alright, Nancy.'

The organist begins to play, prompting the congregation to rise as one, all heads turning to the bride and her grandfather advancing slowly down the flower-decked aisle.

'She looks exquisite.' Delia dabs her eyes with a handkerchief, saddened that illness has prevented her mother and sister from attending the wedding. Liz squeezes her free hand.

'Ron would have been so proud,' Nancy Peirce murmurs, making no attempt to hold back tears.

Delia smiles although she can't imagine Ron approving of Carol's decision to marry at twenty-one and waste her marine biology degree by working on a dive boat. Memory stabs, reminding Delia that Carol wouldn't have had to abandon post-graduate studies if her father hadn't gambled away the family's savings. Wisely, she refocuses on the handsome, soon-to-be son-in-law, as he turns to greet his beautiful bride.

Following the ceremony, tension slides from Delia's skin along with parental responsibility; Carol rests secure in Marti Tonelli's arms. Momentarily, she wishes that Joanna would marry Peter Eames, then rebukes herself for abandoning feminist principles. Her daughters aren't chattels to be handed from father to husband, or in their case, grandfather to husband.

Twenty-one years of motherhood have sapped her strength; she needs some respite before wholly committing to a relationship that only months earlier wouldn't have seemed possible, or even desirable. In the past, the exhilaration of an affair would ensure temporary rejuvenation, an excess of adrenalin-stimulating research activity at double her usual speed. She would emerge from these liaisons exhausted but fulfilled, a scan of her research papers soon dispelling any regrets.

Musing on her new love affair, she acknowledges there is no longer a place in her life for brief passionate encounters with virtual strangers. Her friendship with Liz spans more than a decade, any surface gloss discarded years earlier. Together they have experienced a range of emotions from delight in shared interests to the depths of despair engendered by Ron and Kay's untimely deaths. She turns to watch Liz, commandeered by Mrs Tonelli, whose loud voice and expansive gesticulation belies her short stature. Liz listens attentively, her demeanour calm, with no visible sign of the shyness she often experiences amongst strangers.

Impressed, Delia hopes she can absorb some of Liz's serenity and learn to be less volatile.

As Delia watches her lover's auburn hair dip towards a creamy neck, Joanna rushes over. 'Mum, the photographer wants a few more shots of the family before we go to the reception.'

'Good, that'll get Liz away from Mrs Tonelli.'

'Family, Mum, not friends.'

'Liz is almost family, darling.'

'I suppose so. I did call her Auntie Liz when I was young.'

Delia opens her handbag to retrieve compact and lipstick. 'I'll fetch Liz in a minute.'

'Mum, he wants us now. Grabbing her mother's free hand, Joanna drags her towards the church porch where Carol and Marti are sheltering from midday sun.

'Hurry up, you two,' Carol calls. 'I'm getting hot in all this gear.'

Marti murmurs something about stripping her when they get out to sea. Descending the porch steps, he offers his hand, a mischievous smile playing around his generous mouth.

'Oh dear, you are a bit pink,' Delia remarks as she and Joanna take their places either side of the bride and groom.

'Nothing to do with the sun, Mum.'

'It should be a bit cooler on the boat,' Marti says to his new mother-in-law.

'I don't know about that,' Delia answers. 'Honeymoons aren't usually tepid affairs.'

The camera clicks as Carol blushes for the second time. 'Oh no, please take that again. I must have looked terrible!'

'Beautiful,' the photographer contradicts. 'I need a few natural images. Let's have mother and daughters now.'

Marti steps to one side, leaving Delia to stand between her daughters, her arms around their slender waists.

'Thank you, ladies. That's it for now. See you at the reception.'

Following the speeches, Joanna rises to her feet and hurries over to her grandparents, seated at a nearby table. 'Wonderful wedding, isn't it? Carol looks beautiful.'

Nancy Pierce beams at her favourite granddaughter. 'So do you, dear.' She pats the empty seat beside her, Liz having adjourned to the ladies. 'I haven't seen you for ages. Tell me all about life in Toowoomba.'

Delia pricks up her ears as Joanna slides into the chair, saying, 'Can you keep a secret, Gran?'

Nancy turns her back on husband, George, to answer in a quiet voice, 'Of course. What is it, a new boyfriend?'

Joanna blushes. 'Not really a boyfriend.'

'Just a friend, then?'

Joanna shakes her head. 'Remember I wrote to tell you all about the church and Pastor Eames?

'Yes, dear.'

'Well, we've been, er, together for ages.'

Nancy frowns. 'I thought the pastor was just a friend. You've only known him for a few months.'

'Five months and two days. Anyway, he loves me and wants us to be together forever.'

Nancy looks aghast. 'But this is your first year of university and you're very young. Has he spoken to your mother?'

Joanna shakes her head. 'Peter says it's a private matter between us and God. But I wanted you to know, Gran.'

'Thank you, dear, but I really do think your mother

should be consulted if there's to be a wedding. I know Carol and Marti arranged all this but that was because...' She picks at the hem of her sleeve. 'Because things were a little difficult at the time. What with Delia having to sell the house and then move in with her friend, Liz while she looked for a unit.'

Joanna pouts. 'I don't want Mum to know. Not yet anyway.'

'Know what?' Carol asks, materialising behind her sister's chair.

'Where did you come from?'

'The bridal table, of course. So, what don't you want me to know?'

'I was referring to Mum, not you.'

'Matters of the heart, dear,' Nancy explains. 'Leave it at that, Carol, there's no need to pry.'

Carol gives a winsome smile. 'It must be the season for love. The whole family's smitten.'

Sister and grandmother look puzzled.

'I noticed something different about Mum today. She has that special glow of someone in love. So, I asked her if she had a lover.'

'Really, Carol!' her grandmother admonishes. 'That was rather impertinent!'

'I'm a married woman now,' Carol replies, as though new status entitles her to formerly confidential information. 'Mum said yes, she has a lover and it's a very special relationship, unlike anything she's ever experienced before.'

'Well, I never! 'Nancy reaches for her barely touched glass of champagne and drains it rapidly. 'I didn't expect her to find someone new so soon after your dear father's death.'

'I believe it's quite common for the widowed to remarry

quickly,' Carol remarks, casually. 'However, it's usually men that seek out a new partner.'

Joanna turns to glare at her insensitive sister. 'Married for five minutes and you're an expert on relationships. Not everyone wants the white wedding and bridesmaid business, you know!'

'Girls, please, no arguments today!'

'Don't worry, sis, your secret's safe with me, but I hope to God you know what you're doing.' Carol sweeps away in a flurry of white lace to mingle with her guests.

A secret safe with a young woman more interested in the heady rush of church and state-sanctioned lovemaking than her younger sister's ludicrous obsession with a pastor who most likely wants to dominate body and soul rather than enter into an equal partnership.

Half-listening to Mrs Tonelli heartily extolling Marti's virtues, Delia has more on her mind than either daughter's love life. She's attempting to reconcile her desire to rush headlong into Liz's arms at every opportunity and her acknowledged need to slow the development of a partnership that could last *for as long as we both on earth shall live*. So far, she hasn't raised the subject of relocation to her unit following settlement, too afraid that Liz will misconstrue the move as evidence of cooling passion, or a wish to engage in an open relationship. Fidelity is important to Liz; she didn't even look at another woman during her years with Kay, and although she always appeared non-judgmental when listening to tales of infidelity, Delia sensed that deep down, her friend did not approve.

TWENTY-NINE

Liz has hired a car for the journey south to Airlie Beach where she has booked an apartment for a week. Their original idea of staying on Magnetic Island, a short boat ride from Townsville was rejected in favour of the Whitsundays with its opportunity for exploring some of the numerous islands located in the centre of the Great Barrier Reef. Eager to reach their destination, they decided to drive the almost three-hundred-kilometre trip in one day, sharing the driving and stopping only for short food and drink breaks.

'We can have a honeymoon too,' Delia says dreamily, as they drive alongside cane fields on their way to the rural town of Ayr.

'I don't think so. A honeymoon is a holiday spent by a newly-married couple.'

'That's where you're wrong, Ms Librarian. According to the Macquarie dictionary, a honeymoon can also be any period of happy or harmonious relationship.'

'Well, if that's the case.' Liz turns her head to flash a smile. 'And I imagine you looked up the definition recently,

I ask why we are spending time and money on a holiday when we can experience happy and harmonious at home?'

'Simple, we both needed a break and wanted to take advantage of being in the north.'

'Agreed.' Recalling her lover's advice during the road trip from Toowoomba to Brisbane, Liz suppresses the dark thought worming its way to the surface. November's court case might be only weeks away but there's no need to spoil the sunlit present.

Hours later, weary from a lengthy journey, they take a bottle of champagne to bed – a double ensemble with garish bedspread and clashing striped sheets. 'To assorted alliances,' Delia cries, recalling recent journey dialogue. She raises her glass but Liz holds hers close to her naked breasts; her thoughts having revisited an earlier conversation. 'To the union of bodies, minds and spirits. May the goddess bless them all!'

Mismatched glasses clink.

———

Next morning, they board a yacht for an eight-hour taste of sailing. A former America's Cup challenger, *Gretel* has been refitted for the tourist trade to spend her days plying the waters of the Whitsundays. As they motor away from Shute Harbour, the captain – weathered as an ancient mariner, unlike his youthful crew – invites passengers to assist his crew in raising and lowering the massive sails. 'This will augment your sailing experience, but don't worry, clear instructions will be given at all times. Hands up those who want to volunteer.'

Four women, including Delia, raise their hands. Male passengers study their feet.

'Thanks, ladies.' The captain beams, his eyes alighting on the tanned legs of three young women stretched out on the forward deck.

The yacht slices through turquoise water, sending spray-showers over those sitting in the bow with their backs hard against the guard rail. No one minds, the September day is warm and lightweight clothes dry fast in the breeze. But when the captain cuts the engine, all eyes turn to the stern, uncertain whether there's a problem. 'Crew, prepare to hoist the sails,' he calls, adding details for the benefit of novice sailors. Rising quickly, the four women assemble adjacent to the main-sail boom, their feet planted firmly on the deck. At the captain's command, they begin to unfurl the heavy main sail as the crew wind the grinders. Grasping white canvas, they guide the sail up the mast.

Sitting mid-ship, Liz is bemused by Delia's atypical behaviour. Usually, she must be coerced into physical exercise, although she has tried to firm her physique in recent months and looks good in new white shorts. Another recent purchase – a lightweight cotton shirt – hugs her upper body, accentuating ample breasts. Arms rise above her head, exposing a strip of tanned midriff, the result of sunbathing in a sheltered corner of the rear deck. 'I can't attend the wedding with a pasty winter complexion,' she'd explained when Liz queried the sense in striping down to underwear outdoors before the advent of spring.

Wind fills the main sail, sending the four women scurrying portside as the boom swings out over the water. Crew attend to the remaining, smaller sails. Sliding into her previous position beside Liz, Delia tilts her face to cloudless sky, her expression one of sheer delight.

———

In the early evening, Delia and Liz saunter along the beach adjacent to their accommodation, relishing the smell of salt that clings to clothes, hair and skin. On returning from their sailing trip, they felt reluctant to disturb sea-memories by taking a shower, so dumped their bags in the living room and set off for the shore.

'I felt so much at peace out there,' Liz remarks as they stand watching shadowed water dribble over sand. 'I could have stayed on that boat forever, sailing with you into the sunset across uncharted waters.'

'Hardly uncharted, Captain Cook was here over two hundred years ago. Don't you remember the captain telling us which islands Cook named?'

'I was speaking metaphorically, thinking of our onward journey together. That's uncharted waters.'

'True, but as we both know from experience, the future is out of our hands. So, why don't we enjoy the journey whatever its duration?'

Liz shivers at the memory of police on a doorstep, caps in hands, unspoken tragedy evident in their sombre expressions as the older officer asked for Mrs Delia Pierce. Why bring up past sorrow when they ought to be celebrating the end of a glorious day? Death doesn't belong in this tranquil place, even though Liz is forced to acknowledge the incoming tide will soon erase present-day footsteps.

'In fair weather or foul,' Delia continues, oblivious to Liz's discomfort, 'I trust we never lose the thread of loving friendship.' She hesitates, then adds, 'Apologies for the mixed metaphor, I should have said, rope.'

'The crew called them sheets,' Liz snaps, eager to revert to language unencumbered by emotion.

'What's wrong, Liz? I thought you enjoyed the trip.'

'I did. I'm just concerned about the immediate future.'

'You mean the court case?'

Liz shakes her head. 'I'm thinking about your ability to deal with the conservative society we inhabit. What will you say to those that say our relationship is immoral, that I enticed you into an unnatural partnership?'

'I have never cared what the world thought of me, so I'll walk away from homophobic gossip with my head held high!'

Liz manages a smile. 'I admire your tenacity. I've always been afraid to face a hostile world, chosen instead to lead a quiet life. Few outside my small circle of friends realise that I'm gay.'

'Why would they? You've never made a big deal of your sexual preferences and you don't dress like a dyke.'

'I don't like that term, Delia.'

'Sorry. Lesbian then.'

'Or that one either. They're both labels and I don't want to be categorised. I'm just a woman who happens to prefer sex with women.'

'Woman in the singular, I hope,' Delia teases, trying to lighten the mood.

'You know perfectly well what I mean.' Liz folds her arms across her chest and stomps towards the water's edge.

Delia opens her mouth to give a glib retort, changes her mind and hurries to join her affronted lover. Wrapping one arm around a tense shoulder, she eases the other under Liz's baggy shirt to cup a familiar breast.

'Not here, Delia, someone might see us.'

'Relax, there's no one around. They're all eating dinner.' She strokes warm skin, inching towards a firming nipple.

'Why don't we go back to the unit? I can be uninhibited there.'

There's no response from Delia, she's too engrossed in what remains a novel and delightful deed.

'Please stop, we're too exposed out here.'

Delia removes her hand and turning Liz around, points to a tree with overhanging branches further up the beach. Basic benches in the form of single planks raised on stumps, encircle the broad trunk. 'How about over there?

Against her better judgment, Liz allows herself to be led over to a sea-facing seat, where she sits primly, legs together, hands clasped in her lap.

Kneeling in front of Liz to shield her from view, Delia gently shifts joined hands to access buttons, then slowly peels shirt and bra from thin shoulders.

'I feel foolish,' Liz remarks, staring down at her white breasts.

'Concentrate on sensations,' Delia murmurs, leaning forward to kiss each nipple in turn. 'Close your eyes and listen to the rhythm of water lapping the shore, breathe deeply, taste salt on your lips, feel the warmth of the setting sun on your skin.'

Evening air caresses and ocean-song comforts, transporting Liz to a place far from human-made regulations. Leaning back against a weathered trunk, she's barely conscious of her remaining clothes slipping from her body. Powerless to reciprocate, she listens to exhaled breath leaving her parted lips, tastes the perfume of deep desire.

Later, she hears Delia's voice as though at a distance, the words indistinct except for her own name. Opening her eyes, she blinks rapidly as though sunlight has struck her upturned face. Delia is leaning over her, clothes in her hands.

'Sorry to wake you, my love, but we need to go before the mossies arrive.'

'I wasn't asleep. Dreaming perhaps.'
'Of sailing ships?'
'And sealing wax and cabbages and kings.'

Delia holds out the clothes. 'Come on, Alice, it's time for tea.'

A smile coats moist lips but soon recedes, leaving Liz trembling. Grabbing her clothes, she turns towards the tree, dressing hurriedly as though ashamed of her naked body.

'What's up, Liz?'

'I feel guilty now.'

'Why, only sea birds witnessed our intimacy, and I'm sure they weren't offended.'

'It's not that. I've been completely selfish; I didn't consider your needs at all. I'm so sorry.'

'Don't be sorry.' Delia bends to hug. 'I wanted it that way. It was your time, yours alone to treasure. I needed to show how much you mean to me.'

'Then I am truly blessed.'

———

A second sea voyage offers a different perspective, a powerful catamaran carrying them at high speed to the outer reef where a spacious pontoon has been anchored to the ocean floor, providing a firm base for passengers to don the facemasks, snorkels and flippers stored in plastic bins roped to each corner. On one side of the pontoon, a covered stairway leads to an underwater observatory where the faint-hearted can view brightly-coloured fish and corals without getting wet.

Standing on the pontoon dressed for snorkelling, Liz shivers as the breeze freshens. 'Hurry up, Delia,' she calls, 'I'm getting cold.'

'No fat on you, that's the trouble.' Delia takes a step forward to slap Liz's slender thigh.

'I thought you were trying to get rid of yours.'

'Not all of it, darling.' Brown eyes brim with mischief. 'Besides, you enjoy burrowing into soft flesh.'

Liz blushes, and resisting a smart retort, quickly puts on her facemask before waddling to the edge, her flippers slapping the deck like freshly caught fish.

Beneath the surface, she enters a strange and silent world. Tiny fish flit through coral fingers, giant clams open and close, their fleshy mouths fluttering on the ocean floor. A flash of silver catches her eye, she watches a school of Long Toms dive into nearby depths. Trailing the fish, two turtles swim languidly, their flippers barely agitating the water. Entranced, Liz inhales and dives deep. Angelfish, brilliant in black and gold stripes, pass within centimetres of her facemask, parrot fish in shades of blue and green play amongst the coral. In the distance, she notices the shadowy form of a giant grouper, slows to observe it slide silently through turquoise ocean. None of the marine creatures exhibit any fear of the human intruder, and enclosed in their watery world, Liz feels utterly secure.

A streak of turquoise flashes past as she surfaces, followed by pink flippers. The gleam of familiar thighs confirms it's Delia, swimming just below the surface. After ascending slowly, Liz expels water from her mouthpiece and gulping fresh air, turns on her back to float, relishing the sounds of her surface sphere. Before long, the underwater world beckons again, but now Liz wants to share the experience, so flips over to search for Delia, forgetting her partner is afraid of deep water.

Snorkelling a few metres from the pontoon, Delia almost sinks when Liz touches her arm. 'What the hell,' she splutters, fearing the arrival of a deadly shark. Removing her facemask, she squints at Liz treading water beside her. 'Are you okay?'

Liz nods before shifting her mouthpiece to one side. 'It's incredible down there, I felt caressed by smooth, silky water, accepted by the environment and its inhabitants.'

'You've got water on the brain!' Delia wraps the facemask strap around her wrist. 'I'm getting cold. See you back on the boat.'

Liz squeezes her shoulder. 'Please come down with me, I want to share the experience with you. Just a little way, I promise.'

'Well, I suppose.'

'It's easy, take a deep breath and dive. I'll hold your hand if it will help.'

Despite long-held fears, Delia reaches for her facemask.

———

Chilled to the bone, they sit on a damp seat in the stern, sipping hot coffee from polystyrene cups. They stay too long in the water, diving repeatedly to exquisite coral gardens. Delia nurses an earache and Liz's extremities feel numb, yet neither regrets lengthy exploration and they have already decided to take another trip if time permits.

'At last, I can understand Carol's obsession with diving,' Delia muses, staring over the rim of her cup at the now shadowed sea.

'You're not thinking of taking up scuba diving?'

'No way! But I'm no longer an outsider living on the periphery of her world.'

Liz frowns. 'How can a mother feel that way?'

'Easy, Carol lived and breathed for Ron. From the time

she could walk, they shared a love of the natural world. He taught her to respect Planet Earth long before conservation became fashionable.'

'Then you must be pleased she's found Marti. Watching them sail into the sunset after the reception, I thought how fitting it seemed.' Looking over Delia's head, she adds wistfully, 'They belong out here with only the ocean and sea birds for company. Here they can find true freedom.'

'Freedom from people like me, you mean, concerned by the difference in their ages?'

'Surely you're not still bothered about that?'

'A little. Don't misunderstand me, I like Marti very much, but I worry that Carol has simply replaced her father. Marti needs a wife, not a daughter.'

Liz thinks of the clearly defined roles she and Kay adopted, almost from the start. 'Does it matter what parts people play in relationships?'

'Only if one person wants to alter the script and the other one disagrees.' Delia winces at the memory of bitter arguments.

'Is your ear hurting?'

'A bit.'

Liz retrieves an old cotton scarf from the depths of her beach bag and hands it over. 'Here, wrap this around your head.'

'Are you psychic? When we packed you couldn't have known I'd get earache.'

'Of course not, I must have forgotten it was there,' Liz says, unwilling to reveal the real reason the scarf remains in her bag. A gift from Kay for visits to Alexandra Bay, it shielded pale shoulders from the sun if strong wind prevented the use of a beach umbrella.

THIRTY

In the kitchen, Liz leans against the breakfast bar, staring out at the garden beyond the deck. Neither trees nor flowering shrubs register in eye nor mind, Delia's phone call having confirmed her growing apprehension. Ever since they returned from the Whitsundays, Delia has deemed it necessary to inform her family in Perth, close friends, colleagues, and even mere acquaintances that she and Liz are no longer just good friends. As far as daughters are concerned, Liz understands that Carol, on reading the news – Delia considered a letter more appropriate – wished her mother every happiness but Joanna's reaction remains unknown. Then, last week, Delia decided to join a lesbian group and wanted Liz to accompany her this evening.

It isn't that Liz disapproves; on the contrary, she acknowledges that such groups can be an important avenue of support, especially for younger women struggling with their sexuality. From what she's heard, they also offer advice on dealing with the homophobia that pervades conservative Brisbane. But Liz has always recoiled from such gatherings, her stomach heaving at the thought of entering a roomful of strangers who wish to discuss what to her is an intensely private part of life. What have members of the group in common, except their preference for same-sex relationships? There may as well be support groups for the left-handed, she thinks, recalling problems in primary school.

Determined to forget the matter, she moves out of sight of the phone to begin washing up. Dishes and cutlery absorb her attention for a short time – Delia's portion sits in the microwave – and she hums a favourite tune as her hands agitate soapy water. After drying and putting away, she decides to work on her latest poem, so carries a cup of coffee into the study.

The small room seems oppressive as though it's been sealed up for months rather than a couple of weeks. She opens the window wide, but silence hangs heavy, caught in still evening air. Listening for the familiar night sounds of possum and bat, she's disappointed to discover her front garden devoid of activity, so bends her head to the keyboard to retrieve last Friday's creation. The hard disk hums, fingertips tap the keys; small sounds that comfort, reminders of living, breathing occupation. Yet, as she attempts to edit the poem, she finds herself concentrating on externals rather than the cadence of her verse. Sighing, she pushes the keyboard aside to retrieve her coffee mug, sipping and swallowing to clear her mind.

A tiny flicker trembles on the fringe of thought, but as words birth, she realises they bear no relationship to her poem. Hard as granite, they threaten to crush delicate expression, render the screen blank. Touching her forehead with the tips of her fingers, she wills them to withdraw, leave her free to explore perceptive possibilities. Taunting her with growth, they reverberate within her skull like the pain of migraine.

Closing her eyes, she further shields her eyes with her hands but darkness is deceptive, providing a backdrop for unwelcome images rather than oblivion. Helpless, she watches Delia address a group of strangers, sees their expressions alter from polite interest to compassion as the unusual tale unfolds. *Elizabeth* is mentioned three times in one sentence, and she wants to rush into that room, shut Delia's mouth before intimate details emerge of their life together. 'You are mine,' Liz cries to the open window, 'I refuse to share you!'

Breeze sighs, stirring the thin curtains as goosebumps pepper her bare limbs.

———

Dancing energy, Delia recounts the evening's activities, while her microwaved supper cools on the table. 'Wonderful women,' she exclaims, 'you have no idea how some of them have suffered. But far from destroying them, anguish has empowered them to reach out for what had once seemed impossible.'

Liz recalls Leah's revelation of past violation. 'Do you mean a fulfilling personal relationship?'

'That of course, but I'm thinking of more than love or intimacy. A rewarding career, motherhood, the joy of finding a place to call home. Or even,' she pauses to smile at Liz, 'a spiritual relationship that offers comfort and hope.'

Liz struggles to return the smile.

'I'm not saying that suffering is a pre-requisite for successful personal relationships or a satisfying career,' Delia continues, 'and I pray I never experience rape or domestic violence. But sometimes a tragic situation, and I'm thinking of us now, can morph into something positive.'

'Is that all you told them? Liz asks curtly.

Delia chooses to ignore hostility. 'I said that out of grief and despair grew hope and love. I spoke of our friendship, the long years of comfortable conversations...' She pauses to glance at her supine lover, notes with relief that Liz appears more relaxed, hands unclasped, limbs stretched out. 'I spoke of a damp summer morning when our worlds crumbled and we held one another as tears flowed freely. And a cold winter's night when fate intervened and we discovered more than friendship in each other's arms.'

Tension returns, forcing fingers to curl into fists, a thin torso jerks upright. 'You told those wonderful women how we got pissed and fell into bed. Couldn't keep our hands off each other, could we? Obviously, celibacy didn't suit us. Masturbating doesn't really cut it!'

'What's the matter with you? I didn't say that at all!'

'Like hell you didn't. I know you, Delia. You love an audience, especially a captive one. I bet they lapped up your story, it's so much more interesting when a woman's swapped sides. Did you adopt an academic tone or did you play the helpless female? That one used to work well with guys, although I'm not sure a group of lesbians would fall for it.'

Leaping from the chair, Delia rushes to the sofa and grasping Liz's shoulder with one hand, slaps her face with the other. 'Get a grip, Elizabeth, you're acting like a jealous adolescent.'

Liz's cheek stings, but it's the use of her full name and a tone associated with mother's displeasure that prompts her to dig nails into the hand still clasping her shoulder. 'You bitch!' she yells. 'How could you betray me?'

Delia doesn't flinch. Instead, she kisses Liz's forehead, which proves the catalyst to complete reversal. Sobbing, Liz crumples in a heap. In between sobs, bursts of self-reproach bruise the air above their heads but Delia remains silent, gently massaging the tense neck and shoulders with strong, steady hands.

Gradually, hot tears diminish, an occasional whimper the only sign of continuing distress. Liz yearns to apologise for her deplorable behaviour but each time she tries to speak, Delia says now is not the time for talk. When shoulders relax and a yawn escapes, Delia relinquishes her tender hold. 'Come, I'll help you to bed,' she says, holding out her hands.

Childlike, Liz acquiesces with a nod of the head, swinging her legs around to aid the transfer from lounge to bedroom.

Birdsong and the rustle of wind in tall trees rouse her. Promise of a beautiful spring day, Liz thinks, noticing the strip of morning light streaming through the gap between curtain and window frame. Stretching her still sleepy body, one hand touches the neighbouring pillow and she realises with a start that the pillowcase is cold. How long has she been alone in bed? She blushes at the memory of her childish and unwarranted outburst. Did Delia leave before dawn, or did she pack her clothes – still hanging in the spare room wardrobe – last night? Surveying the room for signs of a hasty departure, she sees underwear, a shirt and a pair of red jeans lying crumpled on the floor, Delia's usual preparation for bed.

'Morning. Cup of tea?' Delia calls from the kitchen as running feet pound polished floorboards.

'Can you ever forgive me?' Liz pleads, rushing to fling her arms around her lover's neck.

'There's nothing to forgive. You overreacted a bit, that's all.'

'More than a bit, I fear.'

Delia raises her eyebrows. 'Let's just say you weren't your usual refined self.'

'It sounds pathetic, but I really don't know what came over me. Probably I spent too long envisaging you revealing intimate details to complete strangers.'

'Silly goose, I wouldn't do that.'

'But I'm sure you mentioned a cold winter's night when...'

'Listen and don't interrupt.' Delia detaches the hands still clinging to her neck. 'Yes, I did talk about you and me but not in the way you assumed last night. I told a story about four friends that were suddenly two, a story about grief and guilt and anger. The painful process of rebuilding, the priceless value of friendship, the joy of new love. I used allegory, non-specific words and phrases. Language is a powerful tool, Liz, you of all people should know that, and I employed it expediently, I trust. I may have spoken from the heart but I allowed my head some input.'

'Wise woman,' Liz murmurs.

'No, not wise, just sensitive to your needs, although I still don't understand why you're so anti-lesbian groups or anti-coming out for that matter.'

'I don't see that it's anyone else's business what I do between the sheets,' Liz says defensively, then confesses in a worried voice, 'I'm scared to death of what will happen when you come up against real prejudice!'

'Don't worry, I'll handle it, I'm a big girl. I've copped plenty of flak in my time and still come up smiling.'

'Can you cope with a full-scale war?'

Delia grins. 'If I've got you fighting alongside me.'

'Right up there with you, Sergeant!'

'General,' Delia corrects, and they both burst into peals of laughter.

THIRTY-ONE

Relocation day comes around before Delia has made a definitive decision regarding a temporary move to her Toowong unit even though she and Liz have discussed the matter. Reluctant to invoke further stress – the court case is due in less than a month – she favours leaving the unit unoccupied until Joanna returns from uni at the end of November, her daughter having expressed a wish to spend some of the long summer holidays in Brisbane. Nothing more has been mentioned about the relationship with Peter Eames, leaving Delia to hope that passionate emotions have cooled.

 A phone call from her solicitor advising that settlement proceeded without a hitch, prompts immediate action, Delia arranging for a removalist to transport her belongings from the storage facility to Toowong the following Saturday. Items such as her study furniture can be transferred to Tamarin Street when appropriate, that is, once a judicial decision is handed down. Privately, Delia believes the case will be thrown out on the first day, probate having been granted and inheritances distributed long before Colin

Masters decided to contest his sister's will on his mother's behalf.

Saturday dawns overcast but dry, much to Delia's relief. As the removalists are due to arrive at ten, she and Liz make certain to arrive at the unit by nine-thirty. Sitting cross-legged on the living room carpet, they discuss the placement of furniture and whether excess items could be stored in the garage until a charity can collect them. The second bedroom is too small to accommodate two single beds, a wardrobe and a desk – Delia has decided renting to university students is her best option – so one bed will have to be disposed of or swapped with the double she installed months earlier in Liz's spare bedroom. A phone call to Roger has solved the problem of a surplus lounge suite; he's happy to take the larger one, his soon-to-be ex-wife Gloria having removed their lounge room furniture to her rental unit when they separated.

A knock on the front door – left open to air the place – prevents further conversation, Delia jumping up to greet the removalists, but it's Roger standing on the doorstep looking as though he's just got out of bed. 'Hi, Roger. I didn't expect you so soon.' She ushers him inside. 'I can offer coffee and fresh croissants. We brought the jug and a few mugs with us and called into a bakery on the way.'

'Thanks. I haven't had any breakfast.'

Liz rises to greet him. 'Morning, Roger. You're early.'

He mutters something about waking at dawn these days, then shuffles across the room to slide down the wall into a sitting position. 'Good size living area, Delia. You shouldn't have any trouble renting it.'

'After Christmas,' Delia calls from the kitchen. 'Jo's coming home for a few weeks first.'

'Right.' Roger lowers his head to study the carpet.

Depressed about his business or the imminent divorce, Liz ponders, and loath to instigate small-talk, she retires to the kitchen.

Before long, the truck arrives and two young men bearing a striking resemblance to rugby union players – Neanderthals in Delia's opinion, with their thick necks and almost square muscular bodies – begin unloading furniture. In between loads, they talk sport with carton-carrying Roger, which seems to elevate his mood.

By noon the removalists have departed and all the furniture is in place, with Carol's single bed and two small side-tables stored in the generous garage. Labelled cartons remain stacked in the appropriate rooms, Delia eager for lunch before beginning to unpack.

'I'll fetch some ham and salad rolls from that bakery on the corner,' Liz offers. 'One or two, Roger?'

'One is fine.'

Delia licks her lips. 'Jam doughnuts for afternoon tea would be good.'

Liz nods and hurries out of the door before Delia can think of any other sugary treats.

'Are you staying here tonight?' Roger collapses into a grey armchair placed at right-angles to the sofa where Delia lies stretched out, her head resting on a plump cushion.

'I doubt it. We can come back tomorrow if we don't finish unpacking today.'

'You're not concerned about security?'

Delia frowns. 'Why would I be? This isn't a rough neighbourhood.'

'No, but you hear about unoccupied houses being broken into and stripped of their contents.'

'Roger, this is a unit, not an isolated house. I'm sure the neighbours would hear anything untoward.'

'All the same, it wouldn't hurt to let them know.' Roger closes his eyes and soon succumbs to sleep.

Listening to intermittent snores – Roger's mouth opens and closes like the giant clam witnessed on the reef – Delia mulls over the events that have altered the course of so many lives since the year began, each one the consequence of accident and addiction, secrets and exposure. A domino effect that could be unstoppable, she fears, affecting not only her family and close friends, but also those outside her immediate circle. She doesn't believe in the wrath of God, how could anyone when so many innocent lives are lost during wars or natural disasters? Nevertheless, destiny seems an inadequate explanation, almost a belittling of human suffering.

The sound of a car entering the driveway breaks the dark thread of thought. Grateful, she vacates the sofa and walks onto the balcony to see if it's Liz. A red car has parked close to the fence opposite her garage, but it isn't Liz's Mazda. Leaning on the balcony rail, Delia waits for the driver's door to open and reveal more than a side view of a brown-haired woman hunched over the steering wheel.

Voices in the living room alert her to Liz's return. She must have parked in the street rather than manoeuvre around the parked car into the garage.

'Lunch, Delia,' Roger calls from his armchair.

'Coming.' Returning inside, Delia hurries to relieve Liz of some packages. 'I'll make the coffee now.' She heads for a kitchen bench, depositing the bags before switching on the electric jug. 'Sorry about the parked car,' she remarks as Liz materialises beside her.

'No problem. I parked in front of Roger's ute.' Liz glances around the kitchen. 'In the absence of plates, we could just rip open the bags.'

'There's some packing paper in the main bedroom, from the carton that held the bedside lamps.'

'Substitute tablecloth,' Liz murmurs, turning on her heel. 'We don't want to damage the tabletop.'

'After twenty-odd years and two kids, it's too late to worry about that.'

They're sitting at the table hoeing into overfilled rolls when there's a knock on the front door. A timid knock this time, most likely a curious neighbour.

'I'm nearest.' Roger gets to his feet and disappears down the narrow hall.

Delia doesn't catch the name but hears him usher the visitor inside.

'I hope it isn't Gloria,' Liz whispers. 'She's bound to spoil his mood.'

'Does she know the address?'

'I mentioned the street at work last week, and you know what a stickybeak she is. She was probably driving around and recognised my car.'

Delia puts a finger to her lips as Roger appears carrying a small suitcase. What the hell, she almost asks, the question dying on her lips when she recognises the woman standing behind him.

Sisters exchange muted greetings, Delia brushing crumbs from her t-shirt as she moves away from the table to give the expected hug. At least the suitcase is small, so the visit should be brief, but what on earth has brought Anna from Perth at the start of the school term? Daughter Angela is at high school yet still a small child in Anna's eyes.

'Church conference in Brisbane,' Anna says brightly as sisters disengage. 'I phoned months ago to tell you about my plans to spend a few days with you afterwards.'

Delia frowns. 'Are you sure?'

'It must have slipped your mind.' Anna offers a perceptive smile. 'I'm not surprised with your having to move twice in less than a year.'

Delia winces at this thoughtless reminder of gambling debts and the implication that Liz has asked her to move out. Fear flutters in the pit of her stomach as she recalls the lack of response to her recent letter. How convenient that a conference enabled Anna to visit Brisbane only weeks after receiving news of her sister's new relationship! There's no question that Anna is a devout Christian – happy-clappy evangelical – but Delia has never heard her express interest in attending a church conference. Liz was right about prejudice; Anna's unscheduled visit has a single purpose: to berate her sister for falling into sin!

'Where shall I put the case?' Roger asks no one in particular.

'In the front bedroom,' Liz replies, grateful for a change of subject.

Delia offers her sister coffee and a jam doughnut, the latter rejected due to calorie concern. As compensation, she tears the chewed end from her half-eaten salad roll and slides the remaining third across the paper tablecloth. 'Won't be a minute with the coffee.'

Anna pulls out the chair, brushing dust from faded leather with a handkerchief before sitting down. Separating the two halves of the salad roll, she examines the contents with a critical eye before extracting a slice of tomato and a lettuce leaf.

In the kitchen, Delia leans against the sink, pondering how to survive until Monday morning. Liz might stay for a few more hours, but it's too much to expect her to return tomorrow, the atmosphere certain to be strained. Then again there's the lack of food. Apart from a jar of instant coffee, a carton of milk and jam doughnuts, the cupboards and fridge are bare. At least Anna has a car, so they can drive to the nearest supermarket.

Steam from the boiling jug draws her attention to the immediate task; she looks around for a spare mug, realises they brought only three and these have been used twice already.

'Use mine,' Liz offers. 'I've finished my coffee.' She turns to handover her mug as Delia steps from kitchen vinyl to living room carpet.

'Thanks. There's no washing up liquid, so I'll rinse the mug in boiling water,' she adds for Anna's benefit.

Her sister remains silent, head bent over dismembered lunch.

'Righto, girls, I'm off.' Roger gets to his feet. 'Gotta stock up on food before the kids descend on me.'

'Thanks for all your help, Roger,' Delia calls from the kitchen. 'Let me know if you want any of the stuff stored in the laundry.'

'Will do. Catch you later.' A wave of the hand and he's gone, the screen door banging behind him.

A glance at Delia's face as she approaches the dining table convinces Liz to take charge. 'I'll start on the boxes in the main bedroom, but before I do, I suggest we eat at my place tonight. I made a pasta bake yesterday and there's enough for three if I make a salad to go with it.' She looks across the table. 'Is that alright with you, Anna?'

Anna lifts her head. 'Fine by me. Is it far?'

'Ten minutes' drive.'

Liz is unsure whether Anna's smile is in response to the dinner invitation or the mug of coffee Delia has placed in front of her.

Standing behind Anna's chair, Delia signals to Liz, her

right hand pointing in the direction of the main bedroom, her eyes flicking sideways.

Liz doesn't hesitate, asking for help in locating the cartons containing sheets, pillows and duvets, all three being essential if Delia and Anna are to spend the night here. 'They could be in the cartons at the bottom of the pile,' she adds, as reinforcement.

'Bound to be,' Delia answers. 'Murphy's law and all that.' The epigram trails after her fleeing figure.

Cartons are stacked against the wall under the large window looking out on the adjacent roof lower down the street. Packing tape rips and paper crunching neutralise whispered truths, but Liz is more concerned with how Anna discovered the unit's address than the authenticity of a church conference.

Delia shrugs in response, her thoughts focused on the days ahead, incompatible sisters jostling for space in a small kitchen, divisive dialogue boxed in by cavity brick walls. And there's no possibility of escape unless it's to the laundry and that's unlikely with rain forecast for the next few days.

'Let's hope bedding for the single bed is as easy to find,' Liz remarks, her voice loud enough to reach the living room.

Delia drops a kiss on the back of her neck.

THIRTY-TWO

Delia escapes to the shower the moment they arrive at Tamarin Street, leaving her sister in the kitchen with Liz. A mean trick, she admits, but she craves time alone to clear her mind and prepare herself for the next few days. On a more practical level, she needs a change of clothes and must retrieve her nightdress from under the pillow and slippers from her side of their bed.

Warm water soothes a weary body, but her thoughts remain scrambled, oscillating between resentment and anxiety. Distress, or even revulsion over recent revelations doesn't give Anna the right to charge across the country to attempt a reversal, if that's what she has in mind. Perhaps she intends to use biblical quotes beginning 'Thou shalt not' to justify her point of view, a pointless exercise, given that as far as Delia can recall, there are no references to women lying with women, in either the Old or New Testaments. But why not telephone or write a letter? Taking the trouble to arrange a flight and hire a car is completely out of character, Anna usually reliant on her husband for organisational matters. So-called flu prevented her from attending Carol and Marti's wedding, a convenient excuse for not engaging with what she dubs *My Eastern states family*. Like their mother, Anna has never forgiven Delia for leaving Western Australia.

———

Halfway through the meal, sporadic conversation ceases altogether, all three women focusing on their food, although Anna seems more interested in picking out pieces of capsicum and placing them neatly on the edge of her plate than eating. She sits opposite Delia, so apart from occasional under the table thigh contact with Liz, there's no opportunity for reassuring touch.

'Men are bastards,' Anna declares suddenly, red capsicum dancing on her fork tines.

Bent over her plate, Liz blushes in anticipation of Delia's response.

'What's Michael done now?' Delia asks, expecting to hear the usual complaints of forgotten birthdays and anniversaries.

'He fucked my best friend. In my house, in my bed.' Capsicum falls onto the white tablecloth. 'And to make matters worse, he expects me to forgive him because he says it was an isolated incident and he swears it won't happen again.'

Delia recalls long ago suspicion, followed by questions and elusive answers, initial anger assuaged by embarking on the same game. 'It's best to forgive and forget, Anna.' She toys with her food to avoid her sister's eyes. 'Think of it as an unfortunate mistake. We all make them.'

'I don't!' Anna's fist thumps the table, sending the pile

of capsicum skyward. 'At least not that kind of mistake. Why should I forgive him when I'm the injured party?'

Delia sighs. 'What do you want then, a divorce?'

'A divorce would be unthinkable. I couldn't bear the shame.'

'Then you'll have to live with the situation, won't you?'

'I guess so.' Anna stabs her fork into a wedge of tomato and lifts it to her angry mouth. An errant seed slides down her chin.

'Cup of tea anyone?' Liz asks, eager to escape the tense atmosphere.

'I would love one.' Anna pushes her plate into the middle of the table. 'Thank you, Liz.'

Delia touches the arm reaching for her empty plate. 'I'll clear up; you did the cooking.'

Liz shakes her head. 'Stay with your sister. There isn't much washing up.' She lifts three plates, taking care not to spill anything else on the cloth. 'Did you want tea, Delia?'

'Yes, please, my....' She covers her error by adding, 'my, that pasta bake was delicious.'

Liz smiles and makes a hurried retreat.

Sisters remain seated and silent, one fiddling with her empty water glass, the other staring out of the window at the shadowed shapes of trees. In a neighbouring garden, a dog bays mournfully at the rising moon. Almost immediately, a woman's voice, harsh with irritation, bypasses trees to filter through taut insect screening. The dog gives a last disdainful howl.

Impatient to learn the truth about Anna's sudden appearance, Delia asks about the church conference.

Anna lifts her head. 'There was no conference, I flew over especially to see you.'

'Because of Michael's infidelity or my letter?' Delia regrets the second query the moment it's out of her mouth.'

'Who you love is your affair, not mine, although I did use the letter as an excuse to come over.'

Delia ponders the sequence of events: letter before infidelity or vice versa? Sensing that Anna has more to say, she acknowledges the unexpected response by reaching across the table to clasp her sister's hand.

'I'm sick of all the pretence, the little white lies, the half-truths told because Anna's not strong enough to cope with reality.' Her voice is tinged with sarcasm. 'It's ten years since my breakdown, so don't you think it's time I could be trusted to think and act rationally?'

'Yes, I do, and I'm certain you'll make the right decision about your marriage.'

'I thought so too, but now I have an added issue to consider.' Anna sits back in her chair, twirls a lock of shoulder-length hair in her fingers.

The ensuing silence disturbs, yet Delia feels reluctant to tease out details. Anna will speak when she's ready.

'I was at Mum's the other day,' Anna begins, her voice returned to its normal pitch. 'We were sorting out some old photographs she keeps in a biscuit tin. She wants to de-clutter now that she's thinking of moving into a retirement village.'

This is news to Delia but she prefers not to comment.

'The old place is getting too much for her, even though she has a cleaner and a gardener. I take her shopping once a week and drive her to any appointments, but she feels a change of scene would be beneficial and provide greater security, plus the company of others in her age group.'

A nod and a smile seem sufficient response.

'Anyway, all that's beside the point. At the bottom of

the biscuit tin, I discovered some letters from you to Mum. Letters written shortly before Angela was born in seventy-eight. January thirty-first, in case you've forgotten her birthday.'

Delia ignores the gibe. Yes, she had overlooked her niece's birthday this year, understandable given Ron died only weeks earlier.

'Perhaps I shouldn't have,' Anna continues, 'but I slipped the letters into my pocket when Mum went to make some tea. Don't happen to remember them, do you?'

A flurry of heated correspondence, followed by months of silence. How could Delia forget? 'What do you want me to say, Anna?'

'You don't have to say anything. It happened years ago, so I'm taking sisterly advice to forgive and forget. But it does raise further questions that need answering if I'm to make a rational decision.' She pauses to focus on the soiled tablecloth. 'Were you Michael's first, er, mistake?'

Delia considers her options – feign ignorance or tell the truth. Either way, Anna is going to be upset. 'I doubt it, but I can't provide any proof unless you count a conversation overheard at one of your New Year's Eve parties.'

'Before or after Angela was born?'

'Does it matter?'

'Absolutely! If it was before, then there's no excuse. We couldn't get enough of each other when we were first married.'

'Michael was talking about the advantages of what he dubbed, "party fun fare," such as no repercussions and no need to continue the relationship, but that could have been bragging. Men tend to do that when speaking to their mates.'

'True, but now it's hard to believe that Maggie was an

isolated incident.' Brown eyes flash anger. 'There was no party on this occasion, it was the middle of a weekday!'

Delia considers whether to invite Anna to stay for longer than a few days. It would give her time alone to mull over her options before flying home to inevitable argument and a distraught teenager if she decides to evict Michael from the marital home. By tomorrow night, unpacking could be completed if the three of them muck in, leaving the unit fit for sisterly occupation. Three days or ten, Delia is under no illusion that she can return to Tamarin Street during Anna's visit. The hire car could be returned – it's only a short walk to shops and buses, including the one that transports students to St Lucia. Anna could join her for lunch at the Staff Club or they could buy sandwiches at the café on the ground floor of the Biological Sciences library opposite her office and sit at one of the courtyard tables. Afterwards, Anna could take a walk beside the river. 'You're welcome to stay with me while you make plans for the future.'

Anna manages a smile. 'Thanks, I might take you up on the offer, but it would mean changing my flight.'

'That's easy as a phone call.'

'Two phone calls. I must let Angela know where I am. And Michael, I suppose.'

'Why don't you sleep on it?' Delia glances at her watch. 'We'll have tea and then leave, you look tired.'

'I hardly slept last night.'

'We can go now, if you prefer?'

Anna shakes her head. 'You have tea with Liz, but if you don't mind, I'd like to lie down for a bit. I feel a headache coming on.'

'Sure, go ahead. My bedroom's the one next to the bathroom.'

'Thanks.' Anna struggles to her feet and heads across the living room to the hall.

———

In the privacy of their bedroom, Delia voices her concern for Anna, who remains sound asleep in the room opposite, a gentle nudge having failed to rouse her. 'I don't know how she's going to handle this, Liz. She has never performed well in a crisis. Instead of standing up to Michael, she's likely to burst into tears and crumple in a heap or say nothing at all and withdraw into herself.'

'At least she's agreed to stay for more than a couple of days. Any idea how much longer?'

'No, but I can't imagine her staying away from Angela for more than a week.'

'Over-protective mother,' Liz mumbles, recalling her own mother's odd behaviour following Kay's death.

'I'm sorry to desert you, my love, but Anna really needs me.'

'There's no need to apologise. I understand.' Yawning, Liz glances at the digital clock – it's flashing zeros. 'Let's hope Anna finds the strength to act wisely. Her battle's just begun. Goodnight, my love.'

After embracing tenderly, they curl together one behind the other, but Delia needs face-to-face comfort, Anna's disclosure on the short journey from the unit continuing to haunt her. Michael's reaction to news of her relationship with Liz – unwisely Anna showed him the letter – was appalling! He maintained that Delia was blatantly immoral and unfit to be a mother or a sister. Fearful of the effect on their daughter, he would not allow Angela to visit her aunt again whatever the circumstances. 'Liz,' Delia whispers into a slender back, 'can we talk a little more? My own battle to combat prejudice has just begun.'

Soft, even breathing answers her question.

Sleep eludes her, despite attempts to count to one hundred forwards and backwards, numerals merging into one another to create an unwelcome cacophony. Eyes drooping, she tries to concentrate on the tree shadows flickering in the slight gap between curtains. Moonlight is brilliant tonight, thanks to a cloudless sky. Senses on high alert, she hears something scramble up a nearby tree. Possum, she thinks, easing herself out of bed. Standing between curtain and insect screen, she searches dark branches but fails to see any sign of the nocturnal creature that often favours them with its presence. Dusky leaves flutter, stirring whispered speech. 'I wish I knew which way to twist my leaves.' Reproof is instant. 'Foolish woman, she thinks, leaves don't decide which way to turn, the wind determines their course.' Breeze blows balmy, stroking her upturned face; a withered leaf brushes the screen, it will fall with the next strong gust. If not for the screen, she could reach out, crumble it to dust in her hand.

'Ashes to ashes, dust to dust,' she intones to the tree, her words filtering through screen mesh to nestle flower-like between living leaves.

THIRTY-THREE

NEXT MORNING, THERE'S NO RESPONSE TO DELIA'S knock, so she opens the bedroom door quietly to check if her sister is still asleep. Peering inside, she sees Anna sprawled across the bed, empty blister packs and an overturned glass lying beside her outstretched hand. Resisting the urge to scream, Delia shouts for Liz before rushing into the room to place her ear against Anna's chest. Her sister's breathing is shallow but even, so Delia slaps pale cheeks and shakes narrow shoulders. Anna's head flops forward like a rag doll. Reaching for pillows, Delia elevates the limp body.

'What on earth's the matter?' Liz calls from the hall.

'It's Anna. She's unconscious.'

Liz appears in the doorway. 'I'll call an ambulance.'

Delia shakes her head. 'It might be quicker to drive her to the hospital.' She gestures towards the bedside cabinet where two torn pill packets rest against the lamp.

Stepping inside, Liz notes prescription medications, the patient's name ripped in half but still recognisable. 'I'll stay with her while you get dressed.'

'Thanks.' Delia hurries across the hall to retrieve last night's clothes from the bedroom floor.

———

The steep stairs seem insurmountable, but Delia and Liz manage to carry Anna down to the car in a few minutes, where they lie her on the back seat. Slipping in beside her, Delia cradles Anna's head. The hospital is a fifteen-minute drive, but traffic is light on a Sunday morning, enabling an almost non-stop journey. On arrival, Liz ignores no parking signs to stop the car directly in front of the main entrance. 'Go and find a nurse,' she directs.

'Back in a minute.' Delia steps from the car and races to double doors that open automatically. Regaining her balance, she rushes over to the reception counter. 'Drug overdose, help please. My sister's outside in the car.'

'One moment.' The receptionist reaches for her phone.

After what seems minutes but is merely seconds, a nurse appears pushing a stretcher.

'In the car.' Delia points to the red Mazda almost blocking the entrance.

Nurse and sister ease Anna from the back seat onto the stretcher, and leaving Liz to park the car legally, they re-enter the hospital. A long corridor leads to Casualty, where half a dozen people sit on plastic chairs awaiting their turn. Anna is wheeled into a cubicle, Delia feeling helpless as the nurse draws curtains around her patient. Uncertain whether to wait, she's about to head for a vacant chair when a doctor approaches. 'Drug overdose?' he barks in her direction.

Delia gestures towards the curtained cubicle. 'My sister, Anna Gibson.'

'We'll need more details than that. Come with me.' Pushing past her, he pulls the curtain aside and steps into the cubicle. 'What did she take and how much?' He leans over Anna.

'Valium and Rohypnol. I'm not sure how many.'

'Haven't you any idea?' the nurse demands.

Delia struggles to remember how many tablets she took during the bleak nights following Ron's death. 'At least three-quarters of a packet. Both packets I mean. Packets of twenty-five.'

'Thank you, that's a great help. Please wait outside.' The nurse turns back to her patient.

Delia wants to ask a host of questions, wants reassurance that Anna will survive this latest suicide attempt, but she dares not disobey, so retreats quickly. Loitering a short distance from the sacrosanct space, she struggles to hear muted voices but learns nothing advantageous. A hand taps her on the shoulder; startled, she twists around, almost knocking into a nurse.

'Cup of tea, dear? You look very pale.' The nurse takes her arm.

'My sister will be alright, won't she? I would never forgive myself if anything happened to her. They were my tablets, you see. I shouldn't have left them in the desk, I should have thrown them out months ago. I don't need them, not now. I don't know why I kept them.'

'Don't worry, she's in good hands.' The nurse leads her over to a vacant chair.

'I found her about nine,' Delia continues, breathlessly. 'I don't know how long she was lying there. If only one of us had gone in earlier, but we didn't want to wake her, she'd had a long journey the day before.'

'Don't distress yourself, dear. Wait here while I fetch some tea.' The nurse scurries away.

Delia slumps in the chair, her chin touching the crumpled t-shirt, her head churning with contrition. Why did she leave strong tablets around when she knew Anna was distraught? Truth is painful – she forgot all about them, didn't even think to check the desk when tidying up after she decamped permanently to Liz's bedroom. Some of her clothes remain in the wardrobe, there being insufficient room across the hall, but she can't excuse not throwing tablets down the toilet, as she intended to back in January.

A second truth hits her with all the force of a clenched fist. Confirmation of Michael's serial infidelity was preventable; she could have feigned ignorance when Anna probed. Lights flash behind closed eyelids; she blinks rapidly to forestall headache, raises her head slowly as the doctor emerges from Anna's cubicle.

Struggling to rise, Delia calls out, 'Doctor, is my sister going to be alright?'

He advances towards her, clipboard in hand. 'She's sleeping peacefully.'

'Can I sit with her?'

'Soon.'

Delia resumes her seat.

'I need some further information,' he continues, taking the vacant seat beside her. 'Has your sister a history of psychiatric disorders?'

Delia glances at the clipboard resting on his knees. 'You might need several sheets of paper.'

'Begin at the beginning.' He extracts a pen from his pocket.

———

THE YEAR OF LIVING RAINBOW

Delia sits by the bed, waiting for signs of wakefulness. She holds Anna's left hand, a cannula having been inserted in her right arm to administer a saline drip. A smudge of black encircles Anna's pale lips, charcoal the nurse said. Delia grimaces at the thought of swallowing the viscous substance. She ponders the reason for the drip; was Anna dehydrated? The nurse left in a hurry to attend another patient, so Delia hesitated to detain her with further questions.

Minutes pass, she manoeuvres the chair forward to get more comfortable. Resting her aching arm on the thin blanket, she contemplates the Monday morning conference she and Charles have scheduled with the Dean and the Head of Department to discuss their joint research. If Anna is discharged tomorrow, it may not be possible for her to attend; she must call Charles to alert him to the family emergency. She wouldn't want him to think she's having second thoughts about continuing the project next year in England. Charles has already spoken to the Dean of Arts at his home university and received verbal approval. It remains for Delia to request a secondment.

Last week, when she broached the issue of spending several months in England, to her surprise, Liz expressed immense enthusiasm, volunteering to take her long-service leave to fund her absence from work. They discussed travelling in Europe first – Liz would have accrued a month's recreation leave by early ninety-three – and looked forward to pouring over holiday brochures once Delia has sorted out her unit. A stopover in Singapore was muted, cocktails at Raffles high on their agenda.

Immersed in the prospect of exotic locations and working overseas, Delia fails to notice fluttering eyelids.

'Dee Dee,' Anna murmurs, using the childhood name unspoken for decades. 'Dee Dee, where are you?'

Overcome with gratitude, Delia leaps from the chair to embrace. 'Here, darling. Dee Dee's right here.'

Anna opens her eyes and tries to lift her head from the pillow.

'Lie still, darling. You don't want to disturb the drip.' Delia drops a sisterly kiss on a furrowed forehead.

'Drip, drip, leaky shower.'

Metal curtain rings slide along the rail. 'It's good to see she's awake at last.' A much older nurse slips inside and approaches the bed. 'Move away from my patient, please.'

Delia obeys instantly.

'Drip, drip,' Anna repeats.

'Yes, we need to maintain hydration.' The nurse checks Anna's pulse, then shines a light into each eye. 'Right, my dear, we need to know what happened last night, so we can work out a course of treatment. Why did you take so many pills, especially when they were prescribed for someone else?'

'Sleep.' Anna turns her head away.

'Couldn't you leave the questioning for a while? She's only just woken up.'

'Are you a relative?'

'Her sister, Dr Delia Pierce.'

The nurse reddens and begins to adjust the drip. 'Sorry, doctor, I didn't realise.'

Delia decides not to reveal her Doctor of Philosophy status. 'That's perfectly alright.'

Backing away from the bed, the nurse almost collides with the young doctor who attended earlier. 'Sorry, doctor,' she repeats and leaves the cubicle.

'Has she spoken?' Dr James asks Delia.

'A few words. She's still rather groggy.'

'Understandable.' He sits on the edge of the bed. 'Anna, would you like to talk about last night?'

'Go away,' comes the muffled reply.

'That's okay. I can wait until you're ready.'

Anna turns her head to study him with narrowed eyes. Charcoal-stained lips tighten into an angry line.

Delia rises from the chair. 'Would it be better if I left?'

'Maybe. If you could wait across the corridor.'

Delia slips away before Anna can turn to face her, but before she can reach the waiting room, a piercing scream assaults her ears. Running back to the cubicle, she sees Anna sitting up in bed, pummelling the doctor's chest with her fists.

'Stop it at once, you silly little girl,' Delia commands in the dictatorial older sister tone used frequently during childhood. 'Dr James is trying to help you.'

Anna retracts her fists and hangs her head in shame.

'Please cooperate, darling,' Delia continues in her normal voice. 'Then I can take you home.'

Anna sniffs. 'Don't go away again, Dee Dee. I want you to hear this. All of it.'

Delia dreads intimate revelations but manages to ask the doctor if it's okay to stay.

'Certainly, although you need to be prepared for irrational statements.' He reaches down to retrieve his clipboard from the floor where Anna threw it.

Delia need not have worried; Anna's disclosures are completely self-centred. Her speech is hurried, as though time itself is running out, her return to consciousness a temporary reprieve. She speaks of elusive sleep, unfamiliar night sounds, the press of dark trees intensifying her towering despair. Snapping on the bedside light, searching the room for something to read, finding sleeping tablets and tranquillisers in the old desk, along with a Gideon New Testament inscribed *Kay Masters, Form 6a, 1960*. A choice of solace, both previously employed, yet neither proving wholly satisfactory. Flimsy pages fluttering in night air, light invading dark spaces to erase the broad sweep of tenebrous thought.

Ripping pages from their binding, tossing them over the side of the bed, wishing she could whip out the fly-screen to send them high over treetops. She has no further need of them, the Promised Land lauded in their lines will soon be hers. There can be no going back to God the Father, no retreat to the so-called sheltered world of patriarchy. Absolute salvation, the saving of mind, body and spirit rests in her hands. A beautiful new life, free from desolation and the sordid machinations of men.

Speech slows, then halts altogether. Anna falls back on the pillows, her face devoid of colour, her eyes empty as a maroon book binding once opened by a Brisbane schoolgirl.

Doctor James replaces the pen in his coat pocket. 'I'm admitting her to our psychiatric ward. It's for the best, you understand.'

Muzzled by her sister's anguish, Delia can only affirm her agreement with a nod.

———

Anna has been hospitalised for three days before Delia plucks up sufficient courage to make the long-distance call to Perth. Forbidden to contact Michael – *he's no longer part of my life, so has no right to know my whereabouts or my mental state* – she protests that Angela will be concerned by her mother's prolonged absence. A fruitless exercise, Anna remarking tersely that like all adolescents, her daughter isn't the slightest bit interested in her mother's affairs. Reluctant to risk argument, Delia changes the subject. Someone else in the family must be notified of Anna's condition, so she decides to telephone their mother.

Jean Andrews catches the next available flight to Brisbane, arriving in the early evening laden with luggage. Delia groans inwardly at the prospect of a lengthy stay. The following afternoon, they visit the hospital, Anna greeting them in the small Visitor's Lounge with hugs and kisses. She appears calm, engaging in small-talk and laughing over her mother's description of the disastrous church bring and buy sale, washed out by a sudden storm. Jean extracts a small package from her handbag, handing it to Anna with a beaming smile. Angela has sent a small gift – scented soap – together with a hand-made card decorated with red hearts. Anna's mouth trembles. Sniffing, she turns away from her visitors to pull a tissue from her skirt pocket. Delia glances at their mother, but she's too engrossed in admiring Angela's gift to notice sudden mood change.

'Lovely of her, wasn't it dear,' Jean remarks to the back of Anna's head. 'Such a thoughtful girl. Naturally, I didn't tell her the real reason for your hospital stay. We wouldn't want to cause her any distress.' Jean gives a nervous cough. 'I made up a little story about women's problems. Angela understands that sort of thing.'

Yes, Anna's got those, Delia thinks. The kind almost every woman has – problems with men!

'I told Michael the truth, of course,' Jean continues, still oblivious to Anna's distress. 'You may have had a silly quarrel, dear, but he has a right to know. Poor man, devastated he was, absolutely devastated! Told me he couldn't think of a single reason why you would want to...' Coughing again, she pulls out a handkerchief, holding it to her mouth as though trying to suppress the distasteful phrase.

'Commit suicide is the expression you're looking for,' Anna says, turning to face mother and sister.

Delia notices there's no longer any eye-contact, and Anna's mouth hangs half-open. Does she want to say more, or like mother, is she afraid to utter the words? 'Are you feeling ill again, darling?'

Anna's mouth moves slightly but no sound emerges, prompting their mother to discard the cake of soap to raise both hands. 'There, there, everything will be alright,' she soothes, reaching out to stroke flushed cheeks.

Lips tighten around the hard curve of teeth; arms rise to dislodge aged hands. 'Get her out of here, Dee Dee,' Anna growls before curling into a ball. Rocking from side to side, she moans like a sick animal.

'I'll fetch a nurse,' Delia calls, rushing out of the room. Screams follow her along the corridor, so she dives into a nearby room where a nurse is administering medication. 'Hurry, please. My sister's having a meltdown and our elderly mother is with her.' She races back to the Visitor's Lounge to rescue her mother.

THIRTY-FOUR

After an hour's bed rest, Jean reappears in the living room looking relaxed and almost cheerful, so Delia suggests tea and cake on the now-shaded patio. They can watch rosellas feeding in the tulip tree next door, chat about Carol and Joanna.

'Such a pity you couldn't come over for Carol and Marti's wedding, it was beautiful,' Delia begins once they are settled in comfortable cane chairs. She hasn't mentioned Joanna and the pastor, hoping that relationship is over.

'Yes, it was bad luck catching the flu. The photos you sent were lovely.' Jean smiles wistfully. 'Never mind, perhaps there'll be another wedding before too long.'

Christ, has Jo confided in her grandmother? Delia gulps her tea. At least Joanna will be in Brisbane soon, so she can ask her directly.

'Well, dear, surely you don't expect to remain single for the rest of your life? You're only forty-eight and it's almost a year since Ron died. Soon, your thoughts will turn to the future.'

'They already have,' Delia murmurs, forgetting that her mother possesses perfect hearing.

'Oh, do tell, darling.'

Delia hesitates, loath to raise what's sure to be a contentious subject.

'Go on, dear. You can confide in your mother.'

A withered leaf lands on the small table between their chairs, courtesy of lively rosellas and early evening breeze. Lifting it onto her palm, Delia traces brown veins with her index finger. 'Sometimes you need a new beginning, so you turn away from the familiar to tread a different path. At first, you're afraid of what's around the corner, but if you find the courage to look, you discover tranquillity and realise it's the right place after all.' She looks across the driveway to neighbouring trees. 'You discover another dimension, a previously hidden aspect of your psyche, and then you understand there can be no going back to the old ways, no more travelling the old road. That path has collapsed and your former self lies inert among the debris.' Fingers curl over the leaf. Stiff and cold, she thinks, like Ron on that sterile hospital bed.

'Why did you crush that leaf? Now, you've made a mess.'

'Perhaps it was a subconscious gesture, a concrete rejection of old values.'

'I'm sorry, dear, but I don't follow you.'

Delia looks over to her mother. 'Anna's tossed out the old ways, too. Before she swallowed those pills, she tore all the pages from the Gideon New Testament she found in Fran's old desk.'

'Maybe she has, dear, but all this business about paths and tearing things up is downright confusing. Are you trying to tell me you won't be getting married again?'

'That's right.'

'Oh well, it's fine by me if you live together. Everybody seems to do that these days and it isn't as though there will be any children. Not at your age.'

A laugh tickles Delia's throat. She covers her mouth to prevent its escape.

'So, when are you planning to move in with this new love?'

'The deed's already done.'

Jean looks puzzled. 'But you've only lived here for a week.'

'This is a temporary move, although I'll be staying on while Jo's here. She can help me decorate. The place needs a face-lift before I advertise it for rent.'

'You bought the unit with no intention of living here yourself?'

'It's an investment, Mum. Uni students are always looking for furnished accommodation.' Delia thinks of the court case, suspended over 6 Tamarin Street like a summer thunder cloud. Sharing the unit would be feasible for a few months but not as a permanent solution. Liz needs a garden.

'So, where will you be living next year?'

England is another possibility Delia doesn't wish to share with her mother until her secondment is finalised. 'Kenmore.'

'Oh, that's unfortunate. I hope you don't have to pass your old house to get there. That could stir up so many fond memories.'

'No, it's a few minutes' drive away.'

Jean leans towards her. 'Any chance of meeting him before I return home?'

Wrong personal pronoun, Delia thinks, swallowing the correction before it reaches her lips. A little white lie must suffice for the present. 'I doubt it, inter-state work commitment.'

'Do you have a photograph?' Jean persists.

Delia terminates the conversation with a shake of the head, followed by a retreat to the kitchen.

Dinner passes without further reference to new love or new location, Delia encouraging her mother to speak of church matters and the bridge club. As agreed earlier, Anna's illness and the incident at the hospital remain off-limits, both mother and elder daughter in need of a good night's sleep before tackling whatever tomorrow brings.

After settling Jean on the sofa in front of the TV, Delia clears the table and begins to wash up, hoping her mother will fall asleep soon. Having promised to spend weeknights with Liz once family members depart, Delia needs to report that Anna's hospital stay is likely to be longer than first thought.

When the phone rings – Delia is used to a wall-mounted phone, so it remains on the coffee table until she decides the best position – Jean leans forward to lift the receiver. 'Doctor Pierce's phone, can I help you?'

Delia strains to learn the caller's identity, but her mother appears to be listening intently, suggesting it could be a doctor or nurse. 'Everything alright, Mum?'

In response, Jean raises her free hand and points it at the TV, ignoring the remote control lying beside her.

'I'll do it,' Delia calls, dashing from kitchen sink to living room sofa.

Evening sounds intrude via the patio screen door, the hum of traffic circling the roundabout at the bottom of the hill, the screech of cockatoos flying in to roost in nearby eucalypts. Determined to eavesdrop, Delia slips behind the sofa, her soapy hands dripping on green carpet.

'I agree, it must have been a dreadful shock for her,' Jean says in a low voice. 'Don't worry, I'll deal with the situation and bring Anna home to you as soon as she's discharged from hospital. It might be best if Angela remains at her friend's place for now.'

Shit, it's Michael. Mother must have given him the new number.

'Yes, of course I understand that you can't take time off work at the moment.'

At least he won't be catching the next flight from Perth.

'Bye, Michael. Yes, do call tomorrow.'

Scurrying back to the kitchen, Delia plunges her hands into cooling water. Cutlery clatters on stainless steel – the dish drainer still buried in a cardboard box – and plates balanced earlier against glasses threaten to topple, anger despatching concentration. Home to Michael, that's the last thing Anna needs! Having failed to escape permanently, she must reassess without the distraction of an allegedly contrite husband and a moody teenage daughter. If Angela were older, Anna could stay in Brisbane while she regains her mental health, plan her future in a quiet space.

Head bent over the sink, Delia jumps when a hand touches her shoulder, sending dirty water splashing over drying dishes. 'I'll make some tea in a minute, Mum.'

'Never mind about tea, we need to talk now.'

Reluctantly, Delia turns around. 'I assume that was Michael?'

Jean ignores her question. 'I shall speak to Anna's doctor tomorrow. Her illness is understandable given what she learned recently.'

'I agree.' Delia wipes her hands on the tea towel draped over the oven door handle. 'She told me all about Michael's latest affair.'

Jean bristles. 'Purely a figment of Anna's overactive imagination. *You* did the damage, Delia, you sent her over the edge. Writing about the joy of loving a woman! Michael was appalled when he read your letter.'

'So, I'm to blame, as usual,' Delia counters angrily. 'God forbid your sensitive daughter should learn that intimacy isn't confined to married couples! How distressing to discover your sister's new-found happiness! Besides, Anna said who I love is my business; Michael's infidelity is of more concern. She found him in bed with her best friend!' Delia steers her mother back to the sofa, waiting until she's seated before moving to the armchair. 'We both know Maggie wasn't the first, Mum,' she says in a milder tone, 'and she won't be the last. Anna's had enough. She wants him to leave.'

'Anna would never break up their home. The effect on Angela would be devastating.'

'I doubt it. Angela's almost sixteen and self-absorbed like most teenagers. I'm certain she would cope well with separated parents once she'd recovered from the initial shock.'

Jean fiddles with a blouse button. 'I suppose that's how you imagine your children will react when they learn about you and that woman?'

'Her name is Liz, Mum. I spoke to Carol last week and she wasn't at all shocked. Grab some happiness while you can, she advised.'

'I'm so glad she's married,' Jean remarks, raising her head to stare at a point on the wall above the TV.

'What's being married got to do with anything?'

'Marti will take care of her. It's obvious you're no longer capable of parental guidance.'

Delia digs her heels into the carpet to prevent a leap from armchair to sofa. Fingers grip the arms of the chair until her knuckles turn white. Prejudice and a complete lack of understanding come as no surprise, but to maintain that her new love invalidates parenting skills honed over decades is intolerable! Anxious to appear hurt rather than furious, Delia ponders a suitable response, focusing on the constancy of her maternal role and the desire for some compassion from her own remaining parent. Present contentment should be valued not scorned; her mother should be pleased that the scar of tragedy has begun to fade.

'What about Joanna? I don't suppose you've even considered the effect your immorality could have on a sensitive girl. She's had so much anguish to deal with this year.'

'So have I,' Delia says under her breath.

'Losing her father at such a difficult age, almost grown up but still needing his support. Ron was such a good man, so sensible, so straightforward. There were no hidden sides to his personality.'

Oh no, that's where you're wrong, Delia wants to shout. What about the cheques written to the owner of an illegal casino, the unpaid bills, the lack of consideration for his family's future? What about the colleague he fucked when his two little girls were sleeping in an adjoining room? His jealous rage when he found out I'd played the same game, his hand gripping my wrist so hard it left a bruise. Her thoughts fashion a fitting reply but it remains unspoken; she cannot speak ill of the dead.

'Nothing to say, have you? Can't deny what a wonderful husband and father he was. Ron put up with a great deal from you, Delia. Most men would have left years ago. You were a spoilt, domineering wife. And now you besmirch his memory without a second thought.'

'It's of no consequence to Ron who I sleep with,' Delia retorts. 'In case you've forgotten, he drove too fast on a wet road.'

'Don't shout at me, Delia, and don't be so naïve. You should know by now that one's partner reflects one's standing in society.'

'Who gives a shit about that sort of status? Being known as a competent university lecturer is what matters to me. No one cares whether I live with a woman or a man.'

Jean squirms in her seat. 'It's not your career I'm concerned about.'

'Oh, I get it.' Slowly, Delia gets to her feet, wearied by fractured emotions and her inability to curb contempt. 'You're afraid they'll chuck you out of the Ladies' Auxiliary or the church choir if they learn your daughter is gay.'

'Don't be silly, Delia. The church is very tolerant these days. Our organist is gay. A very pleasant young man. He plays beautifully.'

Delia moves to stand in front of her mother. 'Then why can't you accept *my* gay relationship?'

'Because of the effect on our family. Look what's happened already to my poor Anna.'

Still struggling with her conscience, Delia sits on the sofa to stroke her mother's cheek. 'Stop fretting, Mum. Anna will be alright. She just needs time to adjust.'

Jean sniffs, her eyes brimming with tears.

'Catching Michael red-handed knocked her for six,' Delia continues, suddenly resolved to speak the whole truth and nothing but the truth. 'But infidelity isn't the end of the world. When Anna acknowledges this, she'll be able to put it behind her and look forward to a bright future without him.'

Quiet descends, swift as tropic nightfall, Jean closing her eyes while Delia goes to draw the curtains. Grateful for an end to heated argument, she's contemplating how to fit visits to the hospital around her work schedule when a fresh burst of hostility shoots from sofa to patio doors. 'All her life Anna's worshipped you, Delia, but when she needed you the most, you snapped her spirit with your debauched behaviour. I can never forgive you for this wickedness, never, never.'

Stunned, Delia clings to thick curtains as her mother beats a hasty retreat to the front bedroom.

THIRTY-FIVE

A PERSISTENT RINGING TONE REVERBERATES AROUND the house, shattering Sunday evening peace. Praying that it isn't Delia with further reports on her challenging family, Liz inserts a bookmark before closing the borrowed novel – UQ Main Library PR section – and laying it carefully on the coffee table.

A spate of sobbing greets her hurried hello. 'Is it Anna?' she asks when sobs subside. The response is barely comprehensible, Liz unsure how *snapped spirit* relates to *wickedness* or a *hostile mother*. 'I'll be there in ten. Please try to calm down.'

Waiting at the intersection with Moggill Road for traffic lights to change, Liz reflects on a straightforward decade with Kay. From the start, Fran Masters accepted their relationship without questioning its validity or its place in society. A welcoming smile, plump arms hugging them both, a thoughtful gift for their future. Her own parents felt a little apprehensive at first but didn't allow it to interfere with the parent-daughter relationship, and before long they were welcoming Kay into the family.

An invitation to the holiday house that later became her parents' retirement home followed, a memorable January fortnight that cemented already warm relationships. Golden sand, lunch under the beach umbrella, her mother's cake soft and sweet, melting in smiling mouths. After the meal, when Kay stood in foaming shallows to throw a line, Bill Coney – usually averse to fishing – would amble down the beach to join her. Liz remembers shrieks of protest as a slippery fish slapped his bare legs, his cheeks pink with laughter.

Moonlight over the headland, standing with Kay fronting the wild ocean, wind whistling through their hair. Waves crashing over rocks, racing each other down the steep cliff to sink their toes into sun-warmed sand.

Memory scene-shifts, and suitcase in hand, she stands at the bottom of steep steps gazing up at Kay's hillside home among flowering eucalypts. On the footpath, noisy minors quarrel in a flowering hibiscus while lorikeets gossip in a tall tulip tree. The rest of her belongings will arrive later in the day, courtesy of a friend's small truck. She leaves behind an empty rented flat and years of loneliness.

Green lights propel her to present-day problems. Memory is sweet but unreliable, only now does she remember an aggressive brother and the looming court case.

Parking on the street, rather than the driveway to enable a swift departure, Liz walks along the path by the side of the building, preparing an appropriate greeting in case Delia's mother answers the door. With luck, Jean will have gone to bed, exhausted from argument. Liz is about to climb the steps leading to all six units, when light spills from the first doorway and Delia emerges, looking around furtively as though she's a grounded adolescent trying to escape. 'Down here,' Liz calls from below, refusing to engage in juvenile subterfuge. 'Did you hear me arrive?'

There's no response, Delia focused on descending quietly – the study/spare bedroom windows open directly onto the walkway.

'Thank God you've arrived,' Delia breathes into Liz's neck when they meet halfway.

'Can I come up?' Liz loosens the arms that threaten to crush her windpipe.

'Yes. She's in bed, snoring like a trooper, though how she can sleep after her hysterical performance this evening is beyond me!'

Liz agrees, thankful to hear that despair has morphed into irritation. Perhaps she can salvage Sunday evening peace once Delia has recounted her dramatic tale. No matter how much Delia pleads, Liz has already decided she won't be staying the night.

———

Next morning, Delia carries a suitcase down the stairs to the waiting taxi, then retraces her steps to assist her mother. Jean Andrews is moving to a motel close to the hospital, despite her daughter's suggestion that they put their differences aside to concentrate on Anna's recovery.

'I don't blame Liz,' Jean remarks when they reach the taxi. 'It's not her fault she prefers, er, feminine company. I imagine she was born that way.'

Delia refuses to continue the conversation, a necessity if she's to remain calm. Following an almost sleepless night – Liz rejected her request to stay – she must cast her mind back to Victorian England and a motherless boy barely surviving in a bleak orphanage.

Automatically, she helps her mother into the taxi, holding her handbag until Jean is settled with the seatbelt fastened. 'See you at the hospital. I'll be there late afternoon after work,' she offers by way of a truce.

Jean sits facing forward, clutching her handbag with both hands as if Delia is about to snatch it.

Stepping back a pace, Delia watches the taxi driver execute a perfect three-point turn, then guide his vehicle to the end of the driveway. A rear window lowers – is she about to receive a motherly farewell?

'And don't think this is the end of the matter,' Jean calls in a shrill voice guaranteed to wake any neighbours still sleeping. 'I intend to make Liz see sense. Unlike you, she seems to be a level-headed woman.'

Scarlet with rage, Delia rushes down the side of the building, but her knees almost buckle at the thought of steep steps, so she grasps the handrail to assist her ascent. Once inside her unit, she prepares for the day's duties, grateful for an unshared space. Two hours alone will focus her mind on the titular protagonist, Oliver Twist, drawn from the author's real-life experiences of poverty and abandonment. Despite the pain of recent maternal rejection, she gives thanks for social reform and the accident of birth that sees her living in a more enlightened society.

———

At the nurses' station, Delia gives her name and relationship to patient Anna Gibson as requested, then makes her way to the Visitor's Lounge. The room is empty, it's four-fifteen, so most visitors are either still at work or on their way home. Anna soon arrives, bright-eyed and smiling as she crosses the room. Sisters embrace warmly before sitting side by side on a sofa that's seen better days.

'I'm going to be discharged the day after tomorrow,' Anna announces. 'Dr James is very pleased with my progress.'

'That's good news.' Delia ponders whether to ask a pertinent question.

'I'm going straight home, in case you're wondering. Mainly because he'll be away on business and Angela's staying with her friend's family until the end of next week. Mum would prefer I spent a few days with her first, but I've decided the best post-hospital therapy would be time alone.'

'Very wise,' Delia murmurs. 'Alone, you can do as you please, without the pressure of family life.'

'Spot on, sis.' Anna rummages in her jeans pocket to retrieve a folded sheet of paper. 'But it won't be all lying around watching TV and ordering takeaway. There are certain tasks I must deal with at once. I've made a list in order of priority.' She thrusts the paper into Delia's lap. 'Dr James suggested it. He says the brain requires discipline to function properly.'

Unfolding, Delia's eyes are immediately drawn to the top of the list: *1. Contact locksmith to arrange for new locks.*

'As you can see, I've made some important life decisions,' Anna continues, her voice showing no sign of strain. 'Contacting the Education department is at number two because I need to let them know I'll be available for a permanent position after the Christmas holidays rather than my usual relief teaching.'

'Full or part-time?' Delia manages to ask, an innocuous question that belies the astonishment building inside.

'Either. I won't have to pay rent until the house is sold or he buys me out.'

Still reluctant to make eye contact, Delia keeps her head down. Last on the list is *Ask Angela whether she wishes to live with me or her father.* Christ, is Anna rejecting every aspect of her current life? 'Have you said anything to Mum?'

'No way, not after she threw a hissy fit over your new relationship! She told me about your argument. Anyone would think you were sixteen, not a middle-aged woman!'

At last, Delia raises her head. 'She didn't even say goodbye.'

'Silly bitch!'

Shocked, Delia feels compelled to stand up for their mother. 'It's not her fault, Anna. She was brought up at a time when no one went public about same-sex relationships. Do you remember my uni friends, Alison and Georgie?'

Anna shakes her head.

'They were lesbians, but when I mentioned this to Mum, she said women often shared accommodation for economic reasons and told me I shouldn't listen to hurtful rumours.'

'I imagine she'll be the same with me when I tell her I've had enough of *his* affairs. She believes divorce is shameful but I now know it's just another lie concocted to keep women in their place. There's nothing shameful about freeing oneself from a cheating husband.'

'Certainly not.' All the same, Delia wonders how Anna will cope with their mother's pleas to keep the family intact or whispered gossip in the church hall. Ripping pages from a Gideon New Testament that didn't belong to her doesn't mean Anna has abandoned Christianity. Along with swallowing a quantity of someone else's tablets, her actions were cries for help. Handing back the sheet of paper, Delia decides not to broach the subject of church attendance or remind Anna that last week she recoiled at the mention of divorce. 'I'm so proud of you for grabbing new life with both hands.'

'Having been given a second chance, I had no choice. Wallowing in self-pity doesn't achieve anything.'

'No. Moving on is imperative.'

'And thanks to your example, I can. It won't be easy, there's Angela and Mum to deal with for a start, but if I'm tempted to regress, I'll picture you embracing a flexible future with Liz.'

I give thanks for a flexible future, Delia muses, recalling the concluding line of Liz's latest poem, *Act of Goddess*. Earthquake and destruction followed by rebuilding, using materials more suited to a challenging site. Metaphor for lives turned upside down through human error.

THIRTY-SIX

Against her solicitor's advice, Liz takes time off work to attend the first day of the court case, which he says will comprise opening comments from the applicant's and respondent's solicitors, so is unlikely to supply new material. Unwilling to risk encountering Colin or Fran Masters in the foyer, Liz times her arrival at the Law Courts Complex in George Street for just prior to the ten-thirty timeslot, slipping quietly into the seat next to Mr Melling. At the adjacent desk, Colin sits beside his solicitor, whose name Liz can't recall.

All stand as directed when the judge enters, both Liz and Colin avoiding a glance at one another. Liz knows the judge will have the final decision, there being no jury in a civil case, so once re-seated, she focuses on the applicant's solicitor. As expected, Mr Giles confirms that Frances Hilda Masters has signed the document giving her son the authority to contest on her behalf the Last Will and Testament of Kay Frances Masters. He then proceeds to outline the case, most information a repeat of Colin's words during his visit to Liz's home months earlier.

'To sum up,' Mr Giles begins, but a commotion at the court door prevents further speech and heads turn to watch an elderly woman struggling to shake off a court official's restraining hand.

'Let go of me,' she demands. 'I must speak to the judge.' Righteous indignation succeeds, the woman freeing her arm to march across the court to the judicial bench.

Liz places a hand over her mouth to stifle astonishment. It's Fran Masters, dressed in her signature *going out for lunch outfit* of lilac suit, matching hat and handbag and black court shoes.

'What is the meaning of this interruption?' the judge demands.

'I was coerced into signing that document, your Honour,' Frances Masters states clearly, 'by my son's bullying. I wish to withdraw my case.'

'Madam, you cannot burst into my court seeking judicial changes,' the judge replies, in a condescending tone. 'You must speak to your solicitor.' He gestures to the court official hovering behind her. 'Usher, please escort the lady from court.'

'Of course, your Honour.' Stepping forward, the usher takes Fran's arm. 'Come along, madam.'

Fran concedes defeat, but as she's led past Mr Giles, turns her head to exclaim in a loud voice, 'I'm Mrs Frances Masters and I know my rights.'

'May I have a moment to consult my client, your Honour?'

'Certainly, Mr Giles.'

A slight bow and he's crossing the floor to lean over the desk where Colin issues whispered instructions inaudible to those seated nearby.

'May I speak, your Honour.'

'Approach the bench, Mr Giles.'

'Your Honour, my client advises that his mother is suffering from dementia, so is mentally unfit to exercise any influence over this case.'

Liz wishes she possessed the courage to refute this statement, but unlike Fran, she feels bound by court procedure, so can only listen as the solicitor adds further false comments, explaining that his client is contesting his sister's will to ensure his mother receives sufficient funds to enter an appropriate Aged Care facility.

The judge nods, his expression grave. 'I order a medical assessment of the said Frances Hilda Masters. Case adjourned until the result has been received.'

Outside the court complex, Liz scans the street for Fran but she's nowhere to be seen. Most likely Colin has whisked her away in a hire car for immediate transfer to a psychiatrist! Liz prays for an assessment that takes no account of CM's opinion.

A train takes her to Indooroopilly Station, where she can catch a bus to uni, there being little point in returning home first to collect her car when she can request a lift home with Delia, who has lectures today.

―――

On campus, Liz detours via the English department instead of heading straight to Main Library. She's desperate to share court case news, but Delia isn't in her office and the departmental secretary has no idea when she'll return. Deflated, Liz returns to work, answering her nearest colleague's query with a little white lie. When requesting time off, or time-in-lieu as it's known in the library, she told her immediate superior, Senior Librarian, Pam, that she had an appointment in the city. Although Pam is one of few colleagues to have visited Tamarin Street and never asks awkward questions or engages in workplace gossip, she remains unaware of the ongoing issues with Colin Masters.

Work hours pass faster than envisaged, one of the library assistants bringing a pile of literature for cataloguing, each one containing a pink *urgent* slip, which means they've been requested by an academic or post-graduate student. Apart from leaving a brief message on Delia's phone requesting a lift home at five, if possible, Liz works steadily, completing the urgent items by four, then moving on to religious study material.

A late-afternoon call from Delia supplies details of Daisy's parking place. No mention is made of day one in court, a relief to Liz, the telephone available to all staff being in the centre of the open plan office within earshot of half a dozen desks. A ploy by management to keep private calls to a minimum, Liz assumes, although lack of privacy doesn't deter some staff. She concludes the call with a cheery, 'I'll see you soon,' and returns to her desk for a final ten minutes.

Delia is already in the driver's seat when Liz turns left at the roundabout near the library's rear entrance – staff only – so she lengthens her stride, reaching Daisy's passenger side as the engine coughs into life. Poor old girl, her days are numbered unless she has an engine transplant. Liz slips inside, responding to Delia's smile with a squeeze of the hand resting on the gearstick.

A slow journey down Fred Schonell Drive – during vacations, most vehicles leave campus at five o'clock – is of little concern, Liz launching into her report of the morning's extraordinary events the moment Daisy pulls away from the kerb. For once, Delia remains silent, her responses limited to exaggerated facial expressions and the occasional thump on the steering wheel. By the time they reach the traffic lights at Toowong, the story is done and dusted with Liz suggesting they detour via the unit to collect Delia's toilet bag and a change of clothes. She can't bear to spend the night alone.

They embrace in the hall, ignoring the unmade bed in the study. 'I miss you so much,' Liz whispers, her breath tickling Delia's neck.

'Same here. I'm not sure I can wait until after Christmas to move back in.'

'It's only a few weeks. In the meantime, we should be able to spend the occasional weekend together. Joanna will want to spend some time with her friends.'

Delia gives a wry smile. 'That's if she hasn't completely disowned me by then.'

As Liz feared, Delia hasn't spoken to her younger daughter about their relationship. 'What happened to telling the truth?'

'I can't tell her over the phone.'

'Are you afraid she'll stay in Toowoomba?'

'I need to get her away from that man. He's turned her head with his talk of sin and divine retribution.'

Liz has had bad vibes about Peter Eames since their first meeting. 'Forget about it for now, we've both got too much on our plates at present to waste time and energy on a pudgy, pasty-faced pastor.'

'Good alliteration, darling,' Delia declares, disentangling herself to usher Liz into the living room. 'If you don't mind, I'd love a cup of tea before we go back to yours.'

'Sure. Have you got any biscuits; I didn't have any lunch?'

'Tim-tams.'

'Good. I need a sugar hit.'

At least Delia hasn't suggested a drink, Liz thinks, settling on the sofa. Proof she's sticking to her newly-imposed rule of no drinking during the week. Self-control despite the family issues she's had to deal with recently is a positive move, alcohol her usual port of call in a crisis. Sister and mother returned to Perth two days ago, leaving new lovers free to be uninhibited but tonight, Liz won't offer wine with dinner.

'Tea's up.' Delia places a tray on the coffee table. 'Two Tim-tams for you, in case you notice there are odd numbers. I don't want to spoil my dinner.'

Liz smiles her approval. Food restraint is a first for Delia and evidence of real change. 'Still on the diet, then?'

'Sure thing! I want to look good for my girl.'

Tea cools in pottery mugs, although they demolish all the biscuits first, citing a need for energy.

Afterwards, Delia rustles up dinner for two from yesterday's leftovers, neither of them willing to make the move to Tamarin Street. Conversation over salad and cold chicken centres on domestic matters such as whether it's worth installing air-conditioning in the unit's main bedroom. The ceiling fan is old with flecks of rust decorating its white blades and tends to squeak when turned on high.

'I suppose I should start thinking about Christmas,' Delia says as they clear dishes from the table. Her voice lacks enthusiasm, she's focused on a first anniversary one week later, rather than a festive season without Ron. She's been there before, unlike Liz.

'My parents will expect me over the Christmas New Year break,' Liz replies, anxious to push Kay-thoughts aside. 'Have you decided to go north?'

'It depends on Jo. I won't leave her alone.'

'Surely she'll want to see her sister?'

Delia shrugs. 'We'll see.'

———

Thunder wakes them around midnight, followed by a flash of lightning that illuminates the entire bedroom. They're lying naked on top of the bedclothes, hot limbs stretched out to catch the fan's warm wind. Torrential rain pounds the corrugated-iron roof, accompanied by the occasional ping of small hail. A return to sleep seems impossible, so they embark on a game of make-believe, envisage snow falling softly, blanketing their world of torrid heat. Play features next, snowballs flying through frigid air to land with wet smacks on winter-weight clothing. A snowwoman takes shape, black pebbles for eyes, orange carrot nose, smooth breasts. Exhausted by nocturnal exercise, they lie on their backs, limbs extended in snow-angel pose.

'Shit!' Delia exclaims, adjusting her legs to sit up. 'What with courtroom drama and luscious lovemaking, the meeting slipped my mind.'

'What meeting?' Liz murmurs, loath to leave her soft-snow bed.

'This morning's with Charles and the Dean. My secondment's been approved. We're going to England!' She bends to drop a kiss on Liz's hot forehead.

'That's wonderful! Now, I can speak to James about my long service leave.'

'You don't anticipate any problems?'

'No. I've already hinted I might be taking extended leave next year. James thought it was a great idea, said I should travel while I have the opportunity. I sensed a tinge of envy.'

'What's to stop him taking an overseas holiday?'

'Twins, due in March. They'll change his life for sure.'

'I'm looking forward to a change of scene. Life will be much easier for us in another country.'

It's only four months, Liz wants to remind her, but keeps the thought to herself. 'Yes, I've heard the English are more open-minded about gay relationships. They're not isolated at the end of the earth, minds closed against change.'

'The tyranny of distance.' Delia sighs. 'But I was thinking about us, not British society. Life will be easier because the people we meet will have no knowledge of our pasts. We'll be Delia and Liz or Dr Pierce and Ms Coney, the English being more formal than we Aussies.'

Liz recalls Charles Powell's stiff handshake, his polite greeting when they met on campus.

'Over there,' Delia continues, stroking Liz's warm breast. 'Over there we'll be a secure unit, just the two of us without the trappings of former relationships.'

'We can't forget the past entirely, Delia.'

'No, and neither should we. Memories are important but we can't allow them to dominate our present.'

'The past is another country,' Liz murmurs, misquoting the opening line of a novel catalogued years earlier.

'Time to write a few pages of the new narrative.' Delia shifts her hand to the warmth between thighs.

'In the morning,' Liz answers, removing the hand. 'I feel cooler now. Let's try to get some sleep.'

'Goodnight, sweet princess, may flights of angels speed thee to thy rest.'

Prince, Liz corrects in her head.

THIRTY-SEVEN

An overcast sky and the absence of an alarm ensure they sleep for hours, waking only when someone knocks on the front door. 'Who on earth could that be?' Liz swings her legs out of bed to grab yesterday's clothes hung neatly over a chair.

'Ignore it,' Delia answers sleepily. 'It's probably just a neighbour.'

Liz glances at the alarm clock. 'Delia, it's nine o'clock!'

'Oh shit!' A second knock propels her out of bed and over to the wardrobe, where she pulls a dress from its hanger, before remembering that underwear is stored in the bedside drawers.

The knocking persists, triggering rapid dressing followed by a sprint into the kitchen for Liz, while Delia scoots down the hall to the door. Fumbling with bolt and key, she asks the caller to wait a moment, then flings the door open to reveal daughter Joanna standing by the railing, a suitcase at her feet.

'Hi, Mum. Sorry I'm a week early but as I'd finished exams and Peter had to come down, I thought I'd grab a lift.'

Delia reacts by stepping out of the door to scan the walkway. 'Where is Peter?'

'He had to go. Church business. He'll call in this afternoon to say hello.'

'You'd better come in.' Backing into the hall, Delia glances into the spare bedroom. Thank God the bed looks as though someone slept in it, though she has no idea how to explain Liz's presence at this hour on a weekday. Short of climbing over the balcony railing and risking a leap to the concrete driveway below, there's no way for Liz to leave the building without using the front door. She's about to call out that the visitor is Jo, when Liz appears at the end of the hall, clothes tidy and hair brushed, her outsize work bag slung over one shoulder.

'See you, Delia. Thanks for calling me about the book. I'd forgotten I left it here. If I hadn't returned it today, I would have copped a fine.'

'No problem,' Delia answers, grateful for an excuse, even if it is on the flimsy side. With luck, Joanna won't ask what prevents her mother from dropping a book into the library on the way to her office.

'Must go now. Lovely to see you, Joanna. Catch up later.' Squeezing past mother, daughter and suitcase, Liz hurries outside, where she executes a neat right turn to access the steps for a swift getaway.

'Shall I drop my bag in here?' Joanna gestures to the half-open door on her right.

'Bring it into the living room, we'll sort things out later.'

'Okay.' Joanna steals a glance at the space her mother has described as a study/bedroom. A single bed is set against the far wall with the small desk she used during schooldays tucked under the frosted windows. 'Is there a wardrobe, Mum?'

'Yes, the one from Carol's bedroom. It's in the corner. The bed and desk are yours.'

'I can see that.'

'Want some breakfast? I was about to make mine when Liz dropped by.'

'Tea and toast, please. We left so early; I didn't have time to eat anything.'

Delia turns into the kitchen. 'Have a seat. I won't be long.'

Behind her, Joanna stops to survey the living room. 'Everything seems to fit, Mum.'

'Sorry, darling, I can't hear you over the jug.' Whistling stops, enabling Delia to fill two mugs with boiling water. Jiggling tea bag strings, she focuses on an explanation for the unmade single bed. Prior to Liz's excuse, she'd intended to comment, if asked, on a shared meal with too much wine, obliging an overnight stay. Breakfast demands attention; she fetches milk, butter and marmalade from the fridge, her mind wavering between mentioning Anna or her mother, Joanna unaware of their recent visits.

'Shall I sit at the table?'

Delia turns away from the counter. 'Sure.' She notices the two tablemats left from last night's dinner, the salt and pepper shakers. Shit, why can't she learn to be tidy like Liz?

'The dining table looks alright in here, Mum.'

'Not bad. It's a bit of a tight squeeze if it's extended.' Delia returns to buttering toast.

'Where did you put the other two chairs?'

'In the bedrooms.' Lifting a plate and mug, Delia heads for the table. 'Here you are, darling. There's more bread if you want another slice.'

'That's fine, Mum.'

Delia smiles before fetching her own breakfast and

taking a seat opposite Jo. Further questions remain unasked, mother and daughter intent on breakfast. Truth filters through lies, longstanding family relationships supplanting nascent love. Sister or mother, Delia ponders, anxious to shield Jo from the unpalatable subject of attempted suicide. Both, she decides, recalling Anna's church conference lie. Sisters sharing a double bed for one night; mother in the study. Left yesterday, no time to remake the single bed, or for them to travel up to Toowoomba to visit niece/granddaughter.

'I'm afraid I have to go to work soon,' Delia says, courage deserting her. 'Lectures have finished but I need to see a colleague about some research.'

'No problem, Mum. I can amuse myself. When will you be back?'

'I'm not sure. I'll certainly be home by mid-afternoon. Help yourself to lunch or you could walk down to the shops. It's only a ten-minute walk.'

'I'll stay here, thanks.' Jo yawns. 'I might have a lie-down on the sofa before I unpack.'

'Good idea.' Delia reaches across the table for Jo's plate and mug.

'Leave it, Mum. I'll clear up later.'

'Thanks, darling.'

―――――

Delia returns at two-thirty, having spent the lunch hour with Liz eating café sandwiches at a table in the shade. Taking lunch back to her office where the absence of most staff should ensure privacy was her preference, but Liz wanted to stay outside, saying she needed a bit of warmth after hours spent in the over-chilled Cataloguing department. 'Are you here, Jo?' she asks from the hall when there's no response to her 'hi, darling' greeting.

'Where else would I be, Mum?' Joanna calls from the living room. 'This is the only home I've got.'

Disappointment with the unit or the usual teenage sulks? Before leaving the hall, Delia fixes her face with a caring smile. 'Did you have a good rest?'

'No!'

'Noisy neighbours?'

'No, a lazy mother.'

Delia frowns. 'Look, I'm sorry your bed's not made, but Anna only left yesterday.'

'Aunt Anna? What was she doing in Brisbane?'

'Church conference.' Delia crosses the room to sit in the armchair adjacent to the patio doors. 'Anna had one free night before her flight to Perth.'

'Pity, I'd have liked to see her.'

Kicking off her sandals, Delia tries to think of something to say. She could prattle on about the joy of seeing her sister, report on cousin Angela or Grandma Andrews, but an escalation of lies doesn't seem fair to Jo when *her* sister knows about Liz. If only she hadn't been so hell-bent on telling all and sundry about their relationship, the truth could have remained safely hidden until they returned from England. 'Jo, I need to...' she begins but her daughter interrupts, asking probing questions about two still-damp towels in the bathroom and a man's handkerchief embroidered with the letter K discovered in Delia's bed. 'So, a new lover, Mum. Is his name Kevin, Karl or Kenneth?'

Delia recalls last night's sneezing fit – most likely the result of pollen from shrubs in the front garden – searching under the pillow for a tissue, Liz handing over the handkerchief she'd placed on the bedside drawers when they went to bed. 'K is for Kay Masters, she preferred men's handkerchiefs. She maintained women's were too small to be of any use.'

'She also preferred to sleep with a woman.'

'Yes, and Kay was a devoted partner to Liz for over ten years, which is as important as a long-term loving marriage.' Delia takes a deep breath and, leaning forward, embarks on a second attempt at truth.

'I know it's difficult for you, but please try to understand,' Delia concludes gently, when the expected tears, outrage and references to the wrath of God fail to eventuate.

Joanna sits expressionless, looking over her mother's head to tall trees swaying in the neighbouring garden. 'May I use the phone?' she asks following an uncomfortable silence, rising from the sofa before Delia can answer. 'Peter gave me a number to call in case I wasn't going to be here this afternoon. He should be able to pick me up in half an hour. I'm sure he said the meeting finished at three.' Without a glance at her mother, she moves to the kitchen, where the cream, push-button telephone sits in its new position on the bench nearest the dining table.

Numb with grief, Delia watches as Joanna extracts a piece of paper from her jeans pocket and places it carefully on the bench. Smoothing the paper with her fingers, she appears unhurried and devoid of emotion, as though she's a casual acquaintance phoning for a taxi, rather than a daughter arranging to leave her mother's home, perhaps forever. An index finger presses buttons, a polite request is made, a message given. Satisfied with the result, Joanna returns to the sofa, where she picks up a library copy of the literary magazine *Meanjin* that's lying on the coffee table.

Mother-daughter dialogue remains absent during the

forty minutes it takes for Peter Eames to travel from the CBD to Toowong, Joanna continuing to read while Delia busies herself with bedmaking. She's in the bathroom, placing crumpled sheets in the laundry basket, when a loud knock announces his arrival. Refusing to answer, she pushes the bathroom door with her foot until it's almost closed, then sits on the toilet with her ear pressed to the wall.

Footsteps pound the hall carpet; the front door opens, and at last Joanna finds her voice. 'My mother's a...' she begins, followed by the sniff of barely suppressed tears.

'A what?' Peter prompts.

'I can't say the word, it's too appalling.'

'How can I comfort you if you won't tell me what going on? Is it because she's going to England? I know you were upset when she mentioned the possibility. But there's no need to feel deserted, my love. You have me now.'

'She, she's sleeping with that woman!'

Silence follows, although Delia can hear rustling, implying the pair have moved closer together. Perhaps they're praying.

'All will become clear,' the pastor says slowly. 'The Lord will counsel you. For the present, it's best you return home with me. My spirit is strong, I can assist you to deflect this evil.'

'I don't think she'll change her mind. Once Mum decides to do something, that's it.'

'Faith, Joanna. Remember the Lord is omnipotent.'

'His will be done.'

Two sets of footsteps move down the hall and into the living room, probably to collect Joanna's suitcase. Delia listens for further dialogue but none arises, so she contemplates whether to challenge their homophobia, not with shouted indignation but calm statements. A pastor must know *his* God condemns male homosexuality, not two women finding love and a reason for hope in one another's arms. She's about to emerge when running feet halt her steps.

'I don't want to lose her!' Joanna cries. 'There mustn't be another accident!'

'Come, Joanna, no loving God would wish a child to lose her mother. Remember the power of prayer. I shall secure her salvation.'

'I didn't mean to doubt your faith, Peter. I'm upset, not thinking straight.'

'Let me soothe you, my angel.'

Behind the bathroom door, Delia shudders. She can almost feel his soft white hands fondling firm young breasts. 'Joanna, we mustn't part like this,' she calls as the door slams, but there's no sign of daughter or pastor when she reaches the steps. Descending at speed, she races around the corner of the building and down the driveway, where his 4x4 waits to turn into the street. 'Joanna, don't go!' she shouts as the Land Rover takes off in a cloud of exhaust.

THIRTY-EIGHT

Outside the Magistrates' Court, Liz steadies her nerves by mouthing phrases gleaned from a book on feminine theology. *I place my soul in your hands, Mother of my heart.* Text becomes a healing mantra when repeated, and soon, she senses respite from the shock of finding a distraught Delia sitting at the top of the front steps on her return from work the previous day.

Following an impassioned retelling of afternoon trauma, interspersed with bursts of sobbing, Delia proposed advancing the date of their departure for England, claiming she felt defenceless against the rising tide of homophobia. Liz managed to convince her that running away wouldn't solve the problem but had to acknowledge her own inability to effect a change of opinion, especially when dealing with a fundamentalist preacher.

The descent of darkness brought further problems, Delia pleading to stay the night and seemingly deaf to the suggestion that returning to the unit would be preferable in case Joanna phoned. In the end, Liz was forced to remove clinging arms and speak bluntly, reminding Delia that court would be reconvening the next day and she needed an uninterrupted night's sleep.

A glass of wine and watching a mindless movie helped Liz to relax, but wakefulness prevailed when she tried to sleep, heightened by high humidity and the absence of breeze, so towards midnight she got up to draw back the curtains in the hope of admitting a little air. Bathed in soft moonlight, her garden offered solace from fevered desolation, sturdy trees promising protection from human intolerance. How she longed to feel gnarled bark graze her frail body, grey leaves anoint her damp hair. 'I am afraid that prejudice will tear us apart,' she whispered to sleeping eucalypts. 'And I cannot bear to lose her.' Leaves fluttered against the screen, sending a draught of cool air over clammy flesh. *Trust and all will be well,* Liz heard in her head, encouraging a return to bed.

―――

Buoyed by midnight counsel and morning wisdom, Liz walks into court to take her place beside Mr Melling. He greets her with a smile and eyes brimming with confidence. Does he possess knowledge of the medical assessment, or is he trying to boost her morale should she be called to the stand? Liz dreads the thought of cross-examination, the sight of Colin Masters just metres away, his arrogant pose and countenance assuming victory before she has uttered a word.

A slight tap of her elbow and she's on her feet, watching the judge cross behind the bench to take his seat. This morning, his presence is no longer daunting even though his expression remains sombre. Papers rustle as she resumes her seat and an air of expectation hovers over the heads of those facing the bench. A glance at the public gallery takes Liz by surprise – Delia is sitting alongside Fran Masters despite plenty of empty bench space on either side of the elderly woman! Fran clutches the handbag resting on her knees with both hands and her expression betrays trepidation, while Delia appears relaxed, hands loosely folded over a smart jacket Liz hasn't seen before.

The judge raises his head to survey the court before returning his attention to the papers arrayed in front of him. Beside her, Mr Melling shifts in his seat and it takes immense concentration for Liz to remain still. She won't risk a peek at the adjacent table, though she assumes the Applicant's solicitor, Mr Giles, is also becoming impatient. On the bench, papers are shuffled into a neat pile, a throat is cleared and at last, judicial speech begins.

———

Afterwards, she can only recollect two of the judge's words, *case dismissed,* although Delia tells her that he spoke at length of the folly of making assumptions without professional interpretation, followed by an order for the Applicant to pay the Respondent's costs.

Outside the court building, Fran can't contain her delight, rushing as fast as her aged legs permit to enfold first Liz, then Delia in a tight embrace. 'Thank God justice has prevailed,' she declares, freeing herself to stand beaming at the younger women. 'My Kay can rest easy now, her wishes have been endorsed!'

'And I can continue to live surrounded by my beloved trees.' Liz steps forward to take Fran's arm. 'A celebration is in order, even if it is just coffee and cake at the café round the corner.'

Delia moves to Fran's other side. 'And with your permission, Mrs Masters, I shall forget about my diet and order the largest slice of gateau available!'

'Fran, please, my dear. Any friend of Liz's is a friend of mine. We girls must stick together!'

———

Less calorific celebrations take place at 6 Tamarin Street that evening, Liz having to go back to work following their café stop. Delia has made good use of the afternoon, preparing salads and barramundi to be served with Moet & Chandon champagne. Dessert is circles of fresh fruit displayed on a glass platter with a small jug of light cream alongside.

Lovers toast the present, delightful as they can begin to plan a future, which in turn is thrilling because unknowable, new experiences await in a faraway land that neither have visited despite their British heritage.

A diet may have been abandoned earlier, but both women restrict their alcohol intake, a reasonably clear head needed for the day's final celebration.

———

Two weeks pass quickly, Christmas presents are purchased – more from a sense of duty than enthusiasm for the festive season, the forthcoming anniversary a cloud that seems to follow them in and out of shops swathed in gaudy decorations. At Liz's insistence – being together for part of the day and all night will help bolster our flagging emotional health – Delia remains in residence at Tamarin Street, returning to her unit each morning to prepare the rooms for repainting.

Washing walls, skirting boards, door and window frames with sugar soap provides an extensive workout, ensuring further weight loss and excellent sleep.

On campus, buildings assume their seasonal somnolence, stone, concrete and brick baking in December heat. Cool cloisters no longer reverberate with the sound of feet rushing to lectures and tutorials, or noisy conversation in shady corners. In the various libraries, a general lack of students – some post-graduates remain – enables some front-line staff to take recreation leave, while others begin the annual tasks of tidying bookstacks and deciding which titles to send via the Cataloguing department for online record adjustment and physical relocation to the off-campus store.

Liz is thankful for the peaceful environment, the ease of finding a shaded bench for lunch with Gloria or sitting beneath a leafy tree using pieces of cardboard to avoid soiling their light-coloured summer clothes. At Roger's invitation, Gloria is spending Christmas Day at her old home, a last hoorah as the house will go on the market in January. Divorce must wait for two years' separation but financial settlement can proceed, a relief to Gloria who wishes to purchase a three-bedroom townhouse so the children can live with her. They will miss their old home with its large garden and swimming pool, but Gloria has promised to take them to a public pool or the beach on weekends. Roger's plans aren't mentioned, although Liz imagines he will remain in Brisbane for the children's sake. She considers asking him to house-sit if his place has sold by March but changes her mind when envisaging two energetic children charging through her garden. Instead, she'll employ a gardener once a fortnight to mow the grass and check on her plants. Watering shouldn't be a problem as there's plenty of rain over summer and into autumn. Informing the local Neighbourhood Watch that the house will be vacant for three months and installing time-clocks to turn on a few table lamps at night should keep her home safe.

———

There's no word from Joanna, and Delia's letters addressed care of Peter Eames' residence remain unanswered. Phone calls every other day also fail to elicit a response, the pastor always lifting the receiver, then, on recognising Delia's voice, declaring that Joanna is out or unavailable. Fourteen days of silence convince Delia that Joanna won't change her mind and accompany her to Townsville, so she calls Carol before purchasing a return flight from Christmas Eve to New Year's Day. Carol encourages her to stay longer, saying she could help on the boat after Boxing Day if she gets bored, Barrier Reef excursions and classes having been booked until the end of January, even though summer isn't peak diving season. The thought of preparing food for hungry tourists in a stuffy cabin while bobbing about on the ocean doesn't appeal, so Delia declines graciously, citing the need to finish refurbishing the unit and visit her in-laws up the coast. George and Nancy Pierce will find Christmas without their only son particularly challenging in the absence of grandchildren. Being present for Liz on her return from mid-coast New South Wales is another consideration, but Delia keeps this thought to herself. They will spend New Year's Day apart, each in the company of close family, which seems appropriate for this first anniversary of their former partners' untimely demise.

Delia's return flight departs at six in the evening, giving her ample time to participate in the ceremony Carol has planned for earlier in the day. An acknowledgment of her father's love for the natural world, a homemade wreath comprising native plants, lowered carefully from *Reef Star*'s forward deck to the ocean's turquoise surface. On their return to the harbour, a late lunch with Marti's mother at her home, before heading to the airport. A fitting end to a Christmas holiday that would have been inconceivable one year earlier. Lifting her paintbrush to finish the bedroom skirting board, Delia can only trust there are no more shocks in store for her as a turbulent year moves to its inevitable conclusion.

THIRTY-NINE

The university will be closed between Christmas and New Year, giving general staff like Liz an extra three days paid leave to add to their annual allocation of four weeks. The nine-day break, which includes four public holidays, isn't a magnanimous decision on the part of management, rather an economic response to the cost of opening an extensive campus for a few days.

One week before Christmas, the remaining cataloguing staff – some are already on leave – attend to mundane tasks previously set aside due to lack of time, so Liz is surprised when her immediate supervisor, Pam, requests a meeting at noon in the corner office used for private dialogue. The usual monthly cataloguing meeting takes place outside manager James' office, with staff standing around or perching on the edge of desks, clutching notebooks in which to record procedural changes or imminent departures and arrivals.

Liz assumes the meeting with Pam concerns her long service leave to which she's added at Delia's request, two weeks recreation leave. Fourteen weeks is a lengthy absence, so perhaps James has decided to employ another librarian for the period instead of dividing Liz's work between the other cataloguers as planned. March is a busy month for the department with boxes of books arriving from library suppliers ready for the new teaching year. The first few weeks of semester are extra busy with cataloguing staff expected to take a turn teaching the new intake of students how to use the online catalogue. Always anxious to avoid the 'public', Liz dreads these sessions, especially if she encounters know-it-all students.

At five to twelve, she's standing outside the office waiting for Pam to admit her, as if they were strangers, not long-term colleagues and friends.

'Why are you hanging about out there, Liz?' Pam calls from the far side of a small table. 'Come on in.'

Liz steps inside and takes the chair opposite, murmuring an apology.

'I have some exciting news.' Pam indicates the sheet of paper in front of her but doesn't hand it over. 'There'll be a temporary vacancy in Fryer from the end of April until mid-December, as Jennifer is taking maternity leave followed by unpaid leave. James has been asked to recommend someone from cataloguing, an in-house replacement being preferable.' Pam pauses to offer a warm smile. 'Given your interest and expertise in Australian literature, James would like to recommend you, Liz, and in his absence, he's asked me to sound you out.'

If there's one library on campus where Liz would feel comfortable, it's Fryer, with its extensive collection of Australian literature, including manuscripts and cultural ephemera – library speak for non-print items – sourced from bookshops and collectors along with numerous donations from grateful alumni. The atmosphere within Fryer is always tranquil, reminding Liz of an era when patrons addressed library staff in subdued voices and wouldn't dream of uttering a word when conducting research in reading rooms. Suddenly, she realises that a change of scene would re-focus attention on her career, somewhat neglected during the past decade, as she strove to create a comfortable home and garden for a partner with no interest in domestic matters. 'I'm flattered to be considered,' she says, recalling Delia's desire for equality in all aspects of their relationship. 'Working in Fryer would be fascinating.'

Pam is delighted, pointing out that gaining experience in a different area will be beneficial should Liz seek promotion in the future. Almost as an afterthought, she mentions the need for Liz to take up the full-time position in mid-April. 'A handover period is essential as I'm sure you'd agree.'

'Absolutely.' Thoughts swirl as Liz anticipates revised holiday plans and a partner who is already disappointed that she won't take unpaid leave to extend her stay in England. 'I'm happy to alter my holiday dates,' she adds to reinforce new-found confidence.

But back at her desk, excitement and tension vie for dominance, resulting in stupid mistakes that, fortunately, she picks up during the final check made before uploading a record. Abandoning thoughts of making up time-in-lieu, she leaves the library at four-thirty.

―――

The evening meal passes without their usual comments on the day – Delia weary from physical labour, Liz preoccupied with how to phrase her secondment news. Over washing and drying dishes, they argue about whether to purchase a dishwasher – Delia for, Liz against – even though the subject hasn't arisen before.

Retiring to the living room with mugs of tea, they sit at opposite ends of the sofa, staring at the ABC news without comprehension. Grumbles from Delia accompany the weather forecast – heavy rain with the chance of an afternoon storm will upset her curtain-washing plans. 'Curtains can wait, Delia,' Liz snaps, grabbing the remote control to turn off the TV. 'You've got weeks before the unit needs to be rented out.'

'I want the refurbishment done before Christmas.'

'Why?'

'Because January is for planning our trip.'

'Talking of travel, I had an interesting meeting with Pam today.'

'Is she going away?'

Measured phrases blur as Liz shakes her head. 'I, I have some, er, exciting news. Exciting for me, that is.' She hesitates, uncertain how to continue without provoking another argument.

'Go on, I'm listening.'

Leaning back against the cushion – more to appear relaxed than for comfort – Liz describes her meeting with Pam, emphasising the qualities that led James to recommend her for the position. When this fails to elicit any response, she concludes by disclosing her start date and waits for the inevitable explosion. But Delia remains tight-lipped as though she can't quite decide how to react. Is she about to storm out, fling herself on the bed in a fit of selfish sobbing, or does she plan to leave the premises in a huff? The latter would require a degree of cooperation, for some reason she's parked Daisy under the house instead of in her usual spot on the driveway behind the Mazda.

When silence persists, Liz ponders whether to express regret that their holiday must be curtailed, but on second thoughts acknowledges it won't make much difference to Delia. By mid-April she'll be engrossed in research and giving the occasional lecture, Liz's only role the preparation of meals and keeping house in a tiny university bedsit, or flat if they're lucky. 'We have the first few weeks to travel,' she ventures, hoping to provoke a reaction even if it is derogatory.

'I thought we were equal partners,' Delia says, so quietly that Liz must bend forward to make out the words. 'But now I find you've accepted a new position without discussing it with me at all.'

'A new *temporary* position,' Liz counters, recalling that it hadn't occurred to her Delia would object to her working in Fryer. 'An increase in my working hours won't affect you in any way.'

Delia pouts. 'It might. Think of the Fridays when I don't have lectures: mid-semester breaks, the week or two before exams. We could have gone away for long weekends.'

'That would be true under normal circumstances. But next year you'll be working in England for three months.'

'Correct. Three months, not nine!' Delia retorts in the manner of a primary school teacher.

'What difference does a few months make?'

Delia sighs. 'I suppose I could alter my secondment. Originally, Charles suggested I stay until the end of the academic year.'

'Okay by me.' Liz offers a smile to stifle the scornful response building in her brain. Talk of equality is a token gesture; as usual, Delia will do whatever suits her.

'Right, that's settled. I'll speak to the Dean in the New Year.'

A second smile is genuine, Liz eager to resume normal relations. All her life she has avoided conflict and can't comprehend why she almost extended their dispute with a thoughtless remark. A partnership requires compromise.

FORTY

On Wednesday morning, Delia continues her new routine of breakfast with Liz, then leaving Tamarin Street for her Toowong unit ahead of Liz's departure for work to save shifting her car twice. Today, she'll pack a small suitcase and leave the unit tidy before flying to Townsville early the following day. The bulk of her personal items, including clothes, remain where they were stored on and after moving day, although larger furniture had to be repositioned prior to redecorating and the sofa is still shrouded in an old sheet. Downstairs, the laundry is littered with painting equipment, the result of a last-ditch attempt to finish redecorating the study, which proved unviable given self-imposed time constraints.

Deciding to begin upstairs – it will be cooler in the garage later in the day – she's restored order in the living room and has her suitcase open on the bed when a car pulls into the driveway and stops opposite her garage. Probably a taxi, she's noticed drivers seem reluctant to pick up or drop their fares further down. Ease of turning around, she assumes, the driveway narrowing slightly at the rear. Crossing to the wardrobe, she selects two sundresses and carries them over to the bed. Shorts, tank tops and a lightweight shirt to wear on the boat are next, to be followed by underwear, swimming togs and a spare pair of sandals. She refuses to wear the white deck shoes favoured by Carol and Marti; apart from rubbing her feet when wet, Volleys are most unattractive.

A car door slams and tyres slip on damp concrete as the vehicle reverses into the street. Taking a bloody risk, mate, Delia thinks, traffic often speeding up the steep hill from the roundabout at the bottom. She listens for the screech of brakes but, hearing nothing untoward, turns back to her suitcase.

The front door has been left wide open to increase ventilation, so Delia fails to hear the quiet footsteps that cross from hallway to study or the sigh escaping pursed lips. But she does hear a thump as something or someone hits the study wall. Fearing an intruder, she looks around for a weapon and, finding nothing, remembers the ironing board stored under the bed. She meant to take it down to the laundry, then forgot in the flurry of repainting. After sliding the board across the carpet, she grasps folded legs to hold it against her body like a shield. Tiptoeing into the hall, she halts before the doors leading to bathroom and study. 'Come out, whoever you are. I'm armed and not afraid to use my weapon.'

Girlish giggles alert her to an unexpected but welcome visitor. 'Joanna?'

'Sorry, Mum, I should have called or at least knocked on the door, but I'm so...'

Still holding the ironing board, Delia takes a step forward to stand in the doorway. 'What's up, darling?'

Instead of answering, Joanna launches herself from the bed, triggering a rapid sideways movement to shove the ironing board against the study door. Metal leg-locks scrape, but Delia has more on her mind than paint damage, the arms around her neck threatening to strangle, the tears hot against her cheek. 'Come into the living room, Jo, we can't talk here.' Gently, she loosens the clinging arms, murmuring comfort phrases used during a childhood that suddenly seems recent rather than years before.

On the sofa, Jo curls foetal-fashion, resting her head on her mother's generous thighs. Sanctuary for a troubled adolescent, Delia thinks, stroking the thick brown hair that tumbles over pale flesh and pink shoulder straps like an old woman's shawl. Shifting her fingers, she checks for signs of fever, but although the skin around Jo's eyes is red and puffy, her forehead is cool. Stroking resumes, Delia mindful that patience is required; Jo will speak when she's ready. The problem must be Peter Eames, she assumes, rather than fear of failing end of year exams. Perhaps the relationship is over, its intensity a figment of imagination or the muddling of sex and religious fervour, powerful emotions, especially for an inexperienced teenager. Joanna was easy prey, a timid girl lacking the self-confidence of her older sister. Living in Carol's shadow for nigh on eighteen years, no wonder Jo responded to a pastor's passionate conviction that *her* spiritual health mattered to a revered deity. Delia trusts both church and man will be discarded when Jo returns to Toowoomba for her second year of nursing.

Jo stirs, stretching an arm to wipe a lingering tear, but she appears no closer to exposition.

'Can I get you a cold drink?' Delia tucks a stray lock behind a pink ear.

'Not yet,' Jo murmurs. 'I want to stay here where it's safe.'

'Of course, you can stay here, darling,' Delia answers, thinking of tomorrow's flight. She'll have to cancel; it's doubtful a spare seat would be available on Christmas Eve. Carol will be disappointed, but she has Marti and his large family for company. Her first Christmas as a welcome addition to the Tonelli tribe; distraction from an initial festive season without her beloved father. Witnessing Carol's anniversary ceremony would have been poignant, but Delia must concentrate on the present; Jo can't be left alone. Murmurings beneath her hands shift images of foliage fragmenting as wind and waves weave their endless dance. Alert, Delia bends to hear her child's tale of woe.

At first, Jo speaks of loving care, compassion and reassurance, of gentle hands caressing and whispered words promising salvation. Peace of mind and body – no threat to almost restored equilibrium. Then, her tone changes, becoming matter-of-fact as though she's trying to block harsh truth with crisp sentences devoid of emotion. Intimacy sanctioned by a higher power, reward for restraint, an angel's pure gift to her saviour.

Religious imagery that belongs in a consecrated space, not a pastor's bedroom. Delia swallows hard to banish the anger simmering in her throat. Tight-lipped, she waits for simpler language to surface.

'He didn't force me,' Jo continues in her normal voice, 'so why do I feel violated?'

'Persuasion can seem equally distressing. There's the fear of pregnancy or concern that, by succumbing, you've forfeited respect.'

Jo lifts her head to snuggle into her mother's soft breasts. 'I'm not worried about pregnancy; he used a condom.'

All the same, Delia will be relieved when Jo's period arrives. 'That's good, but you should think about going on the Pill now, darling.'

'I see no point, Mum.'

Delia frowns. 'Did he ask you to leave?'

'No, it was my choice. He doesn't even know I've gone. Too busy thinking about his Christmas service and whether Jane Donovan will sing a solo.'

Delia resists a sigh of relief. At last, Jo has come to her senses, acknowledged that Peter Eames is in love with his role as pastor, not a girl twenty years younger. A saviour-seducer who has no intention of offering marriage or even a long-term relationship. Having achieved his goal, it appears he's already moved on to another young woman seeking sanctuary within the walls of his church. 'Who's Jane Donovan?'

'She's a new member of the choir. Calls herself a refugee from the Catholic church.'

Unable to think of a response, Delia drops a kiss on her daughter's forehead. The next few weeks will be tough, but at least Jo won't be sitting in church on Sundays watching a repeat performance. Back home in Brisbane, she can work through her distress without fear of appearing naïve. A visit to grandparents would help, Jo has always been close to them, perhaps they'd welcome two extras for Christmas Day.

'I'll have that cold drink now, please, Mum.' Lifting her head, Jo ties her hair in a knot before shifting sideways. 'Bit warm today for a long cuddle.'

'It's never too hot for TLC.' Delia recalls small hot bodies seeking comfort over numerous Brisbane summers. She moves into the kitchen, quickly followed by Jo.

Over lunch – Sao biscuits with vegemite and a wizened apple the only available fare – Delia raises the Christmas issue, reassuring Jo that a flight can be cancelled or postponed. They could both fly to Townsville after the Christmas/New Year break. In the interim, she offers two choices for Christmas Day: picnic in a park or asking George and Nancy to join them in a picnic on the beach near their home.

Jo considers her options by resting her head on folded arms.

Following a lengthy silence, Delia begins to clear the table, figuring Jo has fallen asleep. Most likely she spent half the night awake, worrying about the aftermath of sex and whether to risk a return to her mother's home. Since her arrival, Jo has apologised threefold for storming out weeks ago, blaming herself for being unduly influenced by a man whose principles she once trusted. For her part, Delia hasn't mentioned Liz or living at Tamarin Street for the past week. If asked, an almost empty fridge and pantry can be easily explained as pre-holiday preparation. As for Jo's attitude to gay relationships, time will tell; so far, the subject hasn't arisen. Acceptance would be preferable but Delia won't push the issue. Over the next few weeks, alone-time with Liz could prove difficult, if not impossible but that's a small sacrifice when they have three months in England to enjoy one another's company. Reminded that Jo has yet to learn the secondment has been finalised, Delia makes a mental note to disclose the details once Christmas Day arrangements have been settled.

'Neither option suits,' Jo answers, raising her head. 'I don't want to wreck your plans, Mum, or let Carol down, so

I'll call Gran and Grandpa to see if I can spend Christmas up the coast and the following week if they're willing.'

Astonished at the sudden transformation from troubled teenager to thoughtful adult, Delia can only watch open-mouthed as her daughter leaps up to grab the phone from the adjacent kitchen bench.

FORTY-ONE

THIRTY-TWO CELSIUS AT SIX-THIRTY IN THE EVENING, the seven-two-seven beached on the runway like a bloated tourist after a lavish lunch. Irritated by the unexplained delay, Delia stares out of the window, wishing she had earplugs to supress the noise of a fractious toddler sitting across the aisle.

Musing on an atypical Christmas, she recalls the siblings and cousins vying for her attention, Eva Tonelli sitting at the head of the table, issuing directions to daughters and daughters-in-law about the mountain of food laid out on kitchen benches. Seafood figured prominently at the Christmas Eve meal, along with baked pasta and a host of sumptuous desserts, meat absent according to Italian tradition. Delia dreaded getting on the bathroom scales when she returned home!

When the family raised their glasses to absent fathers – Giovanni Tonelli had passed away in 1980 – Delia struggled to remain dry-eyed, but grief soon lost its intensity as the family showered her with loving kindness.

New Year's Eve meant another family feast at the huge

wooden table, Eva Tonelli once more relishing her role as matriarch. For Delia, Italian exuberance brought new meaning to the saying *eat, drink and be merry*, but when she went to bed in the early hours, the subsequent phrase, *for tomorrow we die* pierced the mask of cheerfulness like red-hot needles. Pushing her face into the pillow, she, sobbed and sobbed until she thought her heart would break.

———

Beneath silver wings, Brisbane suburbs doze in warm night air, elevated timber houses creaking as the temperature drops. Familiar with recurrent contraction and expansion, their inhabitants rest undisturbed, bathed in bay breezes. The single-storey brick veneer homes mushrooming in outer suburbs are slower to cool, hugging the earth a distinct disadvantage in a sub-tropical climate.

From her window seat, Delia envisages a wide brown river meandering past the houses and high-rise built close to its banks and a university campus contained within one generous bend. Further east, the river passes industrial complexes and wetlands on its final journey to Moreton Bay, but Delia prefers to focus on beginnings not endings. Beyond bay islands lies the wide Pacific, conduit to all the other oceans that surround distant shores, affording a fitting label for a small planet spinning in space. This first day of the year nineteen-ninety-three promises novel experiences in an Old World land, an opportunity to fully embrace her new reality.

Further down the east coast, a small village slumbers beneath starry skies untarnished by the light pollution found in cities. Here and there, pin-pricks of light reveal modest houses nestled in dense foliage, with caravans and cabins perched on the rise overlooking a beach and tiny creek where low tide reveals oysters clinging to rocks and sandbanks provide easy access to the ocean.

Earlier in the day, as the sun rose over a murmuring ocean, Liz walked empty streets on her way to the shore. Raucous cockatoos greeted the dawn from their roosts in tall eucalypts while in front of her, a pair of crested pigeons cooed to one another as they waddled towards the patch of bush behind the beach. When she joined them, dry leaves crunched beneath her sandshoes, and she heard the call of silver gulls standing on sandbars. Ordinary sounds from the natural world, and all she needed on this anniversary morning.

Stepping onto sand, she was relieved to find herself alone – no sign of other early walkers or even the surfers often seen cresting the waves beyond the estuary. A flash of red caught her eye, a plastic cylinder discarded by a small child and overlooked by a careless parent. Bending to retrieve the toy, she brushed it clean, then stood facing the ocean reliving childhood holidays on beaches up and down the east coast. Wearing home-sewn shorts and a sleeveless shirt – at her mother's insistence, she wore dresses to school or on visits to relatives – she blew bubbles into a cerulean sky. Some hovered in front of her, shimmering for an instant before the wind carried them out of sight. Others flew towards the sea, a stream of brilliant spheres; she squealed with delight as one landed on her outstretched hand, closing her fist to prevent its escape. But soon, a damp palm attested its impermanence. She remembered tears and an empty container flung into the sea.

Memory moved through the years as she rock-hopped across the creek to access the path leading to the grass-topped headland. Emerging from tangled bush, she relished cool breeze on her damp neck, salt air filling her lungs. She climbed steadily, careful not to slip on foliage and rocks still moist from last night's shower. On reaching the top, she raced over wind-whipped grass, her arms raised to the sun, savouring freedom of movement and solitude. She had intended to climb down to the surf beach but hesitated when she reached the worn patch marking the start of a steep path created by generations of surfers, swimmers and sunworshippers. The elderly fisherman might be down there, eager for a chat, but she cannot cope with human speech.

 High on the headland, close but not too close to the edge, she sat hugging her bare knees, staring at undulating ocean beyond the breakers yet sustained by memories of a different stretch of coastline, where the sound of the sea filtered through an open window and a golden lover curled beside her. Waves of desire surged through her; she sought to capture the climax, hold it within forever, but passion retreated like the tide, and she lay beached on the shore, breathless and brimming with love. 'A damp patch on the skin is all remains when the bubble has burst,' she cried, her words spiralling over the edge to lie broken on jagged rocks at the foot of the cliff. Closing her eyes, she prayed for patience, perseverance and the ability to embrace new experiences without looking over her shoulder.

To David and Andrew with gratitude for love, laughter and marvellous meals!

ACKNOWLEDGMENT

Many thanks to Miika and the Next Chapter team for their continued faith in my fictional creations.

ABOUT THE AUTHOR

Originally from England, and now living near Melbourne, Sue worked in Australian university libraries until taking early retirement in 2008 to concentrate on writing novels. Since then, Sue has had ten novels published, six of them by Next Chapter.

Sue's latest books, 28 *Days, Next Step,* and *Exposure* (*The Reluctant Doorkeeper Trilogy*) are set in Melbourne between 2100 and 2106. They explore the problem of overpopulation and extended life expectancy in an increasingly climate-challenged world and the inhumane solutions adopted by a government determined to rid Australia of unproductive citizens.

For her current project, *The Year of Living Rainbow,* Sue has returned to 1992 with a narrative focusing on one year in the lives of friends, Delia, 48, and Liz, 38, following the deaths of their partners, Ron and Kay, in a road accident on New Year's Eve.

Sue's goal as a fiction writer is to write for as long as possible, believing the extensive life experiences of older writers can be employed to engage readers of all ages.

To learn more about Sue Parritt and discover more Next Chapter authors, visit our website at www.nextchapter.pub.

Printed in Great Britain
by Amazon